I0788451

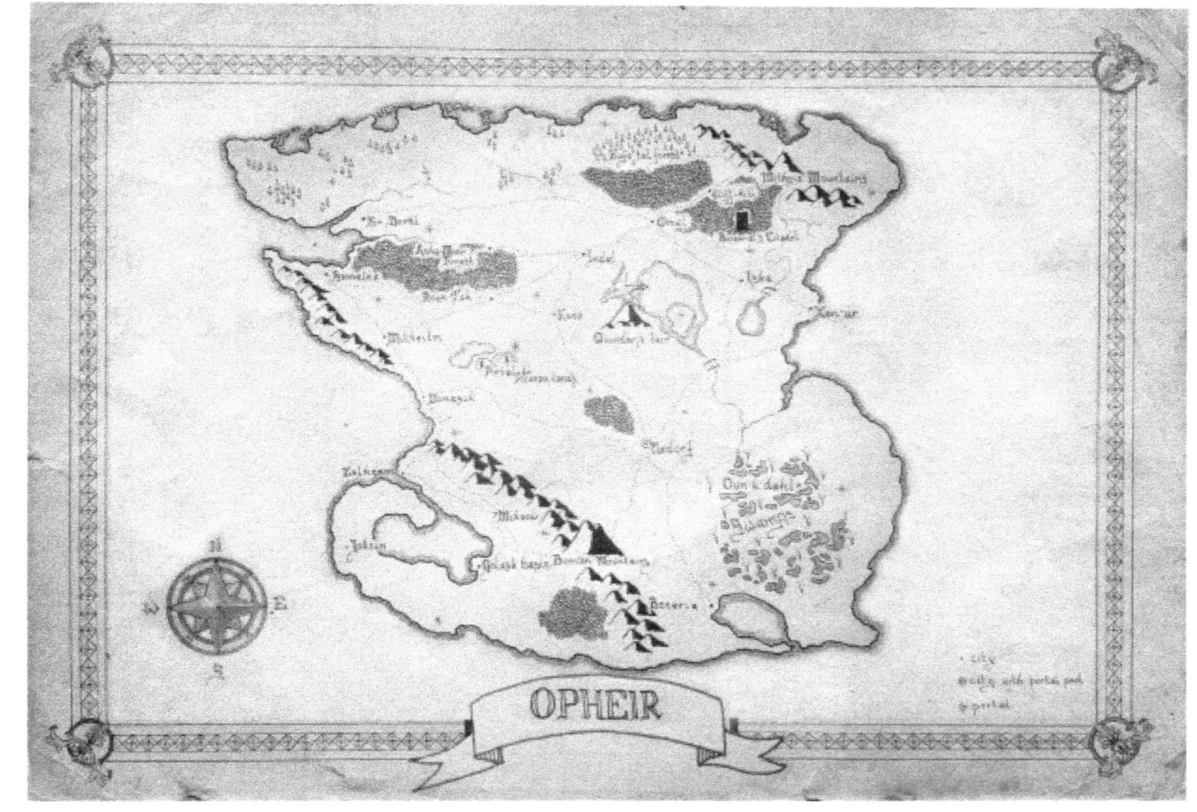

Mahren Mountains
Raver's Castle
The Bowl
Badal
Ashe
Wilhelm
Blangnak
Zultrann
Mahren
Splash bay
Banter Mountains
Asteria
Oun'k dahl
St. Laren
Gnurlan's lair
OPHEIR

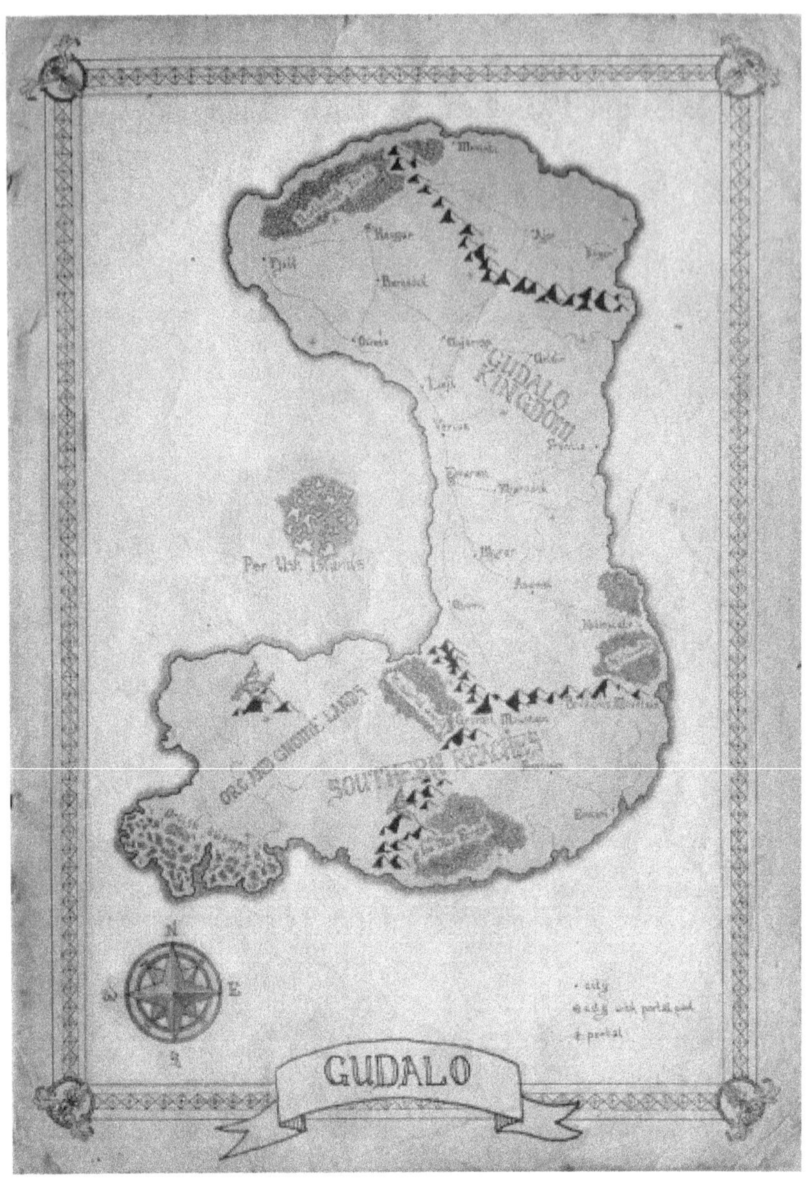
GUDALO KINGDOM
Per Ush Islands
SOUTHERN REACHES
N
S
E
W
GUDALO

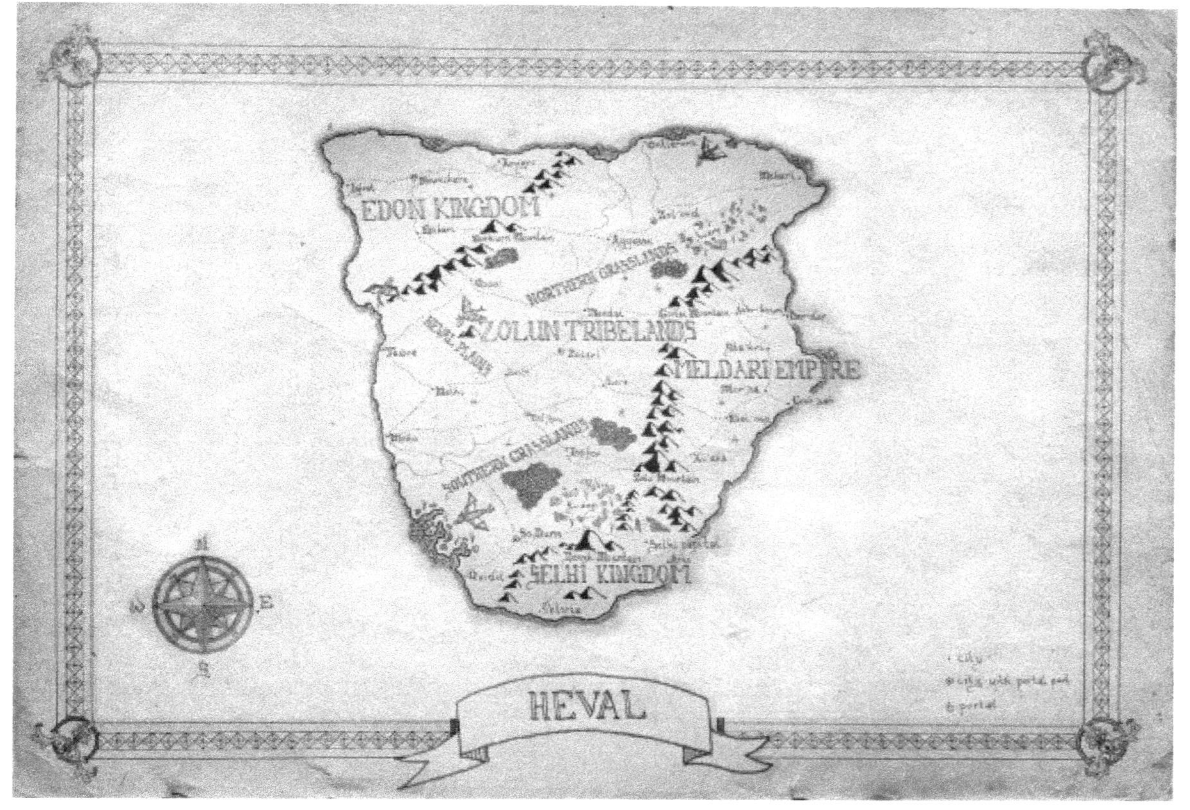
EDON KINGDOM
NORTHERN GRASSLANDS
ZOLUN TRIBELANDS
MELDARI EMPIRE
SOUTHERN GRASSLANDS
SELHI KINGDOM
HEVAL

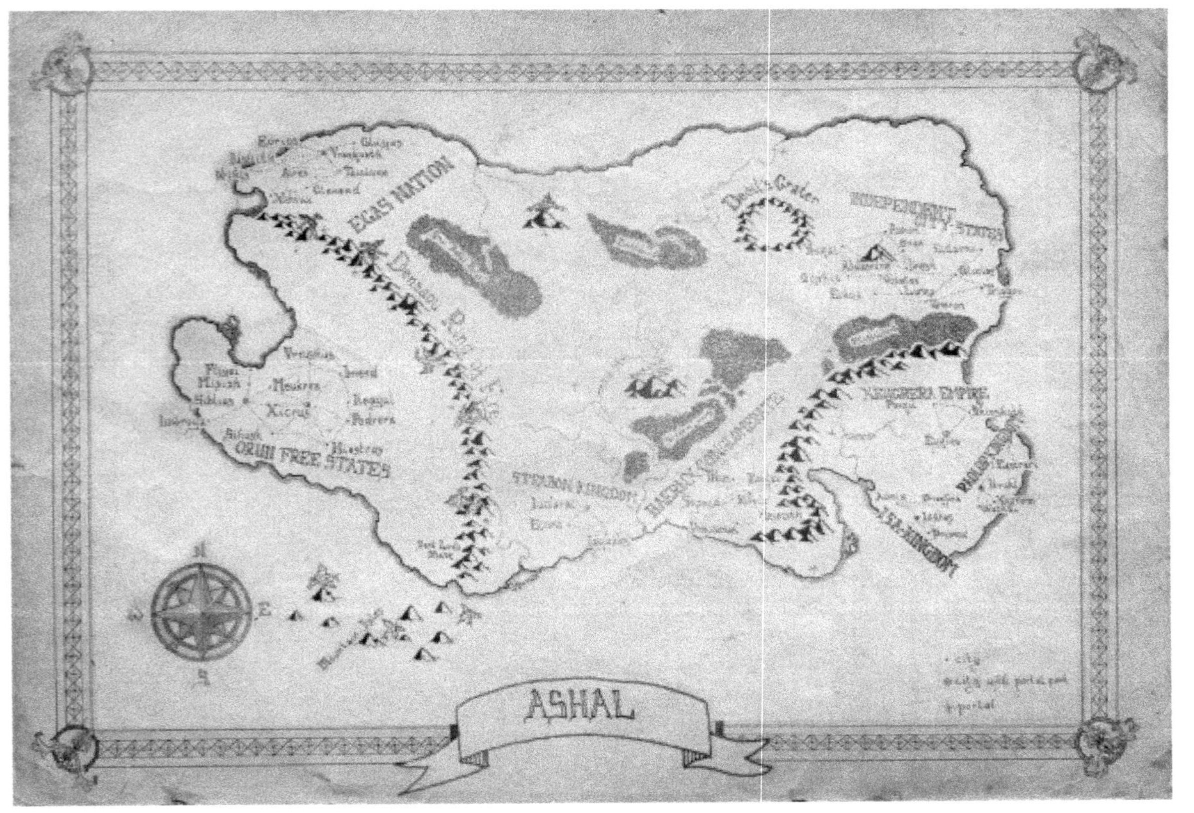

EGAS NATION
ORUIN FREE STATES
Demsen Ring
INDEPENDENT CITY STATES
Death's Crater
STEMBON KINGDOM
NACHOBERA EMPIRE
ASHAL
· city
city with port, port
portal

Want a bigger map of Emerilia and the continents? Check out **http://theeternalwriter.deviantart.com/**

Character Sheet is located in the back of the book for reference.

Emerilia

Stone Raiders' Return

Prologue

Bob sat on what looked like Dave's back porch in Cliff-Hill, sipping on a glass of bourbon.

Dave flashed into existence within the Mirror of Communication conference room. "You look like you have something on your mind," Dave said. A pint of beer appeared in his hand as he sat in a muskoka chair near Bob.

"The Dark Lord and his sudden power increase worries me. I don't know where he's getting it from but it's a hell of a lot of power." Bob sipped from his glass, looking out over Cliff-Hill but not seeing it.

"While we're talking about power, I was wondering about something." Dave's tone made Bob look over. "If I was able to make a nuclear power plant, what would the empire do?"

Bob's eyebrow raised in surprise before he chuckled. "I should stop being surprised by your actions at this point."

Dave might not be his child, but he was as proud of him as a father might be of his son. "The Jukal will look into explosions that are over a megaton. They will also look into any massive nuclear decay emissions. Even all of the armor dissipating at Devil's Crater wasn't enough to set off sensors, because they released so quickly and weren't all at the same time. If they had been at the same time or a constant release over a few hours, then the AIs might have picked it up. What are you thinking?"

"I could use runes to dissipate that energy and stop the Jukal from sensing it, though, right?" Dave asked.

"Yes," Bob agreed.

"Okay, well, I'm thinking about a lot of things. The biggest one right now is that when I destroy one of my conjurations, it falls apart in nuclear decay. If I was to slow down the breakdown of that process, I could make a nuclear reactor. As I was thinking about that, I figured that I might be able to make a fusion reactor. Look, we know how it works—we just don't know why. With the right kinds of magical runes and conjurations, I could recreate the conditions found within the sun," Dave said with growing excitement.

Bob rubbed his chin in thought. "Why do you need so much power? I know that Malsour completed the drop pad for the power station," Bob said. "Shouldn't that be more than enough power?"

"The ley lines of Emerilia are a finite resource. If everyone pulled from it, then it would not be able to compensate for the energy loss. I know on Earth that we ran into problems from burning up our natural resources. The reactors will stop that before it happens. I also have different projects that I want to work on that will require power but drawing that amount of power from the ley lines will arouse the Jukals' interest. I'm not just thinking of making fusion power plants either. With your help, we can maybe make Mana wells." Dave held Bob's eyes.

"Mana wells?" Bob's voice made his interest clear.

"Nuclear batteries made from the waste of nuclear reactors," Dave said.

Bob sat back in shock. He knew something of the theory behind the nuclear batteries, but he had never thought of making them. He had just needed to manage Emerilia. It had been too long since he had really needed to think scientifically, making his problem-solving skills sluggish.

Bob smacked his head. "Damn, that could work. They don't give off radiation at levels that would be detected, but if you, say, rigged up a conversion box—maybe code in something that changed that decay, waste, heat and such, and turned it into Mana..." Bob whistled.

"That was what I was thinking," Dave said, getting excited.

"So what's your plan?"

"First, I need to train up other people to code—doing this all by myself isn't simple and I have too many projects. Why is it when I learn something, I always feel that there's so much more to figure out?" Dave released a suffering sigh and leaned back into his chair.

Bob laughed. "Ah, the age-old dilemma of those who seek to innovate and improve; there's no upper limit, no end, though it is a hell of a lot of fun to just chase those ideas and dreams."

The two of them sipped their drinks and looked out over the peaceful simulation of Cliff-Hill behind Dave's house.

Sato appeared from thin air, wearing his normal attire: a white space suit with blue accents and an emblem on his shoulder that showed his rank.

"Hey, Sato." Bob conjured a seat for the man.

"Bob, Dave." Sato nodded and smiled to them both.

"Seems I'm not the only one who can conjure items." Dave snorted.

"I have a little problem with the fine control. Need to get a better sensory skill or spell for it." Bob grinned and looked to Sato. "So, no Edwards today? What's he up to? Hopefully not using those damned gravity spells."

"Ouch." Dave winced and looked to Sato, who cringed.

"That was last week. He overdid the area of effect, got most of the station with one point five Earth gravities."

"Well, that has gotta suck." Dave shook his head.

"It wasn't the most fun, and we've put new rules on him using it in the station. He gave me this file, however." Sato tapped something out on a screen on his arm. The Mirror of Communication received the file and transmitted it to Bob.

"Got to love faster-than-light download speeds," Bob said.

"Wish I had that when I was playing games in my parents' basement," Dave muttered, drinking his beer.

"How are things going with the Stone Raiders, Dave? It's been awhile since we last talked." Sato relaxed and let his upright military posturing fall away.

Dave conjured him a beer and looked to the roof above the porch. "Well, we cleared out the occupied Aleph facilities. They moved in and started getting everything up and running. They've got a low population, so it's taking them some time. They're focusing on getting more automatons online. We saved the older generation of Demons and the Beast Kin. We're in the middle of building a city for our main guild hall and we're in the process of solidifying our alliances with different countries and groups."

"Sounds pretty impressive." Sato sipped the beer and let out a pleased sigh. "Damn, that's not half bad." Sato looked at the beer appreciatively.

Bob noticed the look on Dave's face. "What are you thinking?"

"Well, I've just started teaching people how to make magical code."

"You've taught one person," Bob inserted.

"Yeah, but it won't be long till he's pretty damn good at it and taking the responsibility off my shoulders. I still have a whole bunch of Aleph, Dwarves, Stone Raiders, my own smiths, and Devil's Crater Army to teach..." Dave trailed off, deep in thought. His frown started to widen as his pursed lips turned into a grin.

He clapped his hands together, jumping out of his seat, and looked to Sato and Bob. "How many Mirrors of Communication do you have?" Dave pointed to Bob.

"Maybe a hundred of the smaller ones and twenty of the long-range ones like the one you have in the seeder." Bob shrugged.

"Sato?"

"We have a few," Sato said.

"Ugh, fine! Keep the numbers to yourself; you're going to be using them a hell of a lot more if I have my way!" Dave said, clearly excited.

"Dave, words," Bob said.

"Okay, so I need magical coders to deal with the things I don't want to. I have ideas I want to work on, but there's also a ton of weapons, armor, walls, frigging toilets and showers that need magical coding as well. I can have a lot of them coming down to the city and helping me out, but that's a lot of resources and things that could go wrong. The Mirrors of Communication give us a place where we can experiment with things without fear of blowing ourselves up. It also means that people from all over Emerilia, or even beyond," Dave gave a pointed look to Sato, "can join in on the lessons, or work with others to gain the skills they need. My only cost will be that they either help with the city, that they continue working for me for two years, or that they make five short-range Mirrors of Communication and one long-range, which they are then to pass out to others who are interested in learning. We expand the lessons to include conjuration or other magic. Do you think we can rope Fire into having some of her professors teaching through the mirrors? I think I can get the Aleph college to join in. They want to learn more, but they're kind of scared to go to the mage's college. This bridges the gap," Dave said.

"So, we basically make an online and interactive virtual reality college?" The words spilled from Bob's mouth in excitement.

Dave clapped his hands, clicked his fingers and pointed to Bob. "Give the Gnome a prize!" Dave smiled, his excitement infectious.

"An online virtual reality college, within reality being framed as virtual reality!"

"So, my people could take lessons directly from you on how to use their abilities?" Sato asked.

"Yes, though those who don't have the implants would only be able to learn the magical coding. But those with abilities could learn every type of magic with enough knowledge, and even conjure items," Dave said.

"Then, as more people learn, more Mirrors of Communication are passed around. Maybe the mage's guild could run it; anyone who wants to learn can go to a mage's guild and learn anything. We could teach farming and agriculture, or even how to control a ship," Bob said.

"And the Jukal won't be able to see a thing." Dave smiled.

Bob's face went slack, his eyes glossy. "With just learning any of that, the median strength of a person on Emerilia could skyrocket."

"Yes, and what would happen if we were to have lessons after the basic studies to teach people how to gain classes? Kind of like a Master's Degree program on Earth, but instead of getting a piece of paper, they get a class that only takes time and effort." Dave held Bob's eyes.

"It's so simple, but the impact it could have, giving education to any and all that desire it—I can't even try to guess what will happen," Bob said.

"A revolution." Dave looked over to Sato.

Chapter 1: To The Grind

Suzy got out of bed. Walking to her balcony, she looked out over the Per'ush islands. They truly were beautiful. Even though the sun had yet to fully rise, people were already moving around in the early morning. There was a kind of energy to the place that was hard to find anywhere else.

A sense of excitement, hope, and opportunity, as if anyone and everyone were just on the cusp of some great achievement and were pushing themselves and their peers to new heights.

Induca made sleepy noises, stretching in the large bed the two had shared. Suzy smiled and looked back to her girlfriend. Induca was flighty and seemed to be something of a rogue, but when Suzy and Induca were alone, they had shared their fears and insecurities. It had made them stronger in their relationship and as people.

"Earth wasn't all that great," Suzy muttered to herself, wandering over to Induca, who rolled over, still not ready to embrace the coming day. Suzy took a few more minutes looking at her girlfriend, studying her body as if to memorize it forever.

"Close the blinds," Induca complained.

"Come on, baby. Time to wake up." Suzy moved over to Induca.

Induca pouted and buried her head under a pillow. "It's dark now," Induca said in a proud voice.

Suzy let out a long sigh, a smile on her lips at Induca's antics.

***

Induca toweled off her hair as she walked back into the room.

"Goddammit, Dave, what the hell were you up to when I was gone?" Suzy yelled.

Well, I guess the vacation is over. Induca pulled on her clothes as Suzy continued to have a one-sided conversation with Dave.

"All right, since we're in Per'ush right now anyway, I'll see if I can get a meeting with Deia's mom and run this by her," Suzy said, defeated.

"Yes, I know, you wouldn't be able to do anything without me. I swear, anytime I get even a few days off you go and turn the damn world on its head!" Suzy sighed. "Okay, go and make your power station. I just got your file; we'll talk later."

"Everything go well?" Induca wrapped Suzy up in a hug from behind.

"Well, it seems in the time we've been gone: Dave has spent millions of coins worth of gold in order to increase his mining manager class level, he's come up with several new patents, and founded a new school for people to learn anything they want. He's also figured out how portals work. Oh, and he somehow got his hands on more materials than the Dwarves have." Suzy sighed again as she leaned on Induca.

"So, where do we start?" Induca asked.

"We talk to Deia's mom to see if she and the mage's guild want in on the online school. Having more educated mages is something they're all about and I know that they want to learn this new way of magical coding. We get a whole damn flock of birds with one stone with just that. Going to be a pain with the contracts and trying to figure out how to manage it, though right now we just need to make sure that the POEs are strong enough that they can defend themselves and their families. Dave is overworked with it and if we can get more people to understand magical coding, then we can increase production and maybe make some real factories, not just one of Dave's conjuring thingies. Might also get him to make that summoning hall," Suzy said.

"You're smiling," Induca said into Suzy's ear.

Suzy looked to Induca and then back out of their room and out onto Per'ush. Her smile grew as she placed her hand on Induca's encircling arms. "He might be half mad and drive me up the wall, but he knows how to light a fire under anyone's ass, including his own. It's going to be a lot of work, but damn if I'm not excited to get started." Suzy chuckled.

"Well, let's go change the world." Induca kissed Suzy's head.

"Back to the grind," Suzy agreed.

***

"Let's start, shall we?" Hamdir, the leader of the Aleph Council and a Half-Elf, Half-Human asked, looking to the rest of the Aleph Council. "So, Meda, you said that you have something important to tell us?"

"Yes," Meda said. She was also a Halfling, but Half-Elf, Half-Dwarf, and the council member in charge of managing food within the Aleph cities, from the various greenhouses and vertical wall gardens to their distribution. She looked as if she were about to jump out of her seat in excitement. "Dave sent over a plan he came up with to improve our growing abilities. I had a look at it and, while we would need to change a few things, once we adapted the various magical coding systems, we could be growing a full harvest of foods faster than ever before!"

"How much would these plans cost for us to use and how fast are we talking?" Hamdir asked.

"We could half, maybe even quarter, the growing time and the plants would be healthier and better than any other we can grow. For cost, I don't know. Dave hasn't put a price on it; he gave us the plans to test out and tell him what we think. Instead of just focusing on one area, this system works on all aspects of what the plants will need. It uses different magic from all of the Affinities. Combining them is hard, but Dave seems to do it seamlessly."

"Why don't we ask him if we could maybe build one of them at cost to test it out?" Koza, a Half-Human, Half-Elf, and the leader of the Aleph's security, asked.

"Maybe offer our help in their attempt to create a true factory at Zol'Ord?" Frenik, the Dwarven council member in charge of Aleph's mining, forges, factories, and all manner of building and expansion, added.

Hamdir nodded. "I agree that sounds like a good plan. Meda, continue with your best judgment. I know that with winter coming, people across Emerilia will need food more than ever. If we can supply them food throughout the winter months, we can start making trading partnerships and growing our alliances."

"I'll see to it," Meda promised.

"Good. Sela, I heard that you had something to share." Hamdir addressed the only Gnome in the room.

"The Stone Raiders are building a power station. They have created a drop pad where they want to put their teleport pad. Josh is pulling funds together and it seems they will start building immediately. I have also been told that they are nearly ready to start spinning their city." Sela, who looked after the various Aleph power systems, looked to Frenik, who nodded.

"Dave has been in the city for just three days, but he and Malsour have been doing the impossible. Dave's been mass conjuring and destroying, carving out the city. Malsour has been emplacing the rollers. The other Stone Raiders have been helping out; they could have it spinning within the week. Then, their only problem becomes power. They need that power station up to keep the city spinning. That, or they keep powering it with their vault-classed soul gems." Frenik shrugged and looked to Sela. "I don't think many groups could meet the power needs of a spinning city, but I think they might have enough to keep it going for maybe a month or two."

Sela nodded in agreement.

"They're damn fast." Koza leaned back in his seat and tapped his hand on the table.

"That they are. I expect that they're going to be changing quite a few things as they build their city. How are we looking for security?" Hamdir asked.

"We've got more automatons up and online. Ela-Gal has been training and testing out our controllers. Josh sees the Stone Raiders' Guild Hall as a hub, a place for Players and POEs to meet and fulfill any need that passerby's had. It's also clear that he thinks of it as a staging area for the coming war. That said, I think it's clear that our role in the coming fights will be to move troops and supplies. For that, I think we should focus on trying to learn magical coding to improve our factories and production times. Just like with food, we're going to need bandages, arrows, spears, Health and Mana potions. All of that is going to be our contribution." Koza looked pained to admit it, but it showed an inner strength that few military people had: knowing when to back down.

"Understood. I agree with Koza's assessment as well. I also know that Ela-Dorn, who is off trying to find out more information on the portals, agrees with Koza." The nods around the table showed that the rest of the council did as well.

"How are we looking on those new bracelets and the shipments to Devil's Crater?" Hamdir asked.

"We've retooled the factories. We've got the weapons coming out at a regular pace. The bracelets shouldn't be too hard; they're very easy to manufacture and we can just copy the magical coding right over."

"Good," Hamdir said, impressed with Frenik and his people's efficiency.

"So, what about the trader's, mage's and adventurer's guilds?" Koza asked.

"I have talked to the mage's college and guild. I'm leaving the discussions to Ela-Dorn, but it seems that we will be sending some people to Per'ush to learn at the college, a sort of trial. There will be people on exchange from the mage's college coming to ours as part of the deal. The trader's guild we've talked to about a trade charter. They think of themselves as the most powerful group and want us to bow down to them. I don't think they understand what we can do with our factories. Once they start realizing how many decent items we can create in a short time period, well, I don't think that many of the traders will be happy with our undercutting their products. The adventurer's guild is interested in learning from our own controllers, doing trade for weapons, armor and simple things. It's going to be a heck of a lot cheaper if it's from us than regular smithies. Also, we've had a number of kingdoms that are voicing some interest in us supplying them with consumables like arrows and crossbow bolts. The Dwarves have also agreed to share their plans for their magical artillery, but they want to buy all of our stock until their clans are fully armed. Then, we have agreed to not make any more without getting their approval," Hamdir said. "Now, I think that covers all of the really fun meet, greet, and politicking things. Does anyone have anything else to say?"

No one looked as if they did. In fact, Meda was eyeing the door like a hundred metre sprinter looking at the finish line.

"Very well. I know we're all busy and we have a lot of work to do." Hamdir clapped his hands together, pushing his seat back out from the conference table, and ended the council meeting.

***

Kol walked through Unity. The city was growing quickly; every day, more people and materials came through the teleport pad.

Adventurers made up the bulk of the numbers, but there were still others who were laborers and people looking to make a start in Ashal with the protection that Devil's Crater boasted.

There were also a large number of Players who were coming to see the place where the Stone Raiders' battles had taken place and looking for rare dungeons. The Stone Raiders' live streams were some of the most popular videos on Earth.

Kol looked around with his eyes, his real eyes, not just his senses and his sensory spells.

An energy ran through the city—a sense of progress, a sense that anyone could put a stamp on the future. From here, so many great things could form or start.

Kol was smiling without realizing it as he walked through the curving main trading street that passed through the various sectors. Inns and shops selling anything from prepared foods to clothes or armor lined this main road.

Kol came to a stop and tucked his thumbs into his belt as he looked at the growing industrial sector. There were homes here and there, but for the most part there wasn't much built on the land. Two massive smithies were being built: one was complete; the other would be done in a few days.

With Earth and Dark mages on the payroll, as long as someone had a plan, it was easy to throw up a building.

Two smithies on the opposite sides of the world. Kol grinned proudly.

"What you doing out here, old man?" Gurren's voice cut through the noise of people going about their day, the market hawkers and the growing buildings.

"Hey there, kiddo," Kol said, finding Gurren, Lox, and Steve walking down the street toward him. Gurren and Kol clasped each other in a hug.

"How was the adventuring?" Kol asked, as they stepped apart.

"Good. Right now, we're just going out there, finding out where the dungeons are, and identifying what's in them," Gurren said.

"You keep him out of trouble?" Kol looked to Lox and Steve.

"Ah, well, we tried to," Lox said.

"Wouldn't let us get into too much," Steve said, almost sounding as if he wished they'd gotten into more trouble.

"Damn adrenaline monkey," Kol said.

"Not true! No adrenaline in these veins!" Steve's frown turned into a proud smile as he hit his arm. The sound of metal on metal rang out.

"So, what you doing out here? I thought you would be in there getting ready for fitting the first DCA soldiers with armor." Gurren pointed to the smithies.

"I was just heading down there. All of the contracts and everything are lined up. Walk with me." Kol headed for the smithies. "We've got the steel coming in from the Aleph to Cliff-Hill. There, we've got our people turning it into the different armor pieces. We've gathered our most skilled smiths here to fit the roughly shaped armor pieces to the soldier. We can make everything a lot faster than one smithy doing every single piece. All of the smithies are going full bore and we're hiring anyone who can swing a hammer the right way. But the sooner we get this done, the faster we can go on to armor other groups and get ready for the repair jobs coming in."

"You sound really excited," Gurren said, smiling with his grandfather.

"Well, we're going to have three locations, all accessible by teleport pads, and we're able to repair and make Weapons of Power and items that use Mithril. Other than us, you'd have to go to a Dwarven mountain. I've even got a few of the council who might be interested in joining the smithies. They want to travel more and we're innovating a whole hell of a lot out here! Dave made this thing called a carver; you can use it like a pencil to carve runes into any metal. Enchanting and making magical code takes minutes, not days."

"Damn. You think the council will go for it?" Lox asked.

"I think so. You haven't been near a Dwarven mountain in a while, but Dave's shaken things up. Every day, people are figuring out new things. Dave started a fire and now those embers are catching onto other hearths and setting them ablaze. As Suzy said, we're going through a revolution." Kol shook his head. "It feels like every other minute, something is coming to light that changes practices that were held for centuries."

"Would you be able to fix my right arm? It's been a bit funky," Steve said.

Kol looked over to him. He put his hand on Steve's casing. "Hmm, yeah, looks like it's a bit messed up. I can get that fixed. Shouldn't take me all that long," Kol said. "Those Aleph are a smart bunch." The intricacies of the metal man were as complex as they were elegant.

"Halt!" a Beast Kin crocodile barked.

A formation of DCA coming down another road stopped as one. All of their feet slammed into the road at the same moment.

"Starting to not only act like a real army, but look like it." Lox's veteran eyes looked over the ranks with approval.

"Their training was enough to get them to work together and understand a lot about tactics. Now they're specializing and becoming true soldiers. I saw that they're training for guerrilla tactics?" Lox's statement came out as a question.

"Dave made something, a bracelet you can put on your hand—it allows the user to fire a spearhead. A spearhead that can convert to a Mana bomb on impact," Kol said.

"Their close-in support would be pretty impressive, despite their magical abilities. Also, great for hit-and-run—smash them with a few dozen Mana bombs and run away," Steve said with approval.

"I would have called them cowards before. With the Dwarven Warclans, you're taught that doing anything but having a straight-up fight is dishonorable. Though, the more I fight, the more I realize that anything that keeps you alive and puts the bad guy down is fair game," Gurren said.

Kol nodded. *When did he grow up to be a veteran?* Kol thought, a bit sad at the trials his grandson had gone through.

"Well, pass off your weapons and armor to the clerk running the counter. Steve, come with me and I'll get that arm fixed up. We'll go get a meal later tonight? I think Dave will be coming back," Kol said.

"Sounds like a plan," Lox agreed.

"See you later, Granddad," Gurren added.

"Try not to break my smithy with your big damned head," Kol said, Steve following him.

Gurren and Lox laughed as they walked away.

Kol guided Steve back to an unused area of the smithy. They had built the smithies to be two-thirds the size of the ones in Cliff-Hill, but they only had enough people to fulfill a third of the roles. Recruiting was up and with the incentives, people were joining, but training them and seeing whether they were any good took time.

Steve walked into the high-ceiled smithy and looked around. "Bit different than the Aleph smithies. Looks more like a small machine shop."

"We don't mass-produce. Everything here is of the highest quality and materials." Kol pointed to a place on the ground. "Stand there."

Kol grabbed a ladder. Using a hotkey on his interface, his apron and belt appeared on him. He used the ladder to get level with Steve's shoulder, sitting on the top and pressing his hands to Steve's metal shoulder. He hissed and shook his head.

"Damn apes," Kol growled.

"Something the matter?" Steve asked as Kol pulled out tools and opened up the maintenance hatch in Steve's arm.

"They used Mithril to make your casing, but when they did so, they used their rollers and heaters. This must've been a pain in the ass since they didn't properly break the bonds in the Mithril. The way that Mithril bonds, it makes it the strongest material out there. If it isn't bonded properly, then it'll have weaknesses and stress points. Dave told me about it. He worked out the worst points in your armor, but he wasn't able to do everything." Kol worked his tools on the gears in Steve's shoulder.

"So, my Mithril armor is messed up?" Steve asked.

"Yes. It will fix itself over time, but that could take years," Kol said. "Mass-producing items makes sense, but you're a one-of-a-kind item. You can see it in your structure that they adapted the behemoth body to you, instead of creating a body around your core. Oh, no, you don't," Kol grunted, his wrench turning and freeing something in Steve's arm.

"Are you sure it's the best to have you working on my gears?" Steve sounded a bit worried.

"Dwarves were the first to use gears and pulleys; it's a force multiplier. We use them to move our artillery and in our elevators as well as a bunch of other mechanical items. I've been brushing up on it recently after Dave started spouting something about a 'car' to me one time we were working. Your gear systems are really complex and it makes sense. If they or your magical coding fails, you have a backup in the other." Kol fiddled around with a gear and then pulled out a rod with a spinning bit.

"That feels weird," Steve said as Kol used the carver on some runes that had been worn away slightly.

"Just a bit more and we'll be done," Kol said, enjoying working on Steve. His core was linked to the rest of his body through magical coding that converted his commands into actions. His magical coding acted as nerves while his gears acted as muscle.

There were none as complicated as the ones in Steve's face. Kol finished with the carver and pulled out a silver ingot. He rubbed the silver; it covered his finger as if it were paint. He rubbed it over the runes, the silver flowing into the carvings.

"How are you doing that?" Steve asked.

"It's my smithing art. It's called Blind Man's Touch, though a lot of my fellow masters call it finger painting." Kol sighed and ran his finger over a gear that showed signs of stress. It was as if he massaged the weakness out of the gear.

"Okay, how does that feel?" Kol asked.

Steve rolled his shoulder, rotating it through three hundred and sixty degrees. "Pretty good!" Steve's arm opened up; his hand collapsed inward, a repeating ballista replacing his hand and forearm.

"Hmm." Kol tapped his chin in thought.

Steve looked to Kol. "Why do I get the feeling that was a 'mind if we try something out' hmm?"

"Because, I think we could make that a heck of a lot more powerful," Kol said.

"Okay, what are you thinking?" Steve's repeater once again changed back into a hand.

The fluidity of the change impressed Kol but his mind was on other things. "So, you know that bracelet thing that Dave's made for the Devil's Crater Army. I think we could adapt that to your hand, maybe that and the lightning ball thing he had? No, probably not the lightning ball thing. He said he got a shock every time he used it—don't want to know what that does with your inner systems. You have a shield on your other arm, right?" Kol got down from the ladder.

"Yeah." Steve sounded curious but wary.

"Okay, so I've been working on making a force shield. It's basically a simple system where you have a small shield but then a magical shield that extends outward whenever you're under attack. Also, you could see through the shield and fire your weapons at whatever's attacking you." Kol walked deeper into the smithy until he reached a worktable he'd claimed for himself, pulling out books and other materials.

Steve followed him. "What about power draw?"

"Ah, not just an amazing piece of engineering!" Kol said with approval as he pulled out a piece of paper and then flipped through a book.

"Isn't that Dave's book?" Steve asked.

"Yep, his damned complicated runic system for the purpose of magical coding," Kol said, "but for power..." Kol found what he was looking for, pursing his lips as he read the description.

"I think we can add in a magical enchantment similar to the one Dave uses for gathering power in an area. You will naturally draw in magical power from all around you. If a spell slams into your shield and fails, we can enchant it to take in a percentage of the failed spell's power." Kol started to note things down on an interface notepad he'd "stuck" to the desk.

"Well, I can absorb information really fast. If you give me those books, I can memorize them in a few seconds and help you out that way," Steve offered.

"Always good to learn a little bit more about yourself." Kol pushed the book to the side so Steve could read it. "How good are your senses in regards to your body? Might need to do diagnostics on the move."

"Umm, well, the circuit looks like this." Steve used his left hand to draw the runes on his interface, picking up the book with his right and flicking through it.

"Wish I could do two things at once." Kol looked at the magical circuit Steve had drawn. He stared at the completed design silently for a few minutes.

"Well, we are going to be changing *that* piece of garbage!" Kol declared, writing out another series of runes as Steve put down the book. "First, we'll get you a better way to sense yourself and things around you. Then, you can probably upgrade most of the code in you with the knowledge you now have." Kol bent to work.

"Wow, I thought I was near my peak, but damn this is a lot of information." Steve flipped through the book's pages at an alarming speed.

"Good, then tell me if this would work." Kol let Steve see the code he'd written down.

"That should work, much better than the last." Steve winced.

"Good. Can't have my people going out with you when you're only half functional!"

Chapter 2: In High Towers and Back Rooms

"Next!" Jules yelled.

A Demon walked in through the door, his face nearly split in half by a scar that cut through the Demon's eye, nose, and mouth. He walked with a limp; his right knee looked to be shattered and his right arm had been torn apart, with only a small nub holding onto the crutch that held him up.

Jules was running the healing clinic within the Stone Raiders' Guild Hall.

"Please take a seat." She waved to the examination table.

He slumped onto the table, his one eye glazed over as if he were headed for the executioner's block.

Jules pressed her hand against the Demon to better sense his injuries. The damage was pretty bad and it would take some time, but with what she'd been able to do for Kol and the other mangled patients who had come to see her, she simply rubbed her hands together, preparing herself for the task ahead.

"Okay, the head's going to take some time. The arm will be something you need to come back here regularly to get checked on its progress as we'll have to grow it from something else. Good thing for you that here, with the Stone Raiders, we've created the skill to clone people's anatomy. I also see that your wing is a bit messed up. If you want, we can start today. We can get everything but your limbs sorted out right now," Jules said.

The Demon looked up to her as if fearing to believe her.

"I'll take that as a yes. Make yourself comfortable and we'll get started in a few minutes. I need a few supplies." Jules pulled things out of cupboards and put them onto a rolling table. She pulled out more items from her bag of holding.

"Why are you doing this for me?" The Demon spoke slowly so that he didn't mess up the words with his broken jaw and torn lips.

"Back on Earth, I took an oath to help anyone when I can, no matter what, so that's what I'm doing. Lie back please." Jules wheeled the table over.

"Thank you," the Demon said, tears in his remaining eye. Although the Demons seemed to have gotten over most of the conditioning that made them think that unless they were a fighter they were useless, the ones in the DCA didn't know anything else. Having their bodies torn apart and made useless terrified them. As they had criticized one another for weakness to get stronger, they were now the weak ones. Jules wasn't just healing their bodies; she was giving them back the life that they had devoted themselves to.

"When you wake up, this is just going to be a bad memory." Jules smiled to the Demon as tears fell from his face. Jules cast a sleep spell on him. His eyes closed and Jules rolled up her sleeves. It was her seventh patient today. While others fought and warred to gain their levels, she toiled away with the wounded and broken.

Whether it was farmhands from Verlun or those who had been injured in Devil's Crater or in Cliff-Hill, they all had wounds that they wouldn't normally be able to heal. For some, it was because it was too expensive. For others, the wounds were too severe for POE medics to deal with.

It was a small thing, but to them, it was huge. When Jules had suggested it, Josh had given her access to the treasury and all the support he could muster.

"We might be visitors to this world, but the POEs, I can't help but feel protective of. Help the worst and those who are allied with us first, but heal whoever you want and get the supplies you need. A bit of goodwill here can mean a lot in the future," Josh said.

As I look around, I keep thinking that we're not becoming just the most powerful guild on Emerilia, but an empire.

She pushed the thoughts from her mind and pulled out a scalpel. First, she needed to remove the dead flesh and then she could work on regrowing healthy tissues.

***

Oson'Mal finished repeating Dave's idea to the mage's guild Archmage, Alamos.

Alamos tapped his chin in thought. "Well, I think the college's Archmage, Jelanos, will go with the plan. After all, it is rather ingenious. I know that there are several people who want to learn this fabled magical coding. It seems that Dave has made something here that could completely revolutionize Magical Circuits and make them available to everyone to learn and make, though I do not know how he is going to have so many people produce Mirrors of Communication. They can take months to make by master craftsmen."

"Well, he can make one in about ten minutes, if he wants to, so a normal person might need a week if he's teaching them," Mal said.

Alamos raised his eyebrow in interest. "Very well, I will take this to Jelanos and we should have an agreement made within a few weeks. Now, onto the matter of the Stone Raiders becoming an affiliate of the mage's guild and college. We accept this and we can make you a valued retailer. This means that we will decrease the costs of buying goods from us and we hope that you will reciprocate. It also means that any of your people are welcome to stay at one of the guild's inns. They can also teach, learn, and take on mage's guild and college contracts. Does this sound amenable to you?"

"I can't make those decisions, but I can pass it on and put you into contact with Josh," Mal said.

"Please do," Alamos said.

Mal shared Josh's contact information, as well as sending Josh a message of what Alamos had proposed.

"Well, I must get back to my studies. Thank you for hearing me out." Mal rose to leave.

"My door is always open, Mal, and the Stone Raiders are a force I would prefer to have on the mages' side." Alamos came around the desk and guided Mal out.

A prompt jumped up into his vision.

Your Guild has joined the Stone Raiders Guild

The Stone Raiders are now affiliated with the Mage's Guild.

You gain:

Discounts for mage's guild members in Stone Raiders' affiliated shops and locations (discounts can increase based on guildmember's level, contribution to Stone Raiders and stats).

Affiliation will be dissolved:

If the two guilds go to war with one another.

There is a break or breach in contract and people from one guild treat the others with hostility (refer to affiliate guild relationships).

"Something the matter?" Mal asked.

"No. Just Josh accepted my proposal—didn't think he would act this fast." Alamos laughed.

***

Josh sent his own guild affiliation screen out of his vision with a flick of his hand, finding another waiting for him.

You have earned a new class: Guildmaster

You have taken on one of the hardest roles in all of Emerilia. You have led your guild through thick and thin and they have placed their faith in your leadership. Don't fuck up.

Status: Level 1

When fighting with a group of your guild members (over 5 people), you all gain a 1% boost in stats.

50 people, 2% boost

Effects: 100 people, 3% boost

200 people, 4% boost

400 people, 5% boost

600 people, 6% boost

Josh whistled to himself, looking to the next pop-up.

Quest: Guildmaster 2

Have 1,000 guild members

Rewards: Unlock Level 3 Quest

Gain +2% base to guildmembers' stats when defending

Josh checked the wiki. His eyes opened in alarm. *It would be a base two to the five people, increasing by two for every larger group. Damn, it doesn't sound impressive, but with people's stats that is a hell of a bonus!*

"That could be useful if this Lord Esamael decides to act. Wasn't long ago that we were fighting in Devil's Crater. When you get to the top, there really are snakes all around looking to take your position." Josh sighed to himself.

Since Lucy had been able to foist most of her responsibilities to others, she had been focusing on gathering information. The image her information was creating was a scary one. Esamael's people were powerful and he had large forces backing him. Josh wouldn't care what he did as long as he left the guild alone, but it was readily becoming clear that he didn't care for the Stone Raiders and wanted to destroy them.

Josh's hand curled into a fist as he remembered Selhi Capital. *We won't be stepped on again.* He sat like that for a few minutes before Florence entered her office that he was temporarily using during his stay in Verlun.

"I hope my seat is comfortable. I heard we're affiliated with the mage's guild now," she said.

"That we are, Florence. I have something I want you to look into for me." Josh leaned forward, a cold look in his eyes.

"What is it?" Florence's eyes thinned as her excited atmosphere from moments ago disappeared.

"While we can't attack Selhi Capital for what they did to us, I want you and Lucy to come up with a plan to make them and the world know what happens to someone who screws with the Stone Raiders," Josh said.

Florence nodded. "It won't be easy, but I can think of a few ways we can do it. Lucy and I should have something planned out within a week."

Josh's eyebrow raised.

"This is my guild and they treated us like shit because they thought of us as nothing more than a bunch of first guild amateurs. I lost a lot of gold there. I've often thought of a few ways to repay their kindness." Florence's smile didn't hold any kindness.

A predatory smile crossed Josh's face.

***

Lady Merguine didn't pause in her steps. The royal guard let her into the king's office without hesitation.

King Sigaird sat at the large desk that took up the majority of the room. He barely glanced up from his interface before going back to work. As soon as the doors closed behind Merguine, runes glowed, showing that protections were working.

Most wouldn't notice them, but Merguine had a keen eye for the smallest details.

"From your report, it doesn't sound good." The king looked to Merguine as she took a seat.

"No, it doesn't," she said, a picture of regal beauty. "It seems that all of the towns between us and Verlun are controlled by Esamael's forces. From what we can tell, he has control of a number of guard units as well as roving bandit groups. There have been no survivors from the bandit raids for more than a year. I think at that time, he started taking over. It also seems that the cities around Per'ush's harbor are also with Esamael. Geldir, Frentia, and Asamal are on our side. We've confirmed this through truth seekers," Merguine said, referring to the men and women who practiced mind magic to reveal the truth of people's words, Merguine's hunter-spies.

"What about Verlun?" Sigaird asked.

Merguine straightened out her dress, wondering the best way to proceed. "Different elements within Verlun are allied with either Lord Esamael or the Stone Raiders."

"They're just a guild—what can they offer them?" King Sigaird looked skeptical.

"Protection and a way to make a living,"

"They are my subjects, under *my* protection." Sigaird slammed his fist against the desk.

"Where were you when they were being stepped on by Esamael, when they were being taxed so that they could barely feed their families even if they had a good harvest? Who hasn't had a real presence in the area for years?" Merguine said, her tone cutting. "Your brother might have been the king, but you were second prince. You went off adventuring, not caring for the people until your brother died and you were forced to return."

Sigaird made to reply, but the fire in Merguine's eyes and the shifting air in the room made him pause.

"Through this, Verlun and the fields from Geldir down to Asamal are now worked by fierce Stone Raiders' supporters. They have provided jobs, education, training, a place in their guild, a new influx of gold, protection to those who support them as well as medical that most nobles are barely able to afford. People who have lived in Gudalo for generations are uprooting their lives, moving to Cliff-Hill and Devil's Crater. The Stone Raiders give them options and don't try to control them unless they become part of their guild. Stop thinking of the Stone Raiders as a guild. Think of them as an empire, one that has the backing of the Dwarves, Aleph, Demons, Beast Kin, a number of Elves and kingdoms. They are also now affiliated with the adventurer's, trader's and mage's guilds. You are not working from a position of strength. In fact, you are the weakest of the three players in this fight. I have it on good account that the Stone Raiders are *not* to be underestimated." Merguine stabbed her finger into the armrest of her chair.

King Sigaird, a bit shocked with the vehemence of her words and her tone, recovered after a few minutes. "So, what do you suggest?"

"I think it's time that you stopped treating Gudalo like a kingdom. You've been trying to keep it going all this time, but your brother screwed it up and it's coming apart. Talk to the races to the south. It's about time we had peace; bringing them to the table will allow us to make real progress. Lord Esamael wants to tear everything down? Well, if we build ourselves up enough, his support is going to start to wane and fall to the wayside."

"How long do you think until he moves?" Sigaird leaned forward, finally hearing an option that could keep Gudalo out of a war.

"With winter coming..." Merguine paused and looked to Sigaird.

"He won't do anything until spring. Fighting in the winter is a pain in the ass. Make sure we have reinforcements moving from the southern borders at the time. We can't go to the Stone Raiders, as that makes us look weak. They're a guild, after all, and they have no loyalty to us. Anything we say to them, we can assume that Esamael will hear. Uniting all of Gudalo—now that is a monumental task. However, if we do it, then Gudalo will finally be stable. It might not be a kingdom anymore, but I'd be fine with that. All this responsibility weighs on a person." Sigaird showed his weariness as he let out a tired sigh.

"Well, it looks like we have a plan and a few months in which to do it. I suggest we get started." Merguine stood.

"When this is all over, will you still go adventuring with me?" Sigaird asked in a quiet voice

Merguine smiled and leaned on the desk. "Of course, I will, you big idiot."

Sigaird leaned over the table himself, kissing her.

"Now, let's get your stupid country sorted out," she admonished, pulling back.

"All right." Sigaird rolled his shoulders.

"The Lady of Air is hopeful for our success and for Gudalo coming out of this as a nation instead of a tyrannical kingdom," Merguine said.

Sigaird raised an eyebrow in interest. "Well, good to know we have some people in our corner." Sigaird looked reassured by Merguine's words.

"Hurry up and make Gudalo one nation." Merguine walked out of the room. The door opened for her, letting her out into the castle.

In minutes, she was out of the castle through a hidden entrance and moving quickly for a temple. She was admitted through a side door. She stepped into a courtyard where a young lady sat in a chair. White hair spilled down her shoulders, while her foot bounced erratically.

"Air," an elderly Elf said from his seat along the side of the courtyard.

"What is it now, Venfik?" she said in a perpetually bored tone.

Merguine cleared her throat.

"Woo-hoo, something fun!" Air jumped from her seat and glided to Merguine. "So, did you pass the message to Sigaird? The man is as stubborn as he is cute." Air winked and giggled at Merguine's expression. "Don't worry—he's all yours." Air walked around Merguine, her feet never touching the ground.

"I told him," Merguine said. Faster than she could think, Air was right in front of her with her hands bunched together under her chin as if she were some child hearing a bard's stories.

"Well?" She squealed.

"He is for the idea of unifying the rest of Gudalo," Merguine said.

"Woo-hoo! Who's the best? I am, that's who!" Air jumped ten feet into the air with her hand raised in a victory pose before she came back down. "Good. The leaders to the south are also for it. Should take a few months, but when Esamael attacks, the country will come together as one. Nothing like a little fight to bring people together," Air said.

"Are you sure he will attack?" Merguine asked.

Air's eyes held Merguine's, as if judging her worthy of the information she held or not.

"You are my Champion and I have trust in you, but I know my Champions and some information should not be shared. If you find out on your own, then do with it as you will. However, I can only guide you so much." As fast as she had been serious, she went back to dancing around the courtyard, making Merguine wonder whether it had even really happened.

"Okay, Venfik, so who's next on the list?" Air asked.

Venfik stood from his chair with a more elegant air. "Markolm," he said with a tired voice.

Air pouted, letting her shoulders slump as she waved her arms around lazily. "The Elves are always so boring with how proper they want everything, though!"

"They are also where the Angels will most likely be released. The alliance needs the Elves to fight what is to come. Either that, or the various entities in Ashal?" Venfik asked.

"Fine! Markolm it is. See you later, Merguine!" Air shot up into the air in a white blur.

"Look after yourself, Champion." Venfik gave her a bow before following his lady through the air.

Merguine watched the two's display of Air control in slight shock before she shook her head. "Sigaird and I just had to become Champions of Lady Air."

Chapter 3: Advances

Josh hit the buy button, committed to the action that took out a massive chunk of resources from the guild's treasury.

Moments later, there was a prompt. He changed to it.

New Item in Treasury

Teleport Pad

Josh selected it.

Place Teleport Pad

There are 2x Drop pads under the Stone Raiders' ownership that these teleport pads can be placed at.

Do you wish to place a teleport pad at:

[Verlun]

[Possible Power Plant Location]

Josh clicked the second location.

The Verlun location had a drop pad at its location as it was cheaper to use than a full-blown teleport pad.

"Teleport pad's in the right place," Malsour confirmed. Throughout the buying process, he had been focused on the drop pad he had made hundreds of kilometers away.

Josh was still a bit awed by the man's patience and ability.

"Road trip!" Dave yelled, pointing to the person up in the guild hall's teleport pad control room.

"Connection made. Powering up teleport pad," the controller said.

Darkness seemed to greet them on the other side of the portal.

Dave clicked his fingers. A miner that had been brought into the teleport pad room powered up and started to move forward. A cart followed behind.

As soon as the miner passed through the event horizon, its front end powered up, lighting up dozens of lasers and immediately slicing up debris and material. A gravity tunnel pulled the debris into the miner and out to the cart following behind. Another gravity plate underneath would keep the miner attached to any surface, even if it was on the ceiling.

Spike wheels moved the large thing onward.

In just a matter of minutes, it had cleared out around the teleport pad and started to carve out what would be their first power station.

"Well, I guess this really is going to become a reality." Josh chuckled.

Cassie's fingers found his and she looked at him proudly.

"Yep! Now, just need to get that damn city turning. I've got the gardens being worked on, but I want to leave some of the development to my students as a project," Dave said.

"Teacher Dave—that's going to be weird." Malsour chuckled.

"Thanks, man. I'll remember that, jackass." Dave grinned and watched the miner as it continued to move steadily forward. Lasers from around its body started to cut through the rock; more gravity funnels poured materials into the following cart. Three more miners were off to the side, waiting to go through the teleport pad and help with carving out the power station.

"Well, we're going to have to figure out a name for this city sometime. Just calling it *the* guild hall isn't going to swing it," Cassie said.

"What about Earth? You know, our home before this? Too weird?" Dave looked at them, seeing their less than enthusiastic reactions. "What about Terra?"

"Terra doesn't sound bad—kind of like it," Josh said.

"Not really all that much thought behind it, but it works." Cassie shrugged.

"We'll put it to a vote. Don't want Boaty McBoat Face," Josh said.

"Who the hell would name anything Boaty McBoat Face?" Malsour asked, puzzled.

"Have I got a story for you!" Dave said.

Josh snorted, leaving the teleport pad room as Dave told Malsour the story.

Cassie put her arm in his as they walked. "Something on your mind?"

"Just, all of this, it's—well, it's way more than I ever thought would be possible. We're basically making a damn empire for ourselves. It's pretty crazy."

"And exciting," Cassie added.

Josh smiled and looked over to her.

"That it is, love." He bent over and gave her a kiss. "Dinner at the tavern? I heard that it's to die for with the cooks all being masters at their skill."

"Oh, you romantic." Cassie giggled as they walked on.

***

Alkao stormed through the government buildings. Anyone who saw the look in his eyes moved out of his way, sticking to the walls.

You need to do this—no, you HAVE to do this. Alkao firmed his grip on his sword as he walked.

Guards opened the doors to an office with a single desk and a large window that looked out over Unity and Devil's Crater.

"Alkao?" Anna sat on one of the twin couches in the room, cleaning her blade while looking over information on her interface.

"Anna'kal, I ask if you are interested in going on a date with me." He said the words so fast that he couldn't back out of it.

Anna's wolfkin eyebrow arched in amusement and the corners of her lips curled upward.

"Friggin' Party Zero," she muttered. Alkao barely caught the words.

The guards closed the doors. Alkao would have seen the excited and confused looks of those in the hallway, but all his attention was on Anna as she rose from the couch, her tail swishing back and forth.

She twirled her sword around. "Why do you want to ask me out?"

No room to back out now!

"You are smart, strong, sexy, and I can't get you out of my damned mind. When I'm with you, I want to do anything to keep you around, to continue talking, even making myself look like a complete idiot." Alkao scratched his head awkwardly. "I wanted to stop hinting at my feelings and put them out in the open. That way, there are no problems between us."

"Okay," Anna said.

Alkao looked at her, her face unreadable as Alkao's stomach dropped. After a few moments, he brought himself upright.

"I'm sorry for wasting your time. I will never talk of these matters again." Alkao turned. There was a whistling through the air. Alkao turned and ducked, his training instinctively kicking in. He always believed that if he was leading an army, he needed to train as hard as, if not harder than, the lowliest private.

He turned to find Anna flying through the air toward him. He stumbled backward, crashing through a table, and fell on his ass.

"I'd like that." Anna smiled and kissed Alkao's lips before she jumped off him, a wicked grin on her face as her tail whipped back and forth in an excited manner.

"Could you have told me that before I broke the damned table?" Relief flooded through Alkao as a weight felt as though it were lifted from his shoulders.

Anna gave him a hand to help him up. "Well, if you play your cards right, then we might break a lot more than a coffee table with me jumping on you." Anna wormed under his arm.

Alkao's blood drained from his brain as he forgot how to reply.

"Now, I'm picking where we go for our first date." Anna pulled away, capturing his hand in hers and towing him toward the door. Alkao half stumbled, still in a state of shock.

***

"I've got to go soon; got a lesson to teach." Dave sat down at his seat with the Council of Anvil and Fire.

"Good to know that you enjoy my hosting of the bi-weekly meetings." Quino's smile took out any bite in his words.

"Dude, aren't you coming to the class?" Dave asked.

"Okay, so getting along with matters at hand. Materials have been distributed—you'll see that in front of you. We've had a number of people express an interest in working for the Cliff-Hill smithies; they're interested in learning these new techniques and expanding their horizons. The Aleph have made an agreement with us to transfer students between our groups. We will be doing twenty to start, all volunteers, but anyone who wants to go above those numbers is free to do so! The Aleph will also be making various parts for us: artillery, shields, and consumable ammunition. We are looking to follow more in the Aleph's steps of setting up factories while also keeping our ability to make singular items at a much higher quality level. Cliff-Hill smithy is acting as a test bed in that capacity. Anything that they will learn, they have agreed to share with us. Dave, it's been said that you have a new income of raw materials?" Quino rattled off.

"I do; I put all of my gold into Mine Manager so that we would have a resource pool not from the Aleph and the Dwarves, because I know most of this council's resources are already spoken for, and you are in deals with the Aleph to increase the amount of resources you can use," Dave said.

"The Stone Raiders have been storing a lot of resources. Should we be worried about a market drop?" Quino's voice was serious.

"Josh knows markets; he will release it so that the markets don't crash. Also, we have most of those materials already spoken for in different projects," Dave said.

"Awesome. Okay, any other issues or problems?" Quino asked. "Nope. All right—see you in class!" He grinned and disappeared.

Dave rolled his eyes as he exited the conference room, using his interface to change to another. He appeared in a massive auditorium.

Already, people were there, talking to one another in different groups. Races from all over Emerilia and those with hundreds of different garbs depicted their allegiances, country, or kingdom.

Thankfully, he had also set it so that they couldn't see him until he wanted to, kind of making a veil between the class and his stage.

Dave moved to the front of the classroom. Sitting at the desk that was off to the side, he opened up his interface, posting different windows around him. He tapped his chin in thought as he looked at the different runes and information.

His level caught his attention.

Level 222

You have reached Level 222; you have **366** stat points to use.

He moved around. Feeling that he was okay, he moved to his stats and started allotting points.

"Intelligence—let's move 20 there; 20 to Endurance and another 20 to Agility." Dave updated the stats.

Character Sheet

Name:	David Grahslagg	Gender:	Male
Level:	160	Class:	Dwarven Master Smith, Friend of the Grey God, Bleeder, Librarian, Aleph Engineer, Weapons Master, Champion Slayer, Skill Creator, Mine Manager, Master Summoner
Race:	Human/Dwarf	Alignment:	Chaotic Good

Unspent points: 306

Health:	26,300	Regen:	11.06 /s
Mana:	8,180	Regen:	23.55 /s
Stamina:	3,240	Regen:	22.00 /s
Vitality:	263	Endurance:	553
Intelligence:	818	Willpower:	471
Strength:	324	Agility:	440

Dave closed his eyes as the feeling of power passed through him. It lasted for a few minutes before it dissipated.

"I'll sleep good tonight." Dave snorted and moved his hands around to get used to the new Agility and Intelligence stats. His Endurance was so high that he needed only four hours of sleep a night. With everything that was going on, he felt as if it was going to be needed.

A massive metal man appeared in the room, drawing everyone's attention.

Dave was brought out of his thoughts by the sudden silence.

"I know—I'm usually shocked by my own handsomeness in the morning, too!"

"Steve, what are you doing in here?" Dave asked, breaking the veil.

Steve jumped off what must've been a twenty-meter high landing, down to the front of the stage, leaving a massive crater in it.

Dave shook his head and then rested his temple on his fingers.

"Huh, this place does break like the real world." Steve got out of the crater.

"Is this *the* Steve?" Quino said, appearing faster than a raincloud on a bad day.

"Steve, Quino." Dave waved between the two of them. The floor repaired itself, the conference room working.

"So, you're the automated man? Damn, those Aleph are a smart bunch!" Quino looked over Steve.

"Hey, watch your magical senses, pervert!" Steve complained, crossing his legs and placing his hands over his groin.

"You don't even have two shiny metal balls," Dave said.

"Got more balls than a Orjin whale!" Steve shot back.

"Gross. So why you here again? Other than seeing if the Mirror of Communication conference rooms can break?" Dave asked.

"I came to learn. I downloaded all the information in your book, and while I can see where many of your solutions come from, I'm interested in learning more from the master himself," Steve said.

"Any particular reason?" Dave asked.

"Might need it sometime. I am made of Magical Circuits and gears. Kol opened my eyes to that," Steve said.

"You see the old geezer?" Dave asked as he looked over to Quino talking with Endur in excited voices. *You'd swear they were oversized, hairy, excited schoolgirls talking about their crush.*

"Yeah, he's working on getting the DCA fitted with their armor and repairing the high-leveled weapons of the adventurers coming through. I'm in the city right now," Steve said.

"Nice!" An alarm went off on Dave's interface. "We'll catch up afterward in the Aleph Guild Hall. If you enjoy this, then you'll enjoy what we've done."

"See you afterward." Steve went to find a seat. A big group of Dwarves battered Steve with questions, Quino leading them.

Dave rolled his eyes; he stood up from his desk and moved to the lectern in the middle of the stage.

He'd hated presentations when he was a younger man, but he'd had to get over that fear with Rock Breakers. Here and now, he was excited to open minds and teach everyone a passion that had driven him to this very spot.

"Hello, everyone. Please grab a seat. My name is Dave Grahslagg. I created this little skill called magical coding and I think it could change Emerilia as we know it. I hope you're ready for it!" Dave looked at those faces and dozens of races representing hundreds of cities, towns, and villages. They were Emerilia, from the highest Player to the lowest POE.

They were his brothers and sisters, the prisoners of Emerilia and the future of the Human race. Dave's eyes drifted over them as he smiled.

"Well, let's get started, shall we?"

Chapter 4: Date Night

Dave worked the armor into its correct form. He put the hammer down, pulling the heat from the metal, and settling it back into a wearable state. He placed it on the bunny Beast Kin soldier.

"How does that feel?" Dave asked.

The bunny moved and turned, checking its movement and the new knee armor Dave had given them for their larger knee joint. "Damn, feels comfortable." The bunny moved through a few practice movements.

"Check it out for an hour or so. If you like it, then tell your lieutenant. If not, come back here and I'll fix any issues," Dave said.

"Thanks, man!" The bunny got out of the way of the next soldier coming in.

"Well, you are one big bastard, huh?" Dave looked up at the gorilla Beast Kin.

"And you are small, but thick," the Beast Kin said.

Dave laughed. He moved to the racks of pre-made armor and grabbed the different parts he would need. "I'm guessing that you like being able to take a few hits and smash through those fighting you?"

"I have this body. I might as well use it."

Dave nodded and started to form pieces of armor with the blow-torches and anvil behind him.

"Why are you already altering it? Don't you need to size me?" the gorilla asked.

"All in my head," Dave said, his hammer falling rhythmically on the armor. "I have a high Intelligence stat, so doing something like looking at another person and figuring out their dimensions isn't that hard. From there, I just shape this as best as I think, then give it to you, do some personal alterations and then good to go," Dave said.

"Master Dave is a machine," another smith veteran said to Dave's right, where they were hammering out their own armor for their customer.

"That is impressive," the gorilla said.

Dave picked up on the sadness in his voice. "You ever thought about becoming a smith?"

"I did at one time, but I am all strength and no form. I can hammer metal flat easy enough and I want to do the detailed work, but I've never been able to," the gorilla said.

Dave looked to the gorilla with a frown. "Hasn't anyone ever taught you?"

"Well, no. I am too big and clumsy. I make a lot of problems in the smithy," the gorilla said, as if the idea was idiotic.

"But you hammered metal out?" Dave asked.

"It was the closest I could get. Having someone to make metal sheets is rather useful." The gorilla sighed. "I wanted to do something with my life. I'm big and strong; I can fight or labor. If I fight, then I can maybe do something with my life and attract a mate."

"Well, I don't see why you can't learn smithing. I know that there are a bunch of Demons and other Beast Kin doing it. I don't see why you couldn't. If you're in a military contract, then I know that Devil's Crater is in need for skilled armorers to keep this stuff in the best condition and perform repairs on it," Dave said.

"You think that they would have me?" the gorilla asked.

"I know that here, with Cliff-Hill smithies, we will accept anyone who is willing to learn the craft. We have an agreement to teach Devil's Crater armorers. You could get in through that program, if you want to talk to your lieutenant?" Dave said.

"Uh, I think I might do that." The gorilla rose from its squat.

"I never caught your name," Dave asked.

"George." The gorilla smiled.

"Well, hope to see you around the smithy more, George." Dave smiled and held out a hand. George took it, shaking before leaving to find his lieutenant, his new armor slung over his shoulder.

A whistle blew in the distance, the afternoon shift being replaced by the early night crew. The Cliff-Hill smithies never slept. The DCA platoon marched off, a new one arriving and moving to the smiths, ready to start fitting their armor.

Dave cooled off the pieces he'd been working on and put them back on the various piles around the smithy. He sat down at a work-bench and took out a carver and a soul gem covered in a thick ebony band.

Kol found him not too much later, sitting down at his own work-bench, drinking from his canteen and wiping the day's sweat from his brow.

Dave cracked his back and smiled, remembering his class the other day. He opened his skill menu finding his Teacher skill.

Active Skill: Teacher

Level: Journeyman Level 9

Effect: You can teach people skills that you have prior knowledge of, up to your level of ability. Your students are 10% more likely to understand what you're teaching them. Teaching on subjects you have a higher knowledge on will yield higher results. Teaching skills you have mastered or created give higher chance for students under-standing your lessons.

"So, seems that the effectiveness of the skill only increases when it goes up by entire grades. So, I will probably see it only increase when I make it to Expert level," Dave said.

If the level was to increase every time, then he could essentially speak in a different language and people might be able to understand him. With teaching, it was not only about the information but the way it was presented, putting a lot of pressure directly on the teacher. No stat or boost could completely solve this.

Dave stepped into a part of the smithy he had made his own. He dismissed the skill screen and pulled out a soul gem wrapped in ebony metal.

"What you working on there?" Kol asked Dave.

"Little side project. Right now, our most powerful smithy is in Cliff-Hill. I don't want us to have to go back there every time to do our best weapons so I'm hoping to upgrade or make another smithy with its abilities."

"It's a soul gem though," Kol said, intrigued.

"Yes, but soul gems are made from crystals. I'm hoping that I will be able to make this grow or form according to what I'm coding. I've also enchanted it so that if it does work, people will feel less tired, more focused, as well as have increased Strength, Intelligence, and Endurance. Tinkered with the magic of the thing to provide a boost to all Affinities. Took a lot of studying the portable smithy, but just like it, this smithy *should* grow in power the more items that are made on it," Dave said.

"So, is it going to be one of those soul gem-powered items like your factories in Terra?" Kol said.

"Yeah. And how do you like the new name of the guild hall?" Dave asked.

"It works. 'Bout time the damned hole in the ground got a name." Kol huffed.

Dave grinned, looking to Kol and back to his work, carefully forming new runes in the ebony band. "So, by my estimate, I think we're ahead of schedule with the DCA's armor."

"For now, we are, but there's always the possibility of something messing up along the way and we fall well behind. Yes, we're getting four companies done in a day instead of two and a half, but it will still take three and a half months to get them all properly fitted." Kol pulled two wrapped objects out from his bag of holding.

"Still plenty of time," Dave said. "What are those?"

"These are yours." Kol put them on his workbench. Dave moved closer as the cloth was pulled away to show two familiar-looking rods.

"I didn't code them because I know that you'd want to do that, but there is a core of soul gem, then an ebony sleeve, silver layer for the coding, and an outside layer of Mithril. Each layer has soul gem shards embedded in them." Kol smiled.

Dave looked at the rods. They looked like Roman pillars. Three-quarters up their length, they looked as though they had been twisted apart, showing the white of the Mithril, the silver and ebony layers, and the soul gem core that shifted with contained power.

The lights played off the different layers. It was only when looking close, someone could see the beauty of the piece, formed into a complex tool and piece of art.

Beating Rods

Formed by Dwarven Master Smith Kol for his unofficial second grandson, Dave Grahslagg, to magically code into tools to defend himself with.

Quality: SSS

Abilities:

(???)

Soul Bound (not currently bound)

Charge: 750,000/750,000

Durability: 10,500/10,500

Dave read the description. A small smile came to his face. He started to blink faster as his eyes became itchy and hot.

Kol cleared his throat and looked away.

"You ornery old bastard." Dave wrapped his arms around Kol.

Kol hesitated for a minute and then hugged Dave back. There was no need for them to say anything.

After a moment, Dave let go.

"So, you made the damn thing and left all of the hard part about magical coding to me?" Dave sighed as he studied one of the rods.

"Ha! It was a pain in the ass to make those with the different layer—had to do each on top of one another and then run the crystals in a certain matrix. Compared to those two conjured batons on your hip, you'd be surprised with the amount of power you can get from them. Also, you might find that you can actually hit someone who's suppressing magic without your weapons half dissolving," Kol said.

Dave scratched his head awkwardly, remembering his fight in Selhi Capital.

"Lad, you make some of the most impressive items I've seen, but other than the runes on your body and your armor, you haven't augmented yourself all that much."

"Well, if I augmented myself, then sure I could be really damned powerful, but the thing I'm doing is to empower the largest group possible. I am but one person. However, if I can give an item to two or three people instead of myself and allow them to do great things, then it could cause ripples, changes further out there that I can't even imagine but can only hope for." Dave looked out to Unity, over the smiths who were carving magical coding into their breastplates for the bomb drop ability, hammering and forming armor for the DCA.

"What is your end goal for all of this?" Kol asked.

Dave pursed his lips in thought. "To let people decide what they want to do with their lives." Dave looked around and sighed.

"You miss Deia?" Kol smiled, sitting back.

"Yeah. She's been training her brains out and I understand that, but I do like seeing her." Dave smiled.

"Well, go and surprise the girl. You two need some time off anyway. You've been making things and fighting creatures since Boranal's Citadel. I think having a few days off is warranted," Kol said.

"But there's so much to do!" Dave complained.

"There is a lot to do, but there are a number of things that are more important than work. Having a personal life and being with the woman you love are a few of those things." Kol's voice was firm.

"Bu—"

Kol cut him off with a wave of his hand. "But nothing. Everyone else is back and working their brains out. I can talk to Suzy for you. You go and take Deia out on the town. All work and no play makes life pretty boring." Kol gave Dave a smile.

Dave took a deep breath and let it out. Kol had a point. Just working all the time—it was a habit he'd fallen into with the Rock Breakers and Deia had the same with training. Both of them were always striving forward for more. That motivation and drive was one thing that attracted them to each other, but without the other there, they were liable to grind themselves into the ground.

"And when you get back, leave the fitting to us lot. I know you're working on several different projects. We can fit armor just fine and we'll get the smiths we need for it. Your research is of more help than all of this, and while you're working on that, maybe just go do some things for fun?"

"I think you might have a point. I'll finish up this first, though, and then set off for Per'ush." Dave smiled.

"Fine. Don't leave it too long." Kol stood. "I'm going to get some darned sleep!"

Dave waved good-bye to Kol. He finished carving out the runes on the ebony band before he headed out for a space that had been left for expansion of the smithy.

"Going to have to alter that thing's makeup; could boost the power a bunch," Dave muttered to himself, putting his creation down.

Portable Smithy

The portable smithy shakes with power. Do you want to use it?

Cost: 3,500 Mana

Y/N

"Seems the Mana cost has increased, compared to the portable smithy in Cliff-Hill. Probably because it's more powerful," Dave thought out loud before he hit the Yes button.

The soul gem seemed to unfurl. Its glowing light released calming light as it unfurled outward, creating a floor of smooth crystal and rising up into workbenches. A forge flared to life with blue flames; glowing soul gem crystals made up the anvils, racks, basins, and other items that were part of a smithy.

Black supports with silver runes grew upward and above. A roof grew together from the supports, attaching to the adjoining smithy. Its progress slowed considerably, but the items in the adjoining smithy had been turned into soul gem crystal.

"Wow." Dave looked at it all.

The glow faded. Inside, it was easy to see swirling patterns moving over the different surfaces. The floor felt more like wood instead of crystal, with no chance of slipping.

It was warm, but not the burning heat of a normal smithy. Dave moved about, feeling inspired by the beauty and workmanship of the building.

You Have Created a Soul Gem Construct

A soul gem construct is a building that has been formed from a soul gem. They constantly gather ambient Mana and channel it inside, to keep the interior at optimum conditions. According to the orders given to it, it can supply this power to the users of the area, or use it for other things like expansion.

The original creator of the construct may choose what is done with the construct.

You have gained [Soul Gem Smithy] in your buildings tab.

Dave changed tabs, looking to his buildings. He minimized the ones under [Terra], opening the tab [Cliff-Hill Smithies] and finding [Soul Gem Smithy].

Dave made excited noises as he looked over the information there.

"Going to need to change the programming some, but this is awesome! Imagine what I could do with the greenhouses! Do that later, once the farmers come back to me with their recommendations. Now, hmm, what should I tell it to do? Keep the base stat increase and bonuses—that's a given. Any extra energy this puppy stores up to its full charge goes into covering the other smithies. Damn, okay, that's useful." Dave read over a part where the smithies could be altered at any time. Moving items would be as easy as doing drag and drop on his interface. Growing things cost Mana but the smithy could store up to 10,000,000 Mana. It was a small four-person smithy right now, but with time and power, it could expand over the other smithies. It would be less of a power draw with other facilities already there.

"Well, what's the use of having toys if you don't use them? First, I should get that power situation sorted."

Dave looked around the smithy, studying it. He pulled out pieces of steel, whistling to himself and carving out some simple runes. He heated up silver over a blowtorch, using it to fill the runes.

It didn't take him long to make a few dozen of the items. He conjured metal over them. They spread outside the smithy, burrowing into the ground. They spread out in a net around the smithy, covering a massive area.

He destroyed the conjured metal. The runes on the metal activated, turning heat into Mana or capturing free Mana and routing it all toward the smithy.

"Okay, so next." Dave put the twin rods in the furnace. Just a few feet away, it was still warm, but once you got within a foot, then it felt as though you had stepped into Hades.

He grabbed another scrap piece of metal from his bag of holding.

Having something for him to make magical code on honed his skill and could be used in all kinds of situations.

He put it in a pocket in front of his belt. It made the heat manageable as his arms were covered in Mithril. He reached into the furnace; each of his hands curled around a rod.

Runes flared across Dave's body, his eyes silver as he focused completely on the metal in front of him. The Mana flow amplified the waves of heat that the furnace gave off.

Ten minutes later, Dave pulled his hands from the furnace. Hitting a button with his elbow turned its flames off, and the runes in the smithy converted the heat back into Mana.

Dave dismissed the conjured Mithril and looked down at the twin rods. Runes could be seen within the opened sections, running along the different layers, the soul gem's light playing over them.

If one was to look really close, they would see bands at the bottom of the rods.

"Damn, these are beautiful." Dave looked at them both.

A prompt appeared in his vision.

Quest Completed: Dwarven Master Smith Level 4
You must craft 2 weapon of SS quality (2/2), or 100 of S Quality with your Smithing Art (0/100).
Rewards: Unlock Level 5 quest
+10 to all stats (stacks with previous class levels)

Quest: Dwarven Master Smith Level 5
You must craft 3 weapon of SS quality (0/3), or 150 of S Quality with your Smithing Art (0/150)
Rewards: Unlock Level 6 quest
Increase to stat gain

Class: Dwarven Master Smith

Status: Level 4

Effects: Allowed access to all Dwarven Mountains and smithies.
Allowed to take on smithing apprentices.
+40 to all stats
Access to special quests.

Using a hotkey, he changed into his fighting gear. Dave slid the rods into the loops in his belt. He looked at them proudly.

"Okay, let's go and see if I can't wrestle Deia away from some of that training."

***

"Okay, so you know about my family, but what about yours?" Alkao asked Anna as they sat at a table in an up-and-coming restaurant.

"Oh, I'm pretty similar. I was created by my father; he's using the name Bob right now. Uh, I guess, I kind of technically have a kid. I helped Shard and the Aleph make Steve." Anna tapped her chin in thought and sat back in her chair, shrugging. "Yeah, think that's about it."

"So, Steve is your kid?" Alkao asked, a confused look on his face.

"In a way. To Shard and me, it was more of an experiment to see if we could actually make another separate and intelligent creature." Anna shrugged.

"What's he think?" Alkao asked.

"We're pretty good friends, though he bugs me at times, calling me Mom." Anna shook her head.

Alkao chuckled and his hand covered hers.

She entwined her fingers in his, looking up at him with a smile that seemed to make her eyes sparkle.

"You are beautiful," Alkao said.

"Thanks," Anna said, shyly.

"Haven't been on many dates?"

"Have you?" she shot back.

"Not really. Being a Demon Lord was more fighting than anything like this." Alkao waved at Unity and Devil's Crater.

"Same with me. At first, I went around trying to solve everyone's issues. I saw the futility of it and just started to look after my Beast Kin. We were hunted down like yours. Thankfully, Dad saved us and then gave us a second chance, a chance to change this system." Anna's eyes fell to the table before moving back to Alkao's, and she gave him a small smile.

"Well, you've already changed it quite a lot with your actions," Alkao assured her, squeezing her hand.

"Oh, the things you will learn," Anna said, sounding sad.

"They are my things and burdens to learn, but hopefully I have a sexy little wolf next to me." Alkao leaned forward.

"Oh, so I'm a sexy little wolf now?" she asked playfully, also moving closer.

"Personal opinion." Alkao's eyes traced Anna's body. "Definitely." His serious tone was broken by the grin that spread across his face.

"You know I could kick your ass?" Anna asked.

"Hmm, kinky." Alkao laughed, raising his free left hand to place his forefinger under her chin.

"I am *much* older than you," she warned, not fighting as he drew his forefinger back, half beckoning, half pulling her forward with an invisible and immaterial force.

"I'm a big boy. I can deal with it," Alkao said. Their eyes closed as Alkao kissed her gently. After a moment, he dropped his finger, their lips parting as they opened their eyes.

"I heard that the Grove is great this time of night. Come on." Alkao stood. Anna rose with him, a complicated expression on her face. Alkao led her out, grabbing their coats, and headed for the Grove, where the oldest, rarest, and most beautiful trees had been gathered by Fornau. There were many parks across Unity, but the Grove was the largest. It seemed to have been perfectly sculpted by Fornau. The collection of trees was more beautiful than most ruling castles' flower gardens. Glowing vines ran between the trees, giving off light, while certain bushes and other plants gave off heat to fight against the fall weather.

"I hope my kiss wasn't that bad," Alkao said as they entered the Grove. Others moved about, from people running to those finishing up picnics. There was a party happening in one of the larger gazebos; couples walked along the paths.

"No, it wasn't that. It's just that I know what is going to come and I do like you, but I don't want to get close to someone and lose them. I know that it is really hard to kill the others, but they're not as visible as you. People are going to come after you and I don't want to have things to distract me when I'm fighting," Anna said.

"I think the same thing." Alkao sighed. "But that is life. If we don't take a risk on this, whatever it is and whatever it might become, well, I feel like we're going to regret it when we get older. As for the being weaker stuff, well, then count me as a willing student. I have my own things I want to defend and I can see that you're one of the best swordswomen I have ever seen. The Air seems to react to you as if it is a part of you. I don't know how you're so in tune with an Affinity."

Alkao's words weren't from jealousy or anger in his own inability, but the sound of a man who saw a dream and wanted to chase it.

"Okay, if you become as strong as Suzy, then I'll think about it," Anna said.

"As strong as Suzy? She commands nearly a company of creations!" Alkao sputtered.

"And?" Anna asked.

Alkao opened and closed his mouth a few times before he sighed. "Okay, very well, but I want your help."

"You're going to need it. Can't have you getting all worn out away from prying eyes," Anna said. The look she gave Alkao made his brain short-circuit for a short while.

***

Fire had a confused look on her face as she looked in the direction of the teleport pad that had just activated. The look wasn't for the teleport pad, but for the person who walked off it. She activated her monitoring system, moving to a mage light to watch the teleport pad.

"Something the matter?" Mal said in her room.

"Our son-in-law has arrived. He's been getting stronger," Fire said with approval, leaving the mage lights and pulling up her interface to send Dave a quick message.

"Both he and Deia are pretty driven," Mal said.

"Someone sounds like a proud father." Fire looked to where Mal was reading a book as blue orbs of Fire circled above him.

Mal simply smiled.

"Do you think they're going to have children soon?" Fire asked.

"You're about to become a mother for the second time and you want to know if you're going to be a grandmother as well?" Mal went back to reading.

"I'm already a grandmother!"

"Not of Elves and Humans," Mal countered.

"Well, the Dragons are kind of Humans, just with really big changes in their biology," Fire countered.

Mal looked over the top of his book with a quirked eyebrow.

"Fine! But, what do you think?" Fire looked back to Dave as he grabbed some flowers before he headed for the library where Deia was cooped up.

"I think the hormones from being pregnant are playing with your head," Mal said.

Fire threw a fireball at him.

He made it dissolve without looking up from his book. "And *I'm* the hothead," Mal muttered under his breath, but Fire still heard it and threw another, which he defeated again.

"I think that they are doing things at their own pace. We don't need to worry about them; they've got everything sorted," Mal said.

Fire sighed, releasing control of the mage lights, and frowned as she turned in her chair.

"What's the matter?" Mal lowered his book.

"I think they'd look so cute with kids." Fire pouted.

Mal rose up, smiling as he made his way behind Fire and hugged her from behind. "Don't worry; you'll have a litter of children to worry about sooner than you think. Aren't Fornau and Quindar's children just getting into their rambunctious phase?" Mal kissed her head.

"We should organize a visit!" Fire said defiantly.

"Okay." Mal hugged her tight.

"You going to let me go?" Fire pouted, moving her hands around, making a T. Rex impression.

"Nope." He grinned and kissed her cheek, laughing slightly from her antics.

***

Deia rubbed her eyes again, adjusting the Mana light on her reading desk by pressing in a Magical Circuit switch.

A sudden aura surged out behind her. She turned to find the focus of the powerful aura moving through the library toward her.

Her tired expression evaporated in seconds as she saw Dave approach with a large bouquet of flowers and a massive smile on his face. She ran from her chair, jumped up in the air, wrapped her legs around Dave and kissed him.

He stumbled, but held his footing. The two of them smiled as they kissed.

"Hey, babe. Thought I'd take you away from all this...flowers?" Dave asked, turning and walking back the way he'd come as if it were the most natural thing to have a female Elf attached to his chest.

"But I have research to do!" Deia said in a rising panic.

"Nope, *we* have a date night to do!" Dave said defiantly, proudly marching toward the doors.

"Let me down, you dolt! Everyone is looking!"

"I didn't notice." Dave smiled as he waved to a few of the bewildered library patrons.

Deia laughed at the people's expressions, hiding her face in Dave's shoulder. The weight and pressure of her training seemed to ease off her shoulders with Dave around.

Outside, he let her get off him before he passed her the flowers. "So, have you seen any of the sights yet?" Dave asked.

"Well, the first time, we just saw my family, really. Since then, I've been just researching something for my next training session," Deia said.

"As a fellow book nerd, I am proud of you! As your boyfriend, I think we should start going out more often. We're starting to sound like a pair of hermits! Off to the enchanted falls we go!" Dave declared, pointing his finger into the air and walking forward.

Deia giggled like a little girl. Dave's smile widened as she wrapped her hand around his arm and buried her face in it to muffle the giggles.

"First! Shower! Then, clothes! Time we got you out of that traveling gear and into a nice dress. I do love time changes and not needing sleep," Dave said.

"Shopping?" Deia did enjoy nice clothes, but she hated how much work went into trying to look good. And there were so many types of clothes! How could she even start to try to understand them!

"Don't worry. I learned a few things being a CEO. How to dress and evaluate people on their clothes were a few of them!" Dave smiled. "And I can't think of anyone I would rather put my skills at their disposal—though you look good in anything." He moved closer so only she could hear him. "However, I like it best when you don't have anything on." He gave her a devilish wink.

If he keeps up, my cheeks are going to melt! She shook herself. Her eyes darted to his wide smile as he led her on. Unable to really express how happy she was, she held onto him, never wanting to let go again.

***

"How does this look?" Deia asked.

Dave looked up from his interface. Even with his higher Intelligence, it took his mind a few minutes to restart and then pick his jaw up off the ground.

He let out a whistle as he looked at Deia. She wore a vibrant red dress that seemed to bring out her smoldering eyes and her hair that draped over her left shoulder. The dress had a plunging neckline that stopped at her sternum. The material looked as though it had been molded to her, accentuating her bust before slightly pinching in to the waist, and finally coming down in a long skirt. Down her right leg, the dress split at mid-thigh, showing off her toned and tanned legs.

Deia looked upward. Her makeup highlighted her high cheek-bones and her eye color. She turned to the side, checking the fit of the dress.

Dave's brain gave out again as he watched the way the dress clung to her while accentuating her beauty without being too revealing or skin tight. The leg cut was to the back and side to allow freedom of movement and make sure that there wasn't a wardrobe malfunction.

"Babe?" Deia looked to Dave.

He stood up, looking her over, and walked closer.

"You okay?" Her mouth rose in a smile.

He dropped to his knee. "Can I propose to you again?" Dave asked from on his knee.

Deia let out a satisfied giggle. The fitting ladies tittered at Dave's antics.

"You look like the goddess you are." Dave rose up as she put her arms around his neck. He gripped her side and their lips joined.

"You charmer." Deia looked into his eyes.

He gave her a wink, his boyish grin firmly in place. "I'll take the dress and her—thank you, ladies and gentlemen." Dave picked Deia up in a princess carry before she could react.

"Put me down!" Deia squealed, her arms still around Dave's neck.

"Have a good night!" the head saleslady said. The others smiled at the two's clear happiness.

Delilah's Dresses
Do you wish to purchase:
1x Custom dress
Cost: 62 Gold
1x Clutch of holding
Cost: 54 Gold
Y/N

"Hell yeah!" Dave said, making for the door. The dress cost more than a full suit of iron armor and the clutch was as much as a high-quality enchanted steel sword.

Dave couldn't give a damn, seeing the smile on Deia's face. Some things were worth it.

"Put me down," Deia said. "Pleeeease."

"Okay." Dave sighed and lowered her to her feet.

"Thank you." She kissed Dave. Holding his hand, she adjusted her black clutch on her wrist, which held all of her gear and pouches of holding she used. "Now where do you want to go?"

"Somewhere expensive and tasty!" Dave led her out of the store.

"Aren't you going to dress up?" Deia asked. Her clothes radiated heat to fight the breezes of the city.

"But I have." Dave pressed one of his hotkeys. He changed into a simple suit—decorative black shoes, a light-blue blazer and pants with darker blue lapel and a crisp white shirt opened up at the collar. His Dwarven Master Smith necklace hung there. On his wrist, he wore his spear-bracelet.

He pulled out a comb, pulling his hair to the side, and fixed his beard scruff into something a bit more presentable with a few strokes. He put the comb into his blazer pocket, which was actually a pouch of holding.

"Well?" Dave said, striking a pose.

Deia bit her lip and looked over Dave, whose lips curled into an amused smirk.

She moved forward, just inches away from him, pressing her body against his as she traced his lapel with a finger. "I feel like we won't be sleeping much tonight." Her eyes slowly came to meet his before she gave him a slow, seductive kiss.

It took all of Dave's control to not throw her over his shoulder and run to the nearest hotel. "You are a bad demi-god." Dave's hands moved to her ample rear. "And we aren't going to make it to dinner if you keep that up!"

He kissed her, nice and slowly, taking his time to make up for the time apart.

Deia's stomach rumbled as she looked up at Dave with a guilty expression.

"See, food first. Going to need it with staying up all night." Dave winked.

"Fine." Deia captured his hand in hers as they started to move. "So where are we going?"

"You forgot already? The Enchanted Falls," Dave said. "Now, what have you been up to while away from your doting fiancé?"

Deia and Dave shared all that they'd done apart as they walked through the floating islands, the two of them catching more than one person's eyes as they walked and chatted.

Deia talked about her attempts to make a volcano erupt, as well as her greater control over Fire, and the Dragons she'd come to know, as well as her mother and father.

Dave talked of the progress he'd made.

They used private chat; it was ingrained in the Stone Raiders now, not wanting to let others know about their plans.

They finally arrived at a restaurant. They had to cross a small brook that glowed from magical stones underneath; rare and interesting fish moved through the water and artfully placed plants.

"Hello. Dave Grahslagg. Table for two, please," Dave said to the person waiting at a lectern.

"This way, please." The server smiled and gestured for them to follow.

Dave and Deia looked through the restaurant. It was large, with three different levels, but it was open and airy, with people spread out so that they wouldn't disturb one another. Magical Circuits kept the noise from traveling beyond tables, allowing for a relaxed and relatively quiet dining experience.

A pool linked to the lake outside the restaurant went under the diners' feet before coming out into an opening that spread out of the other side of the restaurant and into a large lake dotted with tiny islands, illuminated with magical stones and gems.

They were led to the third floor, where the server waved them into a private room.

"Thanks," Dave said.

"My pleasure. Please press the activation rune on the table when you are ready to order." The server smiled to them both before closing the door behind them.

Deia let out a breath, moving past the cushions that made up the seating around the low table. Beyond, there wasn't a wall, but open air looking out over the lake that they had seen when entering. A waterfall rained down from an island above, splashing into the lake.

It was a soothing sound, only amplifying the tranquility of the lake and the quiet of the room.

"It's beautiful," Deia said, looking at it all.

Dave walked up behind her and wrapped his arms around her, feeling the light spray of the waterfall.

"Merely a background to your own stunning self," Dave said.

"You charmer." Deia smiled and leaned back into him, with her hands resting on his arms. For some time, they just looked at the sight before them, drinking it in.

Deia kissed Dave on the cheek.

"You want food?" Dave looked to her with a knowing smile.

Deia pouted in a cute manner, making Dave laugh.

"Fine, fine!"

They took their seats on opposite sides of the low table, reclining on the cushions. They didn't take long to figure out what they wanted before they pressed the activation rune. They were greeted in mere seconds. The new server took their orders and left quickly before coming back with both of their drinks.

Dave drank some wine similar to rice wine back on Earth while Deia drank some Elven wine.

They continued to talk about what the other had missed, as well as joke around and poke fun at each other and enjoy each other's company.

Once the food came around, speaking was at a minimum. The food was served in an Asian fashion; there were small pieces of food with chopsticks. They fed each other delicacies they knew the other would like and sipped their wine.

The meal was cleared away and dessert came. Deia moved over to Dave's side, getting him to feed her as she nestled up beside him and they looked over the falls and lake.

With all of it done, they were both feeling slightly tipsy and tired.

Dave sighed, looking over the perfect scene.

They sat like that for a while before Dave kissed Deia on the head. "To the hotel?"

"Mmm, though we'll need some Xer." Deia hit the activation rune. "Feel like I should reimburse my fiancé, someway." She grinned and gave Dave a slow and meaningful kiss.

They separated just as the server returned.

"Do you want anything else?" The server smiled to them both.

"No, thank you. Just the bill, please," Dave said, his arm around Deia.

"Certainly. I hope you have a good night," the server said.

Enchanted Waterfall's Refuge

You owe this establishment 75 Gold.

Do you wish to pay?

Y/N

"Yes," Dave said, rising to his feet and helping Deia to hers.

"Thank you for your service tonight. The meal was wonderful," Dave said.

"Our pleasure. We hope you come back again." The server smiled. "Have a good night!"

They wandered from the restaurant, touring around the park that the water from the waterfall traced through and over small wooden bridges that took them above the streams.

They went to a café to grab some Xer.

"Hey there, little miss. You want to hang out with a *real* mage?" A late teens/early twenties Human sidled up to them as they waited for their coffee.

"No thanks. My fiancé is all the mage I need." She looked to Dave with a smile.

"Pssht, slut." The Human rolled his eyes.

Dave's shoulders tensed. His eyes glowed silver as the mage spluttered and collapsed to the ground under the full brunt of Dave's aura.

Dave growled, a bestial noise as he started to move forward on the college student.

"Babe." Deia pushed her forefinger against Dave's chest.

Dave took a breath, calming himself as he noticed the other patrons were all quivering as they looked at Dave with wide eyes.

"Sorry, but didn't like what he said." Dave sighed and once again suppressed his aura. "Ah, are those our Xer?"

He looked to the hostess holding two cups, still stunned.

"Y-yes, sir." She held them forward with shaking hands, even without the aura pushing on her.

"Thanks." Dave smiled and Deia gave her a beaming smile as they grabbed their coffees.

Dave spotted a Dwarf among the college student's friends. "You should have said something to him," Dave growled, fingering his necklace. The Dwarf looked as if he wanted to do nothing more than dissolve into his seat.

"After you." Dave opened the door for Deia. He'd originally wanted to sit down, but now the night air and the beautiful streets of Per'ush looked much more appealing.

"Why, thank you." She smiled, once again putting her arm in Dave's as they walked the island's roads.

Slowly they made their way to their hotel, the alcohol in their systems leading to more than one flirtatious comment. They were having a hard time keeping their hands off each other as they got to the hotel.

Dave got them in and they took the elevator upstairs. Dave opened the door, only to get hauled in himself. Deia kicked the door shut as their lips mashed together. They pulled their clothes from each other. Their lips and fingers explored each other's bodies as fabric fell away, leaving a trail to a massive bed. Deia fell on the bed and Dave pulled her dress off fully.

She worked his belt, pulling his pants off as he kicked his shoes off.

For the rest of the night, they explored each other's bodies, releasing pent-up excitement.

Dave woke up, looking at the sun coming in through the open doors. He looked down at Deia. She was wrapped around him, her head resting on his chest, while her leg lay over him.

Dave tried to move but Deia's grip tightened.

"Body pillow, don't move," Deia demanded, holding tighter and pouting cutely at Dave.

Dave stopped moving and Deia settled back down.

"Little nymph," Dave whispered, kissing her head. His hands moved downward in order to wake her properly.

Deia groaned and shifted against him.

*****

"I'll make that slut and half breed pay for embarrassing me like that," the mage from the Xer shop said, his face contorted in rage.

"Selyin, you think that is the best idea?" his Dwarven friend Porz said tactfully.

"He publicly shamed me! I will crush him and his family, and then make his woman writhe beneath my legs! With a body like that, she's practically asking for it!"

Porz's face hardened as he heard the words from Selyin's mouth. He'd known that Selyin was a rash young man, but he had been told by his parents to try to make powerful friends. However, Selyin's character dropped low in Porz's eyes.

He had three sisters and four brothers. He was the eldest and was fiercely protective of them all. He closed his mouth, hiding the anger welling up deep within him. *I could take someone cursing at me, but saying such things about women...*

"I must be off. I have an early class," Porz said.

Selyin's waved at Porz, dismissing him out of anger.

Porz turned and walked away, his eyes deep and dark as he opened his interface. He had heard of the Human-Dwarf who had become a Dwarven Master Smith. From the man in the Xer shop's aura, he was indeed a powerful person. And with the necklace he wore with various metals, he was pretty sure that he was that Dwarven Master Smith, David Grahslagg.

He sent a message to his father. His father would know what to do.

He hadn't made it back to his dormitory when he got a message back. His father ordered him to do nothing and to support Dave

Grahslagg in the courtroom, if necessary. From his words, he, too, didn't hold Selyin in high regards. Friends could be made anywhere; friends who were as foul as Selyin were barely worth coming to know.

Chapter 5: Consequences

"What?" Queen Selhi demanded, looking to the Dwarven messenger.

He cleared his throat. "For attacking a Dwarven Master Smith, we're keeping our fucking mountains closed. Fer fuck's sakes, you deaf?" The Dwarf growled.

The guards moved forward, ready to take the Dwarf down a foot.

He pulled out a blade of pure Mithril and released his aura. The guards fell to their knees and it was all Queen Selhi could do to stay upright in her seat.

A Weapon of Power!?

The queen looked over the Dwarf.

Devos Markem

Dwarf

Level 439

He must be one of the hidden experts of the Dwarves. A sense of dread filled her. The Dwarves were a secretive race. Sending out one of their experts armed with a Weapon of Power was a rather loud and firm message.

"Should teach you lot a lesson for attacking the Stone Raiders. Heard from my grandson what they did at Boran-al's Citadel." The Dwarf's hands opened and closed on his sword before he put it away.

"Donsk and Zolu close their mountains to you." Devos turned and marched out the door. As he exited the room, he suppressed his aura, letting the royal court recover from their actions.

It looks like our actions against the Stone Raiders are finally coming to bite us in the ass.

"My queen, we have just received word from the teleport pads. There are guilds pouring through the teleport pad from across Emerilia. They're spreading out to every city to compete in the different guilds' trials to compete in the Dwarven mountains," an advisor said after a few moments.

Queen Selhi rested her head on her hand. "Close off the Dwarven mountains to us, then have their friends and fellow guilds fight in our tournaments so that few to none of our people can make it into the Dwarven tournament, where the winners are rumored to receive Weapons of Power," Queen Selhi said to herself. The disruption of trade, alone, would be immense. Having two Dwarven mountains to trade with and two port cities had made Selhi one hell of a trading hub. Many traders would probably move to other lands in order to survive. Shipments of foodstuffs and supplies coming from other lands would have to be diverted through the treacherous mountain paths that the Dwarves didn't maintain or across the seas.

The guilds friendly to the Stone Raiders would probably beat out the majority of the Selhi people who tried to fight in the government's, mage's and adventurer's tournaments that would sponsor people to enter the Dwarven tournament.

Queen Selhi had not gained and held her position by being an idiot. She could see what was coming and it wasn't pleasant. Selhi didn't have much land with which to grow food on. They made potions and remedies from their swamps, but their biggest thing was trade. With that now in peril, Selhi would need to adapt and quickly.

The fact is that this will tear our country apart in months. Already, the guards of the cities have been talking to one another. While the Stone Raiders did their best to help them, the government threw them out and made the army hunt them down. The people see the Stone Raiders as champions for how they defended Devil's Crater and are creating thousands of jobs.

She hit the armrest of her throne in frustration. She couldn't go to them and ask how she could possibly repair their reputation with one another. To do so would make her look weak to her political opponents.

Instead, she opened up her interface, sending a private message to her spy master. She needed to know what the Stone Raiders were doing and try to figure out a way to repair their relationship. Or else, Selhi was doomed.

***

Dave and Deia wandered through the Per'ush islands, looking over different magical displays and wandering the streets, taking in the vibrant mage's college atmosphere.

They were sitting down on a park bench, reading off their interfaces, with Deia using Dave's lap as a pillow, when a dozen burly mages with an official-looking seal on their chests walked up.

"Excuse me, sir, but we are going to have to take you into custody," one of the men said.

Deia looked over from her interface at the college police.

"Hmm, what?" Dave dismissed his interface.

"Please stand up. Place your hands behind your back and come with us." Lightning gathered in the mage's hand. The other mages had spread out, all of them using different enchantments or spells to gather electricity.

"Ugh, Tasers." Dave shuddered. "What is this for?" He looked to the mage who had been talking.

"For assault on a minor," the mage said.

Dave frowned, thinking about it. He snapped his fingers together. "Ah, that little shit at the café? Are you kidding me? Screw that!" Dave opened his interface and went back to reading.

"Dave." Deia tapped his knee.

He looked down at her as she gave him a look.

Dave groaned and pouted at her. She gave him a stern look.

"Fine." Deia moved her head as Dave stood.

"Okay, where we going?"

"Due to the person in question, we are to take you to the courtroom immediately," the mage said, all of them still with their magical tasers. "Please put your hands behind your back and don't resist."

"Fine, but only because my fiancée said so." Dave did as he was told.

Deia trailed behind. A number of officers watched her as well. As they took Dave through the island, people muttered and whispered to one another as they passed.

They were escorted into a drab but official-looking building, through a number of doors and finally a courtroom where there was a well-to-do family behind one table and a prisoner box opposite them. A judge sitting at the front of the courtroom slammed his hammer against the table as the people in the seats behind broke into whispers and talk.

Dave burped as he was escorted to the prisoner box. The cuffs were left on as runes activated. They were meant to weaken the person inside and seal their magic.

"Silence!" the judge said. The room's noise dissipated.

Dave looked back. Deia shook her head with an amused smile. Dave shrugged and grinned back to her.

His eyes moved to the prosecution. There was the boy who had hit on Deia, as well as a strict-looking man who stared daggers at Dave. From his clothes, Dave pegged him as a noble. A crest of some kind was on his chest. Dave looked to the others behind them. Many wore that crest, sneering or looking at Dave in disgust.

"This court has convened to hear the accusations of grievous bodily harm of Selyin Jakon by the accused," the judge peered over to Dave, "Dave Grahslagg. If the prosecution could tell the court of the defendant's crimes." His tone dismissed Dave already.

"The Jakon family are a pillar of the community and their son is one of the greatest magical prodigies of this island. The accused is an unknown man coming to this city with a lady of ill repute. When Selyin asked for the defendant to leave with his prostitute, he turned violent, harming the boy both physically and mentally," the family's lawyer said.

Dave's eyes latched onto the boy, who smirked at Dave before his eyes drifted over to Deia and then back to Dave, his intentions clear.

"You better think about your word choice about my fiancée," Dave growled. His eyes started to glow.

"Restrain the accused," the judge said, flippantly.

A charge ran through the box and shocked Dave. He gritted his teeth in pain. It went on for some time. Dave's body locked up so he couldn't do anything.

"We do not tolerate whores in our cities, Mister Grahslagg. Arrest the whore, too." The judge pointed to Deia.

Dave saw the boy's smirk increase. Dave started to laugh, embracing the pain as he stood up. His clothes smoked and burned away as his runes started to glow across his body. Gray smoke poured from his body.

Using his soul smithing, his manacles fell apart. His magic and the box holding him warred with one another. Those closest to Dave rushed away as police sent spell after spell at Dave. He closed his eyes. His runes tore power from the world around him, as spells slammed into him, making him grit his teeth.

Just a bit more...come on, trip the fail-safe. His clothes burned with the electrical current running over him.

Dave's armor, triggered by his decreasing Health, activated. Dragon scale armor grew across him; his breastplate and hood appeared over him, growing into the rest of his armor. Spells slammed into his Mana barrier as if they were nothing. People were running and screaming as Dave calmly stepped out of the prisoner box.

"Shut UP!" Dave's voice and aura sent people tumbling to the ground, all except for Deia.

Just then, the doors slammed open, revealing Alamos, Jelanos, Mal, Fire, and a dozen other high-ranked mages by their aura.

"Hold it!" Jelanos yelled.

No one moved as Dave looked to Deia. She, too, wore her armor, her red eyes burning from under her hood.

"Dave, please tell me what is going on." Jelanos took a calming breath.

"Hey, Jelanos. Uh, so, went on a date with Deia here. Grabbed Xer afterward. That kid hit on her, no biggie, but then he called her a slut. Pushed him to the ground with my aura." Dave shrugged, admitting that much. "Now if *anyone* thinks that I'm going to listen to this fucking kangaroo court, where I'm being accused of giving the little fuck a beating and calling Deia, my *fiancée,* a whore—" Dave's eyes locked with the boy's and then his parents', all who had gone pale as he released all suppression on his aura. "That's something I won't stand for."

An aura much more powerful than Dave's extended throughout the entire room. Fire stepped forward, still in her disguise with a slight but visible bump declaring her pregnancy. Her red hair crackled like flames and her eyes were like the very fires of hell.

"Who dared to call my daughter a whore?" Her voice ripped through the room, making people shiver at her bloodlust.

"Honey." Mal put a hand on her shoulder.

She let out a growl, but lessened the pressure on people; a number had pissed themselves and a few had even passed out.

Mal looked to Jelanos. "I ask that this trial be done with the Mage's College Council," Mal asked in a calm voice.

"Oson'Mal, I agree. Dave Grahslagg is a Dwarven Master Smith and both he and Deia are part of Party Zero," Jelanos said.

The Jakon family's faces were already pail but turned milky white. A few fainted from the information.

"Thank you, Jelanos." Mal smiled. His eyes took in the room. Dave and he shared a look before both turned their gazes on the Jakon family and, then, the judge. The judge appeared as if he had looked into the eyes of death.

Jelanos and his people quickly convened the Mage's College Council, bringing those who had been at the original trial to the new one, including the judge. Alamos had muttered something about an investigation and wandered off.

Witnesses from the café were brought forward. They'd been rattled by Dave's strength, but all of them told the truth of what happened.

"So, in the end, you called a woman a slut, in front of her and her fiancé, after she refused your advances. He put a little pressure on you and you ran to your parents who, thinking this was a whole matter of great loss of face, set up a kangaroo court," Jelanos said. He was not allowed to vote with the council, but he was giving his last remarks.

"This is Emerilia. You might be powerful in social stature here, but out there in the wilds where this man and his fiancée thrive, you'll get your ass kicked or killed. Think more with your head next time, you dumbass. As for the Jakon family—it seems that you think that you are the ones who run this college! This is a place of equality!" Jelanos's gaze made his displeasure clear.

"You have highlighted something to me. Next week, we will have magical trials once again. It's been too long since the students of Per'ush proved their ability to stay on this island. Everyone will undergo a test to see what they are working on to improve. We reward hard work here, not back alley deals. If you can't show your drive and progress, you'll have to move to the other mage's colleges. We will be having these tests once every year, starting next week!"

Jelanos looked to Dave. "I am sorry to both you and Deia for what has happened here. The court rules you are free to go, with our apologies." Jelanos bowed his head to Dave.

"Thanks, Jelanos. There are always some bad apples." Dave smiled and bowed his head back.

"This case is finished." Jelanos and the rest of the council filed out a back door as people erupted into talk.

Dave was released. He found Deia and the two of them headed out of the courtroom. Fire and Mal followed behind. Fire muttered darkly about checking up on the families and alliances in Per'ush.

They reached a teleport pad and took it back to Mal and Fire's island. It took some time to calm Fire down.

"Next time, try not to burn the place down," Deia chided Dave.

"I'd burn everything down just to get to you." Dave kissed her.

She gripped his hand tighter, a big smile on her face as they walked.

Mal was also angry, but not enough to think about burning the Jakon house down.

"Mom, can you take us to the Ring?" Deia asked as soon as they were in Fire and Mal's apartment and the runes were activated.

"Why?" Fire asked.

"To show off, of course." Dave smiled and kissed Deia's cheek. She didn't deny it, her cheeks turning red.

"Okay." Fire smiled.

The room glowed before they disappeared and then reappeared inside a mountain. Dave put his armor on; the Mana barrier activated against the heat. Dave was a Master Smith—he'd spent days moving in front of and working with hot forges, but one could always escape the incredible heat by standing off to the side. The heat rolling around the volcano was oppressive and there was no way to escape it. Thankfully, his armor easily handled the extra heat.

Dave whistled as he looked around the storied house that looked out into a dormant volcano. The top had been capped off, but below, there were red streams of magma running through the rock crust.

Dragons wheeled around inside the volcano or disappeared into tunnels or landed on other houses built into the walls of the volcano. Massive wings flapped nearby, before something large gripped onto the side of the volcano and peeked its head into the house.

"Deia! I thought that I sensed you. Did you learn what you needed to from the college?" The massive Dragon's inciting eyes blinked at Dave. "Is that Dave?"

"I didn't find what I need yet, but Dave, this is my sister, Denur. Denur, this is my fiancé, Dave." Deia held onto Dave's arm tighter and smiled up at him.

"Ohhh," Denur said, looking amused and excited. She reached inside the house, her form changing and becoming smaller as she moved into the house until she was in her Human form.

"So, you must be Induca and Malsour's mother," Dave said with a smile, talking to the legendary mother of Dragons.

"They grow up so fast." Denur smiled, an excited look on her face. "Deia has told me so much about you! This is so exciting; we have sooo much to talk about!" Denur sounded and looked like an excited big sister instead of a centuries-old legendary creature.

Dave felt growing anxiousness, looking from Denur, Deia and Fire's hungry looks to Mal's sorrowful one. *Why do I feel more nervous here with my in-laws than in that court?* Dave gave Mal a pleading look.

Mal started to study something on the wall.

No! How could you? I'm never getting you Dwarven whiskey ever again!

"So, when's the wedding and how many children are you two thinking of pumping out? Are you going to build a house in the volcano or keep the place in Cliff-Hill?" Denur started.

"What kind of wedding are you thinking? Temple, public? Something a little smaller?" Fire added in.

Dave was dragged to the couch as Mal excused himself to make refreshments.

Dwarf down! I say again, Dwarf down! Don't trust the Elves!

Chapter 6: Study and Progress

"Come on, you lazy bastards! Git those damn shields up!" Esa yelled out, her words putting enough fear into the mixed POE/Player group as the skeletons rushed them, peppering them with arrows.

Off to the side, Gurren, Lox, and Steve talked about where they wanted to check out on their next scouting adventure.

Esa rolled her eyes as the wall of shields held against the attacks. The new Stone Raiders yelled their defiance as the mages and archers supported and fired over them, killing the oncoming skeletons. After a few minutes, the skeletons were down and the new Stone Raiders were celebrating.

"Stow it! That wasn't even hard; they were only level 120! Where was the communication? Communication is the most important thing. If you don't have your shit together in these small groups, what's going to happen when you're with the rest of the guild?" Esa demanded.

Lox, Steve, and Gurren waded in from where they'd been relaxing.

"Do you know how to use a shield or your blade? I swear, half of you pissed yourselves, cowering behind the damned things, too scared to react. It's about movement; always advance, always have them at a disadvantage. You stop on the battlefield, you lose momentum. You will die faster than the Demon Horde if you are forced backward! ALWAYS move forward!" Lox yelled out, his voice filling the cave system.

"Mages, where was your communication? Archers, don't group up together to try to get a hit. Sure, you might get the kill for experience, but what does it matter if all of your guildmates get killed?" Gurren demanded.

"You've fought across Emerilia and your trainers said you were ready for this! Don't make them liars! Have confidence in your training—work together and you'll make it through! Now, back out!

We're going to do this three more times today until you're comfortable with fighting creatures above your level and can work as a *team*!" Esa said, her words meant to be reassuring.

They moved out of the cave system. The four veterans stuck together.

"Not too bad," Gurren said so that they couldn't hear.

"Give them a few weeks and they'll be Stone Raider material, though they need to come out of their shells. They're like damned scared rats!" Steve complained.

Esa shook her head at them. She changed out of her armor and stretched as they exited the dungeon. A Magical Circuit lay over the entrance. It would let Unity know whether anything left the dungeon that wasn't supposed to. It would also let people know whether there was anyone in the dungeon. There was nothing worse than getting to a dungeon only to know that someone had gone in an hour before and cleared it out.

"I remember when there was just a few hundred in the Stone Raiders. Now, we've got eight hundred veterans and four hundred recruits," Esa said.

"Misery loves company, especially when everyone knows that we're the best prepared for the coming events." Lox clapped her on the back. She was too tall for him to reach her shoulder.

"It should be fun! I heard that there are some parties that are going to open up some portals we know about," Esa said.

"That could be fun." Steve looked to the others.

"If you go, don't forget about me and Jules. This training stuff is fun, but I'll get bored of it in a few weeks," Esa said.

"Can do!" Gurren smiled.

They looked out from the cliff that the dungeon was carved into. Most of Devil's Crater was still a wild forest, but roads connected to all of the main keeps. A wall circled the entire crater. Forests had been cleared in the farming sector.

The greenhouses shone in the distance, plots around them waiting for spring when the orchards could be planted.

Small villages had sprouted up as families had moved to be closer to the land they owned. Unity sprouted out of the ground, its moat now filled with water. The wall was still being worked on and with Esa's sight, she was able to see the signs of building within the city. Representing Unity and Devil's Crater, the government's towers twisted up into the sky; two separate towers circled each other, combining to become one.

Demons, Beast Kin, and people being pulled in magical levitation devices flew around.

Esa looked at it all. A smile appeared on her face, proud of what she had done and excited to see how Devil's Crater would grow.

"Heal, meditate and eat up; we've got an hour until the mobs respawn. If you've got questions, now's the time to ask us," Esa said.

***

Dave and Deia waved good-bye to Mal and Fire as they walked through the teleport pad into Terra.

"Come and see." Dave pulled Deia along through the housing complexes.

Deia laughed at his clear excitement to show off what he had been up to.

Well, it's only fair, the way he was clapping in excitement when I pushed the magma up. I nearly reached the plug at the top! Deia smiled, exhilarated by the enthusiasm and clear pride he'd shown at seeing the work she'd done.

It made her want to try even harder, but it wasn't enough to pull her away from him. She was excited to see what he'd been up to.

They passed the second housing complex, going through large twin doors. Past it, they were greeted with a wall of noise. Miners, both large and small, were hard at work. Repair bots rushed around with materials while dozens of Stone Raiders moved around, helping out. Carts moved in organized lines, carrying materials from the miners off to a side corridor that connected to the refinery.

"Dave, Deia!" Malsour flew in across the nearby corridors that opened up into the city, riding his metal surfboard.

"How was the Ring?" Malsour looked to Deia.

"Fun! I learned a lot, but I realized that I still have a lot more to learn." Deia smiled.

"Mother is always the best in teaching us how to push ourselves." Malsour smiled.

"How have things been?" Dave looked out over the city.

"We're just about to fire up the first run on the power station in the city." Malsour's silver disk expanded as he waved for them to join him on it. Deia and Dave did so, as he took to the sky, looking out over the city.

It was truly immense. When Deia had left, it had been little more than holes in a wall, creating main roads. Now there were blocks for apartment buildings, roads were cut out, structural members met along the length of the city with industrial, residential, and all manner of buildings.

It looked like a clay sculpture of a city back on Earth, just without the cars, people, and refined touches to tell you it was inhabited.

"Once we have the power sorted out here, we can start with the city's massive refinery." Malsour pointed to a massive building with multiple access points and where the industrial areas were located. Smaller miners crawled all over the area, their lasers cutting out the interior of the buildings there.

"The farmers got back to us and they love the design for the growing houses. I thought that we should go with towers placed in strategic positions for backup, as well as a few areas open just for people to enjoy a park. Also, it might be an idea to alter the light distribution devices to give off light that Humans are more likely to thrive in. We do better with sunlight around," Malsour said.

"Wow," Deia said as they moved past a massive ball of stone. Steel bands were being overlaid on it by floating repair bots.

"The ley line power station is under construction. It will take three weeks to complete with our plans. With more miners and Dark mages, I can shorten that down a few days, maybe a week," Malsour said as they glided down toward the power station within the city.

"How are we looking for starting to spin this place?" Dave asked.

"A day or two. If we stop at one kilometer, we can leave the miners working to expand. Then when those sections are completed, we can spin them, sync it up with Terra module one and then fuse them together," Malsour said.

Deia looked over what Dave and Malsour had been up to. It was hard to believe everything he'd been able to do in such a short time.

She squeezed Dave's hand, proud of her hubby-to-be.

He smiled to her as they descended into the power station.

It was identical to the very first power station Deia had entered in Alephir. Miners and repair bots were everywhere, working to create more lines to burn materials for energy. Carts holding Dave's vault-classed soul gems waited nearby. These ones, instead of using teleport pads or the main streets, dove underground to move their loads.

"I felt that it might be good to keep all of that out of sight. They can go on the streets as well, but if we've got people moving around, then we can move supplies down underneath us and across all of Terra," Dave said, seeing what she was staring at. "When I'm done, Terra will have multiple back-ups for everything and safety measures galore. The Aleph security measures are nice, but I like something that doesn't rely on Mana every time and to expect the primary systems to fail," Dave said.

"This is quite the ambitious project," Deia said.

"We don't like to think small here and this is just the interior." Malsour smiled. He and Dave shared a look before Dave pulled Deia to the front of the power station.

"So, Miss Oson, would you do us the honor and start this power station up?" Dave asked.

Deia smiled and conjured pure blue flame that projected from her forefinger in a solid stream. There wasn't any break in the flame, as if it were a plasma torch from Earth.

She played the fires over the burnables that were already in the rune-covered shelter that would convert the burning items into Mana.

The power station started to come to life, the runes releasing a slight glow as different screens started to show the line as active.

"That's my girl." Dave brought Deia close and pat her backside. "We're off to the Aleph college. Deia wants to do some studying and I want to pick Ela-Dorn's brains. Want to come?" Dave asked Malsour.

"Fill me in when you get back. I really want to get working on that power station facility. I have the plans all finalized." Malsour gave Dave a look that told Deia that they were keeping something secret.

"Awesome!" Dave took Deia on a more personal tour and stopped off at what he'd turned into his development office. There were people all over the place, carving up magical coding. Dave looked at a bunch of it.

"You're going to have to teach me that magical coding of yours one day," Deia said as they headed back into the housing complexes.

"Oh, I think I can get you a *private* lesson," Dave whispered into her ear as he grabbed her ass, making her jump slightly and look around to see whether anyone had seen it.

She hit him in the shoulder playfully. "Bedroom only, you ass man." Deia sighed.

"Sorry, couldn't help myself." Dave winked.

Oh, you're so paying for that tonight, Deia thought, firmly and thoroughly head over heels addicted to the man as he was with her.

***

Ela-Dorn was working on a particularly confusing set of runes as there was a knock at her door.

"I said I was to be left alone!" she yelled, not looking up from her work.

"Is that anyway to treat the guy who gave you the sample?" Dave stood at the open door, grinning. Deia was on his arm and smiled at Ela-Dorn as she looked up, wearing magnifying glasses on her head.

"Deia! Dave! Good to see you two. Come in, come in!" Ela-Dorn looked around her large lab. Even with all of the space, there wasn't much room to sit. Every available surface was taken up with some kind of research or parts or copies of different items that came from the portal Dave had traded to them.

"We thought we might drop in and see how things are going. Malsour was finally able to sit me down and explain the basics of the portals and how they function, so I thought that I would come over here to see if I can't get some more knowledge about it all. And Deia is looking for information on Fire skills," Dave said.

"Oh!" Ela-Dorn had an excited smile on her face, happy to share what she knew with Dave. Just sitting and researching was great, but having someone to bounce ideas and theories off and watch them understand the concepts was some of the most satisfying conversation a person could have, in Ela-Dorn's mind.

She looked through piles of paper. "I had one of them around here somewhere," she muttered before she found what looked like a set of glass frames.

"These should work. College associate's eyeglasses—this will allow you to access and save texts from the college and any Aleph information center. While you did blow up the grand library"—Ela-Dorn gave Dave a pointed look; Deia smiled, and Dave looked sheepish—"we have records of everything for this exact reason."

"Thank you, Ela-Dorn." Deia accepted the frames. "I'll leave him in your care. And Dave, remember—you're cooking tonight and we're going over the house's renovation plans!"

"I won't forget, babe." Dave pulled her close, her arms wrapping around him as he gave her a slow kiss.

The two of them looked into each other's eyes as he released her, both of them with big smiles on their faces.

Ela-Dorn smiled, feeding off their happiness. *Hmm, with all of these new places we're connected to, might be an idea to get Gal to take me on a date night.* Ela-Dorn tapped her lower tooth that jutted out.

"Don't get into too much trouble," Dave said.

"Me, get into trouble? Look who's talking!" Deia moved for the doorway as Dave smacked her ass. Deia turned around, her eyes thinning as her lips pursed.

Dave chuckled as she walked away, ogling her rear.

"Damn, you two are like a new teenage couple," Ela-Dorn said.

"It was a good weekend and with her around, it's a great time." Dave grinned, like the love-struck Dwarf he was.

Ela-Dorn shook her head, but couldn't stop the smile that appeared on her face or the feeling in her stomach that made her want to fist pump into the air. Deia and Dave were a special kind of couple who made others happy just seeing them together, their love and affection for each other clear to all.

"Okay, now, to portal things! Lay it on me!" Dave moved farther into Ela-Dorn's lab.

"Okay, so what do you know?" Ela-Dorn asked.

"I know the structure of a teleport pad and I know a ton of runes. I haven't taken a portal apart yet, because I thought that it might be better to do that when I increased my Intelligence to get me firing on all cylinders. That said, I've checked out two different kinds of teleportation spells from different people. I know that a teleport pad works by attuning itself to another one. The teleport pads stop the effects of gravity within their event horizon, then they resonate with each other on the same wavelength. This tricks them into thinking that they are one entity, connecting them across a large space. It's as if you have a big sheet of paper with two dots on it. When the teleport pads resonate, the paper bends, folding just so the dots meet. You pass through one teleport pad—you come out the other. Removing the gravity just reduces the cost of power needed, which is a lot for the two teleport pads to communicate to each other constantly, keeping attuned *exactly*. Now, over something like a planet, the calculations and changes are big, but nothing significant to mess with everything. I'm going to guess that portals, because of the distances in-between, attune to each other constantly because changing attunement from one portal to another takes time to properly sync up and is a massive power draw to open them up. Holding them open, however, is much easier than having to reopen them constantly." Dave looked to Ela-Dorn.

"Bravo. In simple terms, yes." She gave him a smile. "Where have you seen two people using teleport spells? We thought about it, but casting them just takes too much time and calculation. And the incantation is a pain in the ass, so we use teleport pads and their runes to make it easier."

"Some pretty powerful people were doing it, but I'm hoping that when I destroy a portal that I will be able to figure it out," Dave said.

Ela-Dorn spluttered, turning slightly apoplectic at Dave's words. "You want to destroy a portal!"

"Well, it's how I learned how teleport pads are made. It's the easiest way for me to learn how a portal works." Dave shrugged.

Ela-Dorn whimpered slightly, taking a seat on a pile of books and paper.

"Don't worry, I've got a few hundred of them." Dave grinned.

"Would you be willing to trade us some more of them?" Ela-Dorn perked up.

"Yeah, though they are pretty damned valuable, so it's going to cost you."

"We can probably come up with something to trade," Ela-Dorn said.

"Good. I hoped you were going to say that, because I want to speed up the development of Terra, and Josh doesn't want to devote much more resources to it. The city and the power station facility are really damn expensive." Dave sighed.

"That we can definitely help out with." Ela-Dorn nodded, thinking of a few people who would be interested in working on a new city.

"Sweet! They can help me with my summoning hall as well!" Dave smiled and clapped his hands together.

"Summoning hall?"

"Wanted to make it easier for people to soul bind a creature to them, which would really increase our fighting capacity. It's something that I've been thinking on for nearly a year. Who would have thought that combining summoning rituals as well as interdimensional portalling would be hard?" Dave smiled.

Ela-Dorn looked at Dave with a half-stunned look. "I really should stop being stunned at this point, shouldn't I?" She thought of what the Stone Raiders would be if they all had summoned beasts with soul bound contracts to them.

Dave shrugged. "Big ole universe out there—plenty to do and see! Now, seeing as you've already taken one portal apart, could you do it with others and put them back together?"

"Shouldn't be that hard."

"Good. Then we should do that and see if it works still. If it does, then it makes moving them over here and to other places a lot easier.

Do you think you can rig up something that would make the portals able to connect to more than one place?"

"We could. It would take some time and it wouldn't be the most stable. I think making our own portals that connect to other standard portals would be for the best, but then you're just going in one direction. Also, as you said, the power that would be needed would be massive."

"Don't worry. I'm working on that problem. Well, I will be, once I have my lab up and working. We need a system that we could use on any portal to make it able to connect to multiple or other portals. Would they work with teleport pads?"

"It looks like the portals have fail-safes built into them so that only portals that have the right code can connect to one another." Ela-Dorn scratched her cheek. "Though we think there is a flaw in it."

"Oh?" Dave leaned against a table he was next to.

"It looks like they have the option to be changed. Though we went through the portal you gave us and the portals that we recovered—all of them have the same password that hasn't been changed. Now, this could have been a system-wide update that keeps rolling around, as some have said. The problem is, your portals have been in storage and not connected to anything for a long time. We think that once they were tested, they were shipped, making them pristine originals. From that and the older portals and bits we've recovered, we're getting a ton of information." Ela-Dorn stood and waved for Dave to follow her. "We've been looking at their power signatures and while they're high in their active stages, they are also high in their dormant stages. They have massive networks of runes and tap directly into the planet's ley lines in order to be powered. We will need to check when another portal comes online—compare our sensors to check our theories against hard data to confirm that." She pushed into a room with a large screen on the front of it, showing a map of Emerilia and a bunch of points littering it.

People moved around at different tables, talking to one another and discussing things.

"Though, right now, we looked at the portals and the amount of power that they can absorb over time and their highest rate of charge. With that information, we were able to search for places where there is power being absorbed at the portal's dormant energy levels."

Dave looked at the map with new eyes. There were tens of portals already showing on the screen.

"When they power up, they consume a lot more power, pulling ambient energy in the area as well as ley line energy." Ela-Dorn pressed a rune on a table. Five locations were added to the map with green dots.

"There are hundreds of portals in my seeder. Why are there so few portals online or charging?" Dave looked to Ela-Dorn.

"We have two ideas. One, that the portals have been worn out, broken, or destroyed, or that they are already charged and thus not making the same readings."

Dave made a noise of agreement.

"Okay, so could we increase the size of a portal?" Dave asked.

"Sure, but the portal on the other side would need to be the same size and the energy requirements would multiply," Ela-Dorn said.

"Okay, so first, if we had teleport pads that can only connect to one place, would they be easier and cheaper to make?" Dave asked.

"They'd be a hell of a lot cheaper and easier, not only in making them but operating costs. Why?"

"Good. We can get that started. Then, we're going to need to figure out a way to jury-rig a portal to connect to multiple destinations, maybe even make our own versions here in Emerilia. Now, is there a way to, I don't know, stop things coming through a portal?" Dave said, ignoring her question.

"Like defenses?"

"No, like a shield that would go over the event horizon so that they never make it over here," Dave said.

"Oh." Ela-Dorn tapped her cheek in thought as she looked to the ceiling. "I think it would work, if we put it so close to the event horizon that it's hard to tell where the barrier is. I'm not really sure what would happen, but I think that the person would either be thrown back out, or die. We could use our teleport pads to test it out."

"Okay, so let's get started on that and you can get me up to date on all that you've found out about the portals and their runes. I have a plan for the power source, but I'm keeping it close to the chest for now," Dave said.

"Okay, but I want those portals. And why do you want teleport pads that only connect to one location?"

"One, because of cost. Two, to be ready for whatever might come. And three, to make an empire."

Chapter 7: Planning Ahead

"Thank you." Suzy took a long drag of the Elven wine and smiled at the waitress in approval.

"Work, was that fun?" Induca smiled. They were sitting in the original housing complex at the Stone Raiders' tavern.

"Ugh! So Zel's factory is being built. It's mostly done and everything looks mostly okay. However, with an undertaking of that size, there are always problems. We've got most of our trained smiths working in Devil's Crater, working twenty-four/seven in six-hour shifts to get the Devil's Crater Army armored in record time. Cliff-Hill is producing all of the base parts as well as training a veritable army of smiths. Kol hopes that a hundred or so of them will pass his standards in a month, to be turned into a true smith. Dave's accelerated the build on Terra by months and it looks like we're going to need to have that smithy running in time for Terra being opened up to the public. Then, THEN! They tell me that there are a bunch of Dwarven Master Smiths coming over to check out Terra and possibly work in the smithies!" Suzy dropped her head on the table.

Induca rubbed her back, trying to comfort her.

"Resources, we have tons of, as well as gold, but it's crazy!"

"Why don't you get some people to help?" Induca asked.

Suzy sat up and looked at Induca as if seeing her for the first time. "You have a point. Dave said that I can do whatever I want. There are people helping me out but they're working in other roles. Maybe I can hire other POEs interested in it. I don't see why not. Would be some interviewing, but then I would only have to pass on the word, okay them and they can deal with the large issues personally." Suzy's face broke into a smile as she kissed Induca. "What would I do without you?"

"Work yourself into the ground if you could," Induca said.

"Hey you two, what's up?" Steve came from behind them and thumped down into a chair.

"I thought you were off dungeon diving," Suzy said.

"I was, but now I have to watch over a bunch of new Stone Raiders." Steve sighed.

"How are they?" Induca asked as Suzy sipped her wine, enjoying the flavors as they rolled over her tongue and the warm sensation that came with drinking the liquor.

"Not as bad as I thought they might be. Just have to get them used to the runnings of the guild. Right now, it's mostly all about training them with how to communicate and fight. It's optional, but people have to show their skills in a private fight so that they can pass on without doing it. We've got a lot of new people joining who have just started playing the game or were doing other things. We've lost a lot who realized that only people who embrace all of the Stone Raiders' values can join, not just someone using the Stone Raiders because they have a name. Also, you'd be shocked with how many never even made it past Lucy in the vetting process." Steve shook his head and leaned back. "So, when we going on another adventure?"

"Huh?" Suzy asked.

"I know you're all wrapped up in things, but this is the first time in months that we can freely do as we want; form our own groups and go out into Emerilia and do things as a party, not just a guild. I thought you would be interested." Steve looked to them both.

"That does sound pretty fun." Induca looked to Suzy.

"I agree, but right now, we're busy with everything going on. Maybe, once Terra is running, Zel and his ceramics factory are settled in Zol'Ord, and the Cliff-Hill smithies are sorted out. We're going to have to come up with a different name for the smithies," Suzy grumbled.

"Metal and Hammer? Weapons 'R Us? Blades McGee?" Steve offered.

"Metal Beaters? Headache Inducers? Cliff-Hill Conglomerate?" Induca joined in.

"Grahslagg Corporation isn't bad, then have the ceramics and smithy subsidiaries and their respective locations." Suzy twirled the wine in her glass and took a big swig from it.

The others paused and looked to Suzy.

"Has a ring to it," Induca agreed.

***

Dave felt his chair tilt back, someone pulling him away from his desk filled with gadgets and his interface windows stuck to the walls.

Deia turned him around, before she straddled him and crossed her arms behind Dave's head.

"Hey," Dave said. His surprise turned into a smile as he wrapped his hands around Deia's waist.

Deia leaned down and kissed Dave. "How's work?" She glanced at the walls and desks.

"Uh, well, we figured out the teleport pad problems. We kind of hacked it together. I wanted to recode the whole thing, but Ela-Dorn pointed out that I could focus my efforts elsewhere, primarily figuring out the power source I've been talking up. Plus, she now has a whole bunch of people who I've trained in magical coding. So, there is that. How was your studying?"

"Good. I still don't know what's wrong." Deia sighed and bit the inside of her lip.

"Well, talk me through it. I am known to have solved my way through a few issues." Dave smiled confidently at her.

She rewarded him with another kiss. "Okay, so, basically, Denur is trying to train me in not only controlling my Mana in a large area, but to use it with the effect I might do with a small spell. So, she wants me to make the volcano erupt. That means I need to put a massive amount of energy into the magma to cause it to expand and shoot upward." Deia sighed and slumped on Dave's lap.

"Okay, so talk me through what you do when you cast the spell," Dave said.

"I use my Mana directly on the magma, using it in a concentrated blue flame where it's actually magma and not rock. Faster to just heat that up than the rock above. Concentrating on the pure flame and making sure that they're in the right area is really hard and saps my energy." Deia sighed.

Dave's eyes thinned in thought, his fingers absently making circles on her lower back. "Okay, so you're heating it from below, but what about heating it from above as well?"

"What do you mean?" Deia cocked her head to the side in interest.

"Well, thermodynamics—heat rises, right? If you're heating below, then it's always going up? Is there a way to contain that wasted heat, forcing it back down into the magma, not only making the spell really powerful, but containing it, using the environment around you to reinforce it? Could you pull that heat from somewhere it isn't needed?"

"Babe, you're a genius!" Deia kissed him and then tried to get off him quickly, stumbling for the door.

"Don't just focus on using your Mana. Use your environment around you, like you use your sword!" Dave said to her retreating backside.

Dave shook his head and went back to focusing on his plans and the parts he was working on, and on what they were supposed to create.

The kinds of energies he was dealing with could be enough to destroy some nations on Emerilia and here he was dicking around with it with a bunch of half-guessed science, matched with observational theories and magic.

"Well, it sounds like I'm *really* confident in all of this when I put it that way," Dave grumbled as he worked on the gravity core. There were four essential layers. One was the massively powerful gravity core with a surrounding Mana shield. Then there was the hydrogen that was going to be pumped inward. Then, there were the regulating pipes and covering that would enclose everything and where water would turn to steam and through a set of runes be turned into electricity. Also, an opposing gravity field that would make sure that everything wasn't ripped up and pulled into the gravity core.

In that capsule, Dave was going to be creating a miniature sun.

"Time to up the old stats." Dave opened his character sheet. Ever since Devil's Crater, he had been regularly adding stats to his character. It was really helping out with his new projects. Also, with his next idea, it might be a good idea to have some higher Intelligence for it all.

"Putting 30 to Intelligence and Agility ought to do it. With that, I'm just a hundred and six points away from level 200 and a new class." Dave checked his character sheet.

Character Sheet

Name:	David Grahslagg	Gender:	Male
Level:	172	Class:	Dwarven Master Smith, Friend of the Grey God, Bleeder, Librarian, Aleph Engineer, Weapons Master, Champion Slayer, Skill Creator, Mine Manager, Master Summoner
Race:	Human/ Dwarf	Alignment:	Chaotic Good

Unspent points: 246

Health:	27,300	Regen:	11.26 /s
Mana:	8,580	Regen:	24.05 /s
Stamina:	3,340	Regen:	24.00 /s
Vitality:	273	Endurance:	563
Intelligence:	858	Willpower:	481
Strength:	334	Agility:	480

"I should start to think about what my next class should be. I've got big bonuses to my main stats. Maybe I can get something that makes me better at handling people? Delegating, I'm good at, but maybe there's something more?" Dave shook his head. He had more immediate concerns compared to what class he might pick later.

"Now, I just need to get the gravity fields *juust* right, so the core settles in the center, still pulls in the hydrogen, and that doesn't tear the exterior unit inward. Maybe I should work on this in the mirror lab?"

He quickly pulled out his small Mirror of Communication. Placing his hand on it, he appeared in a laboratory with all of the materials that had been in front of him now appearing in the mirror room.

He created his first core with a thought. In the mirror conference rooms, it didn't cost any Mana. It only relied on what you could imagine.

Dave turned on the two units and the room was sucked into the gravity core. Dave refreshed the room before he was crushed and started again.

"Dave?" Malsour walked into the room some time later. It had taken him some time to access the workshop. Only Malsour and Deia knew how to find it as Dave went there to try to escape from people and carry out his most hazardous experiments.

Dave shushed him. A sphere, in the middle of the room, was about the size of a soccer ball. After a lot of annoying accidents, Dave had gone with a smaller version of the reactor. It was easier to refresh.

Dave turned the power on. It held steady before starting to vibrate dangerously. Dave shut it down, remaking it and altering the inputs on the control panel.

"What's up?" Dave turned to Malsour as he worked.

"The power facility is functional. We've got it at twenty percent right now. We're going to increase the power to make sure it can handle it, charging as we do so. Once we test it up to a hundred and twenty percent, we're going to scale it down to ninety-five percent and charge up everything we have." Malsour slumped into a seat with a tired but pleased smile on his face. He had been working around the clock with other Dark mages and miners to get the facility cut out and then operational. The Aleph had lent a hand as per Dave's deal with them for portals, but Malsour had spearheaded the whole project.

"Well done, man!" Dave grinned.

"Don't worry, your secret laboratories are set up and powered as well. No one knows they're there other than me," Malsour assured him.

"Good, but first of all, I need to know how I'm going to make the damn reactor work." Dave looked to his project. He powered it up again. It held steady for a few minutes. Dave saw the hydrogen starting to condense, making layers, and then it fell apart.

"So far, I'm not having much luck." Dave sighed and reset it.

"You want those layers in it?" Malsour asked.

"Yeah." Dave nodded.

"Why don't you have them in there to start with? Might make it easier to start. Doing it all in one go is going to be a pain in the ass." Malsour stood up from his chair. "I'm going to get some sleep. See you later." Malsour yawned and waved to Dave half-heartedly.

"Have a good sleep and awesome work on the power facility!"

Dave changed the parameters of the test and ran it again. "This would be so much easier if I had a quantum computer to run simulations," Dave complained. He rolled his neck and stopped halfway, smacking his palm against his forehead.

"Bob!" Dave demanded, opening his contacts and inviting the Gnome to his lab mirror conference room.

Bob arrived a few minutes later. "Hey dude, what you up to?"

"I have this prototype. It should be working, but the settings and the runes are finicky as hell, so I'm not sure how to balance it all," Dave said.

"I'm guessing this is your new fusion reactor?" Bob studied the soccer ball device.

"Yup. So, I was going to mess around and try to get it to work with a whole bunch of self-made simulations. Instead, I thought that you might be able to help me with that big ole brain of yours, any information you can get from the Jukal, and maybe a quantum computer to test it all out?" Dave sounded more as though he was pleading.

"Yeah, I have something like that I can use. It might take some time though."

"That's fine with me!"

"What else you working on here?" Bob said, his curious mind piqued by all of the different projects strewn across the laboratory.

Dave's smile turned practically evil. "You want to ask a mad wizard what he's up to in his very own lair?" Dave let out his attempt at an evil laugh before he devolved into a fit of coughing.

Bob laughed heartily at Dave's antics. "Oh my, haven't laughed that hard in a while!" Bob wiped a tear from the corner of his eye.

Dave rolled his eyes, and pulled out a soul gem with runes carved in its surface.

"Oh, is that one of those armor soul gems you made?" Bob scooted closer.

"Similar. I got the idea from them at least. No, this is a soul gem-based building. Have you looked at the soul gem smithy that I made in Devil's Crater?"

"You mean the one that is eating the rest of the smithy and the smiths are acting like excited little girls seeing a pony for the first time?" Bob asked.

"I'll take that as a yes," Dave said. "Well, what I did was encode a set of instructions into the soul gem. Basically, it follows a set bunch of commands, like make a sword, or make some armor."

"Or make a house?"

"Pretty much. The smithy was my first try, but these are going to be better. Also, they have a whole bunch of safety features in them, making them perfect for Terra. You can put them anywhere, feed them power and they'll grow into the structure you want. You can stick them together, or alter the coding to change the building as you want, though I am putting a code on it that only someone with the correct access can do it," Dave said.

"What is your aim with this?" Bob asked.

"First, I want to make growing towers from them. They're much better at catching any stray energies, they look good, we're going to need a few of them, and having my coders working on them all is still going to take weeks to get a complete growing tower going. With this, I can pump some almighty power into it and could have it up in a few hours to a day." Dave grinned.

"Damn. If you ever wanted to build another city, all you would need to do is mine the hell out of the thing, then put these soul gems in the right place and voilà! Aleph City in a few hours," Bob said, impressed.

"Exactly! Also, they can store an incredible amount of power. So we will have plenty of storage for any and all energy we produce."

"What is with you and conserving energy?" Bob asked.

"Hey, better to have it and not need it than need it and be fucked."

"Eloquent as always." Bob snorted.

"Though, I also have other plans and those might need a hell of a lot of power, so, over-building everything now so that later, we're not totally screwed," Dave added.

"What kind of plans?" Bob asked.

"Portals." Dave grinned. "Oh, and while we're on the subject, could you make a copy of your teleport spell and one of the one in my house? I'm going to be trying to learn more about it and the more information I have about teleporting, the better."

Bob shrugged as he created the spell and held it, ready to be activated. Dave looked it over. Once he was sure it was memorized, he nodded to Bob, who then pointed to an open space of the lab; runes started to appear on the floor. Dave wheeled over, studying them all, working on memorizing them as Bob looked over the coded soul gems and the various screens of information.

"You're not that bad of a teacher," Bob said absently, the two of them looking over the other's work in interest.

"Oh? You been to one of my classes?" Dave moved to a different Magical Circuit, trying to understand it. Its complexities were not simple.

"Well, with all my copious free time, I thought it would be more interesting to see what all this magical coding is all about. I'm impressed. It's a pretty simple method, but it's really effective. Spells that are more complicated are really easy to mess with a person's mind. By making one system that everyone can understand and is nice and linear, it will push people into a magical coding revolution," Bob said.

"Did you check out any of the other classes in the mirror?"

"Yeah." Bob sat back and looked at a soul gem in his hands. "I wish that you didn't have to run combat classes and others on survival, though it makes sense with all that's supposed to be coming down on Emerilia. With even a few levels that someone just checking out the classes might gain, it's well worth it. The stronger the POEs, the less likely they are to get run over by someone else."

Dave looked up from the runes and looked to Bob. "I've also figured out what to do with the last of the resources you gave me."

"The last of them? You make it seem as if you're scratching the bottom of the barrel instead of having the majority left over!"

"Well, when building teleport pads, that many resources go quick!"

"Okay, that makes sense. You'd get, what?" Bob looked upward, doing some mental calculations. "Thirty or so teleport pads?"

"Yes, if we were building the older generation ones," Dave said.

"Hey, it's not kind to keep old people in the dark! I swear, this newer generation." Bob shook his head, mumbling the second part to himself.

Dave grinned, enjoying Bob's frustration. "So, teleport pads are really expensive, because they're made to connect to each other. Resonating with two teleport pads is a lot of power, even more if it's adjusting from resonating with another teleport pad just moments before. So, what if you had tens of teleport pads and then connected them to just one location?"

"Well, the power cost would go down considerably." Bob shrugged.

"You would also be able to cut down on all of the extras—the complicated runes to dialing different teleport pads and the massive power reserve soul gems. What I've been working on is this." Dave shared a three-dimensional mock-up of what looked like a greatly slimmed down teleport pad. "We will have these in every city, in every village and town. Then we will have them posted at every portal and key locations around Emerilia. Five of them will connect to one teleport pad in Terra. The teleport pads here will be able to connect to any of the pads, which will only accept people coming from Terra. The teleport pads out there will only connect to the teleport pads here," Dave said proudly.

Bob sat there, thinking about it all. "Dave, you're going to eliminate the need for people to work ships. Wagon drivers are going to drop dramatically."

"We need people to handle all of the goods that are going to be passing through here. We're going to have plenty of jobs and with Terra connecting Emerilia, trading is going to increase dramatically. Yes, the world markets are going to be a bit of a mess, but I think that Josh will have a way to get that sorted out."

"Terra isn't just going to turn into a hub of travel—it's going to turn into a hub for *everything*. You're going to have goods, people, services, the best of everything right here. You'll become the trading capital of Emerilia. Do you know how many enemies that's going to make you?"

"Probably a lot, but I've heard that we might be seeing some action soon with someone trying to show up the Stone Raiders. We're not going to stand for that anymore. They come at us, we're going to hammer them flat. We aren't going to do this overnight and we're growing in numbers every day. Right now, we're just making plans for the future," Dave said.

"Well, the damn future sounds a lot more exciting than I ever imagined." Bob laughed, still trying to just understand the impact of what Dave was doing and what Terra would become.

***

Kol wandered through the Cliff-Hill Smithy. With only half of the smithies working, it felt half-abandoned, though with the older and trained smiths moving around, inspecting the new smiths as they worked and the newer smiths doing whatever they could to impress their teachers, it was no less busy.

Kol looked to a stream of carts that were coming in from the teleport pad. There was a constant stream of people hoping to work at the smithy or in Cliff-Hill, as well as materials that traders wished to sell or supply the various industries in Cliff-Hill.

Aleph driverless carts moved to the smithy, dropping off rolled steel. Laborers moved the metal, their increased strength helping them. From there, the metal was cut down and then formed into different parts of armor. Then it was sent to a growing textile mill that Suzy had made a contract with and was a holding under the Cliff-Hill Conglomerate.

"That's a damn mouthful." Kol sighed and shook his head as he worked his way through the smithy. Once the armor was at the textile mill, they were fitted with leather bindings and padding. Sure, the armor could have been fitted with auto-fit coding, but that would take a lot of time and effort.

With Dave's classes, it might become a lot easier. Kol walked through the enchanting area of the smithy. Smiths looked over the shoulders of the higher-level trainees in here. All of them were taking

Dave's classes and learning magical coding first, over the more complicated Magical Circuits.

Many were working on strips of waste metal, improving their skills. Kol moved through.

Shift Manager Yori was one of the first to come to Cliff-Hill from another place. He was an Orc, not a normal sight in Opheir, but no one batted an eyelid with all the races now in Cliff-Hill.

His gruff appearance hid his almost childlike excitement when he learned new things or started work on a new project. Right now, he had that cockeyed grin on his face, his two large lower teeth fully uncovered.

"Yori," Kol said in greeting.

"Hey, boss. Got something you might want to check out." Yori waved for him to follow.

Kol followed as they came to a table where there were parts of an Aleph automaton, specifically a number of arms, that were poised over a piece of metal.

"What is this scary-looking contraption?" Kol asked.

"I took automaton limbs and attached carvers to them. Having our people make the same code over and over again, while good practice, becomes mind-numbing after the first twenty times or so. If we can get more of them trained in fitting people, then we can speed up production. I was there for the talks with the Aleph about making our work more like an assembly line, as they said. I got talking to them about their various practices. When I was thinking of a way to speed up things, I thought of how they use various moving limbs to do welds and move items. Watch." Yori placed the breastplate underneath, just so. Checking its positioning, he reached up into the mess of limbs.

The limbs came online, moving as if studying the metal beneath them.

Then, all at once, they started to carve runes into the breastplate, several limbs working at once to make different parts of the runes. A circle formed, encapsulating the runes. The arms pulled away, leaving a magical code surrounded by a circle.

Kol read the runes, checking their depth and their quality. They would make a contained ball of Mana that would be as large as the circle, what Dave called his bomb-bay.

"How many times can this machine do this for?" Kol looked to Yori.

"As long as it has a charge. The only problem is that it can only take breastplates of a certain size and they have to be placed according to these markings." Yori pointed to lines that framed the breastplate.

"Okay." Kol nodded, impressed. "We can teach the smiths coding later on anyway and they can read the information on it in their free time. The faster we get them trained in making the armor and then fitting it, the faster we can get to making different kinds of weapons and armor. Now, what do you need to make ten of these machines? I want them set up for every size of breastplate we have coming out of the shop."

"Well, mostly, just need people who have a good handle on magical coding, maybe some people who really enjoy it. Then I can get the supplies from the Aleph. These limbs were second-hand ones that they had. The machines were broken, but they still had these replacement limbs. We can get those easy enough and we have the carver factory as well, so nothing too complex." Yori looked to Kol.

"Okay, get to it. You can get fourteen people to help you out. I would prefer if they're trainee smiths, but if you can't find enough of them who are interested or have the skills for this, you can pull from the trained smiths. Once you have these arms all set up, I want you to go around the smithy and see what you can do with speeding production up. I know that Dave has made a lot of things that have increased our productivity, but the man has other concerns. You and your team's job will be to speed up production and the quality of items coming out of this smithy. Once you have a plan, come to me and we'll look it over. If it sounds viable, I'll let you test it out in a controlled area. Even if it fails, it's better to know what we can and can't do than being too scared to try it out." Kol clapped the large Orc on the back.

"Thanks, Kol! I'll go find some recruits!" Yori's childish grin spread across his face.

"You do that." Kol chuckled.

The big Orc went off as Kol looked at the odd carving machine. "The first time it's innovative or good practice, but afterward it's just repetitive. Having people carve the same thing day in and day out is going to kill their sense of creativity. Maybe this automation isn't as bad as everyone's been saying."

Kol shrugged and started his way back through the smithy.

To most, the smithies would look like chaos. To Kol, they were an old and familiar sight, a second home to him. He weaved through it as easily as someone might walk down a street. There was a simple etiquette to follow when in a smithy to make everyone's lives easier and Kol was well versed in it.

He frowned as he felt a familiar presence, a bunch of them. His frown deepened as he growled, marching through the smithy. There was no need to weave as people got out of Kol's way.

"What are you lot doing here!?" Kol demanded, coming out to where a large group of Dwarves were talking to one another and inspecting a pile of armor.

Well, some were talking; most were arguing with one another, growling and pointing to the armor or one another. To many, it would look as if they were about to start a brawl. To Kol, it was just another meeting of Dwarven Master Smiths. Each of them had a necklace or bracelet that showed all of their metals. Some wore it proudly; others tucked it away or hid it under a large beard.

"Well, we did say that your smithies were acceptable! Did you think we just said that we'd stay in the mountains when there's so much going on here!" Quino moved to Kol and slapped him on the back as if they were best buds.

It was all Kol could do to stay upright. He pinched the bridge of his nose. "This is just a nightmare. I'm going to wake up and there won't be twenty Dwarven Master Smiths in my loading bay. Just wake up any minute now," Kol said/prayed to himself.

"Don't worry, we're here to stay," Endur said, a grin on his face with his massive arms crossed over his chest.

"Fine! Though, you're only taking master wages and fitting armor until we're done! We've got some repair jobs, and when we're done with the armor fitting, we've got a list of weapons to be made. None of that 'take materials and work on your pet projects'! You want to work on them, do it in yer own time!" Kol said.

"Sounds good to me," Sola said.

"Where's your nearest tavern? Been awhile since I got employed somewhere! Need to celebrate!" Ankol said, a large smile on her face.

"Up in Cliff-Hill. Don't make too much trouble and be here for first shift tomorrow morning. Give your names to the foreman and he'll get a schedule made up. You'll all be going to Devil's Crater tomorrow!" Kol said.

"You got it, boss!" Quino said. The Dwarves headed off to find the foreman, returning to their arguments and looking forward to exploring Cliff-Hill and the taverns.

If there were gods, then Kol bet that they were similar to Bob in order to drop so many Master Smiths into his lap.

"Well, looks like production is going to go up." Kol sighed. Having one Master Smith was like a hundred trained smiths. With their tricks, smithing arts, and knowledge, they churned out better products faster. It would also mean that the trainees would have a larger information pool to pull from. It would also be a big draw for the better smiths to join the Cliff-Hill Conglomerate in order to learn from the best.

"I just wish they weren't all a bunch of degenerates." Kol rubbed his forehead and turned back toward his smithy.

There was nothing like pounding on some steel to try to forget the mess that had just arrived.

***

Sato, Edwards, and Captain Adams all sat in Sato's office.

Edwards had just finished talking about his new work. He had dozens of scientists working on all kinds of magical coding. Fifteen of them were attending Dave's magical coding class, and another forty-three were attending and testing out the growing class selection available through the Mirror of Communication.

It had been so successful, Sato had asked for volunteers for the combat classes. Many had volunteered and he had people spending hours hooked up to a Mirror of Communication. When they came out, it took them little time to incorporate what they'd learned into their fighting style. His people were stronger and deadlier than ever.

The whole station felt as if it were brighter. No longer were they just sitting on the rim of inhabited space, trying to survive and avoid detection. They were improving themselves and becoming stronger. Tomorrow wasn't as bleak as it was just a few months ago. There was hope, and hope was a powerful drug.

It's also why everyone is pressuring me to let Captain Adams go and check out a few star systems, to check on the validity of Bob's information.

"How does the crew feel?" Sato looked to Adams.

"They're ready; they want to be let off the leash, sir." She paused. "I agree with them."

"The new corvette is operating well?" Sato looked to them both.

"There were issues in the beginning, but Edwards's people went over it with a fine-tooth comb," Adams assured him.

"Everything checks out on our end; she works better than we hoped. These runes are a lot more stable than we thought. They've decreased the number of moving parts by an impressive margin. There's actually not a whole lot that could break that easily. The crew all has a basic understanding of magical coding. If anything breaks, they have the tools and materials to fix any issues. Also, with the Mirror of Communication, we can monitor them constantly."

"What about the slip drive?" Edwards asked. The drive was old Human technology that had been adapted and upgraded with Jukal information in the war. Now, with their better understanding, they'd upgraded it again, trying to make it reach as far as possible while also keeping the corvette-turned-scouting ship as hidden as possible.

"Through the tests, we haven't had a failure," Adams reported.

"We worked the bugs out in the unmanned test vehicles," Edwards said, as he and Adams eyed Sato.

A smile spread across his face as he let out a big breath. "Okay, fine! It looks like you've put my fears to rest or at least forced me to let this go ahead. Captain Adams, prep your crew. You've got three days' leave, then you're going to check up on this map and see if these Jukal installations are where they're supposed to be. Edwards, I want that thing checked and rechecked. I think it's time Humanity started to explore the stars once more." Sato looked to his co-conspirators.

"Yes!" Adams jumped out of her chair and pumped her fist. Realizing where she was, she slowly sat back down, looking at them with an embarrassed face.

Edwards and Sato burst out laughing, and Adams joined in a minute later.

Chapter 8: Sound of Progress

Dave wandered through the testing area of the conference room he'd set up. People from all walks and races worked at their own tables. Carvers hummed as people talked or concentrated.

"Watch the depth at which you carve. If you go too deep, then you will create a weakness in the material you are working with. If those runes heat up, they can melt or burn through the other side and you might never see it!" Dave's voice carried through the large room. People nodded, some writing down notes. Others continued on as they'd already understood this.

A pop-up blocked Dave's vision.

Active Skill: Teacher

Level: Expert Level 1

Effect: You can teach people skills that you have prior knowledge of, up to your level of ability. Your students are 15% more likely to understand what you're teaching them. Teaching on subjects you have a higher knowledge on will yield higher results. Teaching skills you have mastered or created give higher chance for students understanding your lessons.

"Ugh, this skill is so slow at leveling," Dave complained. "Looks like I was right about the increase only happening when I get to the next grade level. Shiny fifteen percent." As he was in his notifications, he checked out his latest skill.

Active Skill: Teleportation

Level: Journeyman Level 6

Effect: Understanding the theories of teleportation, decent understanding of teleportation mechanics.

I'll show you decent mechanics, soon enough, Dave growled in his head. He'd talked to Ela-Dorn as they worked.

Many who studied the portals or made the teleport pads were only Apprentice or Journeyman level. No one actually built a portal or teleport pad by themselves. Each of them made a part, which came together and turned into a teleport pad. It had been why they created factory lines. From the teleport pads, it had spread to every area of Aleph manufacturing.

Dave understood a decent amount about the theories and with his background, he could understand it better than some Aleph who agreed it worked, but didn't truly believe it or try to justify it with their own science.

It was like gravity waves. People on Earth, for the most part, agreed that they were a thing. However, not all of those people knew how the hell they were formed or why and where they were formed, but they could tell you whether the theories had been proved and give you a rough overview and some background knowledge. Moving across light-seconds instantaneously might sound really simple, but they were some of the most complicated systems ever created.

Fighting with a sword, you could become a master in multiple ways and fighting styles. With science, there was only one way: you break everything down until you understand it completely.

Dave didn't have the time for that, so he was going to use some cheats.

An alarm bell went off, signaling the end of class. Many left the class, but several stayed around to continue working on their projects. Here in the mirror conference room that had been turned into a large building filled with various auditoriums, labs, and testing areas, they had access to resources and people that they wouldn't have outside.

Reading and writing was common knowledge throughout Emerilia because of messaging systems. Math, biology, how to defend yourself or use magic: that was either passed down by family, or you went to a school for that. The cost of schooling in Emerilia was nothing to sneeze at. The nobles could do it, but a farmer or a simple laborer? They couldn't afford it.

The academy gave them access to that and more. The various guilds had representatives who went around the school looking for talent that they wished to cultivate.

Dave smiled around proudly, hearing people talk about their different classes and the qualification fights that were happening all across Emerilia.

Every guild and most cities had gotten in on the Dwarven tournament, hosting their own so that only their best made it into the finals.

Dave exited the Mirror of Communication.

A new prompt appeared.

"Hmm, must not be able to do everything while I'm in the Mirror of Communication because the Jukal don't know for sure what's going on." Dave opened up his latest notifications, alarmed by the number of them.

The prompts short-circuited Dave's brain.

Quest Completed: Skill Creator Level 3

Personally teach 10 people your Skill (10/10)

Rewards: Unlock Level 4 Quest

+20 Intelligence (stacks with previous class level)

+20 Endurance (stacks with previous class level)

+20 Willpower (stacks with previous class level)

300,000 EXP

Quest Completed: Skill Creator Level 4

Personally teach 50 people your Skill (50/50)

Rewards: Unlock Level 5 Quest

+20 Intelligence (stacks with previous class level)

+20 Endurance (stacks with previous class level)

+20 Willpower (stacks with previous class level)

400,000 EXP (700,000 EXP)

Quest Completed: Skill Creator Level 5

Personally teach 100 people your Skill (100/100)

Rewards: Unlock Level 6 Quest

+20 Intelligence (stacks with previous class level)

+20 Endurance (stacks with previous class level)

+20 Willpower (stacks with previous class level)

500,000 EXP (1,200,000 EXP)

Quest Completed: Skill Creator Level 6

Personally teach 200 people your Skill (200/200). Or help your students reach the level of Apprentice (1/1).

Rewards: Unlock Level 7 Quest

+20 Intelligence (stacks with previous class level)

+20 Endurance (stacks with previous class level)

+20 Willpower (stacks with previous class level)

600,000 EXP (1,800,000 EXP)

Quest Completed: Skill Creator Level 7

Personally teach 400 people your Skill (400/400). Or help your students reach the level of Apprentice (5/10).

Rewards: Unlock Level 8 Quest

+20 Intelligence (stacks with previous class level)

+20 Endurance (stacks with previous class level)

+20 Willpower (stacks with previous class level)

700,000 EXP (2,500,000 EXP)

Quest Completed: Skill Creator Level 8

Personally teach 800 people your Skill (800/800). Or help your students reach the level of Apprentice (5/50).

Rewards: Unlock Level 9 Quest

+20 Intelligence (stacks with previous class level)

+20 Endurance (stacks with previous class level)

+20 Willpower (stacks with previous class level)

800,000 EXP (3,300,000 EXP)

Quest Completed: Skill Creator Level 9

Personally teach 1,600 people your Skill (1,600/1,600). Or help your students reach the level of Apprentice (5/100).

Rewards: Unlock Level 10 Quest

+20 Intelligence (stacks with previous class level)

+20 Endurance (stacks with previous class level)

+20 Willpower (stacks with previous class level)

900,000 EXP (4,200,000 EXP)

Quest: Skill Creator Level 10

Personally teach 3,200 people your Skill (2,579/3,200). Or help your students reach the level of Apprentice (5/200). Or help your students reach the level of Journeyman (0/1).

Rewards: Unlock Level 11 Quest

Increase to stats

Class: Skill Creator

Status: Level 9

Effects:
+180 Intelligence
+180 Endurance
+180 Willpower
+4,200,000 EXP

Level 225

You have reached level 225; you have **261** stat points to use.

Active Skill: Teacher

Level: Expert Level 2

Effect: You can teach people skills that you have prior knowledge of, up to your level of ability. Your students are 15% more likely to understand what you're teaching them. Teaching on subjects you have a higher knowledge on will yield higher results. Teaching skills you have mastered or created give higher chance for students understanding your lessons.

"Holy crap." Dave stopped moving as his head reeled from the four hundred and eighty stat points.

"I think I'm going to take a nap." Dave closed his eyes, using a simple sleeping spell.

He woke up only a few hours later. As he moved around, he could tell his perception of time was still off, but he slowly started to normalize out a bit.

"Maybe I should take a nap after gaining my stat points more often, instead of breaking Magical Circuits or fighting it out," Dave muttered, moving carefully. His perception of time was still off, making him stumble as he walked.

"This is worse than that time in university when I drank jaeger for a day straight," Dave got to the door. With each step he started to get better, with his higher stats while he was messed up, he was quickly being able to walk properly once again.

He used the railings outside of his room; after about a half dozen steps, he was starting to walk properly.

"Sweet! Not falling over! I'm running late, so that'll help." Dave ran out of the room. Sleeping and having his mental capacity taken up with work leveled him out better than he hoped.

He ran out of his apartment, jumping from the third-floor balcony. People were hanging out in the second housing complex. Everyone who wasn't a Stone Raider was now in the first housing complex.

A number of them were walking through the corridors toward Terra. Everyone seemed in a festive mood.

Dave had a massive grin on his face as he weaved through the people. People yelled out his name in excitement. Dave's grin grew into a smile as he waved at them all. He skidded to a stop in one of the corridors that had been cut out into what was now the growing city of Terra.

Malsour looked back from the corridor. Seeing Dave, his confused face broke into a smile. "Looks like we'll finally get this thing moving," Malsour said.

"How are we looking?" Dave asked.

"We've cleared out everyone from Terra. We've separated module one from module two. We've got the power plant shut down. Everything should be secured. Miners have been anchored, as well as carts. We have all the power we should need and a reserve," Malsour rattled off.

"So, it sounds to me like we're ready to spin this city like a top!" Josh walked into the corridor, his arm around Cassie. Their relationship had grown until it was clear that it was an open secret. They embraced it, something that various news services on Earth seemed to be going wild with. Dave hadn't listened to those news sources in quite some time, so he didn't give a damn.

"Hopefully not that fast." Dave shook Josh's hand as he got close.

"Thought we might as well come and see what you've gone and done now." Suzy held Induca's hand as Deia walked past them, wrapping her arms around Dave's neck and giving him a kiss.

They shared a smile, Dave feeling the pride and confidence Deia felt.

Malsour cleared his throat.

"Hmm?" Dave asked, looking to Malsour.

"Well, I need you to rune the 'on' switch," Malsour said.

"Fine!" Dave said. Deia released her arms from around Dave's neck. He moved to the edge of the corridor before he turned to Terra. He closed his eyes, tracing the command circuits and coding that made up the module. He found the ones he would need; checking their settings, he found everything was set properly. It had been such an immense undertaking that he hadn't been able to replace all of the Magical Circuits with coding.

He placed a hand on the wall. Using a heat spell and his conjuration, a silver button appeared, the coding hidden underneath it.

"Sorry, it's not a big red shiny button, but that will work." Dave put his arm around Deia while he waved for Josh to step forward.

"Well, this has to be one of the most expensive renovations I have ever been a part of! I think it's time we moved in." Josh pressed the button. The wall pushed inward and runes lined up as they sent a signal to Terra's systems.

The air seemed to fill with dense Mana. Everyone's hairs stood on edge as there was a steady but growing hum in the air.

Around the city, miners cut the last pieces of highly dense rock, freeing the city as it sat on the rollers around its circumference.

The hum increased in volume as the city started to slowly move. Everyone held their breath as the city started to turn, at just a snail's pace at first but steadily increasing in speed, becoming faster and faster. The humming and the feeling of dense Mana in the air faded away. The city buzzed as it spun.

"Looking good to me," Malsour said.

"Everything checks out with me," Dave said.

"Rotation is stable and the rollers are working as designed," Shard agreed. "Terra now has functional gravity," Shard said, sounding rather pleased.

He must have been saying it to all of the Stone Raiders as they cheered, more than a few holding mugs high.

Dave's vision was filled with different screens.

Quest Completed: Friend of the Grey God Level 4

Get the Stone Raiders' Guild Hall functional

Rewards: Unlock Level 5 Quest

+10 to all stats (stacks with previous class level)

+400,000 EXP

Class: Friend of the Grey God

Status: Level 4

+40 to all stats

Effects: Access to hidden quests.

Access to the Imperial Carrier *Datskun*

Quest: Friend of the Grey God Level 5

Protect your Guild from Lord Esamael's forces

Rewards: Unlock Level 6 Quest

Increase to stats

Quest Completed: Bleeder Level 3

Get the Stone Raiders' Guild Hall functional

Rewards: Unlock Level 4 Quest

+10 to all stats (stacks with previous class level)

+300,000 EXP

Ability to disable Jukal Link

Class: Bleeder

Status: Level 3

Effects: +30 to all stats
Ability to disable Jukal Link

Quest: Bleeder Level 4

Protect your Guild from Lord Esamael's forces

Rewards: Unlock Level 5 Quest

Increase to stats

Quest Completed: Aleph Engineer Level 5

Help build 1 Aleph City

Rewards: Unlock Level 6 Quest

+15 to Endurance (stacks with previous class level)

+15 to Willpower (stacks with previous class level)

+15 to Intelligence (stacks with previous class level)

+500,000 EXP

Increased access to Aleph College Knowledge

Class: Aleph Engineer

Status: Level 5

Effects: +75 to Endurance, Willpower, and Intelligence
Gain access to Aleph College resources

Quest: Aleph Engineer Level 6

Create your own Aleph Facility

Rewards: Unlock Level 7 Quest

Increase to stats

Increased access to Aleph College Knowledge

Level 226

You have reached level 226; you have **266** stat points to use.

Dave tried to hide his wince at the new stats, adding more projects to the mix that was going on in his head.

Even with all of the experience gained from the three classes, he had only gained one single level. Each level was nearly one point five million experience, making it hard to complete through just normal means.

"Well, that is one hell of an accomplishment," Josh said, bringing Dave out of his thoughts.

"Now, just need to get that refinery and that growing tower sorted and we'll be mostly functional." Dave looked over the city.

"Well done, babe. I knew you could do it." Deia kissed Dave's cheek.

"Thanks, firecracker." Dave squeezed her from the side. "Now, I need to go back to bed. I just got more than seven hundred and fifty stat points in a few hours. I thought that teaching my own skill with the skill creator class was going to be good, but I didn't realize that so many people would pick it up so fast. I wonder if just because I'm in the room and pointing out a few things, if it will count toward me actually teaching them."

Dave tapped his chin in thought, completely disregarding the looks of shock by those who had heard him. "Do you mind taking me back to my room? I think I need some sleep to adjust to all of this?" Dave asked Malsour.

The ground seemed to pick Dave up.

Deia just sighed and shook her head, an amused smile on her face. "Just what am I supposed to do with you?" Her fingers brushed some hair out of his face.

***

As Alkao's shield rang with Anna's hit, he jumped sideways, using his wings to allow him to glide away. The air currents changed, making him pull his wings closed as Anna forced the air to her will. She was on him in seconds.

They traded blows with blinding speed.

Even with two weapons, Alkao was the one on the defense. Anna's fighting style made every motion an attack.

It was clear that if Alkao did anything other than his best, he would die. At first, he had been scared to try to go all out, but Anna had firmly beaten into his head what she would do if he didn't go all out. He had only landed one solid hit on her, cutting her clothes, but she'd moved faster than he'd been able to track. His blade never made it to skin.

His body, on the other hand, was battered and bruised from her hits. New scars covered his body and bruises made themselves known.

Alkao grinned. It had been so long since he felt truly alive, to dance with death. The need to spill blood, the hunger that ached in his very soul, pulled on his mind.

He had felt it when he was fighting the Dark Lord's Champions, but he had pushed it down, needing to concentrate on the battle and stay in control.

He slowly let himself go into his berserker mode. He sped up, slowing his retreat as his muscles bunched up and his veins started to show themselves. He looked slightly mad with the crazed smile on his face and obsidian eyes. He felt the undeniable power of his berserker state kick in.

He pushed back the red state where he would lose complete control. Anna, Kala, and the other trainers he'd had regularly beat into him how useful control was.

Anna and he traded blows. Anna seemed to glide, her hits raining down with power that shocked Alkao. Their hits made shockwaves through the training ground. People stopped to watch their battle as they danced around the training square. The force of their hits shook the very ground.

Alkao heard the noise of a notification after a while and the falling red that would make him lose control fell away. He felt confusion as his finer control came to him, no longer fighting berserker mode, but instead bending it to his will instead of his impulses.

In his confusion, Anna got the opening she needed. A wind blade cut Alkao's leg, making him cry out in pain. He rolled and brought up his shield, defeating her next attack. She jumped over him, assisted by the air around her bending to her will. She let out a shriek.

Alkao shuddered as his body was stunned by the noise. He started to move, only to have the flat of Anna's blade next to his face.

"Well, looks like I lose again." Alkao sighed and lowered his arms as his berserker strength left him.

"At the end there, you seemed to get a lot faster and stronger, though you lost a bit of control." Anna pulled her sword away and put it in the sheath on her back.

Alkao groaned as he rose, putting his sword and shield away.

"Berserker, though it seemed that I was able to control it." Alkao secured his weapons and pulled out a small Health potion. He drank a bit. The wound would heal soon enough.

"I got a notification!" Alkao remembered, opening up his notifications.

New Active Skill: Control the Beast

Look at you, master of control, Zen, and ugh—whatever. Seems you're not just some raging monster, but a more collected and understanding one... Whatever.

Level: Novice Level 3

Effect: Instead of giving into that pesky raging impulsive berserker, you can utilize the buffs of the berserker mode while remaining in control. 11% increase in control when in berserker mode.

"How the hell do I level this up?" Alkao asked, re-reading it.

"What?" Anna asked.

Alkao shared the new skill he'd earned with her.

"Impressive. It's hard to break some of the racial trait abilities. Might actually give me a challenge." Anna smiled at Alkao as he gave her a sour expression.

"Thanks. Good to know I'm a slightly more interesting punching bag." Alkao sighed.

"Don't worry, you're a cute one, too." Anna grinned as she stepped on her tiptoes and kissed Alkao's cheek.

Alkao's frown was erased as he looked over Anna.

"Keep those thoughts to yourself, pervert. We've got a lot more training to do before I even think about going on another date with you!"

"Are you one of those people who love to hurt others?" Alkao asked, stretching.

"Just think of it as lesson reinforcement." Anna laughed.

Alkao groaned as Anna tossed him a Stamina potion.

"Five minutes and we'll go again. Now about your footing—you're not putting it into play enough. You can use your wings with great dexterity, but with the combination of the two, you fall short. You've never really worked on footwork, taking to the air where you have an advantage due to your natural abilities. So, we're going to work on your footwork some more, then we'll work on fighting in the air. Time, you learned how to really fight up there and use tactics instead of just wild melee actions." Anna paused, a thoughtful look on her face.

"We'll have to pass some of these lessons on to our forces, though they should be staying at range, only coming close to target when they're bombing it." Anna shrugged and pulled out her blade. "You ready?"

"As I'm ever going to be," Alkao said, freeing his weapons. He tried to activate his berserker mode, but couldn't. He'd have to see how he could activate it and then trigger it at any time. Having the bonuses of berserker racial trait and the ability to control it would be rather impressive.

"Begin." Anna rushed forward. Alkao's shield was there to meet her. Their blades rang out as the wind around them turned into a maelstrom, dirt and debris flying away.

Alkao was focused, not on hitting Anna, but making her have to use all of her skill. He still felt as if there was a ways to go until he truly saw the upper limit of her abilities.

He felt the hunger for violence and destruction rise as his serious face broke into a grin. His berserker trait activated as their speed doubled. To many, they were slightly blurred as their hits slammed into each other, Alkao defending from invisible blades of air as well as Anna's devastating two-handed sword that she wielded as if it was a rapier through a combination of speed, grace, and strength.

Not how I thought my first relationship would start, but definitely interesting. Alkao let out a growl, actually holding Anna at a stalemate as they traded blows. Alkao took a hit to the side. He turned; his wing flashing out and making Anna dodge and unable to follow up with a killing attack. Alkao's pain was dimmed as they continued the fight.

The two of them smiled like the predators they were as DCA soldiers watched. Many of them saw the strength of their leader and one of the most respected advisors to the DCA. Some doubted their ability to ever get to that level; others took heart in that even their leader trained as hard as possible to protect his people. Others vowed to one day be as strong as them.

DCA officers went around, bellowing out orders and getting them back to training. They fought with a new ferocity compared to before, focused on the future.

Chapter 9: Crowning Achievements

Malsour manipulated the walls with his Mana. There was something incredibly satisfying with building things through his magic. In the space of a few hours, he could do what would take miners, repair bots, and lower-level mages days.

He was working on the refinery within Terra. The refinery in the attached housing complexes was backed up with several weeks' worth of material. The refinery had one complete line of crushers working. Past the crushers, a heating and extracting assembly would pull out the various materials, sorting them into different groups. A number of materials were removed from here, to be used or placed in the Stone Raiders' storage, which had been moved out of the housing complex into a large warehouse that was heavily runed and protected.

Anything that wasn't picked up or thrown out was sent to the smelting area to completely refine down the metals and materials. The heating and extracting assembly was working at thirty percent, with crafters and coding apprentices working on the different runes.

Malsour was working on the smelting area. It was pretty simple. The most complex work happened in the extracting area, with a number of Aleph limbs sensing and sorting out materials.

He just needed to make an area that was capable of moving the sorted materials into various furnaces to be heated so that the slag could be pulled out and the molten refined metal could be poured into shiny new ingots.

He had a ready supply of metals that had been delivered to the area. He willed them into shapes, from smelting crucibles to massive furnaces, cranes and lifts that would move the materials around the area. He compressed the stone to make surfaces that would be okay if some of the molten metal spilled.

He engraved some large runes in different places.

To someone watching, it seemed that the metals were picked up by the ground and formed into various shapes, the different parts of the area coming together like some elaborate puzzle.

Standing on a pillar of stone, Malsour looked over it all with pride. Materials were moved through the facility on rails affixed to the ceiling. Beyond the doors out of the area were the cooling facilities where ingots were magically cooled after they were poured. Waiting for the metals to naturally cool would slow down the process too much. Here, every single metal other than Mithril could be smelted down into its component parts.

When he said every metal, he meant it.

His refinery was the first one ever built with the ability to process all of the rarer materials. Aluminum had its own run, which was much more complicated because of the need to further separate it and combine it with different materials. Iron and steel lines were next to each other. Only five percent of the iron that entered the refinery's smelting area actually became refined iron; the rest would go on to become steel.

He had been studying how different metals were refined and worked with for many years. His Dark Affinity and interest in metals and materials meant that he had dedicated extensive time and effort researching and refining the processes. He'd made a number of trips to the Aleph college and talked to Bob, Shard, and Jeeves, the Dwarven AI, to gather as much information as possible. With everything, Terra would be the largest producer of titanium and aluminum, and that was with just one refinery.

Malsour wiped sweat from his brow as the last of the pieces were put into place. He opened up a hole through the floor and created a ramp upward. It opened up to the underground pathways.

These were an innovation of Dave's.

The underground pathways were the supply tunnels of the city. The carts could move down here as fast as they desired, never having to stop for people walking in their way. They were also without air. So, carts could move even faster without air resistance.

Malsour fitted an air lock to the hole he'd made and started working on the magical coding for the doors and the air tubes leading in and out of it.

I wonder if Dave will get permission to put them throughout Terra? Would be pretty sweet to look out over the city while accelerating in a bunch of carts.

"Though, there would be a massive demand for silicate—that will be pretty costly. Maybe, when we've mined enough resources." Malsour used his finger to carve out a rune; others started to appear around his finger, creating a complete magical code.

"Well, with Dave's sensors, we probably have a bunch of different material deposits that we can find already," Malsour muttered to himself as he looked over his work. He pulled out an ingot of silver and willed it to fill the runes. That done, he left and activated the air lock.

It worked perfectly. Malsour looked out over the smelting area. It had taken him nearly five hours, but it had come together into several smelting lines, all ready and waiting for their materials.

Malsour started working on the magical coding, but the thought of it made his brain feel as if his head was too small. He groaned, holding his temples.

"Damn, dude. I know you're a Dragon and all, but this is some impressive ass work." Steve walked into the smelting area, admiring it all.

"All in a day's work." Malsour grinned and took a sip of a Health potion. His headache lessened, but he was pretty Mana-fatigued.

"How's the coding going?" Malsour asked. Although there were dozens of coders in the refinery, there needed to be some quality control so that an essential part of the refinery didn't break from a wrong rune or line of them. So, looking over their coding was Steve.

After a talk with Kol, it seemed he'd understood just how vital coding was to him. He'd downloaded all of the information Dave could give him, and then went and asked Dave for everything he'd runed. He downloaded all of that and Dave had given him a test: create Dave's one-way teleport pads.

He'd done it within a week and Dave had qualified him as a master coder. Steve had even got a title for it. Being technically a created creature, he couldn't gain skills or increase in abilities other than fighting, the strength of his soul bound master, or having his physical body altered, like with his new limbs.

"Coding is coding. Once you know the symbols and the right order to put them in, it gets pretty easy. We should have most of it done within the next few days. I'm going to get some repair bots working in here," Steve said.

"I heard that you are now using the repair bots in order to code?" Malsour asked.

"Yeah. It's not hard for me to control them and I can work with all of them at the same time. I need to do some changes to my personal coding and circuits, but I think that I'll be able to control more of them after some work. It's simply a factor of processing power and memory, no need for Willpower or any of those stats."

Malsour nodded, impressed. "Well, I wish you luck with that. You going to be ready for those greenhouse units next week?"

"Well, I think that Dave is working on a way to make the greenhouses faster than we thought. Looks like he's been messing around with something like that growing soul gem smithy in Devil's Crater."

"Well, he isn't one to just go with what works." Malsour sighed.

"Ain't that the truth." Steve grinned.

"I'll see you later; I'm going to get some sleep and nurse this damn headache," Malsour said.

"See you tomorrow. Good thing we don't have to walk all the way to the housing complex!"

"Agreed!" Malsour snorted and headed out of the refinery.

***

It had been two weeks since Terra had come online. With the abundance of power from the power station facility, the city had a ton of extra power. In fact, it had been cut to a twenty percent draw while the power station on Terra only had two running power extractors.

It was why Dave found himself working in the location of what would be his third smithy subsidiary, working on a soul gem in his hands.

He carved the last rune into the ebony covering. Blowing the shavings clear, he took a pot of silver resting on top of a torch and poured it on the ebony. He carefully controlled the metal, using his soul smithing so that exactly enough silver fell into the runes.

He conjured metal over his hands, grabbing the soul gem and holding it over the torch. He used his Touch of the Land, and then his soul smithing to meld the soul gem and ebony band together.

He studied what he was doing, making a few mental notes. He was the only person capable of making soul gem buildings currently so he was trying to break down what he was doing and make a spell that could meld soul gem with metals.

The soul gem was large, weighing about ten pounds, thirty centimeters long and ten wide.

He took it, leaving the table he had been working at and moving into the center of where the smithy would be.

It was a wide open area, slightly curved with the city. Smooth stone covered the area. He'd carved runes into the ground; silver filled them. He walked to an indent in the ground in the center of the open area. He put the soul gem into the hole. A bit of Dark magic made the rock close on the soul gem.

"Okay, so let's see how this goes." Dave turned the ebony covering and lined up the runes. He jogged away as he heard a cracking noise behind him, as if ice were growing across a cold lake. He got to the edge of the smithing area where his table was located.

"Uh, well, I guess that's what I get for using a vault-classed soul gem." Dave scratched his head. The soul gem seemed to have erupted from the ground. A floor stretched out around it for fifty meters. Posts grew upward, creating a second story. It grew upward and outward at a rapid pace. Workbenches, tool racks, furnaces, and burners grew from the soul gem's central location.

Dave watched the smithy grow before his eyes, smiling at it. A number of other Stone Raiders in the area came over to have a look at what was going on. Carts with soul gems on them appeared, pouring power into the construct and speeding up the growing process.

It continued to grow as Lucy found Dave working on another ebony band, a soul gem next to him.

"So, I guess this is how you proposed to fix our power-saving issues?" Lucy pointed at the growing multi-floored smithy.

"Well, one way. I was already working on this, pretty much a scaled-up version of what I made in Devil's Crater. We can run our power station at full and it will take just a few days to build this. Once it's done, then it can hold a hell of a lot of power. I've connected it into the power grid I ran so that if the power station is creating more energy than the carts can hold, it will be distributed through the grid and into here. In the later modules, I want to make all of the buildings like this so that they can hold a charge. I hate wasting energy." Dave grinned. "I didn't want to use this on the greenhouses right away. It needs some more testing first. If this fails, then it's not that big of a loss, but if we have it with the growing towers which are supposed to be ten floors tall and all over the place, it wouldn't be the best."

"Agreed. Better to scale up than go from a simple building to an apartment. I knew that they were a smart idea, but I didn't expect that they would look beautiful." Lucy looked over the growing smithy with a smile. "We've come pretty far since we started, huh?"

"Further than I thought possible," Dave agreed as he looked from the smithy to the miners that were carving out places for parks, hollowing out towers for living quarters, training rooms, shops, and banks. Stone Raiders wandered around, helping out where they could or just taking in the sights. There was only a few hundred of the nine hundred and growing Stone Raiders Guild members here. Most had come and checked out the new city, staking out claims on rooms and living quarters.

Despite everything they'd accomplished, there was still a lot more work to be done. The miners were carving out rooms, but they couldn't do anything but massive runes. Dave had found that the repair bots with a light enchantment on their legs were the best at carving out the complex coding.

"I was thinking the other day about Earth," Lucy said.

"Oh?" Dave looked to her.

"How are you able to play so much? You're an E-head, but I keep on seeing that you're making decisions back on Earth," Lucy said.

"Well, that was some subtle questioning." Dave grinned.

"With the amount of questioning and information that I get from pulling apart coded messages or watching through the Aleph scouts we've got posted everywhere, actually asking a straightforward question is pretty nice." Lucy smiled.

Dave laughed. "Well, you do make a good point." He crossed his arms. His face turned serious as he looked at Lucy.

Her eyebrow quirked. "This is the part where you're thinking of whether or not you should tell me something, something that might change our relationship?"

"You're good and I don't know if I can tell you yet." Dave shrugged.

"Do you trust me?" Lucy asked seriously.

"Yes, I trust all of the Stone Raiders, but this isn't something as simple as trust or not," Dave said.

"Well, I'm happy you trust everyone here. Seems we did our vetting right." Lucy smiled.

Dave returned the gesture, relieving some of the tension in the air. "Okay, well, you might as well be my test subject. You want to learn the truth?"

"Yes, I want to know the truth." Lucy held his gaze.

"Come with me." Dave stood, and led her out of the city and toward the teleport pad.

Chapter 10: Initiation

"So, where are we going?" Lucy asked.

"Just need to show you the power station. Stay close—don't want you to stumble into any of the power couplings," Dave said. He was acting odd.

Though, what would you expect when the most powerful man in the world was found out and then I started asking questions about his life?

It didn't take them long to pass through the housing complex. Dave talked to the controllers and they opened a portal.

Dave led the way into the power station. The air was thick with Mana while carts moved with large soul gems on them, each of them carrying a couple of the vault-classed gems.

"We're going to have to make a factory for those. Right now, we're buying them from the Aleph. They're being really nice, seeing as they need them nearly as bad as us. With us both being able to create them, then we won't need to dump so much of it into the city's power grid, and we can also start using them to supply the different nations with power," Dave said as they walked through the large multi-story facility.

"Supplying them with power? As in charged soul gems?" Lucy asked.

"Yeah. Could turn into a new currency—soul gems for different items. Be a bit more stable than coins, which we could use to make things." Dave didn't head into the main area of the facility but a secondary command station to the facility.

"But we'd need something less than a vault-classed soul gem for that," Lucy said.

"Well, we could make grand, greater, and those types with ease. I spent a few months working on soul gems to try to figure out how to make the vault-classed ones. I could use that same information, give it to a bunch of researchers and get them to figure it out." Dave shrugged.

"So, that's why you helped to make that Mirror of Communication school? Have the people who are going there work on your projects that you don't want to deal with?" Lucy laughed.

"Well, it is pretty convenient and I would give them a share of the profits from the royalties, though I made that school for other reasons." Dave activated a hidden rune in the command center. He indicated for Lucy to follow him and pushed a section of the wall, which turned out to be a doorway. Lucy followed. The door closed behind her.

She stopped in complete darkness before lights came on. She stepped out of the short corridor and found herself in a massive room with a soul gem matrix across the walls. There were a few floors to the place, all with what looked like various labs.

"What is this place? It's not on the plans." Lucy looked to Dave.

"Well, I needed a place to make things where the Jukal couldn't watch." Dave headed up to the laboratories. Each were large rooms with a corridor ending in a wall. It looked as if it could be expanded if Dave willed it.

"Jukal?" Lucy asked.

"We'll discuss that soon enough," Dave responded.

Okay, so what are you making in here that is so dangerous? Lucy wondered what the hell he was trying to hide in a video game.

"That." Dave pointed to a large metal box in the corner with runes all over it. "And that." His finger moved over to a spherical object with runes around it but not glowing.

"Okay? Big metal boxes? What does this have to do with how you can play so much and still be out and about in the world?" Lucy shook her head and crossed her arms, thinking Dave was screwing with her.

"Well, for that, you're going to need to sit down and open your mind, because we're going to have a long conversation that you're not going to really like." Dave opened his interface and sent a message before he grabbed one of the rolling spinny chairs that lay around the lab.

"Well, this all seems rather creepy." Lucy took a seat and faced Dave.

"If you were to know what was real and what was fake—would you be interested?" Dave asked.

"Sounds like a line from a movie. Do you have pills?" Lucy snorted.

Dave gave her a sad smile. "For curiosity's sake." Dave leaned back in his chair, his eyes never leaving Lucy.

Lucy thought about it for a while and shrugged. "I'd want to know what was real."

Dave scratched his head and sighed. "Okay, so technically, it's closer to the year 3043 than the early two-thousands. Eight hundred years ago, Humanity was pushing their boundaries, reaching farther than anyone had ever gone before. They wandered into a spacefaring empire. They were called the Jukal Empire, tens of spacefaring races controlled by the Jukal species. Every planet, every race was given a job, compartmentalizing the races. Factories were not a thing and the Jukal controlled the market. The Jukal were used to aggressive species and others that they raised out of the dirt, making them think that they were some techno-gods.

"And here was Humanity. We had multiple star systems under our belt and we didn't want to become a part of their system. We wanted to trade and learn from them. Some nations started stealing from them to get tech, but most of Humanity were just wowed by the Jukal Empire and other races. We weren't alone anymore. The problem was that the more time Humanity got to know the Jukal Empire, the more tech that moved between the two groups and the people who had been supporting the empire saw that there was another way to live, another group that might help them out of their slavery. Do you know what happens when someone shows the oppressed that there is another way?" Dave asked.

"They fight? What does this have to do with anything?" Lucy asked, confused.

"I'm getting there," Dave said. "And yes, you're right. When someone finds out that they have a way out of oppression, they fight. Well, the Jukal Empire didn't want to give up their position. Empires do not go down easily, so they shut down trade and started to mass their ships.

"Us Humans, we've fought thousands of battles since we started recording histories, even more before that. The Jukal tried to hide their actions, but they knew what was going on—spies found out. Humanity started to raid the Jukal and activate their war fleets. The Jukal technology was more advanced and they had numbers. Humanity started training people in VR and building fleets.

"The Jukal, confident in their victory, started pushing into Humanity-controlled systems, intent on subduing us to make us useful or wipe us out."

There was a noise from where they had entered. A short Gnome walked into the room.

"Hey, Dave, Lucy. So, what's going on?" the Gnome asked.

Lucy did an Analyze on him.

Bob McMahnon

Gnome

???

"Who are you?" Lucy asked.

"This is Bob, though we'll get to that later." Dave looked to Bob. "I'm telling her the truth. She's our intel officer, so she might be able to tell me a better way to tell the rest of the Players and POEs. Grab a seat."

"Okay, well, this is sure to be weird as hell." Bob grabbed a chair and pushed over to Dave. "Ha! These *are* great fun! Not as comfortable as my chair, though!"

"Bob." Dave sighed as he looked at the Gnome playing around in his chair.

"Right, serious business and all that." Bob used his small feet that barely reached the floor to move over toward them.

"Okay, so, war took over. The Jukal Empire's fleets hammered Humanity's. While they put up a good defense and took out a lot of the empire's forces, in the end the Jukal Empire had too many ships and they wiped out every Human they came across. Thousands fled in every direction and Sol system was destroyed. Now, the Jukal had a problem. Bob, I think this is your part." Dave sat back.

Bob cleared his throat.

"With Humanity spread across the stars, the Jukal fleets had to go hunting to make sure that Humanity never made it back from the brink. It was a massive undertaking and their ranks were already greatly reduced. The Jukal fleet had been made for two purposes: to destroy 'aggressive species,' those that tried to upset the balance of the empire or actively trying to kill anything they could get a hold of, or conquering races occupying a planet's surface that the empire wanted and didn't agree to their terms. Now, these forces were gone for a few centuries, tracking down Humans and losing many ships in the process. The empire needed a way to fight off these species. I came up with an idea." Bob scratched his cheek awkwardly and took a deep breath.

"I didn't want to see another race as brilliant as the Humans be just another entry in the empire's victory books. I knew a number of Earth scientists and found their ideas refreshing and interesting. Thankfully, my interactions were never discovered by the empire. We needed a way to deal with the aggressive species without using the Jukal fleet. Humans used VR to become some of the greatest pilots and fighters seen. I studied the original VRMMORPG's. Humans lost their inhibitions and acted freely. Caring less and acting on their whims, they were *powerful*. Jukal tech was on the level of magic, an interface made up of a nanoweave around a person's brain and an integrated processor to take your thoughts, translate it through nanites and implants into reality. Appears to be magic, but it truly is just techno wizardry. I proposed to blend the two together: grow Humans and make them think they're playing a game, then watch as they cut back the aggressive species. Sure, they were in a prison they didn't know about, but they would survive as a species, even if it was in an odd zoo. You could continue to innovate and thrive.

"However, with time, it stopped being a secret project and started to become a reality show: watch the dumb Humans as they fight and keep the interesting aggressive species alive for entertainment! For five centuries, this has gone on. The Jukal fleet hangs out in a few systems and moves around the empire, but they aren't the true fighting force of the empire. You are—Humanity's unknowing slave race, the population of Emerilia. Translated from Jukal, it means Trapped Mind. I created a simulated prison, called it Earth and imbued Emerilia with technology to make it seem like a virtual reality game." Bob's appearance changed to what could only roughly be called a frog. It was purple, furry with a large stomach, bulbous eyes, and limbs that looked like hands but moved like seaweed in water.

Lucy looked at the peculiar creature, not overly stunned.

Bob changed back to his Gnome appearance. "I am Lo'kal. I started the Trapped Mind project," Bob said, sounding sad.

"Okay, so, what is this, some side quest?" Lucy asked. "That is some interesting transformation. Wish I could teach my agents that."

She looked at Bob and Dave, who looked at each other. Her smile fell from her lips at their serious expression.

"Can you meet her on Earth?" Dave asked.

"I can do it. Take me a few minutes to set up everything." Bob stood.

"Sounds good," Dave said.

Bob headed out of the room.

"What are you talking about?" Lucy asked.

"Could you log off for me? I can prove that this is real," Dave said.

Lucy snorted and stood. "I just wanted to know how you were walking around and playing this game so much. I didn't know you would troll me this hard."

"I haven't left the game in nearly a year." Dave looked at her.

"So, what? You have a body double?" Lucy asked.

"Just, please, trust me. Log out and you'll see."

"Fine." Lucy opened up her menu.

"Don't do it in here. This is way too heavily warded for the AI to read you," Dave said.

"Okay," Lucy said, getting annoyed with the prank.

They headed out of the secret lab. The door closed behind Dave.

"Is this okay?" Lucy asked.

"This will work," Dave said.

Lucy pulled up her interface to find her logout.

Log off commands

You might be leaving, but your character is still here. Leave commands for them to complete while you're away.

(Beware: if you have your character stray into danger and they die, it will count as a normal death. Only soul bound items will stay with you.)

Lucy didn't put in any commands and pushed the window to the side.

System Message

Are you happy with your commands?

Y/N

We advise sleeping (Saving) before exiting.

Lucy pressed Yes.

Her world went black, before she found blinking LEDs looking down at her. She pressed a button on the hatch of the full immersion pod. It retracted; lines pulled out from her form-fitting suit that looked after her bodily needs while she was under. She got up and stretched. She was only slightly stiff, and not hungry or tired at all. She looked around her pod.

She was in the E-head facility in Japan. There were eight identical pods on the walls around her, all of them humming slightly with their occupants inside. Lights turned on around her. She looked around, sighing and moving to the end of the room, where there were four more compartments of people in their immersion pods.

That was when a Gnome appeared in front of her. One minute, he wasn't there. The next, he was.

"Hello, Lucy," Bob said.

"Hey Bob, funny prank." Lucy rolled her eyes before she stopped. "Wait, how are you here? This—this is Earth?"

Bob grew and changed, turning into a Jukal as Lucy took a hesitant step backward. Bob reached out with his hand, touching hers. It wasn't some hologram or something made up; it was a real limb.

"I won't hurt you," Bob promised, staying still.

"Can you change into your other form?" Lucy asked, not too comfortable with the Jukal form.

"Certainly." Bob reduced in size.

Lucy touched and prodded him. "What is going on?"

"What Dave told you was the truth. Earth is a simulation made to get people to play Emerilia, to fight the aggressive species. Now, it's a source of innovation, entertainment, and energy for the Jukal

Empire. Look, I can even become immaterial," Bob said as Lucy's hand passed through him as if he didn't exist.

"And materialize again."

Lucy's hand was stuck in his head, but as she pulled it out, feeling wet and slimy, his face didn't change at all.

"But? How? Why?" Lucy asked.

"For that, you'll find your answers in Emerilia," Bob said.

Lucy had a thousand thoughts running through her head. She checked; there was no interface. As she thought of logout, nothing came up. Everything that would be in a game wasn't available.

If he can be here and there at the same time and become immaterial here, then Earth and its laws can't be real. I've already left Earth behind. With this, I'm just truly accepting that I am a true E-head.

Lucy nodded, firm in her resolve even with hundreds of questions.

"It looks like you've reached a decision. When you want to leave, just think of yourself waking up in Emerilia." Bob smiled and disappeared.

Lucy closed her eyes, thinking of the power facility. As she opened her eyes again, she looked at Dave, who was nervously playing with a band of ebony.

Dave put the band away. Lucy made to talk, but Dave held up a finger.

He pressed the rune again and the door to his secret lab opened. Lucy moved through; Dave followed.

"How in the fuck is this possible? It—it's fucking scary to think about, frankly!" Lucy rubbed her head and paced, clearly overwhelmed.

Dave let out a laugh and smiled at Lucy. "Welcome to the truth—welcome to Emerilia."

"Holy shit, does anyone else know? What about the POE?"

"My team knows. The POE were born and raised here. This is their land to them and it has been for generations. Players are grown, conditioned and allowed access to Emerilia once their cycle has reached maturity," Dave said, eager to answer any questions Lucy had.

Lucy looked around, her mind moving all over the place. Catching a glimpse of the boxes Dave pointed out earlier, she asked, "What are those big metal boxes with runes on them?" Lucy pointed in their direction.

"One is a fusion generator prototype. The other is a system I hope to use to form Mana wells from," Dave said.

"And since this is real, you're actually going to build a fusion reactor? Isn't that really unstable?" Lucy said.

"Yes, but we can respawn," Dave said.

"How does that work?" Lucy asked.

"This is going to be a long night." Dave sighed and smiled as he sat back in his chair.

***

"Exiting slip stream," Anders called out as the corvette *Phoenix* entered a new system.

"Miko, check our stealth systems," Adams said. It was the third system that they had entered and the first one that was supposed to have the Jukal Empire's presence.

Everyone was tense as Miko ran her tests.

"All systems are functioning within reasonable tolerances," Miko said from her station in the belly of the corvette around the reactor.

"Quinn, Forsyth?" Adams called out to the two other members of her command team. There wasn't a need for many more on such a small ship.

"Sensors are receiving telemetry through passives," Quinn replied.

"Weapons are ready and waiting; shields ready to be deployed within a second," Forsyth finished.

"Immediate area for five light-minutes is clear," Quinn said.

"Good. Take us down to fifty percent readiness. We will wait for thirty minutes before advancing farther into the system," Adams said.

It was one of the longest half hours Adams had ever waited through, looking over her screens and fighting herself as she wanted to just rush into the system, gather the information and bug out.

She had come to learn patience. When there was little to do but train and do more practice runs, sitting on her hands was an acquired skill. She started to read a book, waiting for the timer to go down and making it look as though she were absorbed in her screens.

"We are clear up to one light-hour. Creating map of known system. Comparing to records," Quinn said.

Everyone looked to the main screen and the holographic representation that was growing between the front consoles and the screen. An image of the system, the planets, and different objects the sensors had picked up showed on the main screen. The hologram showed the same image, but presented in a full three-dimensional plot.

"How are we looking on that comparison?" Adams looked at the map on one of her command screens. She observed the steady stream of trading vessels that were between four different planets and out toward two slip-points.

Space stations covered the skies and planetary elevators stretched down to the ground.

Looking for military vessels, Adams found them a few minutes later. They were attached to one of the stations.

She hid her shock well. They weren't just warships; they were flying cities. Four were a kilometer long and five hundred meters wide. They were more ovaloid, with smoother lines than rectangular shapes like Human ships. The fifth dwarfed them at two kilometers long and one and a half wide.

They were much larger than most of the Deq'ual's habitats.

"Comparison complete. Eighty percent possibility. Given how old the information is, I believe it is correct," Quinn said.

Adams saw an incoming message through the Mirror of Communication they were using to communicate in real time.

Without pause, she opened it. A message screen appeared on her station.

Private Message: Commander Sato

Sato> Put out some drones and continue on with the mission.

Adams> Understood.

"Miko, get some of our drones out and about. Anders, as soon as we're ready, let's head out of the system and move to our next confirmation point," Adams said.

"Yes, Captain." Anders turned the ship around and pointed them back toward the slipstream they had entered. They would go around and through supposedly uninhabited systems before poking in again to check out another outpost.

Adams hid her inner thoughts well.

They had finally found the Jukal once again and there was a good chance that the information that they had received was good. Adams had been excited to go out, to fulfill her purpose, and to finally be an actual ship captain. Now, she was thinking about the consequences for Deq'ual due to her actions.

They were building a fleet; the war machine was turning once again.

But do we even have a hope of defeating the Jukal?

They were a massive entity and Humanity had already lost once against them. It wasn't too hard to think that they might lose again.

She cleared her throat, pulling on her uniform to set it straight. She had a job to do. Fears and worries weren't going to get it done.

Once they confirmed that the information they got from Emerilia was in fact real, then it was going to be her and her crew's job to go and pay a visit to their planet.

Adams's universe and reality were changing, and she wasn't sure what it would mean or where it would lead.

Chapter 11: Testing Grounds

"Dave!" Deia yelled, entering into the massive new smithy that he'd created.

He was at a workbench, five vault-classed soul gems around him as he carved out coding on a band of ebony. He looked up from his work. His confusion turned to surprise as she rushed him. Barely slowing down, she hugged him. He barely grabbed the table in time so that he didn't fall out of his chair and onto the floor.

"I figured it out!" Deia said breathlessly, kissing Dave quickly.

"Uhhmm?"

"How to make the volcano explode. I was relying on brute force Mana over using what was at my disposal in the environment. It opens up so many new things to study!" Deia grabbed Dave's hand and pulled him.

"Where are we going?" Dave lurched out of his chair.

"Densaou! If I don't get it, I know you can figure out how to help me with all of your sensing abilities!" Deia pulled him to the teleport pads, and then out into Per'ush and toward Fire and Mal's apartment.

Deia made to charge in the door, but Dave stopped her from opening the door.

Heat rose to his cheeks. "Best to knock first," Dave said, knocking very slowly. "Hey! Just came by for a visit!" Dave checked the door and made it seem as if it were locked.

Of all the things I want to see, it was not Mal and Fire getting it on!

"Be there in a minute!" Fire said in a shrill voice.

Deia looked to Dave with a questioning look.

Dave shrugged. "Good manners. We wouldn't want anyone barging in on us," Dave said diplomatically.

Mal opened the door a few minutes later. "Dave, Deia, good to see you. What brings you around here ten at night?" Mal's shirt was half tucked in as he took his time in letting them in.

"We were just about to go to bed," Fire said.

"I always sleep at my desk." Dave gave Mal and Fire a look and then the door.

Mal grinned awkwardly and scratched his head as Fire went a shade of red.

Deia walked over to Fire, not caring for what they were talking about, as she was focused on her one-track mind. "Mom, can you take us to the Ring? I have a new idea I want to try out," she said excitedly.

"Next time, dude, lock the door," Dave whispered to Mal.

"Well, you get, umm, *busy* and you forget those things," Mal muttered, locking the door.

"I haven't forgotten to lock my door once when I've been preoccupied," Dave rebutted.

"That's a mental picture I don't need." Mal shook his head.

"How do you think I figured out we should knock!" Dave hissed, holding his forehead.

"Let's just make it a rule to always knock and never talk of this again?" Mal asked.

"Agreed," Dave said in a low voice. The two of them shook on it before they turned back to the conversation Deia and Fire were having.

"Okay, gather around and we can head off to the Ring." Fire waved for Mal and Dave to join them. As soon as they were close, Fire called up her spell. Dave used his Touch of the Land, looking around as he studied the ridiculously complex magical formation that Fire created as they disappeared from Per'ush and appeared in the Densaou Ring of Fire. Dave equipped his armor; he'd put in a new line of code that would regulate heat.

Denur, who was sleeping on the cap of stone that lay over the heated magma, moved her head around. Her massive eyes focused on the group. She made a groaning noise, trying to recover her sleepy state. "What is it now? Some of us like to sleep," Denur complained, yawning.

"I have an idea of how to make the volcano erupt!" Deia said.

"Hmm, so soon? I thought that it would take a few months, not a few weeks." Denur rose from her position. "Okay, I'm going to go lie down in an alcove. Show me what you can do," Denur said.

"Good luck, babe. You've got this." Dave gave Deia a kiss and a smile.

"Thanks, baby," she said, nervous, but clearly excited and driven to push onward. Fire used a spell, creating a pocket of heat under them that pushed them up and into Fire's home. Mal, Fire, and Dave took seats facing the volcano. Deia was just a speck on the rough stone cap.

Some of the Dragons came out of their homes from the sides of the volcano or flew in from their volcanoes around the ring of fire.

Dave saw Deia's Mana move out to gain control of the entire volcano.

She rose into the air. Beneath her feet, a hole appeared in the stone cap as the air in the volcano started to rotate. Deia stood in the center of the swirling air as it picked up speed. As the room increased in temperature, Dave noticed the power on his armor start to increase its draw. Although it was so small that it barely affected his overall stores, the ability to increase the temperature over such a large area was an impressive feat.

Deia's reach extended into the stratovolcano, where the volcano broke through bedrock. She started to twist and turn it, much like the air that was creating a cyclone, in the volcano's main vent. Deia looked like the center of an hourglass with two spirals above and below her.

She then created another hole in the cap, breaking down into the stratovolcano, just using an increase in heat to cycle the magma there up and down.

Dave watched; his senses allowed him to see everything. The chamber was heating up more and more. The cap broke in more places as the magma below it melted through, pushing out over the cap or breaking through it. The magma looked like an unsteady sea, starting to bubble and move as it started to rise slowly.

Deia continued at her pace, keeping the two cycles moving and the constant relaying heat path that stretched deep down into the stratovolcano, under the magma heating cyclone.

The magma started to move upward. It was slow and arduous as Deia kept several massive spells going: pulling in heat from the surrounding area, pouring it into her cyclones, and then heating up and cooling the vent she had created off to the side.

Deia moved her hands, creating a complex spell. Suddenly, the volcano went from blistering hot to chilly. Deia had forced the heat down the side vent she had created, down underneath the running cyclone in the magma. The law of thermodynamics came into effect; the heat wanted to rise.

Deia cast the biggest fuel air bomb, and cracked a hole in the vent at the top of the volcano's throat.

The fuel air bomb drew in the air from outside the volcano as well as the freezing air. Within the throat, it ignited, aiming the concussive force at the top of the volcano. It created a vacuum within the volcano, heating the air to throw it outward, pulling on the heated magma of the stratovolcano.

The magma rushed upward in a singular moment. Deia burned runes into the walls of the tunnel, increasing the heat and forcing air upward.

The volcano shook as the magma raced upward, threading through the various vents. The plug was blown free of the volcano's top. Ash blew out into the sky as lava erupted fifty meters into the sky before coming down to cover the landscape.

Deia floated through the volcano, letting her spells fall, her runes being eaten by the rush of magma. She crossed through the Mana barrier that kept the magma from entering Fire's home. "So, what do you think?" Deia smiled.

Fire let out an unintelligible squeal, hugging Deia. "Definitely my daughter! That was brilliant—creating heated currents in the magma and air, then forcing that heat under the magma cyclone to push it upward, then using your explosion to superheat the volcano in mere seconds and create a vacuum to decrease the resistance of the magma's path, and create a heated chimney to increase the magma's flow rate!" Fire stepped away, a proud look on her face.

Deia latched back onto her mother, beaming with the praise.

Mal gave her two thumbs-up, his face split in a wide smile.

"I knew you had it in you, firecracker." Dave grinned.

Deia hugged him tightly.

He hugged her back, happy and proud for her achievements as the magma flow slowed down and decreased after blowing off its magma and cooling down without Deia's aid.

They pulled apart Deia's spells, talking about her strengths and weaknesses. None of them pulled any punches. In Emerilia, it was best to be on top of your game, rather than going into a fight thinking that you were all-powerful. There was always room to improve.

That said, none of them hid their excitement from Deia.

As the magma settled, the Dragons whooped and cheered, flying up to Fire's house and creating an impromptu celebration as they changed into their Human forms. All were talking excitedly about their aunt's abilities.

They were genuinely excited for her, and Dave found himself bombarded by more than one Dragon's questions as they asked about items that Fire, Mal, Malsour, Induca, Fornau, and Gelimah had been talking about.

***

King Sigaird watched the arena in Haugr. It was filled with a number of challengers, people testing their mettle to be sponsored by the city to go and fight in the Dwarven tournament.

A wizard with a Water Affinity was facing off with a barbarian using a two-handed hammer. To Sigaird's eye, it was clear that the Water mage was going to lose. He had the skill, but he was cocky, underestimating the barbarian, who was exaggerating his fatigue and wounds even as he got closer.

The Water caster started an incantation to bring down a pillar of water on the barbarian. In a sudden burst of speed, the barbarian closed the space and slammed his hammer into the mage's barriers. It stopped the hit, but the kinetic force was too much for the barrier's grounding. The mage flew off the stage as the barbarian continued to try to fake his injuries, being declared the winner.

Sigaird rubbed his face, stood and headed out of his office and to the balcony that overlooked his capital. He had thought about not holding the tournament. He didn't want to lose capable fighters when Lord Esamael arrived, though holding them back and denying them access to the tournament would turn public opinion against him and make it all the easier for Lord Esamael to take over.

So, he let the tournament go on. He didn't know how many Esamael had under his command, but they wouldn't be inconsiderable forces if he was daring to start a coup.

"I just wish we had more information," Sigaird said.

Lady Merguine was doing all she could to find out more on Lord Esamael and his forces. It was clear that they had plans for the Stone Raiders in some way, from all of the actions that were being aimed at their guild hall in Verlun.

After Lady Merguine's talk, Sigaird wasn't going to mess with them. He didn't need more enemies, though he wasn't going to ally himself with them either. They were a small group and their military strength wasn't all that great. When faced with an army of POEs, it was likely that they would fall, much like they did in Selhi Capital.

Sigaird shook his head and let out a breath.

"While they might run, they don't forget," Sigaird said. "I wonder if Selhi will ever be forgiven for their trespasses. Cut off from all Dwarven mountains and the Stone Raiders taking out contracts for food in the area around them and not willing to trade with anyone who trades with Selhi. Sure, they didn't go in there and wage a war, but they'll gut the damn country. The government has been trying to shift the blame but the guards and people of Selhi Capital have had months to spread what they saw and their anger at having the Stone Raiders being kicked out. A country on the decline and the population is looking right at the government as the root cause."

Sigaird turned from the balcony and walked back into his office, looking at the paperwork and his interfaces that seemed to float above his desk.

"God, I just want to go back to adventuring. This leadership crap is for the dogs." Sigaird groaned and slumped into his seat.

Chapter 12: Decisions and Movement

Loughbreck looked over the forces arrayed in front of him. There were twenty thousand troops moving around an orderly camp. Each wore weapons and armor without emblems. Groups were off practicing their spells or their fighting abilities. Others were running around and completing different exercises. There was one group of ten who were stationed around the territory that Loughbreck was in command of.

"So, what do you think, sir?" The commander of the forces sounded rather proud of his people and his accomplishments.

"They look ready, but we must make sure that they don't slack in the coming months." Loughbreck gave the commander a look.

"They will be ready, sir." The commander bowed.

"Good." The general looked over the camp. "I trust that you have had no difficulties with any of the king's spies?"

"We have a number of scouts and wards placed to find anyone trying to search for us and our concealing magic has been powered ever since it was created. We also have routine patrols throughout the day and night. I doubt anyone even knows we're here," the commander said.

The general gave the man an appraising look. He didn't embellish his actions and he had done more than his orders asked to secure his position.

A man like that is a useful commodity, indeed.

Loughbreck looked around as they strode through the neat camps, riding on his war cat.

The soldiers saluted and got out of the way of the passing commanders. Only a few flinched away from the war cat as it eyed them like prey.

They had been orphaned, kidnapped, or brought up from peasant farms and forged into fighting men. Everything they had was due to Lord Esamael. They were loyal and they wouldn't be missed.

"How are the mages?" Loughbreck asked in a low voice.

"The mages think they're the Pantheon's gift to man, but they show that they are with us, and our own people among their ranks keep them in line," the commander said.

Loughbreck nodded his head. There were a lot of mages who came to Gudalo in an attempt to gain enough skills, or abilities to gain access to the Per'ush schools. Many didn't make it and settled down into other lines of work.

Mages bred other mages, passing on their information to their children. A number of them became peasants. Lord Esamael offered them training and a position. Many took it eagerly, but mages were prideful and sneaky creatures. There hadn't been any of them who had tried to break their oaths yet, but Loughbreck hated waiting for fear that someone might reveal the locations and extent of Lord Esamael's army.

He took some consolation in the fact that everyone had taken magical oaths within Lord Esamael's army to not reveal information. If someone broke the oath, then they would die. It was not an oath to be taken lightly and it had paid off.

"Sir, if I might ask, when will we start to move?" the commander asked.

"We will first gather our forces and then head toward Verlun and the teleport pad there, timing it along with the Dwarven tournaments."

The commander nodded eagerly. "Only a month and a half to go."

They shared eager smiles. Finally, the day they had been waiting for was fast approaching.

***

Lucy looked at her fingers and the room around her. It looked to be Dave and Deia's house in Cliff-Hill, but it was actually a Mirror of Communication conference room.

Dave and Deia appeared after a few more moments.

"Hey, Lucy." Dave took a seat. Deia sat with him as they looked out over the cliffside from their porch.

"Hey, so, uhh, okay—it really is a pretty big mind fuck dealing with all of this, you know?" Lucy sat back. Her usually calm composure was shot to hell as she squirmed around in her seat.

"Trust me, I know," Dave said.

"Deia, how did you come into this secret?" Lucy asked, trying to put off talking.

"Well, you always hear some odd stories and such about creation and the rest of it. The Elves keep pretty good records and the creation of Emerilia and the races was all a bit weird. There are no signs of races before we seemed to appear on Emerilia. That combined with Dave and Bob's information. Then, me becoming a Player. It all kind of just came together." Deia shrugged.

"Wait, you're *now* a Player?" Lucy asked.

"Yeah, I was a POE before Bob changed some settings and made me a Player. I can respawn and have access the internet." Deia smiled.

"This is a lot to take in." Lucy held her head.

"It's pretty complicated," Dave agreed.

Lucy took a few minutes before saying anything else. "Okay, so I'll keep your secret and I'll help you out as much as possible, but what the hell are we going to tell the others?"

"Nothing," Dave said.

"They're living in a prison and they're fighting an empire that wiped out our ancestors' enemies! You want us to do *nothing*?"

"Oh, we're not going to do nothing, but we can't tell everyone yet. Imagine if we do? The AIs that are watching over this world would turn on us. They would report everything to the Jukal Empire and they would wipe out the Players or they would wipe out the planet. I don't know what systems they have in place to kill us off. But from what Bob and Player's records say, we have some kind of kill switch in our bodies. We need to have the power to fight back. We need our people to be stronger. Bob is right—we lose our inhibitions when we think of life as a game. The longer they don't know, the stronger we'll get. We have our own issues down here. We still need to survive everything that's going to be unleashed on this world and hold off the aggressive species. If we can do that, then we can look to the Jukal. Otherwise, it's a lesson in futility," Dave said.

Lucy could see that he'd thought this through. She wanted to yell out, to argue his points, though she knew that sometimes timing when and where to tell someone a vital piece of information was important. Too late, and it becomes moot; same if it is too early.

"So, why did you tell me?" Lucy looked to them both.

"We trust you and we know that you're a smart woman. You were asking a lot of questions and this was the best way to answer them. If you've got questions, then I think this makes understanding what is going on easier. You're already questioning your environment. Also, with your growing spy network, you can keep us in the loop," Dave said.

"So, how do the Jukal Empire watch us?" Lucy asked.

"The nanites in us that allow us to use the interface and the like—some of them capture what we see and send it to a transmission station in the North and South Pole, beam them through Mirrors of Communications and off to the empire. They can watch anything we do, unless you have the right runes on your body to stop the nanites or the ability to break the link, like I do because I'm a bleeder. I can sense the transmission and disrupt it.

"Mostly, they just use the system when we're broadcasting—they tap into it. If they want to see someone's feed who isn't broadcasting, then they have to vote for it. Otherwise, they have to use the satellites that are above Emerilia. They can zoom in on battles, so it seems that they're right next to the person. Hell, they can even pick up audio." Dave shook his head.

"Okay, so, all-seeing eyes in the sky. They also have the ability to hack our bodies and see through us. Well, that brings up a whole lot of privacy things." Lucy scratched her head, clearly not happy with how much information the Jukal were getting on everyone.

"Okay, so they can see pretty much everything. I'm guessing that we're in here for some special reason, though?" Lucy looked around the room.

"Yes. Aleph cities and facilities already have runes that make it pretty hard for someone to access it. While we're down in the laboratory or what we're nicknaming Pandora's Box. We have a pretty crappy connection to the Jukal servers. I went a little haywire with it, well Malsour, Steve, Bob and I did. If a Jukal is using their cameras, sensors, or trying to connect to our interfaces and nanites, they're not going to be able to."

"Okay, so we've got some options to stop their transmissions. Where else are we safe?"

"When we're within the mirrors of communication like this, specifically inside the conference rooms, they can't access it. It's part of the reason that I wanted to host our lessons in there. People can get stronger and the Jukal don't even know about it unless they act out," Dave said proudly.

"So, beefing up the general population, making more of them capable of fighting and making them more likely to look at the Stone Raiders and our own businesses in a good light—maybe you should be doing my job." Lucy smiled.

"It kind of just worked out that way." Dave chuckled. "Oh, also our private communications to one another, the Jukal can't get that as well. Those two things have safeguards in them that the Jukal put in their own tech. If they were able to listen to that, then they could listen in to one another."

"Okay, so basically you want me to figure out how to disrupt a galactic empire, and allow us to stay under the radar as we build up strength and power? How the hell are we even going to fight them?"

"That's why I've been working on these machines," Dave said.

"Right, fusion reactor and Mana well." Lucy sat back in her chair. She let out a frustrated noise and looked at the ceiling. "Okay, so, no need to be sitting in here and moping around. What allies and enemies do we have here?"

"Party Zero knows what's going on. The Affinities Fire and Water are backing us, as well as the Merpeople and Dragons. The Dragons and Fire know about the truth, but the Merpeople and Water don't. Bob is also supporting us. We have also contacted a small colony of Humans who are hiding out somewhere." Deia laid out all their cards. "Oh, and Air said that she wants to help us and make alliances. I don't know how that is going for her."

"Okay, so, we've at least got some powerful allies." Lucy shrugged. "We're going to need more to fight what is coming. I think it's time that we started to reach out to other groups and talk about entering more complete alliances."

"I should have some of those one-way teleport pads sorted out soon enough! We could have them set up embassies in Terra. That way at least their ambassadors get used to working with one another," Dave said.

"Seems that playing Emerilia hasn't dulled any of your business acumen." Lucy smiled.

"You should see Suzy at work with it all. Anything like getting people to work together—she is the girl to go to. If you can give her an edge and the ability to make those alliances, I think she can do a pretty impressive job," Deia said.

"I will keep that in mind," Lucy said, making a mental note. "Having those teleport pads everywhere is going to help with my information gathering. Dave, how long will it take for you to make an Aleph automaton factory? I can get a lot of different sentient spies, but those automatons are great for recording and watching over locations without needing to ever leave."

"Say a month and I can put some plans together. I have a project of my own that I'm working on right now," Dave said.

"That works for me." Lucy nodded, excited to get more of those Aleph scouts into her hands. *No secrets will be kept from me anymore!* Lucy smiled.

"You okay, Lucy?" Deia asked.

"Yes, why?" Lucy asked.

"Just looked like some devious creature planning the downfall of an empire," Dave said.

"Eh, who knows what the future will bring." Lucy shrugged noncommittally.

Dave and Deia shared a look before smiling and looking back to Lucy.

Chapter 13: A Time to Build

Dave looked over the teleport pads. Well, teleport pads that could only go to one destination.

"So, the factory line is up and running?" Dave looked over the machine that was suspended in mid-air. It was a third the size of the original teleport pads. Removing all the complicated circuits, replacing them with coding, and then taking the options from all across the planet to just between two locations made things a lot easier.

"Yes. The factories are ready to go through production with this immediately. I have to say that Steve's help with this is incredible," Ela-Dorn said.

"Yeah, it's kind of like how webpages used to be. We started coding them ourselves, but then with the advent of AI and quantum computing, we were able to match the two systems. They took over making all of the code; we just input parameters to see if our different ideas would work. People know coding, but it's like comparing knowing how children are made to the biological process that people go through when having a child," Dave said, still looking over the teleport pad intently.

"While I do love your explanation, what is this exactly?" Josh asked.

"You really need to start reading your messages," Suzy growled. All the leaders of the Stone Raiders, as well as Party Zero, were there, minus Anna. Apparently, she was off training the DCA how to use their new weapons.

"These can be put all over the world, in every single city," Suzy said.

"But you said that they only connect to one location, so what use is that?" Josh asked.

"Dave, I officially found someone worse than you!" Suzy said.

Dave grinned, but didn't look back. The coding on the teleport pad was a thing of beauty. While he was looking at it, he compared it to the teleport pad he'd taken apart, the information he had on teleport pads, as well as Bob and Fire's teleport spells.

"We can connect them all to Terra," Suzy said.

Josh opened his mouth, closing it again as his brain started to figure out what Suzy was talking about.

Lucy nodded in understanding. "We would become the center of Emerilia. You need to trade anything, go to Terra. You're a Player looking for the best gear or to get your items repaired? Go to Terra."

"It would also be great for combat power. We could have people from all over the world with a direct line here to gather our forces, then we can send them out to wherever they're needed," Dwayne said.

"Woohoo, more vacations in different places!" Kim said, getting looks from everyone. "What? Don't need to sleep, just go to the next town as the sun is coming up! Be a crazy party!" Kim sighed, stars in her eyes.

"It would be a huge bottleneck. How would we do it?" Josh asked.

"How much would it cost?" Cassie added.

"Extortion." Dave turned around and looked to Suzy.

"Right now, we control Selhi Capital. We get them to pay a fine, and with that we pay for a good portion of the teleport system we're going to set up."

"Then we can take the rest from Gudalo. Their lord's going to attack us. I know you want to make a show out of it. If we defeat them, we claim their territories and anything affiliated with them. Lucy probably has a list of all of that." Dave pointed to Lucy; she nodded.

"Then, we use their territories as collateral. They pay us to leave or we sell them off. Then we should have enough to go on. Stopping a coup and taking out a mass of lords is a pretty big incentive for people to not mess with us and secure us the capital we need," Suzy said.

"I now see why you two work so well together." Deia sighed and gave Dave a look.

He winked at her, making her look turn into a smile.

"Okay, lay the plan out to me," Josh said.

"Well, first we're going to need more normal teleport pads—well, we can get cheaper ones because Steve is recoding them right now in that big ole AI brain of his. Then we move to replacing the Verlun teleport pad and then start moving outward. We're going to need more power facilities." Dave and Suzy ran through a presentation for everyone. The Aleph and Stone Raiders asked for more clarity as the two talked on.

***

"Well, it is good to be home." Dave looked to Deia as they stepped through the teleport pad and exited out into Cliff-Hill.

"I'm so excited to see Fornau, Quindar, and the kiddos!" Induca squealed.

All of Party Zero had joined in for the little trip, even Gurren and Lox. Anna was still off in Devil's Crater. Deia, Induca, and Suzy had been making dangerous eyes at one another when talking about Anna, sly smiles on their faces.

Dave could feel that they were planning something and he was sure as hell not going to get in their way or be anywhere near them when their plan worked.

"Well, Quindar and Fornau talked about moving to Devil's Crater. They're interested in being closer to the rest of the family, but still want their space. Also, it would keep Fornau with his fingers in a project and the children can meet others from different races," Malsour said.

The group moved toward the road.

Dave looked around to make sure everyone was out of earshot. "Well, that would be one hell of a thing, a family of Dragons in Devil's Crater." Dave grinned.

"They are looking for you to put in a good word with Alkao, if at all possible," Induca said.

Dave scratched his chin as they walked the road toward Dave and Deia's home. "Of course, I can do that. I'm just not sure what the conversation is going to be like," Dave admitted.

"Well, that is a problem for later. For now, we can just focus on the here and now, relax a bit and build our home together," Deia said.

"I'll try to keep the work stuff to a minimum, firecracker." Dave kissed her hand as they continued their stroll. Winter was coming and snow was starting to drift down, but all of the party had spells or enchantments to keep them warm as they walked and talked.

Gurren, Steve, and Lox went off to look for trouble while the rest headed for the house.

They got to the house. Deia lit a fire. The house had been kept aired and clean by a group under Dave's employ. Heavy furs were pulled out while Dave used the large teleportation circle with Suzy. Malsour stayed up above, getting a firm understanding of what he was dealing with in the shape of Dave's house. Induca and Suzy went out back, grabbing a few bottles of wine and furs to sit on the porch.

Fornau and Quindar were supposed to arrive the next day with their passel of children.

"Okay, well, I'm off. I don't know if I'll pass out or not, so come find me in two hours or so," Dave said under his breath to Malsour.

"Why is it that I feel you are using me every time you're about to do something incredibly stupid? Like that time, you boosted your stats and then took apart a teleport pad?" Malsour asked.

"Ah, it won't be that bad. I know how a portal works mostly anyway!" Dave grinned, getting a few moments of Malsour trying to say something before he disappeared from the house and reappeared inside his seeder.

He checked his inventory and the vault-classed soul gems that were stored within. He headed out of the command deck and toward the portals. It didn't take him long to reach one of them.

"Well, you look like a good choice." Dave pressed his hand against the portal. A notification popped up in his vision.

Magical Circuits

You have found a complex series of Magical Circuits. Are you interested in trying to learn from them? The Circuits will be destroyed in the process.

Cost: 10,000,000 Mana (Due to your Affinities, cost is reduced to 8,750,541)

Reward: Unknown

Y/N

"Not quite yet." Dave pulled out a carver, and then nine different vault soul gems. They were the first ones from his new factory. It took nearly a day to just form one of them; thankfully he had a massive power grid at his disposal to charge them all.

Dave used the carver to engrave a magical circle with magical coding around where he was standing before making circles with magical coding on the floor around the vault soul gems around him. It took time to carve the runes and fill them with silver.

He checked his preparations and then looked back at the portal. He sat down and opened up his character sheet. "Okay, might as well go for a ride. Let's put 45 points to Intelligence and 35 to Agility." Dave input the stats and checked his sheet.

Character Sheet

Name:	David Grahslagg	Gender:	Male
Level:	188	Class:	Dwarven Master Smith, Friend of the Grey God, Bleeder, Librarian, Aleph Engineer, Weapons Master, Champion Slayer, Skill Creator, Mine Manager, Master Summoner
Race:	Human/Dwarf	Alignment:	Neutral Good

Unspent points: 176

Health:	29,300	Regen:	15.86 /s
Mana:	9,130	Regen:	20.05 /s
Stamina:	5,740	Regen:	26.75 /s
Vitality:	293	Endurance:	793
Intelligence:	913	Willpower:	711
Strength:	574	Agility:	535

Dave felt the rush of new stats fill him. His mind opened to the universe as the desire to run, to be let free of gravity's limits, washed through him.

He equipped his armor for safety reasons.

Thoughts rushed through his mind but he pushed his hand out, pushing it against the portal.

Magical Circuits

You have found a complex series of Magical Circuits. Are you interested in trying to learn from them? The Circuits will be destroyed in the process.

Cost: 10,000,000 Mana (Due to your Affinities, cost is reduced to 8,750,541)

Reward: Unknown

Y/N

"Yes," Dave said.

The soul gems around Dave glowed brighter. The lights within them swirled with energy that lit up the runes and the circle, forcing their way through Dave.

His body lit up with runes, glowing silver through his armor. His eyes also glowed silver. He closed his eyes, their glow still visible as he looked up at the ceiling.

Power ran through him and through the portal's runes. After a few moments, the portal started to fall apart. Millions of singular runes dissolved as heat passed through it, making the entire portal unstable.

Dave's mind took in the influx of information. There was so much, there was no ability to compare it to the rest of the knowledge he held on teleportation.

It was a flood of information. Time didn't seem to hold Dave as the soul gems around him started to dim with the loss of power. His magical circle and runes turned to smoke while the runes across the portal were nothing but charred outlines.

Dave dropped his hand, knowing that he had all of the knowledge of the Magical Circuits contained within the portal.

Dave started laughing, his voice suffused with the powerful Mana that ran through his body. He felt that if he tried to stand, he would collapse.

"Now, onto the really important stuff," Dave said in his deeper and powerful voice. "Now, I should make three different blueprints of the house for Deia to look at—more than three and we won't come to a decision. We'll have to incorporate security measures as well as modern coding. Don't want anyone getting in and using my seeder. Also, Deia would be annoyed if I didn't have showers and some proper rooms for friends to stay. We've got that land from the smithy and ceramics factory being moved away—might as well use it." Dave opened up his interface and began to work. His body gave up after just twenty minutes.

He had a smile on his face as his runes dimmed and his eyes closed. He fell backward, snoring lightly as his body and mind worked to recover from what he'd done.

***

Deia looked up as Malsour reappeared in the house, carrying Dave on his back.

"What the hell happened?" Deia moved away from the small kitchen area that looked out over the porch.

"Seems he took a portal apart and then passed out. Also, going by his higher level, I guess he put some stat points to use." Malsour put Dave on the bed.

Deia sat down beside him and checked him over.

He seemed fine, just asleep. He moved slightly as she touched his forehead. His eyes opened slightly. He opened his interface, using a few commands to send something.

"Night." He grabbed her hand and tried to pull her to bed as he rolled over. Deia pulled her hand back, as Dave fell back asleep.

She looked at her interface that was telling her she'd just got a message. She opened it up to see three files with rather complex blueprints.

"Malsour, this looks like a house to me." She shared them with him.

He opened them up as well. "Well, it looks like he wasn't just breaking portals apart down there. It looks like he made three different designs for your house." Malsour opened different files, sharing his interface with Deia as holograms of the houses appeared.

Deia's eyes lit up with excitement as she studied the different houses.

***

Quindar and Fornau flapped their wings, bringing themselves in to land near the road that led to Cliff-Hill, but not so close that anyone would see or hear them.

Quindar looked at the two sleeping babies who rested in a sling across her chest. She made low clicking noises, her finger tracing over their smooth skin.

Fornau moved close, carrying two more sleeping bundles in a sling.

"Look at them, so cute," Quindar said. Kora and Hormul's little hands gripped each other's as they slept.

Fornau smiled at his children and his wife, put his arm around her shoulders, and kissed the side of her head.

The heat rose on her cheeks as a shiver went down her spine. Even with four children and being married for a few hundred years, with just a look and a kiss, he could make butterflies turn in her stomach.

"They're perfect." Fornau looked at his four kids. They had locked them into their Human forms; it was the best thing to do. They still had access to an abnormally large Mana pool, but four Dragon children wandering around was a recipe for disaster.

"Well, let's get a move on. It's already dark—we don't want to show up when everyone is going to sleep," Quindar said.

"This way, my love." Fornau's Earth magic made the trees and foliage move out of their way as they walked to the road and then up toward Dave and Deia's home.

They found Malsour studying the house, with screens from his interface floating in front of him.

"Uncle!" Fornau said, loud enough to catch Malsour's attention, but not enough to wake the children.

"Fornau! Quindar!" Malsour looked away from the house and greeted them, looking down at the four newest additions to the family. "They are precious," Malsour said, his voice low, a large smile on his face.

Quindar smiled at his clear joy.

"Come, come, let's get you all inside." Malsour guided them toward the house. Inside, Dave was asleep on his bed. Deia sat next to him, eating from a plate as she talked to Induca and Suzy.

They got up to greet their guests, devolving into cooing and ahhing at the four sleeping babes.

***

Fornau had been relieved of Viola and Urvo. The four women, cuddling the sleeping bundles, talked about children matters.

"Fornau, I was wondering if you could help me with something." Malsour jerked his head to the door.

"Certainly, Uncle." Fornau followed Malsour outside once again.

Malsour shared a message with Fornau. It was a hologram and blueprints to an extensive house.

He looked over the designs, impressed with what he saw. "This is beautiful and functional," Fornau said happily, tracing through the designs.

"I was hoping that you could give me a hand with it. I can do most of the structural items but that grand tree weaving through the courtyard might be just your thing. Also, this area out here has been a bit depopulated with the smithy and factory that used to be here. Was thinking you might know something to do with it all," Malsour said.

"Shall we chain spell?" Fornau smiled.

"I'll tell the ladies first." Malsour ran to the house, talking to the ladies quickly, and pulled Dave out of the house and laid him down on the ground.

With a quick spell, he was able to sink the original house—it still contained Bob's teleport spell to the seeder below them. They'd use it as part of the foundation and Dave's laboratory.

"Ready when you are," Malsour said once only the roof of the old house was showing.

Fornau opened his bag and pulled out trays of seeds. He threw a few down, guiding them through the ground to where he wanted them to stay.

Malsour began firming up the cliff-edge, pulling from bedrock well below the cliff, pushing it up and through the dirt to create a foundation. It was much easier to use already existing rock and then command it to grow, instead of making it yourself.

The foundation made the ground shake slightly as it spread outward. A basement formed, growing up and into walls and floors, breaking through the dirt. Malsour made the old house move out of the way and to the side of the house before pushing up the basement below it.

Fornau had his seeds in position and moved the dirt out from the basements and toward where the smithy and factory had been. Grass and trees started to grow over the area, making sure few people could see to the house. He created softer wood trees so that they would absorb noise.

The house was made up of three main sections. The biggest was the one that backed onto the cliff, and then there were two other sections that grew off it at a forty-five-degree angle, making a lazy U-shape. The basements interconnected under the ground. Stone and interwoven steel made up the floor, growing to create the supporting pillars.

Between the three main sections, there were open areas. Fornau created food gardens here, with one of his fruit trees in each small growing space. The trees grew nearly every kind of fruit once every month or two, depending on sun and water.

The three main floors went up just three feet before stopping. Supporting pillars continued on their way up, crossing over to one another for mutual support. Instead of being just reinforcement, they looked like organic supports.

"Malsour, can you give me growing plots every five meters around the structures?" Fornau asked.

"Can do," Malsour said. Holes appeared in the ground. Malsour changed the structure to make sure there were no weaknesses and that water and time wouldn't degrade his work.

Fornau guided another group of his special trees. The building plans called for timber, but Fornau preferred to grow it.

Calling his creation *trees* was a bit of a stretch. They didn't have leaves and could support themselves with just having sun on their bark and some water on their roots.

They grew like wildfire; their branches and trunks wove together, creating walls, using the supports Malsour had created as guides as the first floor and its walls came together. Then the second floor, with balconies overlooking both the cliff and the area in front of the house. Covered walkways stretched between the main buildings.

An elevated deck ran out from the side houses, extending back and toward the cliff behind the main house. Growing pots appeared in the deck.

Within the main house, there was a courtyard in the center. Fornau guided his last seeds there. Tree trunks sprouted from the ground, coming together three meters up and weaving together.

Their limbs stretched outward, creating walkways through the trees on the second floor, complete with railings. The trees parted, creating a passage through them, and came together again. It grew above the house, the six trees' canopy sprouting and spreading apart, leaves grew to cover the courtyard's open roof and spread over the surrounding roofs.

Fornau took a deep breath, looking at the house he and Malsour had formed together.

The tree limbs and organic-looking supports came together in what looked like a massive two-story, three-building home.

The women hurried to the house, eager to look it over.

Malsour clapped Fornau on the shoulder. "Well done. That was impressive," Malsour said with an approving smile.

"It's always a great pleasure to build something as beautiful as this. All I had to do was follow the blueprints and add a few extra flourishes." Fornau smiled as they walked toward the house.

"Well, enjoy your rest. I'm going to work on some magical coding so it's not freezing and we have most of the facilities up and working." Malsour smiled.

"Mind if I join? It's been some time since I've had some adult conversation and I'm interested in this magical coding," Fornau said.

"Always happy to teach, though I guess we should get Dave inside." Malsour moved to Dave, who was still fast asleep on the ground.

"He must've really needed to sleep," Fornau said.

"He boosted his stats and then took apart a portal. Think of it as massive Mana use backlash." Malsour shook his head, picking up Dave and putting him over his shoulder with relative ease.

***

Dave woke up to the sound of people talking and children playing with one another.

He sat up, his body tired from the day before, he remembered what he had done—the portal and the extra stats. His notifications blinked at him angrily. He was about to open them when he realized he wasn't in his old bed anymore. He was lying on a bedroll in a large room.

He focused on his senses and ever-casting Touch of the Land.

"Whoa!" Dave jumped up out of bed, energy coming back to him. While he'd been asleep, it looked as though Deia had picked a house and then someone had worked on it. The signature of Fornau and Malsour's Mana ran through the house.

Dave looked about, noticing there was just one thing missing—lights! Malsour had installed some, but not many.

Dave pulled out a soul gem, some ebony, and a carver. He left his bedroom using stairs and the walkway to make it to the rightmost building and the basement. As he went, he used the carver on the soul gem, carving runes into it. He got to the first floor, which he had turned into a testing area.

He put his tools down on a workbench and looked around the room.

"First rules for laboratories: Mana barriers!" Dave wielded his carver and moved to the walls.

Once the barriers were up, he fixed up a soul gem, placing it in a corner and commanding it to activate. Veins grew from it, spreading outward through the house, creating strip lighting and windows.

It didn't require nearly as much as complete buildings made from soul gems but Dave commanded a number of petty soul gems to travel through the ground, to collect Mana from the surrounding area and direct it into the growing soul gem.

Dave left his lab. Feeling hungry, he ate some jerky as he walked through his house. It would take some work to finish—some coding, furniture, defenses, escape routes. He wasn't going to take any chances with his house.

Active Skill: Teleportation

Level: Master Level 1

Effect: Understand the theories of teleportation, understand teleportation mechanics.

"Damn, guess that there aren't many people who know about how the theories and the mechanics work, probably why I jumped from Journeyman to Expert. Also, might be the fact that I am understanding a whole hell of a lot more about teleporting! Okay, headache." Dave rubbed his temples. The pain slowly subsided before he continued to look through the notifications.

Active Skill: Spell formation
Level: Expert Level 8
Effect: You use 25% less Mana and your spells are 81% stronger.

"Sweet. I miss you, skills." Dave sighed, looking at them, and paused in his walk. He looked around at the house he was in.

A sad but pleased smile passed over his face. His world had changed since he had built his first house. He'd built a life on Emerilia, he'd made a home, was engaged to a woman he loved and he was in the most powerful guild on Emerilia.

"Not bad, not bad at all." Dave smiled to himself, taking a deep breath, and headed into the main house. He entered a large living area where everyone was gathered. He caught Deia's eyes as she bounced a giggling babe on her knee.

"Hey, Fornau and Quindar, sorry I was out when you arrived," Dave said.

"It's good to see you again, Dave." Quindar smiled.

"I have to ask you about your plans. They were great, really well detailed, though I changed a few things," Fornau said.

"I saw that. The walls are actual trees, not just cut lumber. Didn't know trees could be this smooth, or grow in this manner," Dave said honestly.

"They're a special tree I've been working on for building purposes. Don't worry—they're well insulated and resistant to fire. I was working on trying to make them Dragon-resistant. With these four tikes, it's only a matter of time before they start using their Affinity breaths!" Fornau gestured to his four children, who were wandering around the floor on hands and knees or with the ladies, being bounced on knees or fed by Quindar.

With their cute, determined, and happy expressions, it was hard to think that their other form was of a fire-breathing Dragon.

Dave caught Deia's eyes as she gave him a happy smile. The kind that only made his mind hear ringing alarm bells as he caught the way she looked at the baby.

Dave didn't need to read minds to know what she was thinking: *I WANT ONE!*

Dave wasn't against it, but he didn't want to bring a child up with everything that was going on.

"I was wondering if you might be interested in helping me design our new home? If Alkao is for the idea of having Dragons in Devil's Crater." Fornau smiled.

"I'd be more than happy to help." Dave smiled.

***

Alkao and Anna stepped through the teleport pad's event horizon. People stared at the Demon king as he walked out of the pad. His DCA guards moved around, their eyes looking for threats and their hands resting on their swords, ready for an attack at a moment's notice.

They had arrived late. With the oncoming winter, it was already dark.

Alkao shifted his shoulders, taking comfort in his thick and heavy hide that rested around him, keeping him warm.

People talked animatedly about the Demons and Beast Kin that made up the little party. Anna led the way, weaving through the people waiting for the teleport pad or hawking goods around it before people got to the main city. Refreshments and cart rides were the biggest seller.

The party moved through all of it. Alkao looked over the growing city. Forests had been mostly cut down for housing.

"There are people living in those trees?" Alkao said, asking Anna for confirmation.

"Yes. Cliff-Hill has a large group of Elves from the Kufo'tel forest and Dwarves from the Mithsia Mountains. They lie to the north behind a massive enchanted wall they put up for defense after the Dark and Earth Lords attacked them," Anna said as they finally made it out of the plaza that surrounded the teleport pad and onto the four cart-wide road where carts were waiting to carry people off to the side, or racing past with goods to Cliff-Hill, the teleport pad, and Omal.

Anna led them up the road and Alkao took in the sights of the city. At the top of Cliff-Hill, the city was already formed, with people moving lower down the hillside toward the large stone walls that ran from the two cliffs on either side of the sloping hill.

Alkao saw the familiar smithies. They were lower down the hill, close to the teleport pad and with stone roads that connected to the main road passing through the city.

Dave's ceramics factory was off to the side. Carts continuously moved around the factories and smithies.

They walked up the road for a bit, before Anna walked down a small path.

"Hmm, looks like things have done a bit of growing here. Used to be a road in and out of here." Anna led them through the forest.

The guards all looked around. Anna took a turn around a large and thick grouping of trees. They followed and came out into a cleared area.

A massive three-building home faced them; off to the side, there seemed to be a smaller building. It looked like a shed in comparison.

Soul gem threads lay around, lighting up the house.

"Well, that's new." Anna looked over the home.

"I think with Dave, expecting one thing and finding something completely different is kind of a daily occurrence." Alkao grinned.

"You do have a point." Anna nodded and headed for the main door.

Before Anna could knock, Dave was there, opening the door.

"Come on in!" he said with a wide and open smile, a beer in his hand. He hugged Anna and braced Alkao's arm.

"Don't worry—we've got something that can get even the Demon King drunk!" Dave waved everyone, including the protection detail, in.

"Malsour, Fornau, and I put wards up all over the place today while the ladies went off and gathered us a feast and booze. Nothing gets past the tree line without us knowing about it." Dave smiled to the protection detail. "It's a bit cramped here, but one of the rooms upstairs is free for you to have an overwatch of the main grounds. The two side houses are completely free of people, so use them as you desire. The right side one has my lab in the basement so don't go down there—don't want something to blow up!" Dave clapped his hands.

"Thank you. Do you mind if we have a look around?" the guard commander asked.

"Go for it! We'll have some food ready in an hour or two—better than those rations." Dave grinned to the guard commander. The other guards looked pretty happy. A warm house, wards already set up, and warm food! Not a bad protection detail.

"Thank you for your hospitality," the guard commander said.

"No worries. When you're looking around, could you let me know if you spot any ways for me to improve security around here?" Dave asked.

"Certainly." The guard commander and his detail perked up. Doing a favor for Dave Grahslagg—they'd put in their full effort.

"Thanks!" Dave said with a wide smile. "Well, I'll leave you to it."

"Thank you, Mister Grahslagg." The guard commander tilted his head slightly in respect.

"Please, just call me Dave," Dave said in a light tone, waving away the guard commander's serious tone. He left them to do their thing and guided Alkao into a large room at the back of the house. Massive two-story windows looked out onto a large deck with a roof above it. There were four children in states of play or sleep inside the house. Malsour and Suzy were outside talking. Induca and Fornau were talking to each other and tending to the children. Off to the side, the smell of food wafted in. A woman and Deia were talking to each other animatedly.

"Anna!" Deia said in a raised voice, wiping her hands on her apron and coming out to greet Anna.

"Hey, Deia." Anna smiled.

"Come, I need your help in the kitchen! Induca, could you get Suzy?" Deia practically pulled Anna across the room.

"Hi, Alkao! Dave, get the man a drink," Deia said.

"Yes, honey, be gentle!" Dave said as Induca quickly got Suzy's attention and disappeared off into the kitchen with the women.

"I'll get you something to drink. You know Fornau, right?" Dave gestured to the man watching the three children wander around and holding another against his shoulder.

"Hey, Fornau. I'm guessing this lot are yours." Alkao grinned, looking at the kids.

"Yeah, we have rather large litters." Fornau sighed, a smile on his lips as he looked to the wandering children.

"Thank you again for all that you did for Devil's Crater," Alkao said.

"No worries. It was a fun little project. I heard that Unity might be growing again once the winter passes?" Fornau asked.

"It looks that way. We've got inns growing all over the place and people coming to trade, adventure, and do everything under the sun. We're turning into quite the hot spot, it seems." Alkao smiled proudly.

Dave arrived with drinks and Malsour came in from outside.

"Thank you," Alkao said.

"Fornau and Quindar are interested in moving to Devil's Crater. Be a good place for young ones to grow," Dave said.

"Well, you're welcome to move to Devil's Crater. There are certain things we hold our people accountable for—though, I don't know how safe it is for children. It is Ashal still, after all," Alkao said.

"I think our family would be fine, but we're asking not just for a citizenship. With us, there come certain"—Fornau moved his hand around, as if trying to find the right word for what he was trying to explain—"different needs than other settlers might have."

"Oh?" Alkao sipped from his tankard. He grunted in appreciation, holding his mug up in salute to Dave.

"You like that, huh? Some of my own brew, been keeping it in storage." Dave grinned. "And what Fornau is trying to say—he and Quindar have certain different needs and qualifications, because they're Dragons."

Alkao frowned at Dave, expecting the punchline to come as he drank from the mug again.

"Well, not the way I would go about saying it." Fornau laughed awkwardly.

"So, you're saying you're a Dragon?" Alkao tried to keep his skeptical look from surfacing. Fornau had done a lot for him and he didn't want to be disrespectful.

"Ah, you don't believe me." Fornau's smile turned predatory.

"Pass me my grandniece," Malsour said.

"Thanks, Uncle Malsour," Fornau said.

The ladies came out of the kitchen.

"Could you watch the children? I just need to give Alkao a demonstration," Fornau said.

"Okay. Don't use your aura, though," Quindar said.

"Of course not, dear." Fornau gave her a quick kiss.

"I have the perfect place away from prying eyes." Dave waved for Alkao and Fornau to follow him. They went down to the basement, going through tunnels until they came up inside the shed, which was actually a house. Dave put Mana into a circle that glowed around their feet. The shed disappeared and they appeared in a room made of metal. Dave guided them out into an open area that was big enough to fit two of Dave's houses.

"Does this work?" Dave gestured to the room with his glass.

"This should work fine." Fornau walked into the room. He grew in size, wings sprouted from his back, and his legs started to get bigger as his body and arms extended outward. His neck extended; his clothes disappeared and revealed green, brown, and black scales underneath.

Alkao could only watch as Fornau transformed into a Dragon and turned around to look at Alkao. His nictitating eyelids moved over his eyes.

"Do you believe me now?" Fornau asked, his voice deep and powerful.

"So, you're a Dragon," Alkao said, remembering when he'd said the words just a few minutes ago.

"Correct." Fornau laughed and reduced in size, back down to his Human form. His clothes formed back over him again.

Alkao had never seen a Dragon ever in his life, and now he was in a house of six of them! Four children and two adults.

"This is a lot to take in." Alkao tried to get past how he had felt like prey before Fornau's eyes. He knew with a swipe of Fornau's hand, he could be dead.

"Fornau is really interested in working to help develop Devil's Crater. Quindar wants to get her kids more used to being around people of different races. It's kind of a Dragon thing that the younger generations get a bit rowdy," Dave said.

"They start thinking that they're above other races and killing them, which is one reason we have so few children and most of them are sealed up." Fornau sounded sad.

"Right now, I'm a bit stunned—I won't lie. Though, what would a Dragon need?" Alkao asked. Having a family of Dragons living in Devil's Crater was a good way to protect his people. Also, Fornau had already helped them a lot. Having him around would be a great help to the future of Devil's Crater.

"We would need a perch, just a place away from other people that we could set up a home. Probably in one of the tree ranges, maybe in the areas where you want to have mining and timber? That way, if we go hunting, we can kill anything that comes out of the dungeons and continue to train," Fornau said.

"So, a region along the crater wall for you to carve out a home." Alkao nodded, sipping from his drink and thinking.

"Also, Quindar has offered to teach your forces how to fight in the skies. Anna is good, but Quindar was born in the skies and the Lady of Fire has given her blessing," Dave said.

"I agree to the terms. But if you're out in the crater walls, how are you going to get your children into the town?" Alkao asked.

"Well, I can help with that." Dave smiled.

"You can? I was thinking of just flying over," Fornau said.

"I've been brushing up on my teleportation!" Dave smiled. "I can probably whip up a pretty simple pad that will teleport you from your house in the crater walls to another one in the city—that way you've got two!"

Alkao laughed and drank from his mug. "You called Malsour uncle—but isn't he Human?"

Dave gave Alkao a look.

"Right, dumb question." Alkao sighed. It seemed the more he learned, the more he felt he was behind everyone by two steps.

Chapter 14: A Future Discovered

Dave and Deia sat on the porch. The kids were acting up so the Dracul family was dealing with them. Suzy had her creations working on the dishes and cleaning up and was reading inside the house. Lox, Gurren, and Steve had come by for dinner, and then stolen Alkao and Anna for a night of drinking.

Dave leaned down and kissed her head as she lay in his lap. "I love you."

She turned, a smile on her face, and her lips puckered.

Dave grinned and kissed her again.

"I love you too," she said as Dave pulled back. She grabbed his arm and wrapped it in hers against her stomach.

"You sure you don't want a drink?" Dave asked.

"Nope, haven't been feeling that well lately." Deia frowned and nestled into his lap more. Both of them were covered with blankets, a heating lamp keeping the winter at bay.

"Okay." Dave ran a casual look over Deia, checking for anything that might be the issue. "Uh, okay." Dave frowned, concentrating his spell.

"Something wrong?" Deia looked to Dave.

"You find you've been more tired recently, or sick in the morning?" Dave asked.

"Yes, why?" Deia asked slowly. Her eyes thinned.

"Because I think it's time we saw Doctor Jules. I think you're pregnant."

"What?" Deia asked, startled, as she turned her own senses inward. "How is this possible?"

"Well, I guess it must've been when we were in Per'ush," Dave said.

"But how—that rune I made?"

"Well, with a lot of magical energies, runes can become weaker. Did you check it that one night when we went all night?" Dave asked.

"No, but it's really rare for Elves to get pregnant with other Elves! How the hell did two Halflings do it so fast?" She looked around in alarm.

"I'm not sure," Dave said.

"What are we going to do? I haven't planned for any of this! Am I going to need to leave the Stone Raiders?" Deia sat up, her nerves clearly showing.

Dave pulled her onto his lap.

"I'm going to be a mother!" She looked at him, her shock clear.

Dave rubbed her back and brought her into a hug as she held her hands over her stomach. "I'm going to be a dad." Dave grinned. His nerves turned to excitement.

"But, what's going to happen?"

"You're going to blow up like a whale and I'm going to get a bunch of sleepless nights as a body pillow with a kicker in my side." Dave saw the worry on her face. "Babe, Deia, firecracker—we're going to be okay." Dave held her face and kissed her. "I love you and this is a happy moment!"

"I just—it's so sudden. I can't believe it." Deia looked at Dave. His smile seemed to be infectious as her shocked face turned into a smile.

"I'm going to be a mom," she said in a quiet voice, biting her lip and looking down at her stomach.

"Yes, yes, you are," Dave said. In that moment, Dave was struck with her beauty, with the incredible woman that she was. She was smart, resourceful, driven, proud, and kind.

He squeezed her in a hug, but not too tight, and kissed her head. She laughed and shied away from his tickling kisses.

He grabbed her sides, tickling her, making her giggle like a little girl.

"We have to go see Jules and tell the others!" Deia said.

"We'll do a check-up with Jules tomorrow and we'll wait till then to tell everyone," Dave said.

"Okay, but if this is real—" Deia jumped up and down, excited.

Dave laughed and Deia sat back, leaning against him and holding his hands that circled her.

"We're going to be parents," Deia said.

"Damn right we are." Dave's thumb ran over her hands holding his.

***

Jules looked up from the box of medical supplies she was organizing. Her eyes fell on Dave and Deia as they entered her clinic in Terra.

"Hey! Sorry we couldn't make it out the other day. Esa has been swarmed with training and I have been stuck with a bunch of patients." Jules smiled and greeted them.

"No worries, Jules. We were wondering if you could check something for us," Dave said.

"Oh? Did you break something?" Jules joked.

"No. Well, could you look over Deia?" Dave asked.

"Sure." Jules held out a hand; Deia put hers in it. Jules looked over Deia. *No visible trauma—though...that's weird. Okay, that's, well, anatomically it makes sense, but how the hell is that in a game?*

Jules looked up at Deia with a puzzled look.

"Uh, so it looks like you're pregnant. I guess you should talk to Jukal Enterprises to get that bug fixed." Jules shrugged.

"What? Are you kidding? Do you know how hard it is for an Elf to have a child anyway?" Deia held her hands protectively over her stomach as she looked away, leaning into Dave's embrace.

"Well, Players don't have children. This is a game. Only POEs have kids and Players are infertile, with the game's rules." Jules snorted.

Dave and Deia looked to each other.

Dave closed his eyes and mumbled something. After a minute or two, it felt as if there was a heavy pressure in the room. Jules tried to pop her ears but couldn't.

"Deia used to be a POE, and I used to be a Player like you. I guess that when I became a bleeder and Deia became a Player. It changed my biology, but Deia stayed the same. So, that probably made it possible for us to have children," Dave said.

"What are you talking about? POE becoming a Player and you being a bleeder?" Jules asked, looking confused.

"Don't worry about it—just know that we want to keep the child," Deia said.

"Okay." Jules held her hands up in defeat.

"Thanks." Dave hugged Deia tight and they smiled at each other.

A smile grew on Jules's face. She had never before been able to tell two people that they were going to be parents. Hers was always the job of telling people when their friends and family couldn't be saved from their wounds.

***

"Okay, so what's going on? Why the sudden visit? You sounded flustered in the private message." Fire looked at Deia with concern as she and Dave walked into the room.

"Well, we have an announcement." Deia looked to her mother and father, and gripped Dave's hand tight. She took a breath as a smile spread across her face. "You're going to be grandparents."

"What? How? I'm going to be a grandfather?" Mal's face lit up with what could only be described as joy as he moved toward Dave and Deia.

"Yep." Dave laughed.

Mal had tears in his eyes as he hugged Deia.

"I'm going to be a grandmother?" Fire asked, still in shock, looking to the two in mild disbelief.

"Yes, you are, and not just the grandmother of Dragons." Deia laughed and tears ran down her face.

"Woo-hoo!" Fire yelled. Tears fell down her face as her face broke into complete joy. It turned into a group hug with everyone laughing, crying, and in a state of shock.

"Well, looks like we won't be too far apart then!" Fire giggled, looking down at her own slight baby bump that was now showing.

"Well, means that you'll be perfect for babysitting!" Deia laughed.

"How far along are you?" Mal asked.

"About three or four weeks," Dave said.

"A summer baby! I can't believe I'm going to be a father again and a grandfather in the space of just a few months!" He hugged Deia again.

With Elves, it wasn't weird for your children and grandchildren to be having kids at the same time you were. With the whole aging thing, it was just part of the deal. Other societies found it wrong and weird but the Elves had come to understand it. It was part of who they were.

"We have to tell the rest of the family! They'll be over the moon!" Fire used her teleportation spell and brought them into her volcano.

That night, many of the cities that could see the Densaou Ring of Fire talked of how dozens of Dragons had flown around their homes, roaring into the night sky and letting out their Affinity breath, lighting up the night sky.

It was as if they were celebrating something.

***

Bob finished reading the message from Dave, calling upon his teleportation spell before he had completely read it all. His face, in a state of shock, quickly turned to excitement.

In a flash of light, he stood in the middle of Fire's apartment.

Dave, Deia, and Fire sat on a couch in the middle of the room, surrounded by a group of Dragons who had taken on their Human forms. Mal stood behind Fire, his hand resting on her shoulder and her hand over his as she looked at the happy gathering in a world of her own.

"Woohoo! Atta boy, Dave! Nice work there, Deia!" Bob jumped and thrust his legs into the air. The gesture looked ridiculous with the four-foot-tall Gnome's ecstatic expression.

Dave and Deia let out a laugh that seemed to brighten the room. A festive mood permeated the air as well as happiness.

With the Dragons and Elves, having a child was a rare and great event. Here, the Dracul clan were not only celebrating Deia and Dave's pregnancy, they were accepting them into their Dracul family.

Deia was much more relaxed while Dave was flustered and filled with energy. Deia's years had allowed her to gain a maturity, that, although Dave could touch on it at times, he couldn't hope to achieve in his current situation.

Bob watched with glowing eyes as they looked at each other. Nestled into each other's arms, they were a picture of happiness. It took some time before things wound down. Bob found himself with Deia across from him.

"Bob, there's something I need to ask." Deia's face became pinched and serious.

"Go on, my dear," Bob said, with a soft smile.

"If I was to die now, what would happen?" Deia held his gaze.

Bob sighed. His happy expression became darker as he remembered the weight of his responsibilities and the troubles that encompassed Emerilia. "If you die, then you will respawn still. However, I don't think that your baby will be respawned with you," Bob said.

Deia took a deep breath. Her eyes moved from Bob to her hands. A sour expression crossed her face. "I didn't want to have a husband for so long because I feared that having a child would stop me being able to fight. Now that I have a man I want to get married to, he gets me pregnant right when things start to look like they're going to explode in our faces," Deia said. Even with her words, she couldn't stop from smiling, looking over to Dave, who was talking to a group of Dragons in Human form.

"You're going to need to be careful to not overexert yourself as well. That would be bad for the baby. Mana usage, no more than twenty percent of your limit in one go," Bob said seriously.

"Seems you know a bit about babies." Deia looked back to him.

"Well, I kind of made everyone here." Bob waved his hands to encompass Emerilia.

For years, he had worked with different cloning, fertilization, gene therapy, and DNA sequencing procedures to help give rise to the races that roamed Emerilia.

Deia let out a small laugh and smiled at Bob, her eyes misty as her hand went to her belly. In one day, her life had changed—her future had changed. "Looks like I'll have to be careful."

Seeing those misty eyes and that soft warming smile on her face as she looked down at her stomach, something seemed to have gotten stuck in Bob's eye as he coughed roughly.

Chapter 15: Machines That Changed the World

Dave sat down. The last two weeks had been a whirlwind, between seeing Deia's parents and then letting everyone else know what was going on. Then it had been back to work.

The smithies' hiring craze was paying off. They had nearly doubled their workforce. With the constant shifts, they were hiring more and more. Once Terra was open to more than just the Stone Raiders and some select guests, they'd be needed to work in the smithy there.

Dave had been spending his days in the Aleph college, researching with Deia. He'd taken apart the portal, looked at Bob's and Fire's teleportation spells as well as the combined knowledge of how teleport pads worked. He'd even been able to get through the book that he'd gotten so long ago about teleportation.

He had been working with Ela-Dorn on their portal hijacker: a system that could take over a portal, giving them control over it and allowing them to connect to different portals. They had been able to create a shield system that would block anything coming in that they didn't like.

Ela-Dorn and Dave had finally come up with a prototype mock-up.

"I think it will work. It should work, at least," Ela-Dorn said.

"Well, that sounds good enough for me! Let's go test it out!" Dave pulled Ela-Dorn along, going through the grand library and headed out toward the teleport pads. Dave entered his code that allowed them access to the Stone Raiders' power facility.

"Why are we going there?"

"All will be revealed." Dave smiled. They passed through the teleport pad. Dave led Ela-Dorn through the facility into a command room and through a secret door that Ela-Dorn would have missed, even with all of her senses.

As soon as they passed through the corridor and were inside what looked like a multi-level lab, Ela-Dorn felt as if a weight had been lifted from her senses. "Wow, okay, what have you been up to, Dave?"

"Oh, a bit of this and that." Dave grinned, leading her to one of the labs on the bottom floor.

"Is that what I think it is?" Ela-Dorn pointed to one of the rooms on the first floor.

"If you're thinking attempts at making a teleportation spell, then you would be correct. Thinking of all of the variables is a pain in the ass. The farther away, the harder it is to do. I think I'm going to have to make a magical code to take care of most of the basic stuff. Trying to figure it all out in your head is a pain in the ass and takes a *really* high Intelligence. Today, we're just going to be asking a buddy to give us a ride." Dave opened up his interface and sent a message.

A few minutes later, a Gnome appeared in the room. "Argh, it is a pain in the ass to teleport in here. Thankfully, you have that damn coordinates sent to me, or else I might be in the wall."

"You just used a teleportation spell?" Ela-Dorn said, not completely believing what she had just seen.

"Yeah, I wasn't going to walk all the way down from my carrier now." The Gnome grinned.

"How is that possible? We didn't think that a person could do it. There are just too many variables!" Ela-Dorn said.

"Well, looks like this one has just gone down the rabbit hole of teleportation. Don't worry, lass. There is a lot more to learn, and there are a few cheats." The Gnome winked.

"This is Bob, and he also won't tell me the cheats because he wants to see what we do," Dave grumbled.

"What? If I gave you the answers, then it would be too easy. Though, I have to say, being used as the universe's taxi cab isn't all that fun." Bob shook his head. "Though, you Humans keep on coming up with interesting new ways to do things. So, what's to say that you don't come up with a new way to do teleporting? Then, I might be the one using your spells to do all of this!"

"But you can teleport from one place to another with just a spell? What is your range? How can you figure out all of the computations?" Ela-Dorn asked.

"Well, you can't think too complicated. When it's just moving from one place to another across a planet, you can stop thinking about most of the variables that come with, say, a portal. It makes things a bit riskier, but reduces the cast time astronomically. Also, creating a spell formation into different areas, much like your teleport pads, makes things easier. I have one here, but with Dave's runes, detecting it is a pain in the ass, so I figure out the rough coordinates and send myself. Then, the formation here kind of grabs onto me and pulls me into position. That way you can go really long distances with just a rough idea, and a shorter cast time from one place to another. General teleportation from one point to another in your field of vision is a lot easier. Blind casting is risky, but hell, that's why we can respawn, right?" Bob grinned.

"You can talk on the way. Seeder, please. I have a summoning hall to make," Dave said.

"Right. How's Deia doing?" Bob asked.

"Still stubborn as ever." Dave smiled.

"Okay, so with the teleportation spell, how are you moving from one spot to another—dematerialization, atomic resonance, or something else?"

"Something else. Don't worry, you'll figure it out eventually." Bob smiled.

"But—" Ela-Dorn was cut off as they left the hidden lab and reappeared in Dave's seeder, on the bridge.

"Bob, how do the Jukal move their ships from system to system?" Dave asked.

"Well, there are a couple of ways. They can use the gates, basically scaled-up versions of the portals. The slip streams, which are regions around a star system which have a low and constant gravitational force, allow a ship to use their Alcubierre drives to bend space a little to create a gravitational wave that shoots them forward. Not as fast as portals, but it works for systems that don't have the money for a large-scale portal, or gate."

Ela-dorn looked like a fish out of water as she listened to what Bob was saying. "Ships? Gates, solar systems?"

"I'm going to go and test this out." Dave grinned at Bob and Ela-Dorn.

"Come, young one. Let us watch Dave at work and discuss the realities of Emerilia and the empire that controls it," Bob said.

"Don't you mean the gods? The Affinities Pantheon?"

"Well, have you ever heard of the people who control the Affinities?" Bob asked.

"Well, there have been some odd changes with how the gods work. Like how they interact with one another or the POEs." Ela-Dorn looked thoughtful, thinking on what she knew about the Pantheon, how they worked together at times and other times worked against one another. They seemed to be erratic in their actions. Though with the pattern growing in her mind, the more it looked as though they were working together to do something.

As if they weren't always in control.

"I haven't, but as you say it, a few things make sense now," Ela-Dorn admitted as Dave attached what looked like large clamps around a portal and secured them at different points.

"Well, the Jukal Empire controls them and thus Emerilia," Bob said.

"Okay." Ela-Dorn shrugged.

"You don't seem that shocked." Bob studied Ela-Dorn.

"If it is this Jukal Empire or Pantheon that is trying to assert control over Emerilia, it has little bearing on me." Ela-Dorn shrugged.

"They were the ones who ordered the Pantheon to attack the Aleph. They were scared where your study of teleport technology would go. They have a monopoly over trade and the trade lanes. If you could make teleportation cheap, then they would lose that. Right now, with being in your facilities, they haven't been able to sense anything that you're doing with teleport pads and portals. Once you start showing that you didn't stop working with teleportation, they might try to force you to stop once again," Bob said.

Ela-Dorn's eyes thinned as Dave finished attaching the last clamp onto the portal and running tests.

A cold smile formed on her lips. "Well, they're going to have to try a whole hell of a lot harder to try to get rid of us this time."

"Atta girl." Bob grinned.

"So, Bob, who are you? I think it would be pretty stunning to most people to see a Gnome teleporting around."

"Oh, me? I'm the Grey God." Bob smiled.

Ela-Dorn's eyes widened. "You're the one who saved us! You warned us about the coming forces and helped us escape."

"Bingo." Bob winked. "Now, would you be interested in being an agent of chaos?"

"I thought you were the god of balancing," Ela-Dorn asked.

"Well, sometimes the best way to balance things is to add in a bit of chaos." Bob smirked.

"What are you asking me?"

"I'm bored most of the time and I'm always looking for friends. Would you give me the honor of becoming my friend? You are a rather interesting lady," Bob said.

"I have a husband," Ela-Dorn said.

Bob broke out into laughter, slapping his thigh.

Ela-Dorn's eyebrow rose as she looked at Bob, her lips pursed.

"Sorry, just, woohoo—haven't had someone take my words like that in some time. I'm older than Emerilia itself. I was a scientist before all of this. Playing with problems and looking at what you Humans come up with is a lot of fun." Bob smiled.

"Well, I'm an Orc, so I'm a bit different," Ela-Dorn said.

Bob waved his hand. "You all think you're so different. I spliced you all out of the same genetic code, just some different genetic markers to look younger longer, or have more muscle and bone density, or bigger jaws with large teeth. If you saw the other races of the empire, you'd understand what different races looked like!"

Ela-Dorn looked at Bob in confusion.

"He tells the truth. I was grown in a damn pod for most of my life, conditioned in a simulation to think of Earth as real instead of Emerilia. Now, let's see if this works." Dave opened his interface and connected to the portal's controls. "Bob, what are your portal's coordinates?"

"Sending them to you with updates every nanosecond," Bob said.

"Thank you. Inputting," Dave said. The portal started to come alive; runes that were visible glowed with power as the four different clamps started glowing and powering up.

There was a whirring and clicking noise as the runes inside the portal's rings started moving and changing.

"Oh, that is interesting," Dave muttered to himself.

"What?" Ela-Dorn asked.

"The runes and the Magical Circuits within the portal aren't just metal blocks. They are broken up into different segments—ebony cutting up the different circuits, which are made of silver. The portal heats up the silver and forms it into the needed runes within the circuits. It's why it costs so much power connecting a portal. They're literally reforming their innards each time. Also, they have parts where they destroy runes, and remake them according to the positional differences of the two points. The portals exchange information about their positions and their changes. It's why only two portals are usually connected to each other and they never close. If you shift them say a meter, they have to destroy and reform the runes they've made for positional information and change it. The rings that are changing go from light-years down to meters. They're just centimeters wide, with the runes being burned out in a matter of minutes." Dave looked over the portal as it started to make noises that told Ela-Dorn that it was online.

Runes on the cover of the portal started to glow, coming around from under the four points where the clamps were. Slowly, one by one, the various circuits and runes started glowing. All of them moved counter-clockwise until they reached the next clamps, the portal covered in glowing runes and Magical Circuits.

A shimmering surface grew from the inner ring of the portal, meeting in the center. Ela-Dorn watched as an image solidified on the other side of the portal.

It showed a cargo bay filled with various items.

Ela-Dorn walked around the portal.

"Portal is stable. Activating shield," Dave said.

A faint blue covering seemed to go over the portal from the four clamps.

"Looks like it's taking a good draw from the portal's power output. Okay, we can hold this for a few hours, but after that, the portal here is going to be out of power," Dave said.

She released a breath she didn't realize she was holding.

"We just got a portal to work!" she yelled before jumping around. "Hell, yes! Who is the master of portals!" She laughed, unable to get all of her excitement out with a wide smile on her face as she looked at the grinning Dave and Bob.

"We can power it up from my ship—be a bit of a power draw, but if you'd be willing to give me some hydrogen, it won't be a problem. Oh, and I've been working on your fusion reactor and I think that the AI has finally found the right inputs you'd need for it to be stable," Bob said to Dave.

"How can you have something that generates that much power, and what is a reactor?" Ela-Dorn asked.

"Well, I think I have a few things to show you. First of all, Bob, could you teleport us and one of these portals back to my lab?" Dave asked.

"Can do," Bob said.

They disappeared from the seeder and reappeared back in Dave's lab. Bob used magic to hold a portal, moving it into one of the labs.

"Seems someone's been in here a bit," Dave yelled as he walked off to a different lab.

"Been awhile since I had my own place to run experiments!" Bob said, floating off with the portal.

"What are you showing me?" Ela-Dorn asked.

"How we're going to fix that power problem with portals and teleport pads and not be reliant on the ley lines for all our power," Dave said. "Oh, and now that we have the clamps working, I think it's time we started working on our own portals. The Jukal might be able to sense theirs that we're using if they're on the planet's surface or in somewhere not properly protected. If we have our own, they'll have a different energy signature and we can trick their sensors."

"We just figured out how to get a portal to dial another—now you want to make your own!" Ela-Dorn waved her hands around in an exasperated manner.

"Don't tell me you're not excited." Dave looked back with a grin.

"Of course, I am!" Ela-Dorn said. "You know my weaknesses just a little too well, though. Also, it means I'm going to need to catch up on all those lessons you've been giving."

"Don't worry. I recorded them all so that people can listen to them even when I'm not there. I think I'm going to have to get someone to teach people in my place. I've got too much going on still. Maybe Matt," Dave said, talking to himself in the end.

*****

"Well, this is different," Dwayne said.

Josh, Lucy, Kim, and Florence were all sitting in one of the tallest towers that came together to create a central support for the city.

"It's kind of hard to believe all of this belongs to our guild," Kim said, as they looked out at the city. Day by day, the city was changing.

Dave had finally finished with the growing tower soul gems. The first growing tower was extending up into the skyline, structural supports strengthening the tower. The soul gem buildings looked similar to the metal and glass skyscrapers on Earth.

There were a number of buildings that had been made from reinforced stone and simple steel. Like the power station that was now operating at one hundred percent and the refinery that was working overtime to try to deal with the massive backlog of stored materials that hadn't been processed yet.

"I just hope that we have somewhere near the capital that we would need to implement Dave's plan," Josh said.

"We've got Selhi bent over our knee. In the last couple of months, they have not been having a good time. We just need to make sure that we get rid of Esamael and his forces. Once that's done, then we'll have nearly half of the country and their leadership locked up. We trade them to the king as well as control of the different cities for what we still need—perfect," Lucy said.

"Are you sure it will work? It sounds messy," Josh said.

"They fucked us, or are looking to fuck us over. I agree with Lucy. It's about time we showed them what happens if someone crosses the Stone Raiders." Dwayne held Josh's eyes for a minute.

"Also, coming out stronger than ever and with a growing empire, it's going to be really hard for anyone to challenge us ever again," Florence said.

"Am I the only one who remembers that there are going to be things coming back from wherever they were hiding in just a few months?" Kim said.

"Everything we have now—Terra, the teleport pads, our allies and our new members—everything is so that we can come out of the end of these events stronger than ever," Josh said.

"I know, but damn, I don't want to wait two months before we fight Esamael. Isn't there anything else we could do?" Kim sighed.

"Well, we have large groups who could move outside Devil's Crater to go and have a look at what's living out there. Try to track down some dungeons. I think it's time that we went looking for some nice-sized raids," Dwayne said.

"There are always people who prefer big raids instead of just party-sized dungeons," Josh agreed, a grin on his face. He held out his fist and Dwayne punched it.

"Okay, though, we do have a lot of people who are training, or working on different things. I'll try to make sure that everyone is ready for when Esamael comes with his forces. I've also decreased our speed of recruiting. We're nearly double our size after Devil's Crater and I want to make sure that the veterans aren't outnumbered by the new incoming people," Lucy said.

"Yeah, I haven't had many people arguing that we should do things differently. Though there are a few here and there. Most are just looking out for the guild; others are trying to change it from the inside, so I showed them the door," Josh said.

"Ah, is that why our guild is getting such bad reviews?" Kim asked.

"Bad reviews?" Josh asked, confused.

"Well, some people have been saying things about the Stone Raiders. Turned into a thing where people were saying that it was a terrible guild, unorganized, and all of this. Thankfully none of them seem to have got much clearance to know things. Also, seems like there's a whole bunch of trolls just trying to make us sound like ingrates." Kim shook her head.

"Well, they were asking for things like having the guild together at all times, to only let people do their own thing at certain times and have set training with the entire guild. Some of the more military-like guilds, that's fine, but we're all E-heads here. Most people cycle through sooner or later." Josh shrugged.

"I think that we should pull back some of them who are around Gudalo and in other places that we can't be sure of. When Esamael attacks, we might look weak and not have much reach to look after our guild members. The other guilds won't attack us, but the POEs might if they see a weakness. They might also hold people hostage or prisoner," Lucy said.

"Damn, you're thinking pretty far ahead. I haven't heard of a hostage situation with Players yet, just guards extorting us for gold." Josh snorted.

"Best to be ready for any eventuality," Lucy said.

"Oh, before I forget, Dave told me that he had something he wanted to show us tomorrow. He's been working on it for the last four weeks he's been back," Kim said.

"Okay, but how the hell is Deia pregnant?" Josh asked.

Everyone gave him looks.

"What? I know you've all been thinking it. This is a video game! She's pregnant here though! Does she know who Dave is in real life?"

"I've already had a talk with her. It's odd, but looks like they got a custom patch," Lucy said.

"Okay." Josh scratched his head. Why the two of them would want to have a kid in a video game, and why they would deem to have it right before all the fighting started, he had no idea. "Well, I guess that we should go and see what Dave has come up with."

Chapter 16: From Another Land

Alkao looked out of his office and down at the training area for the DCA.

Snow flurries drifted down from the skies, winter in full swing. The heated roads quickly melted the snow, draining it into the large heated moat.

The fields had been shut down, the greenhouses now working through the winter. Still, with the winter, Devil's Crater hadn't slowed down at all. More people came through the teleport pad every day: Adventurers trying their luck. Traders looking for new markets.

His home was growing, and with them, his forces were as well.

Anna had been making a training schedule with the other officers who had the best handle over their flying spells or natural flying abilities. It had mixed results so far.

Finally, the two groups were starting to separate out. Three brigades specialized in aerial combat and two based on the ground.

Quindar and Anna were having the trouble of getting people out of their bad habits when flying and fighting and then building up new habits. The DCA soldiers were ready and eager to learn but it was still going to take some time before they were ready to take to the skies to fight other airborne creatures. First, Quindar and Anna were going to teach them how to properly support forces on the ground and bomb targets of opportunity.

When Quindar had started teaching them all how to use their armor and their abilities properly, everything had changed. She had them flying in formations, moving through the skies in groups, training on how to fly as a group. She'd also made it clear that the forces on the ground were needed as much as the ones in the sky. Krenua had taken over on working with the people who were supposed to be on the ground with General Kala. The rest and all of Alkao's brothers were working to fight primarily in the air, with training to fight on the ground if they needed to.

The ground forces had moved from their original training to fighting with their new weapons and armor. The aerial brigades were each forty thousand strong, while the ground forces were at fifty thousand each.

Alkao and Kala were the official leaders of the ground forces while Malkur and Vrexu led the aerial forces.

Alkao was proud of his ground forces. They might not be learning a new skill, but they were taking what they knew and building on it regularly. None of them were slacking, always pushing themselves to grow stronger. They were not just training with fighting in formation either. The focus had turned from large group fighting to smaller group skills. Learning to fight in a party of ten or less. Doing as much damage as possible to the enemy in the shortest time.

They were specializing in ambushes, trap making, and scouting. They had learned from their fight with the Demon Horde; they didn't have the weapons and training of the Dwarves, who acted like a mobile mountain on the field of battle. They were quick and strong; they could hit hard and fast, making them great for supporting troops and advanced scouts. They could slow an advance and make an army's morale plummet.

Against the Demon Horde, it had turned them from a raging army of nearly ten million to a fighting force of less than two. Without their forward attacks, they would have been torn apart wholesale. They nearly were when they went into a head-on fight with the Horde.

Alkao's jaw worked, remembering the deaths of so many soldiers. He had still been thinking with old tactics. He had tried to be smart, but he'd gone in with heavy-handed tactics. When it reached a straight-up fight, he wanted his enemy to be tired, ready to make mistakes, low on morale and anything they needed to fight with.

Alkao watched as a flight came in against a group of ground forces, firing their training bombs. The ground forces harassed them with bows and arrows, and various spells. Few, if any, of the bombs got on target.

Alkao smiled as Quindar lectured the different flights. She might be a new mother, but she was a fierce lady. A few had challenged her, and she had quickly and easily put them down. Her strength with Air was nearly unmatched; she was only weaker than Anna in her Human form, who still showed deference to Quindar. In her Dragon form, she was unmatched.

Alkao looked proudly down at his forces. His ground troops moved through fighting exercises. The aerial forces, above the different keeps, watched over the crater.

With every day, his people and his forces grew in strength. They were becoming a force to be reckoned with once again.

Alkao rolled his shoulders, eager to be back down with his ground troops and fighting. He was decent at fighting in the air, but he knew how to fight on the ground better. That wasn't saying he wouldn't use his wings or a few aerial tricks here and there.

The new armor was highly effective. Combined with the armbands and the chest piece, it was bringing in a whole new level of tactics never seen before. Every soldier could run in, nailing down an enemy force with overwhelming Mana bombs and spears before fleeing.

***

"Okay, so, what is that?" Josh pointed to the box sitting in the middle of the room.

"That is a Mana well." Dave grinned.

"Like a well that gives off Mana all the time?" Kim said, getting excited as she moved to the box.

"Yep." Dave grinned.

"I thought that the ley lines were the closest thing that this world had to a Mana well?" Josh asked.

"Yeah, it was, but then I changed it." Dave grinned.

"How?" Dwayne asked.

"It's all pretty nerdy and technical, but I made a diamond that will give off energy for the next few million years," Dave said.

"We just built a power facility and then you built this? Why didn't you make it before?" Josh asked.

"Well, you might have noticed that the power facility had a large power draw recently. That was for me to make the containment box and the Mana well diamond," Dave said.

"We've already got a lot of power from other places. What do we need this for?" Josh asked.

"Well, we could use it to power shields at our other guild halls. Also, we can use these to power our teleport pads indefinitely and give us a ready access to power if we need it across the world. Make it a guild secret," Dave said.

"Huh, that is pretty smart and conniving," Josh said.

"Just doing what I can to help." Dave smiled, thinking of the soul gem factory he had in his lab, cranking out coded soul gems that he'd place with every Mana well and basic teleport pad.

Chapter 17: Resolutions

Queen Selhi woke up to a private message from Guildmaster Giles. She read through it. Her eyes became large as she very carefully re-read it.

She sighed. The amount of money that Josh was asking for was incredible. But if she didn't pay it, then her country was going to go from a recession into a depression. Tension was already high. Much longer and she might have civil war on her hands.

"Well, looks like I'm going to need to take a trip to the treasury. Thankfully, he made it into a payment plan and I can trade goods with them," Queen Selhi said.

Her magistrate's betrayal of the Stone Raiders' trust and their goodwill had come at a great cost. Queen Selhi knew that they were using it as an example to others of what they would do if they were screwed with.

She hated it and wished it wasn't true, but she had messed up with appointing the magistrate of Selhi Capital. It might have been the stress from the job or making sure that they didn't spend too much of the treasury, but it had come back on them in a big way.

"I wonder what he means that they would be interested in entertaining ambassadors from other kingdoms and countries," Queen Selhi thought out loud as she got up from her bed.

***

Dave yawned as he sat down at his chair as the leader of the Council of Anvil and Fire.

It was his third week in the position. He would have one more week and then it would be passed onto someone else. The position mostly ran itself; he told people where materials were going according to agreements already written up. Then, he talked over matters with the council. People brought him their issues if they had any, as well as items for the meeting.

"Sorry." Dave's yawn faded away as he looked at everyone in the meeting. Over the last two months, he had found out he was becoming a dad, broken down most of the teleportation secrets that were to be had, helped to get Terra up and running, and was working on his fusion reactor. Bob had done the heavy mental lifting with his AI. Now, Dave was just figuring out outputs and scaling it all up.

His smithies were producing armor around the clock and were now a few months ahead of schedule. In two more months, it looked as if they would have all of the DCA's armor contract completed and they could turn to doing repairs, making new weapons and armor as well as working on the skills that they had gained through their time in training with the smiths.

"All right, let's get this thing started." Dave banged a hammer against the table.

Dwarves grumbled and made their way to the table.

"Anyone have any issues or concerns?" Dave looked around the table. No one raised their hands as they looked around.

"Good. Materials will be distributed according to the treaties. There will be no materials sent to those who are working outside of Dwarven mountains," Dave said.

A few of the Dwarves grumbled, but Dave and Kol shared a grin.

If only they knew how much Mithril and other high-level materials we have saved up. Be a good surprise for when they move into the new smithy in Terra.

"Okay, we have the tournaments starting in just three days. All of the Dwarven mountains that are hosting the celebrations are prepared and ready. We already have people who have finished and qualified in their own tournaments heading for the mountains. Mithsia Mountain has around twenty percent of our Warclans waiting and ready to be deployed to any Dwarven mountain in case of emergency." Dave looked over his speaking points on his interface.

"Okay, that looks like it for business. In other matters, as a guild member of the Stone Raiders, I have two things to bring the council's attention to. First of all. The Stone Raiders Guild has created a city called Terra. They are asking if we would like to send an ambassador or representative to the city. I can't go into details right now, but Terra will become a hub for people all over Emerilia. Second, the Stone Raiders know of a plot by Lord Esamael of Emaren, in Gudalo. He wishes to usurp King Sigaird of the Gudalo kingdom. They have set their eyes on attacking the Stone Raiders' Guild Hall in Verlun. They wish to use the teleport pad there to assist them in moving their forces into Haugr to kill the king and allow Lord Esamael and his forces to take control of the country." Dave's eyes looked over them all.

"The Stone Raiders desire to defend their guild hall, repel the attackers and then lead an assault on the rest of Lord Esamael's forces. They wish to create a show of power, asking for those who are allied with them to support their defense of Verlun. They will carry out the assault themselves. I have a personal interest with both of these items, so if it is agreeable with you, I will give you the information and excuse myself from this conversation and your votes," Dave said.

"Wise choice; we will let you know when we have made a decision on these items," Quino said, his face hard.

Dave nodded to Quino, using his interface and the controls for the Mirror of Communication to move him to a different conference room. He waited there for a while before he got a message to rejoin the rest of the council once again.

"We will wait for more information on this hub before putting an ambassador's position there. For the defense of the Verlun location, we will allow the lords and ladies under the mountains to make their own decisions as the Stone Raiders are allied with the various mountains and not with the Dwarves altogether," Quino said.

"Thank you." Dave looked to those around the table.

***

Light smiled at her high priest in Markolm, spreading word of the coming apocalypse, of following their true god, the Lady of Light. She dismissed the vision from her view and sat back in her chair.

Ever since she had found out that the Demons were released back onto Emerilia and that the different creatures that Bob had locked away over the centuries were going to be released, she had been appearing to her highest priests across Emerilia, telling them to have their congregation prepare for the coming battle.

Who will stand in my way when my Angels return? A cold smile crossed her face.

The Pantheon had not met in months. Water and Fire tended to their Creatures of Power. Bob was off across the world, never staying long enough in one location for her tracking and spying spells to lock onto him. Her expression turned sour as she thought of the Dark Lord. He had disappeared after the battle between his new Demons and old.

Ten million Demons! He must've been working on them ever since the first batch disappeared. Light growled and her eyes shone brighter.

She took a second, calming herself.

"Well, Air is off playing around with different leaders, while Earth is trying to raise an army." Light snorted to herself. Earth wasn't that strong of a god, and he had no forethought. With his sprites in low numbers and now able to get Champions, he was off blessing anyone who would become his Champions.

"Idiot. Does he not know that those POEs will cross him whenever they sense his plans not going in a direction they like?" She shook her head.

"But my Angels, my beautiful and powerful Angels. I must thank the Dark Lord—he did show me one thing. Creatures of Power double their levels when called to be Champions by their gods. No one will be able to stop the tide of Light." She smiled as her long delicate fingers played with a strand of her golden-blonde hair.

"It's time for the Players and People of Emerilia to know why they should fear a true god."

***

Esamael watched as Geswald walked into his office. The old man looked haggard from racing to Lord Esamael's castle and up to his office.

"You sent for me, Lord Esamael?" Geswald bowed his head slightly.

"I have sent orders to my forces; they will begin moving. In one week, we will be ready to return this country to its rightful rulers," Esamael said.

"Yes, my lord. What do you need from me?"

"Keep my people updated on the actions of the Stone Raiders. General Loughbreck will collect his various men and move toward Verlun in force. I suspect it will not take him long before he has cleared out the guild and has the teleport pad under his control. I want your people to watch and make sure nothing unforeseen happens," Esamael said.

"I will have my best people on it," Geswald promised.

"Good; soon this will all be over and Gudalo will be ours." A hungry smile passed over Lord Esamael's face.

"Yes, Lord Esamael." Geswald forced a smile, even as shivers ran down his spine.

***

"Are you sure about this?" Dave asked as he and Deia sat on their deck, looking over the cliffside that their house backed onto.

"I'm sure. I'm not going to leave my party and you all out there on your own. I'm not even showing signs of pregnancy yet and Jules said it will be fine." Deia looked into Dave's eyes.

"If you die, even though you'll respawn, the baby won't," Dave argued.

"I know. I'm not going to be on the front lines. I can stay back, provide support and run if I need to," Deia said.

Dave sighed, knowing that there was no stopping her now. Once she had made up her mind, he just had to accept it. "Okay, but you're wearing all of your armor and not using any of the power in it for your spells. I don't want you getting mentally exhausted or flooding your system with Mana. We don't know what that would do for the baby."

"I won't use above my own Mana pool," Deia agreed, nestling into his side. "Now, pass me that ice cream!"

"Yes, babe." Dave shook his head and passed her a bowl of ice cream into her outstretched hands. "Aren't you supposed to be the adult?" Dave laughed at her childish excited expression as she put a spoonful of ice cream in her mouth.

"Yes, a *cute* adult." Deia pouted and put her back to Dave, eating her ice cream.

Dave laughed, wrapping his hands around her, and pulled her back to him as she tried to be playfully stubborn.

"Noooo, you just want my ice cream!" She tried to wriggle out of his arms as she continued to eat the ice cream.

"I won't steal your ice cream." Dave chuckled.

"Promise?" Deia said, as if she were some five-year-old.

"Pinkie swear." Dave held up his pinkie.

"Okay!" Deia shook his pinkie and got close to him.

He snorted, putting the furs around her to make sure she was completely covered against the cold.

One week to go until Esamael's forces reach Verlun.

The Stone Raiders leadership weren't saying anything yet, waiting until there were two days before telling the rest of the guild and just a day before they contacted their allies to ask for help.

They didn't mean to just show Emerilia that they were not going to just sit back and let the POEs screw with them. They were going to show Emerilia that they were not alone; they had allies and that they stood together against anyone who might attack them.

The Stone Raiders and their new recruits had been busy at increasing their spells, skills, and stats.

Dave opened up his character sheet, checking his stats.

With three days, I should be over the worst drawbacks of upping my stats.

"Should move 40 to Agility and 30 to Intelligence; don't want to be out for a few days recovering," Dave muttered as he input the new stats into his character sheet.

Character Sheet

Name:	David Grahslagg	Gender:	Male
Level:	202	Class:	Dwarven Master Smith, Friend of the Grey God, Bleeder, Librarian, Aleph Engineer, Weapons Master, Champion Slayer, Skill Creator, Mine Manager, Master Summoner
Race:	Human/ Dwarf	Alignment:	Neutral Good

Unspent points: 106

Health:	29,300	Regen:	15.86 /s
Mana:	11,630	Regen:	35.55 /s
Stamina:	3,540	Regen:	28.25 /s
Vitality:	293	Endurance:	793
Intelligence:	1,163	Willpower:	711
Strength:	354	Agility:	565

Pick a new class

Upon reaching level 200, you may pick one more class or change your old classes.

"Nearly at a hundred stat points. Once these run out, my classes are just going to assign stat points. I'm probably reaching the end of how I can alter my stats through just gaining levels." Dave frowned. This was the power of classes. If he had classes that weren't related to the way he played, then his stats would be skewed in a way to not follow his strengths.

Dave went through the various classes, taking his time. Getting to level 300 to pick his next class could take years.

"Okay, summoning master was meant for me to get a better idea of teleportation. It helped me out some, but I think now that it would be of more use for me to learn more about gravity, time, physics, and all that pesky extra stuff that comes with teleportation. So, good-bye summoning master." Dave removed the class, so he could select another. Looking through the extensive list of classes left behind, he moved to the more advanced subjects.

"Master of Space and Time, Master of Gravitational Anomalies—I'll take that." Dave switched out his new classes.

"Wow, okay, ouch." Dave's mind raced with new knowledge. Prompts filled his vision and flashed in his notification bar as he held his head between his hands. Around Dave, the room seemed to distort and change. Cracks formed in the ground that he lay on.

He let out a cry as power wracked through his body. His mind worked dozens of different ideas at the same time, coming together in experiments that he was trying. With his increased Intelligence and the new classes, his mind was making connections with his knowledge and the newly acquired classes.

Stuck in an emotional state, he didn't have complete control over his actions. He had found answers! He had found something that could alter his spells and formations, turn them from just theoretical to possible.

Classes could be earned in two ways: one by completing the prerequisites for the class and then being above level 10. The second was to reach one of the levels where classes were awarded and purchase them.

When someone was rewarded with a class or they bought it, there was an influx of knowledge. The Jukal were basically using an AI to teach a person through the nanites in their bodies.

Someone could buy a class or switch it out only when they had reached level 10, 50, 100, 200, 300, and every 100 level after that. If someone bought a class, then they would have to wait until the next class level before changing out. If they were to dismiss a class, then all of the stats and benefits would disappear. They would naturally keep the experience that they had gained through improving their class level; they would also keep the knowledge they gained.

Raising levels was not an easy task, so although someone could change out all of their classes every time and gain a new one, it was of limited use. Their overall stat increase was going to be low; they would be a jack-of-all-trades but the master of none.

Some classes not only gave new stats and bonuses when they increased, they gave knowledge.

Both the Master of Space and Time as well as Master of Gravitational Anomalies gave more knowledge upon the completion of a class level. The Jukal gave out a decent amount of information but it wasn't close to the level of knowledge that they themselves had on various subjects.

However, if someone was able to combine just the right classes with their own knowledge and high Intelligence, then it was quite possible to reach the level of Jukal knowledge on certain subjects.

"Dave! Dave!" Deia called out as Dave fell from the couch with his head in his hands, screaming in pain from the new knowledge. It was as if he had stayed up for months studying one subject. And the power—the power was something else.

Dave started laughing into the ground as he flexed his Mana and physical muscles. To the people of Cliff-Hill, a chill ran down their spines.

Dave was currently absorbing the information from both of these classes. Much like when he had destroyed Magical Circuits in the past, the information flooding his mind gave him a sort of rush. The world seemed to fade away, time meaning nothing as he combined the knowledge he gained with the knowledge he knew. His high Intelligence linked it together as he quickly advanced his knowledge and passed through the second barrier of the classes with no signs of slowing down.

***

Bob arrived in a flash of light, looking from Deia to Dave. He didn't say anything. Another flash of magic enveloped them as they appeared in Dave's lab.

Parts of the deck rained around them. Bob didn't have the time to refine his spell.

"What's happening?" Tears streamed down Deia's face.

"I don't know." Bob grabbed Dave. With a strength that belied his small stature, he jumped up to a different level. Deia followed as Bob threw Dave into the room.

Deia followed, using just her Strength and Agility.

Once Dave was on the ground, distortions started to fill the room. Runed objects appeared from thin air. The hazy air messed with both Bob and Deia's senses as they watched the various forming items. Some would appear for just a few seconds, while others for whole minutes.

The entire time, Dave held his head, in clear pain from whatever changes he was undergoing.

"Bob, what's going on?" Deia asked.

"I don't know. What was he doing before he collapsed?"

"He was putting some stat points into his character sheet. He just got his new class and was switching out summoning for space and time and another class for gravitational anomalies!" Deia said, not taking her eyes off Dave.

"I told him that he should hold off on that crap, but even I didn't think that *this* would happen."

Dave's armor appeared over him, covering Dave's face under his hood.

"What is this?" Deia demanded.

"I think he had some kind of breakthrough. What it means, I don't even know. His high Intelligence makes him vulnerable to impulses and influxes of information. When he gained the new classes, he must've got a rush of information? Maybe, as he started acquiring more knowledge, he started figuring out more and more. He has a lot of knowledge inside that mind of his. With those stats and the right starting point, it was like lighting a gasoline-covered fire. The match was the new classes' influx of knowledge. Now, his mind is taking on a path. He must not want to leave. I've had a few rushes like it and the more curious you are, the harder it is to get out of a stat binge. It can take hours or days before you fully recover. I don't know what he's learning, but I know he will be fine. Of that, I can promise," Bob said with a kind smile.

"Okay." Deia's hands unconsciously moved for her stomach. Her eyes searched the room. "Where are we?" She took in the sight of the laboratory.

"Oh, uh, I guess he wanted to wait until the big reveal before showing you this place. We call it the laboratory, though the nickname is Pandora's Box." Bob smiled.

"What have you been doing in here?" Deia looked at the different laboratories and intricate runes around the room.

"Things that might change the very future of Emerilia." Bob grinned.

Chapter 18: Into Motion

General Loughbreck certainly looked like a war general on his large war cat.

Lucy yawned as the general wound down his little speech.

"We march for Verlun! To claim back what is rightfully ours!" The general was being broadcasted to all of the cities under his control through the soldiers' interfaces.

Some of the armies were already on the move, leaving their cities that were sealing up behind them while gathering more forces that had been hiding in the forests.

They would gather before reaching Verlun in three days.

Lucy rubbed her eyes and opened up a private message. She attached a number of files, sending it, and opened up the guild's forums. A cold smile appeared on her face as she typed out a message and posted it.

Within seconds, there were replies on the thread. All across Emerilia, Stone Raiders were moving to the closest teleport pads.

They left the wilderness, or their smithies, their mage's colleges and fighting arenas. Finished off their dungeons and started moving.

The Stone Raiders' command had been sent. The guild was gathering.

***

Sigaird looked up from his dinner, checking out the message he had received. Not many got his personal messaging information. He nearly choked on his wine as he read the contents of the letter.

"Are you all right?" One of the guards moved to help the king.

"Seal the cities! Call the lords and ladies loyal to the crown!" Sigaird said, still coughing while he left his table, his meal forgotten as he headed for his offices.

"Yes, my king." The guard used his interface. The other royal guards watched for threats as Sigaird shared the message with Lady Merguine and continued reading the report.

A shiver went down his back at how accurate the information was. He had no idea how the Stone Raiders had been able to get such information. Whoever their spymaster was, they were a master at their trade. Not even Lady Merguine had been able to get this kind of information out of the southern kingdoms.

The main players were named and pointed out. Battle plans were guessed, but there was nothing solid.

Sigaird opened up a personal channel with the southern border army's general.

"General Eckan, we have reports that Lord Esamael's army is moving. I want you to take some of your forces to Emaren to place pressure on Lord Esamael," Sigaird said.

"Yes, my king. I will have my forces moving within a few hours. It will take us a day or two to reach Emaren," Eckan replied.

"Good. I am sending you reports that have just come to my attention. Do not share them with anyone, lest we might give away our abilities."

"Yes, my king. It will be as you command," Eckan said.

King Sigaird could hear him running. "Good. Let me know when your forces are on the move." King Sigaird closed the channel and opened up another with General Tortessin.

"My king?"

"Check the city. I want Haugr to be ready for an attack in the next couple of days. I am sending you a message right now with all the information I know about what is going on." Sigaird looked up as Merguine walked into his office.

"It will be done," Tortessin said.

Sigaird cut the channel and looked up to Merguine. "What are you thinking?"

"I have no idea how the Stone Raiders have so much information on Lord Esamael. They've practically given us the entire roster of every single person who was working against us," Lady Merguine said.

"So, they knew about Lord Esamael and his plans. What the hell are they going to do?" Sigaird asked.

"I don't know, but they must've known for some time. This is not just simple reconnaissance." Merguine shook her head and slumped into a seat.

"So, what do you think is going to happen?"

Merguine looked into Sigaird's eyes. "I think that Lord Esamael and his forces are in for a rude awakening. They could've sent this information to us at any time and we could have removed Esamael and his people a hell of a lot easier. They waited until Esamael's forces were on the move, ready to attack us. I don't think this is a battle. I think it's an example," Merguine said.

"How so?"

"They've clearly showed that they have intelligence-gathering abilities which well exceed our own. If they knew all of this about Lord Esamael, I can only guess how much they knew about what we were doing. They were using this for their advantage. To what end, I do not know," Merguine said.

Sigaird rubbed his forehead in frustration.

Lady Merguine opened up her interface, checking her messages and sending out queries. She paused with her finger in mid-air. "How did they get your personal contact information?"

Sigaird's hand paused as he looked to Lady Merguine. "I have no idea," he answered, his heart troubled at what her question implied.

***

Josh yawned, stretching out fully in his chair before relaxing and looking at his lieutenants. Florence, Jules, Dwayne, Esa, Lucy, Kim,

Malsour, and Suzy were there. Dave was supposed to be there, but Deia said that he was very ill and someone was looking after him. Thankfully, Malsour had been able to replace him. Both Malsour and Suzy didn't have any real power, but they were still seen as advisors: Malsour for tech, Suzy for anything that Lucy or Florence might forget or she had more knowledge of.

"Lucy, you want to start this all off?" Josh asked, still not fully awake.

"Loughbreck has started to move in the north. He is moving toward Verlun, his forces linking up with one another as they do so. They have something between two hundred and three hundred thousand soldiers, including mages, which make up nearly half of their army. Lord Esamael has ordered the cities to the south to prepare to move. The people allied to him are moving to take power from those who are under the king's thumb, while Emaren is fortifying itself. It's rather quiet right now. I believe in two days, they will carry out their attack with Loughbreck hitting us with his forces and Esamael attacking Haugr with his forces. Their plan is to use the teleport pads in Emaren and Verlun to move their troops into Haugr and take the city."

"Sounds like they don't think of us as much more than a stepping stone," Dwayne said, casually, a cold smile on his face.

"Ah well, we'll just have to educate them." Josh chuckled. "How is the recall going?"

"We've got Stone Raiders coming in from all over Emerilia. They're gathering in the city, getting their weapons and armor ready," Lucy said.

"Kol and a group of Master Smiths working the Devil's Crater smithy moved into the Terra smithy to help with repairs," Malsour added.

"Good—don't want to be going in with low durability weapons," Josh said, thinking of his daggers that were hidden away. While fighting, they were awesome, but they were a pain when he was just sitting in a chair. Having a dagger that ate your damn soul to power it poking you in the back, even if it's through a sheath, was not good back support.

"Florence, how are your people doing?"

"The higher-ups have known this is coming for a while. We'll let our people know tomorrow to not cause a panic. I don't think that we will be that bad off." Florence shrugged. "What I am worried for is any of our allies who are in the city, as well as customers."

Josh tapped his fingers on the table in thought. "Lucy, have the Aleph scouts shadow the spies who are in Verlun. Use the scouts, rangers and such as you feel fit." Lucy acknowledged his words as his eyes turned to Florence. "The day before, warn those you trust. A few hours before Loughbreck arrives, kill off the spies in Verlun and pull those people back to Terra. The less people out there, the less we have to worry about using our spells."

"Can do." Florence and Lucy looked to each other, their looks telling each other they would talk about their plans afterward.

Malsour put a finger in the air.

"Malsour?" Josh asked.

"Dave has been working on something that will be of use to Verlun. We also came up with a way to defend the guild hall there a little better." Malsour pulled out what looked like a diamond encased in a soul gem that had runes carved into it.

"What is that?" Kim leaned forward in interest.

"This is a prototype of a Mana barrier generator. Inside, there is a Mana well that constantly gives off power to the soul gem construct, which serves to contain the power and make it available for the covering runes. When activated, it will keep up a constant barrier using any power that is held within the soul gem and fed from the Mana well," Malsour said proudly.

"So how strong are we talking?" Esa asked.

"Not sure, but Dave had this built a few days ago. He didn't know how strong it would be, but he felt that given a few weeks without being used, this barrier could hold up to a god's power." Malsour looked around the room.

Dwayne whistled.

"He also said that there is the ability to link people to the Mana well. It can increase the Mana density within an area, allowing allied people to regenerate their Mana at a much higher rate. However, the more people connected, the larger the power draw and less going to the Mana barrier," Malsour warned.

"Well, I say we just use it as a barrier for now, but that is certainly interesting," Josh said.

"Aw, I wanted to see if it could fuel some of my higher-level spells." Kim pouted.

"Even more reason to put it on defense. I still remember when you blew out Cliff-Hill's Guild Hall with one of your 'tests.'" Josh stared at Kim.

"How was I supposed to know that it would work that well?" Kim muttered, barely audible to the rest of the gathered Stone Raiders.

"Or the time at the Aleph Guild Hall?" Josh added.

Kim scratched her head, an awkward and embarrassed smile on her face.

"You said that there was something else to increase our defenses?" Dwayne asked Malsour.

"Yes, prebuilding new defenses. I have been learning about magical coding and Magical Circuits with Dave for a long time. While he is out of commission, we still have two choices. We can form new walls within the ground. When Lord Esamael's forces attack, we can raise them up through the ground, creating defenses almost immediately that are better than what we have in place. Either that or I can plant a soul gem construct that will do essentially the same thing, but with the walls being made from soul gem crystal. This process will, however, take longer, unless we feed it with energy from Terra—which actually wouldn't be that hard," Malsour said.

"If we go with the soul gem construct, what are our drawbacks?" Josh asked.

"Power needs. We can generate a ton of energy, but right now, we don't have the number of soul gems we need to move it all. We would have to put certain areas on power saving in order to grow it and it would take a few hours. With the pre-made walls, we can make them today and tomorrow, then pull them out of the ground in a matter of seconds. Also, it would be able to buff us some, but we wouldn't have much time to put in complex magical coding. With the other wall, we can rune it and use soul gems to give our defenders some rather large boosts," Malsour said.

Josh scratched his cheek in thought. "Let's go with the normal walls first. The soul gems have too many things that could possibly go wrong and having them appear out of the ground is sure to shock them a little."

"I will talk to a few people and we will begin. We'll try to make it low enough so that the spies can't sense anything going on," Malsour said.

"Perfect. Esa, Dwayne, how are our people looking?" Josh asked.

Esa and Dwayne looked to each other. They had now both become leaders with the melee fighters. There were just so many of them that it was necessary to break them up. Esa had taken over the training aspect while Dwayne took over the ongoing operations, knowing where people were and setting up raiding parties.

Esa nodded and looked to the rest of the people at the table. "Our people are looking good. We've got some good ole Stone Raiders spirit in them. Honestly, this will be a good test for them. Show them what the Stone Raiders do. If they can't crack this, then we can lose them. If they do, then I say that they're true Stone Raiders."

"Our veterans are ready for whatever might come. We've been grouping the older groups up with the newer ones. Some parties haven't agreed to this, so it's been a bit of a pain in the ass. We've kept Party Zero separated from everyone. There is simply no one who can match their strength right now. As people are coming in, we're sorting them out into their fighting groups. It looks to be a smooth transition. Most are excited to get started. We've grouped POEs and Players; there's no discrimination," Dwayne said, proudly.

"Good—that sounds good. Kim?" Josh asked.

"We're ready to rain some destruction down on these asswipes, though I agree that it might be a good idea to have the surrounding city cleared out. We've had three months to just get stronger and train. Few of us have been able to use our full-powered spells, so they might be," Kim shifted in her seat awkwardly, "powerful."

Josh raised an eyebrow, but didn't remind her of how she had wanted to test out her even stronger spells fueled by the Mana well.

"Very well." Josh shook his head. "Anyone else got any points they would like to bring up?"

"I think we should send word to our close allies, like the Dwarves, Kufo'tel Elves, Devil's Crater and Aleph," Suzy said.

Josh waved for her to go on. Lucy said that they shouldn't send out word until the day of the battle so that word didn't make it to Esamael or Sigaird's ears ahead of time.

"These people have shown great faith in us. There is little risk of them going on to tell others about what we're doing. Also, it gives us a chance to let them see Terra, to show off our abilities and assure them that they are held in a deep confidence. We have many people we are affiliated with through trade and various agreements, but with these groups, we answered their call and they answered ours. We've worked well with them before. A show of trust and vulnerability will go a long way in securing ties with our groups," Suzy said.

"Under what pretense do we invite them into Terra?" Lucy asked.

"To establish their embassies, which we can do at the same time," Suzy replied.

Josh looked to Lucy.

"Suzy raises some good points and it makes sense. If we can show the effectiveness of having embassies here and moving troops to support one another, it's going to be a powerful deterrent to anyone who might challenge one of our allies and a reason for others to join us."

Josh checked around the room.

"Okay, let's go for it," Josh said, not seeing anyone overly concerned about the idea. "Anyone else have anything they want to share?"

No one was forthcoming.

"Okay, then, let's go wreck Esamael's plans!" Josh grinned.

Chapter 19: Today's the Day

Florence took a meal out to Malsour, who was crouched inside one of the guard huts, his eyes closed as sweat ran down his face.

"Malsour?" Florence asked. Seeing he was focused on his work, she put the tray of food to the side.

Malsour groaned, moving his shoulders and moving around.

"You okay?" Florence asked as Malsour pushed himself into a chair.

"Fine, just a bit hard to make walls and such underground. All the pressure from the rocks is a big pain in the ass." Malsour's eyes fell on the tray.

"I thought you might be hungry." Florence smiled and took the cover off the tray.

"Oh, you are a goddess." Malsour smiled and grabbed the tray. He started eating, closing his eyes as he tasted the home cooked meal.

"So, do you think we're ready?" Florence asked, playing with her hands.

"I think we will be. The wall will be complete. Lucy thinks that Loughbreck and his forces will group together to make sure that their command structure is solid before they move to attack us." Malsour dug in again.

"When do you think they will attack?" Florence asked.

Malsour drank from the canteen with the meal. "Mmm, nice," he said, cheering Florence.

"Least I could do for the one building us this wall. I've heard from the other Dark and Earth mages that they've never seen anything like it, or someone as powerful as you," Florence said.

"Thanks. You'll make a man blush." Malsour chuckled and took another drink. "I think that they will attack tonight. They don't think of us as that strong of an opponent. They want to establish a beachhead here and then move through us to Haugr. We're just a small bump in the road. They might get wary when their spies start disappearing, but they're confident in their abilities. They've been training for months or years for this. They think they're ready for anything. After all, they've been told as much through their training."

"What do you think will happen once they start taking casualties?"

Malsour chewed on some ham, looking to the ceiling of the hut in thought. "They have been trained rather well, enough that they won't just fall apart under a little pressure. They are pretty strong, but it just won't be enough. It's going to be huge blow to them once we actually start fighting. They thought that they were just attacking a small, nothing guild. However, once we show up with other races backing us, that's going to be something of a shock. I think we're going to have to hit them hard and fast to decide the battle. Otherwise, they can pull back, regroup and come up with a new strategy to fight us. If they get out of our range, we're going to have to chase them down. Giving them time is the worst thing we can do."

"Is there anything that me and mine can do to help out?" Florence asked.

"Well, I've got all of your mages working on building this wall. Once the spies are gone, I do have a few ideas that might be worth testing out. Going to need a few Earth mages, though." Malsour smiled.

"I'm listening." Florence smiled and moved closer.

***

Josh watched the spies sitting in the inn to his front. They were playing cards without a care in the world. One of them even looked as if he was asleep in a chair.

In fact, the spy was using a bird familiar to watch the Stone Raiders' Guild Hall. Josh was relaxed in the shadows of a rooftop, twirling one of his daggers in his hand.

Josh had gone through the apartment last night. The spies regularly sent up owl familiars to do recon on the guild hall. One of them would cast seer or familiar spells, while another relayed the information. The rest would take over, so there was always someone watching the guild hall.

Josh used his dagger to clean his nails. The shadows on the roof covered him, making him all but invisible. A few enchantments that made people look away and boosted his stealth abilities were also at work with his leather armor.

He opened up his interface again and looked over the different maps. There were dozens of Stone Raiders throughout the city. They had hidden in wagons or moved into the city over the last two nights.

Red markers showed where all of the spies and any other allied with Esamael were located. Stone Raiders were out and about in the town, acting as merchants or dozens of other people. Those who were friendly were harboring them as they waited.

Aleph scouts and drones were doing most of the recon work. All of the Stone Raiders scouts were taught how to control the Aleph scout automatons. There weren't enough for all of the Stone Raiders in Verlun, but they took turns, watching over their targets through their invisible spies.

The green dots of the Stone Raiders started leaving their various hiding spots. Josh moved his shoulders, loosening himself up for the first phase of their plan.

He checked the time. *Three minutes to go.* He checked his map, looking at a mass of red in formation.

Several groups had joined together, making larger and larger formations as they moved down the roads toward Verlun. Now, they were headed off the roads, crossing through fields and moving to meet up with the other large groups to create one massive formation.

In a few hours, all of General Loughbreck's forces would be together and just three miles away from Verlun and the Stone Raiders' Guild Hall.

Josh rolled onto his front and moved forward on all fours, climbing across the roof's tiles and staying low as the shadows moved away from him. Josh was to the side of the balcony as one of the spies stepped out of his room, holding up his hand to take in the familiar.

Josh used one of his skills. In a flurry of motion, he jumped from the roof, crossing the fifteen feet between him and his target. His left blade opened the spy's neck while his right grabbed onto the top of the doorway, swinging into the room.

With Josh's skill, people seemed to move as though everything were caught in molasses. Josh disappeared into the shadows, moving across the room. The spies were just starting to look up at their friend, who was turning around, his neck opened up in a bloody smile.

Josh plunged a dagger through another spy's back. With his sneak modifier, the man died instantly.

Three more. Josh turned, holding his blade out as one spy started to stand. Josh opened his neck.

Two.

He jumped, flipping his body over the last card Player coming up behind him.

The spy pulled out his sword, turning to face Josh just as a dagger plunged into his side, punching a hole through his heart and lung.

Josh ripped the blade out and opened the wound up more. The spy dropped to the ground like a puppet with its strings cut.

One.

The last spy, the controller of the familiar, blinked, coming back to reality. Josh threw one of his daggers. It buried itself in the man's chest.

He coughed and blood came out of his mouth. A rush of power filled Josh through his blades, begging for more violence, for more blood and souls.

"We've got plenty more spies to kill," Josh promised, pulling the blade out of the last spy's chest.

With a flick, he cleaned the blades. Time returned to normal as cards settled on the ground and the last bodies fell to the ground, their lifeblood staining the floors.

Josh moved back to the balcony, sheathing his blades and climbing up the wall with ease. He looked out over Verlun, checking his mini-map. The slaughter was underway.

Josh laughed, running across the roof; he jumped onto another and bounced off two chimneys before he reached his next roof, picking up speed as he ran.

All around him, Stone Raiders flitted about, moving from one target to the next.

Josh waved to those he saw. All of them had hungry smiles on their faces. It had been some time since the whole guild had been out on a hunt. Something about it made someone feel so alive.

The wolves, hunting the sheep. They should have never come into a city under our protection.

***

Dwayne looked out over the city, Esa and Kim to either side.

"Well, I knew that they were going to send some people to help us. I didn't think that it would be so many." Dwayne laughed.

"Ten complete Warclans, ten thousand Aleph automatons, three thousand Kufo'tel rangers, and a full fifty thousand-strong DCA brigade with twenty-five thousand ground troops and the same amount in aerial forces." Esa looked out over the forces that were arrayed down the four main streets of Terra.

"That's not including the other forces that are coming from our other alliances and affiliates." Lucy walked up to them.

"How are we looking on that side of things?" Dwayne asked.

"Each of them has sent at least some kind of force—the smallest being about ten people, the largest around a thousand. It was on short notice and the Dwarven tournaments are going on," Lucy said.

"Better than I thought. I'm interested in what kind of magic they use." Kim rubbed her hands together.

"Mana nerd," Dwayne muttered.

"Muscle-brained warmonger!" Kim yelled back.

"Hey, we all know how much you like putting your spells to work on those deserving of your attention," Dwayne said.

"Heh," Kim said, moving awkwardly and blushing a little bit.

Dwayne held his head, shaking it in disbelief.

Lucy and Esa chuckled.

"So, what is this that I hear? Dave is out of the fight?" Esa asked.

"Deia said that he messed up and he was stuck in some kind of loop. I saw him. He's just sitting in a room with all kinds of these distortions around him. It looks really weird." Lucy shrugged.

"Hope he gets better soon. It's always fun to see what the hell he comes up with," Dwayne said.

"Yeah, the amount of times I've heard people saying that he's cheating... He's pretty powerful, but his weapons, armor, and ideas make him a damned powerful support," Esa said.

They all nodded in agreement.

***

Deia looked up as Dave groaned and fell over. Deia checked for distortions in the room; there were none. She ran inside and pulled Dave to her.

"Dave, baby, are you okay?" She held his head on her lap.

"Sleep." Dave's eyes closed.

Bob rushed into the room. "Is he done?" Bob looked to Deia.

"I think, but he's exhausted and he hasn't eaten anything in nearly three days," Deia said.

"Well, his Endurance will tide him over, but I'll hook him up to an IV so he can get some fluids and nutrients in him." Bob pulled out what looked like a Band-Aid.

Deia pulled off his clothes. Dave smelled pretty ripe for not showering in a couple of days.

Bob slapped the Band-Aid on Dave. "I'll look after him; give me a few minutes." Bob wrinkled his nose.

"You sure?" Deia asked.

"Deia, there are some things that men don't want others seeing, even if they are the love of their life," Bob said.

"Okay." Deia lay Dave down. He looked so peaceful compared to the yelling and screaming man of the last couple of days.

Deia would have stayed up the whole time if Bob hadn't forced her to get some sleep. The first night, he forcefully spelled her to sleep and put her in a spare lab.

Deia stepped out of the room. The glow of Mana filled the room and poured outside. After a few minutes, Bob spoke up.

"He's good," Bob said.

Deia looked back in the room, finding Dave in clean clothes as if nothing had happened.

"Thanks." She moved back to Dave. She stroked his hair, moving it into a position she liked, and looked down on his peaceful face. She kissed his forehead and hugged him.

There will be hell to pay when he wakes up! Her eyes thinned and her jaw tightened. Dave didn't react at all as her expression slackened.

Bob cleared his throat and Deia looked up to him.

"Deia, are you sure that you want to get involved with the on-coming battle?"

"Bob, we've been over this a dozen times." Deia sighed.

"And each time you try to argue against my reasoning. You're carrying a baby and Dave isn't going to be there. Yes, your party is very good, but there is always a slight chance or possibility that you might be hurt or killed. You might come back, but we have no idea what will happen to the baby," Bob said.

"I'm not even showing and this is my party. I have led them till now and I will continue to lead them. As you said, they're a great party and I'll be sitting back and running support," Deia said.

"You say that, but I have seen your battles. You're usually right up there next to Anna," Bob grumbled, sighing and rubbing his forehead.

Deia smiled at his distress. "You don't need to worry so much, Bob. I'll be fine."

"There is a very good reason to worry. Do you know what your husband would do if he was to find out that I let you out onto the field of battle?" Bob said with a dry chuckle.

"This is my life to lead and my decisions to make. I will be okay," Deia said.

"Fine. I know there's nothing I can do to dissuade you, but just try to stay back. Don't get yourself on the front lines, okay?" Bob said.

"I'll try my best, gramps." Deia smiled.

"Make a man really feel his age," Bob muttered even as the corners of his mouth betrayed him, lifting ever so slightly.

Chapter 20: Coming of the Dawn

None of the commanders made to move closer to General Loughbreck.

In the last two hours, every spy and informant in Verlun had gone silent. Their scouts were moving ahead to try to get a better understanding of what was going on in the city.

Those damn spies. I should have sent my own people, not just relied on their agents. They must've drawn the Stone Raiders' attention in some way or they went to ground. Idiots!

His inner thoughts must have made it onto his face as a few of the commanders moved even farther away, anxious to not bring their general's wrath down on them.

"We will be in position before last light. I want to have a meeting with all the commanders and make sure everything is ready. As night falls, I want us to be ready to move into Verlun. Our spies have already shown that they're incompetent. We need to act fast before the Stone Raiders can start pulling information out of them," Loughbreck said.

His aides opened their interfaces, sending out messages to the other formations that were under Loughbreck's command.

He shifted restlessly on his war cat. He, like his soldiers, had been training to return Gudalo back to those who would bring their country into the older and more civilized times, times when they didn't trade with every race and had closed their borders to the dirty races to their south.

They were lower beings that needed to be taught their place. Lord Esamael would bring about a time when the Humans of Gudalo once again controlled the beasts of the south through slave collars and physical force. They knew nothing more than how to act like animals and must be treated as such.

Loughbreck nodded to himself, affirming his beliefs as his army moved forward. He looked upon the ranks of soldiers who had been trained for the cause. A holy army, made to drive out the scourge and teach them their position in life.

The Stone Raiders and their love for the dirtier races was enough to earn their destruction. For daring to be in the way of Loughbreck's army and taking the income of hard-working Human Gudalians with their teleport pad, Loughbreck would happily hunt them down.

He spat on the ground, just thinking about the ingrates.

***

"Preparations are complete," Malsour said to Josh as he walked into the guild hall's main office.

"Good." Josh looked out of one of the windows and watched as people fled into the teleport pad. All of Verlun seemed to be emptying through the teleport pad. They all understood that a fight was coming. They had seen images of the Stone Raiders fighting and most just didn't want to be caught in the middle of it.

Some of the fights in the city had gotten out of hand and a few buildings had suffered as a result.

Malsour slumped into a chair.

Josh looked away from the window, grabbing some wine from Florence's liquor cabinet, and sat down. Josh held it out to Malsour.

"If I must." Malsour smiled and sipped the wine. He looked impressed, taking a large gulp before he handed it back.

"I thought as much, she hid it all the way at the back," Josh grinned and took a drink. "Damn, that *is* good!"

"So, what are you thinking of the coming battle?" Malsour moved to get the kinks out from sitting in one position for hours on end to concentrate his powers.

"I think it's going to be a surprise for Loughbreck." Josh passed the wine back.

"He does have some powerful people with him." Malsour took a swig.

"Their strongest is the same level of our veterans, without all the fighting, skill, and weapons," Josh said.

"True." Malsour passed the wine back. "Though, we shouldn't underestimate them."

"Is that why you and Florence's people were hard at work all day?" Josh grinned.

"Well, can't go easy on them and people usually get scared when random uncontrollable things start happening." Malsour smiled.

Josh chuckled and took a drink. "So, how are you feeling? Good for a fight?"

"Yeah, I'll be fine. Feel weird without Dave there to back me up, but he should be good in a few days." Malsour burped.

"Nice." Josh laughed as the door opened.

"I thought I might find you two hiding up here." Florence eyed the wine in Josh's hand.

"Want a drink?" Josh asked with a winning smile.

Florence's eye seemed to twitch for a bit before she let out a deep breath and grabbed the wine from Josh.

"Not even using glasses," she muttered to herself, pulling out three flutes and filling them before she passed them out. "You owe me a new bottle."

"Of course." Josh's smile faltered at Florence's smile. "Just for curiosity, how much does a bottle cost?"

"Oh, it's nothing big to the Guildmaster of the Stone Raiders." Florence sat in the chair next to Malsour in front of her desk, a sweet smile on her face.

Malsour looked amused as he sipped from the glass she had given him.

Josh took a drink from his.

"About one thousand gold," she said.

Josh nearly spat the wine out of his nose and mouth, but recovered and swallowed it. *I nearly spat probably ten gold everywhere!*

"Why the hell did you buy wine that's a thousand gold per bottle!?" Josh demanded.

"We're pretty successful here and I vowed to do what I want, not what I should do. Got to take a break now and then and live in excess." Florence winked, taking a small sip from the glass. "Also, it is highly potent. You won't realize it, but three or four glasses and you'll mellow out and pass out. It takes a few minutes to kick in." Florence smiled.

Josh and Malsour looked at each other in alarm, thinking of how they had been simply throwing it back.

Josh pulled out a healing ring, putting it on his ring finger.

"You have another one of those?" Malsour asked.

Josh pulled out another ring and gave it to Malsour. Both of them sighed in relief. The rings would keep them sober, but it would also keep them from falling asleep.

"You really should invest more in wearable runed items," Florence chided Malsour.

"I've never needed them." Malsour shrugged.

Florence looked over Malsour, studying him. Her eyebrows rose. "You don't have any enchanted item other than that necklace!" Florence said in surprise.

"Yeah. I use this to read up on the items in the Aleph college. Since the mirror school and their connection to you, they've been uploading a lot of interesting books," Malsour said.

"But aren't you one of the strongest fighters?" Florence asked.

"He is, but everything he and Induca do is by their own power." Josh smiled.

Florence looked as if she were in a state of shock. "But how? Your Mana pool must be massive!" Florence demanded.

"A man must have some secrets." Malsour smiled and sipped from his glass.

"Why don't you use magical items?"

"Never really needed to and I usually break them," Malsour said.

"Just a five percent increase in Intelligence would be massive for someone like you," Florence said.

"Yeah, though Dave offered me fifteen percent rings. He gave them to Induca, because she's been working with using magical items. I might give them a go. They've really improved her fighting ability." Malsour looked thoughtful.

"Fifteen percent," Florence said, her eyes wide. She recovered quickly. "The more I learn about the things that Dave makes, the more I'm simply blown away. You can sell one of those rings for a few thousand gold. Anything above seven percent multiplies in cost."

"He is rather good at crafting." Josh smiled and fingered the necklace he wore. It still pulled power from him. All of the Stone Raiders wore them—a simple piece of metal with a basic magical code carved into the back and connected to one of the guild's vault-classed soul gems.

Today, they wouldn't be taking energy but instead pouring it back into the Stone Raiders. Their aim wasn't to just defeat Lough-breck, but to break him and his forces.

Josh looked out of the window; night was slowly coming. With it, the mage lights around the guild came to life. The guild hall and its outlying buildings covered nearly five hundred square meters. Their walls created a simple twenty-meter-tall octagon encircling a square mile of ground. The fields covering the two miles to the city and fifteen miles over all the surrounding fields were theirs.

Verlun lay in something of a valley, the fields around it rising gradually the farther away. It made it harder to see for a great distance in any direction. Trees and crops dotted the landscape, the trees showing the field's boundaries.

Their plans were in motion. Now, they just had to wait and see what would happen. Josh checked his map. Loughbreck and his forces had gathered together and were now having a bunch of meetings to get all the leaders used to one another and ready for the coming operation.

***

Lord Esamael looked out over Emaren. Before him, there were four hundred thousand soldiers, all waiting around the teleport pad. Others were along the walls, making sure that they didn't lose the city if they were attacked by Sigaird's loyal forces.

He checked his map once again. Loughbreck reported that his forces had moved up to a position beyond Verlun and were ready to move forward with the attack when ready.

Esamael took in the sight. The sun was falling, turning the skies red as it dipped below the horizon. "Are our agents in position?" Esamael asked.

"Yes, my lord," one of the aides answered.

"Good. Pass on the order—we strike now," Esamael said.

The aides and generals who were around him talked into their interfaces, orders passing through the ranks.

After a few minutes, there was a connection from Haugr. A flare came through the portal and lit up the sky, the agreed upon signal for the agents.

Soldiers rushed forward, the elite forces. They would secure the teleport pad on the other side as the lower-leveled and weaker soldiers moved out into Haugr, increasing the area that they held and then striking out toward the royal palace.

The soldiers had trained till they had nightmares about it and executed their jobs with precision. Not once was the flow of troops even slowed in the slightest as they charged through.

"Tonight, the revolution begins, and tomorrow will bring a dawn to a new leader of Gudalo." A hungry smile spread across Esamael's face, his eyes hooded as he looked at the teleport pad as if he could see the bounty that lay on the other side.

****

Deia shook her head at the scouts' attempts to sneak up on the Stone Raiders' Guild Hall. They were decent by most standards, but compared to someone who had been a ranger for a few decades, it was easy to pick them out in the flattened fields around the guild hall.

The access to the Aleph scouts and drones doesn't hurt, as well as this thermal vision gear. Those magical coders do come up with some pretty interesting stuff. She looked out over the open fields with the twin glasses that had been magically coded, lighting up any heat signatures.

The scouts had some decent stealth and sometimes looked like heat shadows, but Deia's trained eyes quickly picked out what was a scout and what was a hot spot.

Once she found them, she sent out Aleph scouts, guiding them to the scouts to confirm their position and shadow them. They appeared as red dots on her map, the Aleph scouts faithfully following their prey.

She took off the glasses and rubbed her eyes.

"Looks like the main force is on the move." Steve had been controlling the Aleph scouts, following what she was saying and deploying them through the fields around the guild hall.

"All right—seems these buggers are making a move. Everyone, get ready. They should be within range for us to move in twenty minutes," Josh said over the guild-wide channel.

Deia felt as if she had an itch she couldn't scratch. Not being able to go into battle with Dave at her side just felt odd.

She trusted in Bob saying that he would be fine. If she and Dave were gone, Party Zero could handle themselves, but she didn't want to let them down. If she wasn't there and something bad happened, she knew she wouldn't have been able to forgive herself.

***

Dwayne looked over the assembled forces. Around the teleport pad, Stone Raiders stood in rows of three, waiting for word.

Behind them, Kala waited with her brigade. They each bore new weapons and sturdy leather armor. Beast Kin wore armor that they had from before joining the Demons.

Behind them stood Aleph formations with their commanders.

Behind them, there were ragtag groups of warriors.

The teleport pads had been moved from the housing complex to inside Terra. Trying to exit the spinning city and get into the housing complex would have led to more than one person getting injured.

"Prepare to move!" Dwayne's words passed through the formed-up units. People stood and checked their gear one last time.

The teleport pad opened, showing night on the other side.

"Forward!" Dwayne barked. The formations crossed through the teleport pad, headed off to whatever lay on the other side.

***

Josh rubbed his eyes, drinking out of a ceramic thermos of Xer as he looked out over Verlun. The guild hall was off from the city center. The main hall was three stories tall, with stables and small stores to the right of it. To the left, lay the teleport pad with roads leading in and out. A wall was erected around the teleport pad and around the Stone Raiders' compound.

Along the road that now snaked through Verlun, stores had risen up, peddling their wares.

Josh turned as a red outline seemed to pass through Verlun, headed for one of the farmer cooperative offices that had sided with the Stone Raiders.

Josh capped his thermos, storing it as he grabbed his daggers. He disappeared from one shadow to another. No one saw him as more and more red silhouettes showed themselves. The Aleph drones and scouts did their work to find anything entering the town.

Josh stopped at a new perch atop an Altar of Rebirth building, the tallest building in Verlun.

Around Verlun, thousands of troops were moving into position.

Josh opened the guild chat. "Send the messages. They're coming." He slunk off into the darkness again. Red silhouettes faded to nothing as his stealth types dealt with the assassins sent in the night.

***

"Sir, the scouts report that Verlun looks to be abandoned," one of the lieutenant aides said.

"Abandoned? Well, where did all of those people go? We should have heard something. There are a number of loyal people within the city," Loughbreck yelled.

"I will have the scouts look harder." The lieutenant bobbed out a bow.

"See that you do." Loughbreck dismissed the man from his sight. Loughbreck's eyes glowed slightly as he looked across his lines, using a spell to see through the darkness of the night.

Up and down the field, there were thousands of his troops. There was only the sound of moving armor as the lines advanced through the darkness of night. Stopping them now would mean them having to take an hour just to get the lines sorted out again. Managing two hundred and seventy thousand soldiers in close formation was not an easy task.

The front ranks of the formations started to pass through a dividing row of trees. They spread out, one single body moving into several different forces so that they weren't fighting on top of one another.

Only one of the moons was up tonight, the blue giant.

Loughbreck's war cat lazily followed. Once through the trees, he could see down onto Verlun.

The city still had lights on here and there. Smoke came from chimneys to stave off the last of the winter frost and the crisp spring air.

The Stone Raiders' Guild Hall stood away from the city by two miles. Its dim lights showed a few large buildings and a simple stone wall around it all.

Loughbreck and his forces were just three miles away.

Suddenly there was a flurry of spells from the Stone Raiders' Guild Hall, as well as arrows being let loose.

"Barriers!" Loughbreck called out. He didn't want to lose troops here; he would need them in Haugr.

Mana barriers flashed to life across the formations.

None of the spells or arrows were aimed at them. Loughbreck watched as all of his forward scouts were eliminated.

"What the hell?" he muttered. He snapped at one of the nearby lieutenants, "You, I need more eyes on the guild hall."

"Yes, sir!" The lieutenant opened up his interface, sending orders.

Loughbreck already dismissed him as he continued to look at the guild hall.

His army continued to advance. Nothing else happened, but everyone was wary of what waited for them. They passed the two-mile mark and then started to reach the one-mile mark before anything started to happen.

"Sir, scouts report that the teleport pad is activating!" a lieutenant said to General Loughbreck.

"Well, what's coming out of it?" the general demanded, shifting atop his war cat.

The lieutenant's voice fell silent as he used his party chat.

"Sir, they're saying the Stone Raiders are advancing out of it," the lieutenant said.

"Mages! Fire on the teleport pad. Kill anything coming out of it!" *How the hell did they figure out that we were coming? Is there a spy in our ranks? Who would tell the Stone Raiders, a bunch of Players, about our plans?*

Mages who were moving with the army closing in started to chant and Mana filled the air. Spells illuminated the night sky, racing toward the Stone Raiders' Guild Hall.

A Mana barrier stopped the attacks cold.

The general's army outnumbered them by nearly five hundred times; he was confident in their victory.

"I want mobile Mana barriers at the ready! I want all units to attack. Get me the forward group! We need to know what their spies see and how successful their attack has been. See if they can get into the guild hall and hit the Stone Raiders and their allies from behind!"

He wasn't sure the spies were really lying low anymore. The more he looked at the city with his own eyes, the more it looked as though it truly was deserted.

This was supposed to be a simple mission, but now it had turned into a true battle. He needed to defeat those holed up in the guild hall before they could become entrenched.

The general's armies might have been stationed in different cities, so that the king couldn't find them, but they worked as one to carry out their general's instructions. Their training hadn't been for nothing.

"We have someone linked to a seer stone to show you the teleport pad." A lieutenant held out a seer stone.

Loughbreck took it and looked into the seer stone. He saw the teleport pad. *The hell? I thought that there was only a few hundred of these Stone Raiders. It looks more like a thousand.*

Loughbreck did not like surprises and every second, it seemed that the Stone Raiders were coming up with a new one.

The Stone Raiders quickly marched through the teleport pad, not showing any signs of panic. They looked determined and ready for what was to come.

Loughbreck looked up, staring at the Mana barrier that surrounded the guild hall. It flashed with multiple magical attacks; even focused attacks by a dozen mages didn't make the barrier even darken.

The Stone Raiders broke into groups and moved to the walls. They scrambled up them, the impacts against the Mana barrier lighting up their movements.

"The hell are those?" Loughbreck looked at the various creatures that followed after the Stone Raiders. They all wore identical armor. As soon as they left the teleport pad, they rose up into the air on their wings or spells.

They didn't seem to stop, rank after rank coming out of the teleport pad. The ground started to shake and rumble.

The scout looked at the walls.

"What in the seven Affinities?" Loughbreck looked from the seer stone to the walls.

Stone Raiders stood on the walls like silent guardians. Metal rose out of the ground, forming around the octagon-shaped walls.

The simple wall with a walkway and guard posts grew three times wider as the Stone Raiders were raised upward. Smooth, sheer walls appeared underneath them as their wall rose; dirt and debris fell as they rose from twenty meters in the air to nearly fifty.

The walls didn't look like a rural village's anymore; they looked like the defenses that might be found around the Haugr royal palace.

There were casting balconies and archery slits. Everything was made from polished metal, not giving any sign of handholds. Gates dotted the wall; they, too, seemed to be made of polished metal with no visible cut between the doors.

In minutes, the Stone Raiders' compound had turned into a fortress.

"Stone Rai-ders!" a voice called out from the top of the wall.

"Stone Raiders!" Hundreds of voices came from the guild hall. They checked their weapons, some chanting spells as Mana gathered around them.

"Well, seems that they can yell pretty loud." Loughbreck laughed, to the mirth of his fellow officers. "Seems that their barrier is strong. Walls are a bit flashy, though. We can break them easily with one of our grand workings. Let's show this rabble what a *real* army can do!" Loughbreck raised his voice so the soldiers around him could hear.

Grand workings were pre-prepared massive scale spells that mages imprinted upon specially made soul gems, thus they didn't require a mage or extra power to be used and contained the equivalent power of hundreds of mages.

He felt uneasy looking at the defenses that the Stone Raiders had seemed to have thrown up in just a few minutes. If he let that fear show, then his people would lose their confidence.

Loughbreck looked back to the seer stone. Thankfully the scout using divinity to see into the compound was able to alter their spell, still looking into the fortress.

The flyers landed in groups on the highest positions along the walls. More of their kind wearing identical armor flooded out into the main open area between the guild's buildings, forming up into small fighting formations.

Next, metal humanoids moved out of the portal. They moved as one complete body, not pausing as they moved for the walls, marching up the stairs to take up defensive positions.

"Get our forces moving. We will secure that teleport pad before they can call on any more reinforcements," Loughbreck declared. "Forward march—double time!"

The formations picked up pace, moving forward faster.

"General, we have a grand working that we believe will work best on the Stone Raiders' defenses," one of the mages' leaders said.

"Good. Once we're inside that barrier, let it loose, and take out that damn wall," Loughbreck said. His war cat picked up the pace with the soldiers marching speed also increasing.

Loughbreck kept his eyes glued to the teleport pad.

The metal creatures stopped coming out of the teleport pad. A lone drummer came out. Loughbreck's jaw tightened as the drummer started. The sound passed through the Stone Raiders' fortress and could be heard over the fields that Loughbreck's army was now running through.

The drummer moved onward as ranks of Dwarves walked out of the teleport pad, their boots in sync. Their blackened armor made them look like miniature juggernauts, their shields held out in front of them as their hands rested on their swords.

Each step was in time to their drums as more drummers came out, adding to the noise. Forces with the steel armor in the small formations broke off, moving around the Dwarves.

Dwarven artillery and a group of Dwarven mages walked out.

An entire Warclan?

Another drummer walked out of the teleport pad.

***

Kim looked over the field of battle. Loughbreck's army was closing in. Their ranged attacks were hitting the Mana barrier, but nothing was getting in.

Kim checked the power levels of the soul gem that had been planted underneath the guild hall. It could keep this up for another twenty minutes before it started to degrade.

She stretched and started to gather her power.

"If you want to stream, now's the time to start!" Josh yelled across the fortress.

Stone Raiders all over the place fired up their interfaces, turning on their live stream option that they had turned off since leaving Selhi Capital.

"Ready your spells!" Kim said.

Across the wall, mages started to glow with power, the balconies lighting up. It took a lot of Mana to light up an area with power. Something that made the mages of Loughbreck's army pause as they entered within just six hundred meters of the Stone Raiders' fortress.

"Fire!" Kim yelled. Her word passed through all of the mages under her command.

The world seemed to ignite with deadly spells.

Lightning struck down from the heavens alongside ice spears and columns of light. The ground started to move as if waking from its slumber. Weeds grew to the size of trees, pulling soldiers down. Crops tried to spear them as rocks broke through the ground, creating spears, or turning into golems that raged through the formation's lines.

Mana attacks slammed into the formations. Mages did everything they could to power their barriers and stop the powerful attacks from breaking through and tearing them apart.

"Fire!" Dwayne commanded. His and Esa's forces let loose with destruction staffs, repeaters, and arrows.

The Stone Raiders mages continued to bring destruction down upon Loughbreck's formations. The Earth and Dark Affinity mages were claiming the most lives, attacking from within and under the barriers.

The formations continued to charge onward. The sound of battle rang out, mages and soldiers fighting the elementals that had risen inside their barriers.

The elementals that formed outside slammed against the barriers, tearing at them, their magical constructs unable to make it through.

"Concentrate on the barrier, mages! Reverse the power drain on your amulets," Kim called out. She faced the mages with her and turned a dial on the simple metal necklace she wore. "I'll create the first spell formation, then we'll go counter-clockwise."

They all nodded in agreement. Kim looked over the battlefield. She closed her eyes as golden light started to form around her—at first just a silhouette before it grew more powerful.

She weaved her spell, focusing it. The other mages looked into her spell formation, altering it, refining it and adding their power to it.

Kim had asked Dave about how she could make spells more powerful. She'd taken his ideas and worked to improve them. It took a long time to create a spell and have others alter it to improve its strengths, but it could multiply the effectiveness of the spell.

She felt the last alteration to her spell formation fit together. The entire spell thrummed with power as it was completed.

Power surged outward from her and from her fellow casters as their amulets channeled power from a shared soul gem.

Kim opened her eyes that seemed to be made of liquid gold, shining like beacons in the night. She pushed her hand forward. The night sky erupted into day as thousands of spears made from golden light raced across the sky. They focused themselves into packs.

The air above the formations turned into a sea of magical firepower, counter spells and attack spells annihilating one another.

Kim let out a laugh as she lowered down to the ground.

She had trained her people in groups of five: one to be the main caster, the others to supply power and alterations to the spell formation, decreasing the power draw and allowing them to use some of their strongest spells.

A Phoenix of Fire seemed to force its way out of another caster's chest. Another called down arcane lightning, the blue lightning leaving craters and glassy ground around the Mana barriers they hit.

Loughbreck's mages kept fighting with everything they had; their own soldiers with even a slight magical talent fired off any spells they had to try to counteract the incoming attacks.

"Switch." Kim moved away from the front of the casting balcony. The next mage moved up, Mana gathering around them. Kim cast arcane sight. Seeing the spell formation, the caster had made, she and the other mages went to work, changing the spell, simplifying it, giving it power and greater structure.

The air seemed to distort around their hand, first in a small swirl, and then growing into a massive white hurricane that slammed into the formations.

They had moved forward, now within just three hundred meters.

The barriers started to fail. Anyone who was unprotected was picked off with Dwayne and Esa's forces' long-ranged attacks.

"Minefield!" Kim called out.

Earth mages who had been staying their hands moved up, calling on their spells.

Others cast their power into the walls.

It sucked up the power. The earth shifted under Loughbreck's troops as power activated spells that Florence and her people had been working on for the last day.

Runes and formations seemed to glow under the feet of the on-coming army.

Chapter 21: Shock and Awe

Loughbreck was stunned by the power that the Stone Raiders' casters were able to put out. Though most of his barriers had held, they had been enchanted by some of the best crafters in Gudalo and then fueled with grand soul gems and monitored by mages.

He had thought that the Light spears were the strongest spells that the Stone Raiders could come up with, but that had been merely a cover. They'd used the bright weapons to mess up the formation's night vision as other spells slammed down onto their positions.

Thankfully, Loughbreck hadn't skimped out on the barriers. He had made them a priority, considering they'd need to go up against Sigaird and his royal castle's wizards. Otherwise, his soldiers would have already been leveled.

However, those valuable barriers were being drained by these Stone Raiders, forcing his mages to channel their power into the soul gems and enchantments to keep them active.

He cancelled his night vision; there was little need with all of the Mana that was being thrown around. The ground was smoking. Fires showed here and there through what was left of the fields. Craters of glass showed where lightning strikes had impacted.

"Have that grand working ready to go as soon as possible! We need to crack that fortress open, now!" Loughbreck yelled.

Once they were inside, they could deal with those mages a lot easier.

A massive hurricane projected out from a mage, tearing through the first rank of barriers that were starting to fail.

"Ground attack!" someone called out. The very ground shifted and moved.

Loughbreck's blood went cold as runes and spell formations started to rise. Power glowed through them, filling the lines and runes, and advancing toward Loughbreck's position.

"Traps! Get your mages to break those traps under our feet!" Loughbreck looked to his formations. There was no way of stopping his troops. They were disciplined, but now they were committed to the fight; there was no stopping them.

They surged forward in their own groups, eager to close with the Stone Raiders and get some payback.

"We only have the grand workings left," the mage commander said.

"I don't care if you have to use a grand working! Stop those traps from activating!" Loughbreck yelled.

"Yessir!" the mage said, rattled at Loughbreck's clear anger.

Mages who had been held in reserve cast spells that sank into the ground, trying to stop the progress of the activating magic that filled the pre-made spell formations.

Here and there, spell formations stopped, turning into burnt ground, though there were hundreds of the traps and it was harder to figure out what spell it was and then find a way to break it, than it was for the Stone Raiders to power it.

A barrier-covered group stepped on a trap.

Water spikes flew outward, tearing into anything that was within its area of effect. Mana barriers only stopped attacks coming in; they didn't stop them going outward. Three different groups were within the range of the spell. Only one of the groups made it through relatively unscathed.

More and more traps were activated. Explosions ripped through the air; hexes made people rip their armor off and claw at their faces. Light blossomed, evaporating barrier groups. Every Affinity seemed present and willing to tear into Loughbreck's formations.

His people made it within ten meters when they seemed to disappear, screaming as the ground gave way.

***

"Prepare for bombing run!" Malkur yelled out. His word passed to all of his aerial forces. He cast a glance down to the forces that were now filling the fortress.

Dwarven Warclans were at each of the three gates that led out of the fortress. Around them were the ground forces of the DCA.

Elven rangers moved with four of the Dwarven Warclans. They wore simple leathers and some pieces of armor, but their economical motion and cold looks in their eyes sent an excited shiver down Malkur's back.

A hungry smile crossed his face as he continued to look over the formations.

All of the Stone Raiders stood, waiting for Loughbreck's forces. When he looked over the arrayed people, it wasn't those forces that scared him. It was the Stone Raiders.

Intermingled with the defenders, the Stone Raiders stood ready, their faces full of rage at the oncoming forces.

They had fled at Selhi—they had needed to flee—but here, here they stood their ground.

Mana barriers slowly covered the allied POEs. The Stone Raiders waited for their commands. With one word, they would pull back. Here they trusted in their POE friends and allies. For a Player to trust in an NPC to do their job, it took the Players coming to know the NPCs as their own friends.

This kind of mutual defense had never been seen before in Emerilia.

Stone Raiders' melee fighters held the first floor of the wall, with their mages on the various balconies. Dwarven mages secured the Dwarven artillery and created Earthen pillars, rising up on top of guard houses and other firing positions that Lucy pointed out.

The other forces sent by different powers were talking to Florence, who was organizing and sent them to either the wall or put their formations behind the Dwarves.

Aleph automatons stood in the openings along the walls. All of them now had the same armbands that they had made for the DCA.

They were still using their repeaters. Josh watched the artillery as it fired towards the enemy.

Everything moved with quick efficiency. There was no time for wasted effort or half-attempts.

Malkur looked back onto the formations that were attacking the Stone Raiders' Guild Hall. Their army was nearly two hundred and seventy thousand strong. The forces within the Stone Raiders' walls were close to one hundred and thirty thousand.

The enemy's front lines were now just ten meters away from the Stone Raiders' fortress. The ground gave way. The illusion spells disappeared as the ground crumbled, revealing a ten-meter drop ending in cursed and hexed metal spikes.

"Josh to aerial DCA—clear for bombing run," Josh said.

"Understood." Malkur opened a channel to his forces.

"Launch, launch, launch!" Malkur barked. Taking his own orders, he ran and leaped from the top of the wall. He quickly gained altitude and the aerial forces followed him into the sky.

"High-altitude bombing run. Do not dive in," Malkur warned, banking. Taking them away from the fight, he flapped his wings while moving the bands on his left wrist, which altered the commands for his chest plate.

He wheeled again, coming in lower and faster than before; he pulled his wings in slightly to gain more speed. To his sides were two more flight leaders; the others followed behind.

"Incoming spells!" someone called out.

The Stone Raiders' mages tried to counter-spell most of what was being thrown at the aerial DCA.

Malkur adjusted his right wristband. He held his hands outward. Spearheads flashed into existence, racing toward the oncoming spells.

They impacted one another, pushing some off course or destroying them. Still, a few got through. Barriers flashed into existence, but still some DCA were hit. Their flight partners dove, grabbing those who were wounded, banking away and returning to the fortress.

"Ready bombs! Nearing drop zone!" Malkur called out. The air rushed past him as he banked and dove past spells and ranged attacks. There was now less room between them and the casters, forcing them to take evasive action or get hit.

He fought against air currents altered by spells and dodged the more visible attacks. It was tiring work, but not one of them slowed or even tried to complain. The Stone Raiders had stood with them and they had vowed to do the same. Fatigue was nothing in their eyes; training had taught them to embrace the pain. It showed that they were alive.

"We are entering the drop zone! Release when ready!" Malkur rolled to the side of an exploding fireball. The heat washed over him as his wings snapped back out, catching the air as he twisted his left armband.

Swirled balls of blue light lit up the sky like Chinese lanterns. A few were caught by spells, causing the thin containment spell to rupture and explode in mid-air.

Mages and archers from the attacking formations fired upward at the incoming bombs. They took out about forty percent of them. Another twenty percent went wide of their targets, but there were thousands of the bombs falling.

Barriers took the impacts, showing their expert manufacture as many continued to hold. Others that had been weakened by previous attacks or swarmed with bombs ruptured. The defenders or different flights of the DCA paid them special attention before the now defenseless barrier groups rushed to join another barrier group or be cut down.

Malkur twisted his wristband again, turning the bombs and spears off as he flapped his wings to gain distance between him and the formations that had now bridged the gap over the cursed spike pits.

Malkur wheeled around in time to see a massive stream of water erupt from among Loughbreck's ranks and slam into the Stone Raiders' fortress wall in several places. The wall held on for a few seconds before holes started to appear.

The water turned into minions of all shapes and kinds, charging to meet the formations inside.

***

A savage smile crossed Loughbreck's face as one of the higher-tier grand workings was activated within the Stone Raiders' Mana barrier.

The original spell was altered, creating a dozen arms made of water that seemed to drill through the walls of the Stone Raiders' fortress. Runes flared to life, fighting the power, but they weren't able to contain it all. The water opened up holes in the walls; the spell reverted back to its original function as Water spirits formed from the puddles, and charged through the new openings.

Magical scaling ladders were tossed down, creating bridges through the new holes in the walls. His forces continued to charge onward.

They had only lost thirty or forty thousand soldiers in the entire advance. Loughbreck hadn't expected to lose as many, but he still had three more grand workings and he was confident in his soldiers' abilities.

Some of the Stone Raiders along the walls started to glow with different light, but it wasn't the same light that came with mages.

"They're buffing their forces." Loughbreck's eyes thinned as the buffed forces left their positions, moving within the fortress.

"Buff our forces," Loughbreck said to the mage commander next to him.

The mage commander made to open his mouth, but quickly shut it, sending out the orders.

Loughbreck knew that they weren't supposed to use the enhancements now, but rather against the royal palace. *Though nothing about this fight with the Stone Raiders is going as planned!* So far, they had shown themselves as capable adversaries. It was time that he thought of them as such.

Ground-shaking booms could be heard from on top of the walls, followed by a whistling noise.

"What is that?" Loughbreck turned to the lieutenant who had been relaying scouting reports. "The scouts report it looks like artillery of some kind, but the guns are pointed nearly straight up."

"Power all barriers on this side! Prepare to receive Dwarven artillery! Break out the soul gems for the barrier enchantments!" Loughbreck barked. His orders were passed out and acted upon as a whistling noise filled the air.

Loughbreck looked up to the walls and within the fortress.

Halos of expended Mana created cones around the artillery's fire base.

Loughbreck's face hardened as he looked over the battle, opening his interface to talk to the different groups and see an overlaying map of the Stone Raiders' Guild Hall.

***

"Come on, you lazy sacks of slime! Shift that artillery! My grandmother could do better than you and she's three hundred and seventy-nine!" the Dwarven artillery commander said.

Lox grinned at the familiar sound as artillery cannon's screws were rotated, bringing the barrels down from their elevated position and over to the breaches.

"Rank seven to nine, to your sides! Move!" Warband leaders moved their people out of the way, creating holes between the Dwarven ranks facing the breaches.

"My God! Put your fecking backs into it or I'll have you lifting these damn artillery pieces to put a fecking backbone in ye!" Artillery commanders continued to "motivate" their forces. The burly artillery gunners finished their movements nearly as one, checking their pieces.

"Gun five ready!"

"Gun eight ready!"

"Gun four ready!"

Up and down the line, guns called out their readiness as Water creatures raced across the open ground between the walls and the Dwarven formations.

"Archers, fire!" an Elven commander called out. Arrows flew over the Dwarves, slamming into the Water creatures and slowing their advance.

The Elves had new arrows in their hands and were releasing within just a few seconds, their skill with a bow equal to a Dwarven shield bearers' skill in shield formations.

"Guns ready!" the overall artillery commander of the two Warclans' barked over the command net.

Nearly any other race of creatures would have thought the tactic insane to fire through their formations and would have been blown over by the force of the cannons.

The Dwarves nearest to the sides of the divide made through their formation slammed their shields into the ground, interconnecting them down their ranks.

"Fire!" the combined Warclan leader growled.

The artillery cannons bellowed behind the Dwarven lines, passing through the corridor created through the Dwarves' Warclans. The Dwarves interlocked shields reinforced one another. They didn't move an inch, even with a magical artillery spell passing just feet away from them.

The Water creatures that had been advancing through the breaches in the walls were bowled over by the Dwarven artillery.

"Reload!" the artillery commander called out.

"Archers, fire!" the Elven commander yelled.

Arrows once again rained down on the oncoming forces. Elves fired, and then bowed as their fellows behind them fired. They came up again, pulling their bowstring and firing before they dropped again and repeated the process.

In ten seconds, there were nearly fifteen volleys of arrows let loose into the air.

"Artillery, ready!"

"Elves, stay!"

"Fire!"

The Elves paused their firing, the artillery letting loose once again.

It looked as if they would be able to hold off the attacking forces with their ranged attacks for about five artillery volleys.

Then, the wall started to crumble as the attacking mages opened up the breaches, tearing down sections of the wall. Other breaches started to appear along the walls. Defenders moved away from them.

"Artillery, change to fire directly on the breaches! Elves, clans! Form up!" the Warclan leader yelled out. At different locations, more breaches were opening. The Dwarven Warclans readied themselves for what was to come.

Lox watched the clans move back into position. Dwarves marched out and snapped forward, recreating lines that had been pulled apart for the cannons.

Artillery was adjusted and elevated to fire over the walls and into the enemy on the other side. Artillery commanders talked to spotters, asking for range, height, and various items to change their point of aim.

Lox looked to Party Zero. They were on the second floor of the wall, looking down at the forces moving inside the walls. Aleph watched the stairs, making sure that none of Esamael's second army made it up to the mages who were waiting there.

Dwarves were the best at dealing with large numbers on the ground, so it had been left to them. The Stone Raiders, in the meantime, were moving around, casting spells. The Dwarven artillery broke open barriers with concentrated fire; the Stone Raiders sent in spells to clear out anything hiding under the barriers.

Lox shifted his grip on his sword.

"Anxious?" Anna asked, relaxing on a pillar, a grin on her face.

"Just hate this waiting around crap," Lox growled.

"Don't worry, there will be a use for us soon enough," Deia said.

"We're just used to being down there with them." Gurren gestured at the advancing Warclans with their Elven support.

"When is it our turn?" Steve's axe whistled as he spun it in his hands.

"Once they start trying to pick off the Warclans with ranged magic and they stay inside their barriers, that's when we attack." Deia looked to Suzy. "How about our reinforcements—how are they doing?"

"They're advancing from where they got dropped off, but are going to take some time before they get into position, though. Look, seems that they buffed their troops. I think they're starting to take us seriously." Suzy pointed at the glowing soldiers.

"Now, watch how a Warclan does it," Lox said proudly.

The shield wall of the two combined clans seemed to drop, digging their points into the ground just moments before the Gudalo forces slammed into them.

The war drums beat out a pace as swords flashed, cutting down the attackers. They tried to flank their sides running into the DCA.

Spearheads of Mana stopped any advance; the DCA stopped the enemy before they could advance down the Dwarves' flanks.

"Damn, I know that the Devil's Crater Army were a strong bunch, but we couldn't really see it when they were fighting the Demon Horde. Now, they've got armor and they're fighting a reasonable opponent. They're pretty impressive," Lox muttered, holding his chin in thought.

"The average level of a person in the DCA is about 150—there are higher and lower, but that's normal. The Demons are also Creatures of Power. The Beast Kin have their own racial traits as well as more training and usually higher levels," Anna said proudly.

"Even though they're fighting a buffed enemy, I'd say that they are the stronger opponent," Deia said. "They've been bloodied and they learned from their battles. I think comparing the fighters they are now to the fighters they were just three months ago is hard."

Gurren grunted in agreement. Lox could only nod as the enemy actually reached the DCA. They were shredded by swords. The DCA worked in a group fighting technique: They would fight as individuals, but band together and then draw apart. They were fluid in their actions, knowing what was going on around them at all times and reacting. It allowed them to draw on their warrior skills instead of fighting in formations that didn't fit them. They didn't fight clean either.

The Dwarves acted as a single entity, but the DCA acted like hundreds of them working together, supporting one another and using their full range of skills. They operated best in tight-knit, small groups, not massive formations.

The Dwarven formation moved forward. Their blades cut those who dared to challenge their shield wall. Artillery bellowed overhead, smashing into those coming through the breaches. More and more groups were making it through with their barriers still functioning.

Elves and other groups of archers let loose with their arrows. The forces that came from the Zolu tribe lands rode on their various steeds, firing arrows over their allies and harassing the forces that entered the Stone Raiders' fortress.

The sky was illuminated with the constant ongoing magical battle between the attacking army's and defender's mages.

***

Geswald looked over the reports he was getting in. Esamael wasn't the only person with eyes and ears around Gudalo.

The army at Emaren had moved through the teleport pad, securing it and their foothold in the city, as they advanced forward toward the royal palace. It seemed that someone had tipped them off as they were running into heavy resistance. People were fleeing the city to try to get away from the fighting.

The city was weak with all of their best fighters off at the Dwarven tournaments.

Still, it seemed that no one from the royal guard had gone into the tournament, including the royal wizards, who were putting up a fight against Esamael that was tearing up the city.

It seemed that Esamael had people to clear out the teleport pad and secure it in Haugr as well as others to destroy the magical circle that was running around the city, empowering the guards who served there.

Even without the buffs of being in their own city, the guards, as well as the royal court, were putting up a fight. It seemed that the army based to the north rushed toward them with all speed.

Closer to home, Geswald had received reports that the southern army that protected the Gudalo border were now moving northward.

They were moving with an army of five hundred thousand, with the first group of one hundred thousand already visible on the horizon—the others just hours behind them.

Geswald had seen the war machines that they brought with them. They would pound on the city's barriers and then walls until they secured multiple breaches and then stormed the city.

There were only thirty thousand soldiers within Emaren. Defending a heavily fortified position didn't take a lot of men, but if the southern forces were able to break in, then it was going to be hell within the city.

Geswald had already made plans for that possibility. If Esamael sent back forces, then they could defeat the oncoming forces rather easily. If Esamael took the throne and killed Sigaird, then it might split the southern border army in their decisions to follow a dead king with no heirs or King Esamael.

Even if it only caused mistrust, then Esamael's army could use that to their advantage.

What worried him was Verlun.

He looked up from his interface, looking over to where Verlun lay. Night had come not that long ago, but over Verlun, the ongoing light display of magical spells was easily visible. Whoever was over there was throwing some serious Mana around.

He had lost contact with his various eyes and ears within the city hours ago. After that, he had been relying on those who were with Loughbreck's forces. They had talked about how walls were coming out of the ground and then they had stopped sending messages.

Geswald scratched his face nervously.

There was an army of nearly three hundred thousand attacking the Stone Raiders, but with all that he had heard and seen about them, he didn't feel good about the battle.

"Pete!" Geswald yelled.

Moments later, his trusted aide arrived.

"Find me someone who can do animal possession magic. I need to know what is happening in Verlun," Geswald said.

"Yes, Master Geswald." Pete bowed his head and turned out of the door he had barely walked through.

Chapter 22: Rise and Shine

Dave shifted, groaning. His muscles were all tense, as if he had worked till he dropped and his mind felt as if it was a gear box chugging to start.

"Look who's up," Bob said nearby.

Dave looked around, finding himself in one of the laboratories. It looked as if it had been pretty messed up. "What the hell happened in here?" Dave ignored the angrily blinking notifications.

"You happened in here," Bob said.

"Thank—" Dave started to talk, but his words sounded sluggish to him.

"You?" He finished off. Dave quickly tried to remember what had happened, as well as think of various different projects to occupy his mind and take up his Intelligence so that he didn't feel as though he were in some bad slow-mo movie.

"Ugh, that's annoying," Dave said.

"I would think so. You kind of got stuck in a loop, it seems. Can you remember what it was about?" Bob dropped a book into his bag of holding and faced Dave.

"Hmm." Dave focused on the other parts of his mind that weren't focused on trying to figure out what was going on.

"Okay, so I added some new stats, changed my master summoning to Master of Space and Time, then added Gravitational Anomalies. Then I just got overwhelmed with knowledge; was like I was a light bulb and the information that was supplied was the battery. I started to solve problems that I had and other problems I hadn't even thought of. I got more and more information and I couldn't slow down. There was so much more to learn. It was as if I was holding a damn power station that was feeding me knowledge. All I had to do was reach out and I could connect the dots. I could create a path through it all. I saw it—I saw and understood what was going on.

The theories became not just ideas that I could grasp, they became factors."

Dave took a breath, opening his mind once again to all he had known, all he had figured out. It was a similar moment to when he had completed his house on Cliff-Hill: a sense of accomplishment, a sense that he could do whatever he put his mind to. There were no barriers but the ones he imposed on himself. No more limits to hold him back.

It was as if he had opened a door and looked out upon the world when he could only see it through a keyhole before.

Bob just stayed silent as Dave felt an undeniable power run through him—not of Mana or Strength, but of solving a problem that had irked him for so long, the satisfaction of winning and figuring out what blocked his path.

Dave looked to Bob. "I understand now. I understand the teleportation, how it works, the teleport pads, the portals, the slip streams." Dave held up his hand. A sphere formed out of layers that seemed to appear in the air. It stopped and floated above the ground, suspended in mid-air.

"I understand how gravity works," Dave said, as if not truly believing the words as he looked upon the sphere he had made.

***

Josh looked out over the battle inside the Stone Raiders' walls.

The walls had been breached in multiple locations. The Warclans were doing what they could to try to stop the flood but they were simply overrun with numbers.

Esamael's formations had been halted, smashing into the Warclans and then diverting around the sides, where they were picked off by the roaming groups of DCA soldiers, Elves, or other allies who had come to help.

"Pull back our Stone Raiders to assist the Warclans and forces on the ground. Have them deploy in parties to where they think best. Get Kim and her strongest mages to stay back, as well as the summoning mages," Josh said to Lucy.

He opened the command channel to all of the leaders of the various allies.

"We're going to raise the second walls. Those who are defending the walls, pull back to the secondary walls. We will fall back there in an orderly fashion, bleeding Esamael's army as we go. Once we reach the walls, we'll let them swarm into the fortress."

"What about our artillery on the walls?" a Dwarven artillery commander asked.

"We can pick it up and bring it to the second location," Malkur said.

"Good. Also, once our forces are clear of the walls, anyone with ranged attacks is free to hit that wall with anything and everything they have to kill off these damn cockroaches," Josh said.

The ground rumbled as a wall, much closer to the guild hall and its few key buildings, started to rise out of the ground. It was only ten meters or so tall, with firing platforms, but it was a defensible location.

Josh changed channels. "Malsour, I need you to change the settings on the Mana barrier. We're getting hit by those damned mages. I didn't think that they would be this powerful," Josh said. The Warclans were shrugging off the hits with their combined shields, but the other forces supporting them were getting hit.

A constant stream of people was rushed through the teleport pads and into the ministrations of the doctors on the other side. The medics in Verlun were just there to heal minor breaks and cuts, stabilizing patients to be moved to Terra.

"It will be done," Malsour said. A metallic board seemed to appear out of the ground as a group of thirty or so people stepped onto it. It glided forward, defenders moving out of the way. It settled down behind the Warclans and in front of the secondary wall. Malsour, who had been riding the front of the metallic board, seemed to be enveloped by the ground as he descended into the ground.

"Well, that is certainly one way to do it." Josh shook his head. He studied the ongoing battle. He thought that the ranged magic would have had more effect on Esamael's army. After fighting creatures in Alephir and then the Demon Horde, he was used to people just using their own strength.

Watching a real standing army in action was a whole different fight.

The mobile barriers were stronger than he had expected. Although his forces were stronger in a one-on-one fight, Esamael's army was closing the gap and simply swarming them with well-trained and disciplined forces. They knew how to fight; it didn't matter if you got a blade in the heart from a level 10 or a level 100. This was Emerilia; if you were hit somewhere vital, you were going down.

Also, the Stone Raiders and their allies weren't the only ones healing their people. If there were wounded, they were hauled to the rear, where Health and Stamina potions and remedies were waiting to be administered.

"Where they can, they use consumables, soul gems, enchanted barriers, potions and spells trapped in crystal matrixes. Much easier to use that first before dipping into your reserves of Mana, creating a massive spell on the spot, or healing a complete person with just your Mana. Also allows them to do more than one thing at a time," Josh muttered to himself with grudging respect.

He looked at the forces streaming back from the walls. The area beyond the walls looked as if it were dawn with the explosions of light from the spells that were being unleashed to keep Esamael's army occupied.

"Even though they're better than I thought, I don't think Lough-breck is having the best night." Josh snorted to himself and jumped down from his perch.

"I'm going to coordinate with Florence and the people in support. Let me know if you need anything else," Lucy said.

"Will do. See you when this is all over," Josh said over his shoulder. He stopped well behind the Warclans that were slowly moving backward. It was a slow and precise movement; going backward for a shield wall was tricky business.

Josh smirked as a familiar face moved around the Warclan and made her way to him.

"You look a lot different from your Golden Sabres days," Josh said. Instead of wearing her golden armor, Cassie wore a ragtag outfit of leather pants with armor plates and a fur and armor top. She had changed her swords for an ebony shield with silver runes along the inside and a sword made of silver, ebony, gold, and malachite, tipped with Mithril.

"After seeing you lot waving your damned Mithril weaponry around, I thought it was time to put on my best gear, not my matching set. Also *baaabe,* would you possibly let me talk to one of your smith friends who can use Mithril?" Cassie walked her fingers up Josh's forearm as she pressed against him.

"You know that rubbing your chest plate against me is kind of uncomfortable?" Josh said.

"Tell me about it. I need to ask Deia how she does it. This is killing my girls." Cassie adjusted her breastplate.

Josh shook his head at the ridiculousness of their conversation. "You ready for this?" he asked, looking out over the fight. He had seen some of the injured pulled from the fight. Too many of the POEs wouldn't make it till the next day.

"I am." Cassie nodded and looked back to him. "What's wrong?"

"I know that we set this up to show that we're strong, that we have allies who will fight beside us, but..." Josh shrugged. "I don't know. The more I come to know the POE, be around them, the more I think of them as real people. Hell, I think of them as more real than most of the people from back on Earth. Sure, they might be ones and zeroes in a machine. Hell, we might just be brains in a vat. What right do I have to say that they deserve to live or die for us?"

Cassie squeezed his hand, taking a moment as the fighting seemed to die down while the groups separated from one another, re-forming ranks and lines.

"We fight for what we believe in and I don't think the POE are any different. They are here because they're our allies, because we made promises to one another. The enemy is here because they want to defeat us, to take what is ours, and control this nation for their own gain. If we roll over for the POE, then no one is going to respect us or come to our aid. This is what we *have* to do. If Emerilia has taught me anything, it's that we need to stop treating it like a game. We're E-heads. This is our reality, our home."

Josh took a deep breath.

The walls from the outer fortress were falling, creating new paths for Loughbreck's formations. Overhead, DCA aerial forces carried artillery cannons. Those who weren't encumbered dove and dropped Mana bombs from their chests and raked the enemy's lines with their Mana spearheads.

As mages got into position, they once again hammered the enemy formations, hitting barriers and dueling with other mages among Loughbreck's barrier groups.

"Stone Raiders are in formation and awaiting your orders," Dwayne said over the guild's command chat.

"Our allies are in position or will be shortly. No one on the walls," Esa added.

"Kim, you've got five minutes to soften up those barriers. Then, let the parties fight it out," Josh said.

The incoming fire started to hit the Mana barrier as it retracted, creating a solid magical defense and allowing the defending mages to focus solely on attacking the enemy within the fortress's walls.

"Well, I guess it's about time we showed Emerilia what happens when you attack the Stone Raiders." Josh looked to Cassie. She nodded and the both of them turned back to face the enemy that poured through the breaches and into the open land left behind by the retreating defenders.

***

Deia called down a Mana firestorm onto the Water spirits nearest the Warclans. Mana fire didn't eat oxygen and burnables, but Mana itself.

The spirits dissolved under the spell's workings, feeding it, turning it from a simple Human-sized spiral quickly up to a fifteen-meter-tall tornado.

Deia moved her hands, burning away the Water spirits as the firestorm continued to grow stronger. Loughbreck's mages attacked it, not realizing what it was. The Mana firestorm howled with angry flames; its red funnel came down into a blue flame made from pure Mana.

"Now, we're talking." Induca raised her hands. Fire elementals seemed to erupt in the skies above the fortress. Wreathed in blue flames, they dove toward the oncoming armies.

"I guess it's time we started working." Anna pulled out her massive sword.

Deia released the first Mana firestorm, creating another as she watched Anna out of the side of her eye.

Anna flicked her blade; the holes in it made the whole blade hum. Anna turned and spun. People cleared out a path for her as their movements disturbed the wind around her. She moved, seeming to float through the air as she spun, jumped, and leaped. Her sword rang out a sad and calming tune with her movements. The air seemed to glide, almost calming in nature as Deia's ears popped from the different air pressure.

Anna's body started to become outlined in the white eddies of wind. Her figure blurred with the speed of their movements as she seemed to become part of the air.

Deia's second Mana firestorm rushed forth, carving through the oncoming formations and eating up any free Mana it could find. It ran through the breaches, tearing the walls apart as it went, melting the metals and rocks, before hurling them out as missiles.

Deia, now with an idea, paused, gathering Mana as the flames for hundreds of meters around flickered toward Deia.

Anna's song turned from calm into a raging tempest. Building upward, it sent shivers down the enemies' spines while the Dwarves and Stone Raiders' allies roared, new strength filling them.

Anna's movements quickened. Her blade rang out powerful and true as she rose from the ground; air from across Verlun was pulled toward her. She danced upward and into the air. The air became white with its rapid movements, obscuring Anna as her song rang out.

The wind took shape around Anna, creating what looked like a torso, then legs and arms, and a head. A twenty-foot creature of barely contained air blades covered Anna, her sword's song becoming silent. The sounds of battle slowly returned as air flooded the area.

Anna's creation stood in the sky, surveying the battle below, like a disapproving god looking over its subjects. It turned in the air. A sword identical to Anna's formed in its hands as it struck out at the attackers.

A white blade of wind raced through the sky.

Deia had only ever seen Anna using her invisible blades of wind.

The strike hit. A line a hundred meters across appeared among the attacking army. Where it hit, a three-meter-deep gouge was left in the ground. Barriers that had already been weakened were torn apart, leaving those who they protected out in the open.

Mages started to use their spells on the massive sky guardian, trying to rip the wind that powered it away from the creature or simply annihilate the magical construct with their own magical force.

Anna started to dance with her blade. Her sky guardian moved as easily as she did in her own form—dodging attacks, deflecting them with her sword made of wind, and returning the attacks.

Slashes formed in the ground, crisscrossing the enemy formations.

Induca created her own Mana firestorms to protect Anna, taking away the attacks to fuel themselves and open up barriers for Anna's Air blades.

Deia closed her eyes, focusing on the spells she was building. In her mind's eye, she saw all of the fortress. She started to weave her spell, red glowing around her and her eyes glowing with power. She smiled to herself as she finished the spell formation within her mind, changing the input formation from her to her armor.

After Dave had talked about how he was creating his enchantments and conjurations, then powering them through his soul gems instead of through himself, Deia had tested it out.

Wisps of almost invisible flame flew from Deia toward the breaches. Some slammed into barriers, creating small explosions, but a few made it to the walls around the breaches and buried themselves into the metal and stone of the broken walls.

The metal and stone were superheated within seconds under the power of her highly concentrated fire spell. They exploded in a spectacular fashion, creating grenades out of the debris. Deia guided the spell as those within the breaches were showered with superheated debris.

Barriers took on solid colors under constant attack from the explosions. Those who weren't covered by a barrier or protection strong enough to withstand the exploding rocks and metal were shredded.

Deia would have only been able to hold the spell up for ten minutes or so. With the power coming from the soul gem instead of from her own personal Mana reserves, she wasn't at any risk of going through Mana exhaustion. She could take her time in directing the spell where she wanted her superheated flames to go, using it like an automatic magical grenade launcher.

The ground opened up as Malsour rose out of the ground on his metal disk. "Well, looks like a few things changed while I was away." Malsour looked up at Anna and the exploding breaches.

It was chaos with the Warclans and allies joined in battle, with Loughbreck's army still pushing forward.

There wasn't enough room within the fortress's walls for them to all make it inside.

Broken bodies and people screaming in pain lay across the battlefield as magic continued to wage battles. The Stone Raiders' Mana barrier and the attacking army's mobile barriers were alight nearly constantly with impacts of various kinds.

"Stone Raiders! Prepare to move!" Josh said. The defenders were taking on more and more casualties and had little to no room to move backward.

Dwarven artillery sailed overhead, slamming into barriers or throwing dirt into the air, leaving large craters behind. They broke through the occasional barrier, tearing into the ranks of the attackers, leaving broken bodies and bloody reminders.

"You ready?" Deia looked to the rest of the party. Anna was still in the sky, but her sky guardian had lost quite a bit of power. Although Anna was a master with her two-handed sword, her guardian was simply too large to avoid all of the attacks being sent at her.

"You know it," Lox said, a grin visible through his helmet.

Steve took a few practice swings with his axe as Gurren twirled his sword. Malsour cracked his fingers as Induca rose into the air a few inches. A red aura appeared around her as her eyes glowed red, looking similar to Deia. Suzy twirled her staff before she slammed it into the ground.

Allies and fellow Stone Raiders started to move away from Party Zero as they focused on the enemy in front of them, their auras leaking out.

Chapter 23: When an Unstoppable Army Meets An Impossible Guild

What the hell is wrong with these people? Loughbreck looked at the massive sky guardian that stood above the Stone Raiders' Guild Hall, dispensing blows imbued with the power of the wind, tearing through people and ground alike.

He had two hundred and ten thousand people left. All of the soul gems had been dispensed to the different barrier groups. His mages were all chugging Mana potions and he'd had to bring in his reserve mages as well.

Had to use a damn grand working to open up the walls and they just burned through them with that damned firestorm.

He winced as the breaches exploded again, showering a passing barrier with shrapnel.

"Lord Esamael is demanding a report," one of the lieutenants said.

"Send him the feed from our scouts," Loughbreck growled. While all of the scouts and observers who had been sent before had been killed off, the army's own scouts were providing eyes within the Stone Raider's Verlun location with various long-range spells and scopes, as well as controlling beasts and looking through their eyes.

He had been assured that the Stone Raiders were just a minor bump in their way to Haugr. Now, Loughbreck was thinking that maybe going straight to Haugr and attacking the walls might have been a smarter idea.

"The Warclans are making a path!" a lieutenant said. As the battle had gone on, they'd discovered it was better to tell Loughbreck any developments instead of keeping it in. It had taken Loughbreck killing two aides before they listened.

"Seer stone!" Loughbreck held out his hand. A stone dropped into it, showing the inside of the fortress. Loughbreck was still stuck outside with a third of his men; the rest were inside and fighting the Warclans.

He watched as the Warclans moved to the side as people rushed through their lines. The Warclans' Dwarves moved with an almost mechanical movement.

Groups burst from the Warclans' ranks like damn Dragons racing through the sky.

Loughbreck's jaw worked as the Stone Raiders finally took the field.

Others jumped over the Warclans, showing their Agility and Strength as they got inside the barriers.

"Buff our forces; all buffs, now!" Loughbreck yelled, not taking his eyes from the scout's feeds. His people were putting up a fight here and there, but it wasn't even close to what they'd been doing with the Dwarves. The Stone Raiders were like a force of nature. They waded through the barriers, taking down the groups inside, throwing themselves into battle. They worked in parties of ten or less.

They coordinated with one another, even if they were tens of meters apart. Anytime they got bogged down, they were supported by aerial bombing, their guild members, or the ranged fighters to their rear.

His eyes fell on a man made of steel; his axe cut through any who dared to get in his path. Two Dwarves to either side of him fought with shields and swords. Behind them, four mages glowed with their power.

Loughbreck saw their eyes, shuddering as the male mage that seemed as if the abyss was clinging to him waved his hand. Shadows lurched from his hands and stabbed through openings in helmets or through any other opening they could find. They dropped as he waved his hand in the other direction; metal spheres flew out to meet magical spells, tearing them apart. Souls and free magical energy flowed in toward the party as they moved forward, neither fast nor slow, as if they were on a simple walk.

Loughbreck saw as the buffs spread like a web, outward from the breaches and toward the frontline soldiers.

They put up more of a fight, actually hurting some of the Stone Raiders. The Raiders seemed to constrict; the parties moved together to support one another. Their pace slowed as they took their opponents more seriously.

The Warclans raised their shields, changing out their lines and wounded being funneled to the rear. The new front rank moved forward, their shields up and ready. As they stepped forward, the Mana barrier seemed to grow with them.

Swords and the spikes on the end of their shields stabbed out, killing or maiming Esamael's soldiers who faced them.

The Dwarven artillery was now up and ready, ringing the wall around the Stone Raiders' Guild Hall and within the small square between buildings. They bellowed, their rounds blossoming over the remaining barriers.

Overhead, the aerial Demons and Beast Kin released more of their Mana bombs. They were now rotating flights and moving in groups of no more than twenty, all separated out so they weren't as easy to take out with a large area of effect spell.

Their spearheads and Mana bombs rained down, adding to the growing pressure on Loughbreck's soldiers.

We've lost our momentum. If this keeps up, then they will push us outside the walls and we won't be able to make it in again.

"Ready another grand working," Loughbreck said through clenched teeth.

"Which one?" the new mage commander asked. It seemed she learned from her predecessor's mistakes of questioning his commander's every other order.

"Use the shades," Loughbreck said.

The air seemed to chill with his words.

"Yes, sir." The mage commander turned to one of her people and sent them to get the grand working.

Loughbreck listened to reports, trying as best as he could to get people into place to stop the Stone Raiders and their allies' advance.

The Stone Raiders had pushed out another fifty meters by the time the grand working activated.

Doorways snapped into being between the Stone Raiders and their allies. For a second, nothing happened, and then creatures—horribly disfigured creations made of shadows—their incorporeal bodies raced toward those who opposed Loughbreck's army.

They passed through the barrier, meeting the Warclans' shields as they hastily dropped into a shield wall. The shades attacked them from the front and glided over their shields to attack them from above. Their screams made people drop to the ground in pain. They flowed over the shields and into the supporting fighters. The shades passed through anyone without a Mana shield or a strong enough will, each of them taking a part of their Willpower and draining their soul.

Those who had been passed through dropped to the ground in pain as weaker shades descended on them, causing them so much pain that their bodies gave up.

Those the shades couldn't pass through, they attacked with their screams and limbs, forming claws and tails out of their shadowy forms.

Holy blades and weapons made them cry out in anger, as they flocked toward those who used gear or spells with a Light Affinity, seeing them as the biggest threats.

The Stone Raiders grouped together, letting more of the buffed soldiers through their ranks as they fought not only those to their front, but the shades that attacked their rearguard.

The Stone Raiders stopped trying to hold back their strength. They activated their most powerful spells, racial traits, and augmenting abilities. Buffs flew as parties drained potions and readied themselves.

"Stone Raiders, to death and back!" a voice cried out of the mass.

The seer stone's view changed, looking to a man who was covered in a black miasma, twin daggers in his hand as he danced through the oncoming fighters. Souls were ripped out of those who were hit by the blades. Each hit the man landed killed a soldier or opened them up for an attack that would.

He moved in a blur, his eyes making Loughbreck flare his nostrils in disgust.

He is no man anymore, but a devil in Human form.

"Stone Raiders, to death and back!" The rest of the guild took up the call and surged outward. Auras burst forth and Loughbreck's eyes went wide.

He had thought that they were showing their full strength when they charged out of the Warclan's formation. Now, smaller parties grouped together; the rest spread out, whirlwinds of disaster. It was as if they didn't care for their lives, for the levels and gear they would lose.

"They're insane." A lieutenant said what Loughbreck was thinking.

Never have I heard of Players willing to lose their levels and gear in order to make a point.

It terrified Loughbreck. He still felt that he could win; this last-ditch effort by the Stone Raiders showed that he had the upper hand.

He was scared for what would come when they respawned. They had close ties to the mage's guild. It wasn't hard to think that they would just use a teleport pad there and then cross over the bay and into Gudalo.

They might be weaker, but they could come back again and again, every time knowing more, finding weaknesses.

Esamael underestimated them. He underestimated their resolve. He didn't think that Players could act like POEs defending their land, except these ones won't stay dead if we kill them all.

A chill ran down Loughbreck. The very air seemed to become still, as if not wanting to anger something or someone.

The scout who was controlling the beast looking down upon the guild hall must have had the same thought as Loughbreck. The seer stone's vision changed to show the teleport pad.

A man stood there; a hood covered his features and metal flew around him in different orbits. On his hips, he wore twin rods that glowed with the light of soul gems. He looked up, as if staring into the very soul of Loughbreck and the scout. There were no discernible features under the hood, just two glowing gray eyes. They did not look pleased.

"Well, time we sorted this mess out." The voice carried on the wind, sending shivers down Loughbreck's spine. Not with the anger, or the sadness in the voice, but the cold and calculated interest in it.

***

Dave rushed past the notifications, getting to the summary at the bottom.

Quest Completed: Master of Space and Time Level 13

You have completed the Level 13 quest for this class.

You have exceeded known knowledge. Come up with new possible theory (1/1)

Rewards: Unlock Level 14 Quest

+15 to Willpower

+15 to Intelligence

+15 to Endurance

+15 to Agility

1,300,000 (+7,700,000 accrued)

Quest: Master of Space and Time Level 14

You have exceeded known knowledge. Come up with new possible theory (1/2)

Rewards: Unlock Level 15 quest

Increase to stats

Class: Master of Space and Time

You have shown a dedication to unraveling the secrets of space and time, their effect on each other and on reality.

Status: Level 13

Greater understanding of Space and Time.

+195 to Willpower

Effects: +195 to Intelligence

+195 to Endurance

+195 to Agility

Quest Completed: Master of Gravitational Anomalies Level 9

You have completed the Level 9 quest for this class.

You have exceeded known knowledge. Come up with new possible theory (1/1)

Rewards: Unlock Level 10 Quest

+10 to all stats

900,000 (+3,600,000 accrued)

Quest: Master of Gravitational Anomalies Level 10

Come up with new possible theory (1/2)

Rewards: Unlock Level 11 quest

Increase to stats

Class: Master of Gravitational Anomalies

What some have viewed as abnormalities and anomalies, you have seen a problem looking for an answer. You seek to right the laws surrounding gravity and understand its powerful secrets.

Status: Level 9

Effects: Greater understanding of Gravitational Anomalies. +90 to all stats

Level 229

You have reached level 229; you have **135** stat points to use.

Dave looked at his new character sheet.

Character Sheet

Name:	David Grahslagg	Gender:	Male
Level:	202	Class:	Dwarven Master Smith, Friend of the Grey God, Bleeder, Librarian, Aleph Engineer, Weapons Master, Champion Slayer, Skill Creator, Mine Manager, Master of Space and Time, Master of Gravitational Anomalies
Race:	Human/ Dwarf	Alignment:	Neutral Good

Unspent points: 135

Health:	38,300	Regen:	21.56 /s
Mana:	14,180	Regen:	48.30 /s
Stamina:	4,440	Regen:	42.5 /s
Vitality:	383	Endurance:	1,078
Intelligence:	1,418	Willpower:	966
Strength:	444	Agility:	850

With the loss of his Master Summoner class, he had lost 30 Willpower but with the stats from the Master of Space and Time as well as Gravitational Anomalies, it was easily replaced.

He looked at a space in the room, conjuring a magically coded sphere.

Conjuring now compared to before he leveled up and gained his classes was like night and day. He barely felt any strain. His higher Willpower made it easy to gain a clear picture of what he wanted to make; his higher Intelligence was like working with an AI. Instinctually, he added in and changed parts of the spell formation, making it easier and automatically linking the creation to his soul gem power sources instead of consciously having to think of it.

"So, this is instantaneous casting," Dave said. Around him dozens of spheres appeared, all floating in mid-air.

Bob laughed, clapping his hands together in excitement and wonder at Dave's newfound abilities. "Welcome to the big leagues, son! You're now nearly as strong as Deia." Bob grinned.

"Thanks." Dave looked at the spheres in interest. He changed some of their coding, his mind controlling each of them independently.

They looked like simple metal orbs. They didn't radiate any power but there was a solidness to them that would make many high-leveled people feel the hairs on their neck raise in alarm. The spheres started to rotate around Dave as if planets around a sun.

"By my estimate, you should be beyond what the class system is willing to teach you. This means that as your class level goes up in the future, then you will not gain any more information but you will continue to gain stats," Bob said.

"That makes sense. It's saying that I need to prove my own theories now to increase my class level," Dave said thoughtfully.

"Well, enough of that." Bob stood. "Loughbreck and his forces have made it to Verlun. The rest of the guild is fighting out there. Esamael and the armies around Emaren have moved into the capital Haugr and are currently halfway through the city, fighting off the guards and local inhabitants as they make their way to the royal palace. They haven't taken many losses, but they're taking their time in making sure that no one gets in their lines. Deia is in Verlun." Bob cocked his head to the side, as if seeing something else.

"You should hurry. Loughbreck's mages just activated a grand working that opens a portal to the shade realm, right between the Stone Raiders and their allies."

"Thank you, for watching over me, Bob," Dave said.

"No worries. Now go and kick that idiot Esamael's ass. We have much to talk about when you come back," Bob said as Dave lifted up into the air, floating out of the room and then over the balcony toward the entrance of the laboratory.

"No teleporting or higher gravity changes than point four or weapons more than three kilotons outside of the Aleph facilities unless it's a spell! Otherwise, you'll trip the AI hounds," Bob said.

"I'll try my best." Dave stepped on the ground and activated the door to open as he ran out of the laboratory and toward the teleport pad.

His spheres continued to hover around him as he ran. His eyes glowed as the runes across his body became smaller, forming solid gray lines that traveled up his limbs, joining at the back of his neck in a circle. A single line traced over the back of his head and down his forehead to the bridge of his nose.

Dave blinked and released his breath. Black lines stayed where the runes had been except for the line that traveled from the circle on his back to the bridge of his nose.

With a thought and a surge of Mana, he activated the teleport pad in the power facility. The runes started to move. They finished their changes as Dave entered the teleport room. It powered up, the event horizon snapping into reality, as Dave stepped onto the teleport pad and exited into Verlun.

He closed his eyes, using his Touch of the Land spell. A detailed image of the battlefield filled his mind. He once again called on his power. His spheres moved faster as he saw a distortion in the sky. He stared at it, quickly losing his interest as he saw a group of shades rushing toward Party Zero.

"Well, time we sorted this mess out." Dave took off into the air. He increased the gravity underneath him as well as his weight by activating two of his spheres. Keeping within Bob's guidelines, he dropped to the ground, creating a crater as dust, dirt, and debris were thrown away.

Dave's spheres spread out as fast as bullets, slamming into those around his party, giving them room. Dave rolled his shoulders and grabbed his twin rods. One turned into a golden shield as the sword in his hand seemed to be made of pure Mana.

"Well, it's about time you woke up from your damned nap," Steve said.

"Ugh, think I got dirt down my back from yer landing!" Lox complained.

"Your back? It's down my feckin crack! Fucking mages!" Gurren yelled, taking out a soldier by slamming his shield into them so hard they flew back several feet into their allies.

A flame-covered Elf zoomed into Dave, nearly tackling him to the ground. Deia crushed her lips against his.

"Time and place, you two!" Suzy yelled.

Deia quickly released him and the two of them looked at each other. They didn't need to say anything, but Dave felt there would be plenty to talk about later.

Deia floated upward, controlling her various spells that were causing havoc through Loughbreck's formations.

"Keep them off me for a few minutes. I think I can do something about the portals the shades are using!" Dave yelled over the fighting.

"You heard him—cover Dave!" Deia yelled.

Party Zero moved to cover their last member as Dave closed his eyes. The gray lines of compacted runes lit up under his armor and hood.

Well, let's hope I learned enough from those classes to make this work.

Chapter 24: Game Changer

Dave felt the portals. Understanding their creation, he felt the tears that bridged between Emerilia and the land where the shades had been pulled from.

Power surged through him and his body shivered with power. He started to laugh. The ambient Mana he was drawing in filled the air as he looked to the spell formations that held the portals open.

He recognized and compared runes, learning new ones as he held a hand up and pointed it at one of them. He fought with the spell formation, changing just a few runes. With the grand working, he wasn't fighting against another Human mind that was liable to think of other things and fall into fear or pride.

What he could accomplish by fighting against the mind of the caster, he could do with bringing more power to bear on the spell formation in front of him. Mana shot out of his hand, connecting him to the doorway between realms.

The runes slowly changed, painfully slow, taking seconds before switching to Dave's form. The construct fell apart. There was no one to try to control the power output of the grand working.

The doorway that was open one second snapped shut, cutting apart anything that was crossing through its abyssal event horizon.

Dave focused on another portal. His armor drew in the power of the portal and a soul gem appeared in the air, holding the diverted energy as another doorway snapped closed.

Dave got faster and faster. With different casters, there was sure to be different formations of spells, each one adding their own flair. It was like a piece of art: everyone had a different take and a different idea. This grand working was one idea repeated again and again and then stuffed with enough power to make it work.

Taking down one meant that Dave knew how to take them all down.

Mages seemed to understand what Dave was doing and targeted Party Zero.

Malsour cast a barrier spell, grounding it around them and pulling from the Mana well.

Hits flared overhead as they continued to fight the oncoming soldiers and shades.

"Change the runes on the Mana barrier. Create Light runes—will give off an area of effect," Dave said to Malsour.

"I don't know how to do that without breaking the current coding," Malsour said.

"Good thing you have me here!" Steve's axe cut a mage nearly in two. He opened up his interface, using his left hand to type and his right hand to fight with an axe before sending it to Malsour. Spheres appeared around Dave as he enchanted them, linking them to the soul gem he had conjured and sending them on their way as soon as they had enough charge.

Dave created a band around the soul gem, placing commands into it and the other spheres he was creating.

"Got to love automation," Dave said as he felt Malsour very carefully changing the spells on the Mana well's casing. "Nothing like playing with nuclear waste to make a man nervous," Dave commented.

"What?" Malsour asked.

"Nothing—nothing at all. Don't worry about it!" Dave said innocently as the first of his flying spheres reached a portal. There was a flash of light and the portal collapsed in on itself. Bits of shades that had been walking through turned into wriggling limbs before they fell apart and dissolved into the air.

Spheres stopped forming. There was a line waiting to touch the soul gem in the air to charge before they raced off.

"Now, about those barriers." Dave turned and looked at the barriers that were all over the place, covering Loughbreck's soldiers and mages.

"Okay, attacking them straight on is a no go. Though they do have that handy-dandy siphon feature, I don't see too many safety features on it. Makes sense—less to stop a mage from charging it in the middle of battle," Dave muttered.

"Great—did you fall on your head while you were taking a nap?" Suzy said.

"No." Dave said.

"Then, do something!" Suzy pushed him into action.

"Okay." Dave conjured carvers around the outer formations. They started cutting runes into the walls as he directed.

"And, done!" Malsour shook a little bit as he wiped sweat from his forehead.

The area under the Mana barrier started to glow slightly. The shades' cries became louder as the power of Light within the Mana barrier counteracted their Dark Affinity and pulled apart their bodies. The stronger ones weren't that heavily affected but the wounded and weaker ones were being pulled apart or forgetting about their prey completely as they were destroyed.

"Remember to always have a power output rune on your coding, ladies and gents," Dave said. Any loose Mana, souls, or weak spells within the octagonal fortress started to funnel together into a pure Mana vortex and poured into Dave's armor, diverting out into soul gems that formed around him. New bands started to form around them.

"What is that for?" Induca yelled over the noise.

"Overcharging!" Dave yelled back, a wide smile on his face. Even as the soldiers nearby were pushed back by the force of the pure Mana channeling through Dave's armor, he floated above the ground with his orbiting spheres and soul gems without moving an inch.

***

Loughbreck had finally made it to the fortress walls, but he couldn't believe what he was seeing. Spells were ripped apart as they came near the Mana vortex that had formed within the center, its power overriding the cast spell formations.

Every bit of power was ripped out of the surrounding area, channeling down into a floating man. As Loughbreck watched, he realized that they were items of some kind.

"Take that man out! Get our elites in there now!" Loughbreck yelled to his aide.

The Mana poured out of the man like a fountain pouring water into a pond, reaching floating soul gems as big as a man's head.

Then, the soul gems stopped just taking in power but further diverted it out, reaching out toward the different mobile barriers that had been stored within mages' and soldiers' bags of holding to keep them hidden.

"He's charging them," one of the aides said in disbelief.

Why the hell would the enemy charge our Mana barriers? Loughbreck's face went slack.

In training, they warned to not overcharge barriers. In battle, however, soul gems and mages regulated the amount of power going into them. Even a soldier with a bit of Mana was good enough to charge them.

The first mobile barrier disappeared in a flash of light and the sound of breaking glass. Its runes, fatigued from hours of fighting, overloaded with power that it couldn't regulate.

The group hiding underneath were open to ranged attacks that wouldn't have made it in otherwise.

Mana from the soul gems reached out like tentacles searching for the next Mana barrier and then the next.

Aerial forces took to the skies in force. Dwarven artillery picked up its pace, finding soft targets in their range. Arrows and spells that the Stone Raiders and their allies had been holding onto lashed out at the now soft targets.

Loughbreck could feel it—the fear that now passed through his people as barriers failed across his lines.

The Warclans advanced, parting to allow the Beast Kin and Demon force as well as the Aleph automatons forward. Blue spearheads flew from their hands, exploding on impact with Loughbreck's front line soldiers; there was nowhere for them to go and their defenses were failing.

Shades were being hunted down by parties of people who had Light Affinity. Few remained within the barrier that surrounded the defenders.

Loughbreck grabbed the mage beside him, pulling their ear to his mouth. "Use the mind working," Loughbreck hissed.

The mage looked at him with wide and alarmed eyes.

Loughbreck held her eyes, his sword in hand.

"Yes, sir." The mage pulled out the grand working from her satchel. Few even knew of its existence.

The crystal started to glow as she imbued it with her own Mana and commanded it into action. The grand working flared to life, passing outward and spreading through all of Loughbreck's soldiers.

Mind magic was powerful stuff. If done right, it could make people break down into nightmares, never to recover again, or it could put people into a hallucination for the rest of their lives. It was created by melding the effects of medical ingredients and magical understanding.

This grand working was not made to strike fear into the enemy; it was to strengthen the resolve of Loughbreck's soldiers. It was a hallucinogenic that would allow them to feel no pain and feel confident in themselves and their victory.

Afterward, it might cause people to break down from what they remembered themselves doing.

That was later. Right now, Loughbreck needed to win in order to drive through to Haugr and support Lord Esamael.

His people surged forward, as if seeing a new weakness in their enemy's lines.

"Activate the last grand working and have someone take it within their Mana barrier," he said to the mage.

"Yes, sir." The mage's face was grim as the grand working fell to dust and she sent orders to others holding their last remaining grand working.

Loughbreck's remaining one hundred and ninety thousand soldiers were dying in the hundreds with every passing second now that they had no protection. Their headlong charge forward was slowing. The ranged attackers were focused on their front lines for fear of being overrun and cut down in close quarters. It didn't help with the Stone Raiders who were among the attacker's formations; their melee fighters had a harder time but still easily cut down two or three against one. Their mages buffed them and wreaked havoc on the ranged forces. Even though they were getting mobbed from every direction among enemy territory, Loughbreck saw something that didn't belong on a battlefield: smiles.

The Stone Raiders, even in overwhelming odds, grinned from ear to ear. Their POEs were, for the large part, staying back within the Stone Raiders' allies, but others were standing shoulder-to-shoulder with the Players.

As Loughbreck heard the sounds of thousands of unnatural cries, the hairs on the back of his neck stood up. The cries weren't coming from within the fortress. They came from the fields around it.

***

Dwayne slammed his shield against a soldier's, tossing them back as his sword darted out. A soldier screamed, going down under their fellows' feet. Dwayne tore his blade from them and brought it across. The blade cut through his next attacker's armor as if it weren't there.

Dwayne fought with everything he had, but he had to be careful to not overextend himself.

"They're in some kind of berserker rage; I don't know what's going on. Treat them like zombies. Unless they're dead, they're a threat," Kim said.

"Lovely—always wanted to fight zombies!" Dwayne growled, dispensing with another two soldiers and a mage who got too close for his liking.

"Well, I personally love zombies and it looks like it's about time we started welcoming this little army to our humble abode. Wake up, minions!" Jason, who was with Dwayne, laughed as magic started to flow out of Jason and into the dead that covered the ground.

He didn't, however, raise any of the allies who had fallen. It was seen as a big sign of disrespect by most POEs to do that.

The once-dead soldiers started to rise; their fellows cut them down here and there. They didn't seem to hesitate at all in killing their allies.

Must be that berserker spell they're under, Dwayne thought disapprovingly.

It blunted the mind and the tactics of the soldiers, though it did keep them in the battle and fighting with everything they had.

"Support has arrived," Josh said over the guild chat.

Summoners and necromancers were muttering out spells or moving their hands as fighting seemed to break out in the rear ranks of Loughbreck's formations.

Dwayne watched as a bone juggernaut charged out of the night and right into the rear of the attacking army. Without their barriers, the juggernaut simply crushed or impaled anything that was in its path with the bone spikes across its body.

"Now, we can have a real fight! Oh, I missed you two, skele-toraus," Jason said, as if he were greeting his household cat.

Dwayne glanced back, seeing Jason sniff slightly in emotion as he fondly patted what looked like two skeleton dinosaurs.

"Fucking necros," Dwayne mumbled. His distraction allowed three fighters in close to him. These ones were harder than before. Dwayne's Strength was more than theirs but his Agility only slightly so. Facing three of them with less Strength but nearly the same Agility was proving to be difficult.

"Help!" Dwayne called out.

A mage in the group sent out lightning, making the three shake with the electricity running through their bodies.

Dwayne cut them down, thankful he had leather bindings on his sword so he didn't turn into a lightning rod as well.

The battle was turning, but Loughbreck's soldiers didn't know it, their minds warped by the spell placed upon them.

We're just going to have to take them all out. Dwayne yelled out and charged a few feet forward. He shield bashed, killing one outright and made the others stumble behind them as he turned in a circle. His blade cleaved through anything in his range.

"Worth every damn copper!" Dwayne brought his sword down in a powerful blow, nearly cleaving his opponent in two.

It was taking time, but they were pushing through the attacking enemies.

Dwayne pulled back a bit. Moving forward without support was a good and easy way to die.

***

Suzy linked herself to her creations. They were running mainly on autopilot, using her imprinted Willpower to guide them as they surged out of the darkness and into the rear lines of the attackers. As the Stone Raiders had teleported from Terra to Verlun, their creations had been sent over drop pads that had been placed by Josh's stealthy types.

They'd come out behind Loughbreck's army, moving forward to enclose the army.

Now, their trap slammed shut as nearly seven and a half thousand creations, summoned creatures, elementals, zombies, skeleton creations, and various other minions rushed out of the fields around Verlun and right into the back of Loughbreck's army.

Loughbreck's army started to turn just as the minion army ran through their lines.

It was chaos, pure and simple. The attackers were caught off guard and charging forward. Many were simply cut down, not knowing what was behind them.

Suzy commanded her Air creations forward, dropping off minions in packs. They were all controlled by one master, essentially creating a basic hive mind. Without needing to communicate to one another, their masters gave orders and they all worked to carry it out.

So, while Loughbreck and his people were trying to turn their army to face the new threat, the minions were compact fighting units in complete understanding of not only what they were doing but also what every other creation under their master was doing.

Suzy thought about ordering them more, telling them specific targets to hit, but there was little need. They anticipated her orders and threw themselves into the battle with everything they had.

Suzy looked to Dave, who peered over the battlefield. His face was covered, but she could see a line running down his forehead. His gray eyes seemed to smoke slightly as he surveyed the battlefield.

She didn't know what had happened to him, but his power seemed to have multiplied. He hovered with her Air creations. His spheres had sprouted blades and spun at incredible speeds, turning anything that was within fifteen feet of him into a blenderized pulp.

His eyes locked onto something. A spear appeared from above and slammed into the ground. The Mana construct failed, exploding as raw Mana escaped.

Suzy ducked. Dust and debris showered down on the party as a twenty-meter-wide hole was left behind.

"They're preparing another grand working." Dave's eyes tracked something as spears started to fall from the sky and opened holes in the enemy's lines, following a mage who was charging forward, holding a glowing crystal in their hands as they ran. Runed armor covered them as the air around them shimmered with a powerful barrier.

Dave let out an annoyed noise as spears formed faster and faster, falling from above.

"Bring everything we have down onto that running mage! They have a grand working!" Deia yelled over the guild chat.

Destruction rained down on the mage, but they continued to run. Their barrier faltered as they charged forward, not caring for the destruction all around them.

An ominous feeling filled Suzy's stomach.

Dave let out an angry yell. "Cover me; I need to get to that grand working!"

"On Dave!" Deia called.

The entire party started forward at a walk, then a jog, and then a full-out run. Spears of metal flew through the air; darklings tripped those in their path. Fire elementals dropped from the sky, screeching as fire flew from their mouths and hands.

Anna, sheathed in wind armor, sent out wide Air blades, throwing people back or cutting through their armor. Lox, Gurren, and Steve finished off anything that wasn't felled by magical attacks. Deia called up her nearly invisible flame spell; anything they hit exploded. Suzy cast buffing magic, increasing their speed and reaction time.

Bands appeared on all of their arms. Suzy looked up to Dave as time seemed to slow, but her reactions stayed the same.

She pulled creations from her storage bag. The Air, Water, and Fire creations watched the sides and rear, keeping Suzy updated with any incoming threats.

Mages started to send their magic at Party Zero. A soul gem hovered above them all; a Mana barrier appeared just feet above it, enclosing the entire party.

The soul gem started to dim with the increasing hits.

***

Loughbreck cried out, using his pole-arm to tear apart another Air creation as his war cat shook an Earth creation down to its components.

The battle had finally reached him. His rear ranks were caught in a fight with the minion army while his front ranks continued to charge into the Stone Raiders and their allies.

"Find us a way to get out of here!" Loughbreck said. He might have won against just the Stone Raiders and their allies, but against this minion army as well, he knew that his army would more than likely fall.

He guided his war cat with his feet, pushing her onward. His advisors and commanders who weren't under the mind magic fought alongside him. They knew what was coming and they were looking to save themselves.

The berserk soldiers and mages were acting as a great distraction, throwing themselves into the enemy. Flames burst out from the mage commander, taking out a large group of minions.

Seeing an opening, Loughbreck squeezed his war cat with his legs. The creature raced forward, running over anything that lay in its way. The rest of the commanders followed, breaking free of the army and the few ranks of the minion army to charge away from Verlun.

Loughbreck sat down in his saddle, riding his war cat, watching the rest of his leaders all around him as they tried to get every last bit of speed from their mounts. Loughbreck noticed the seer stone in his hand. He looked at it. The mage who had been sent with the grand working was charging through the lines. There was no need for them to slow as attacks dropped on them from above, killing everything around them.

His eyes shifted to a commotion coming through the ranks. A party of seven charged through Loughbreck's lines as if they weren't there, solely focused on the mage carrying the grand working.

The mages focused on the party, sending in their attacks. A barrier appeared as they continued their headlong charge.

The Stone Raider who had destroyed the portals to the shade realm surged forward. He slammed his shield into the mage charging forward with the grand working in their hands and tossed them to the side. Before they had time to recover, he finished them off with a glowing sword.

The surrounding forces charged through the path of carnage left by the mage's and his party's passing.

There were seventy thousand of the attackers left, under a fourth of what Loughbreck had started out with.

The mages had spent nearly all of their Mana. Still, the Dwarven artillery kept firing. The allies were now taking back the ground inside the fortress that was pitted and broken through spells and near misses.

Bodies covered the ground as minions moved to the breaches, stopping any of the soldiers from escaping.

The Stone Raiders fought like the possessed. Loughbreck had never seen anything like it. All of those grand workings, all of that preparation and hard work, and his army hadn't been able to get past them.

They were supposed to have been some minor obstacle, but instead they had gutted his army.

Loughbreck looked to his interface as the mind magic grand working came to an end. As the spells counter hit zero, some people continued to fight. However, others dropped to the ground, screaming and crying.

The defenders seemed to slow their advance.

He didn't know which group started first, but his once proud and confident army started to surrender.

Slowly, the defenders stopped their fighting, grouping together, wary of some sort of ruse.

Loughbreck knew it was no ruse. They had been ready to flee nearly an hour ago. Now, with the passing of the mind magic and their numbers a third of when they had wanted to flee, there was no hope left in them. They were broken.

He threw away the seer stone; none of the command group said a word as they raced into the night and away from Verlun.

Chapter 25: Other Side of the Coin

"My king!" An aide ducked as another spell hit the royal palace's Mana barrier. The sky was alight with magical forces being thrown back and forth by the mages in the palace, as well as Lord Esamael's mages.

"What?" the king asked. His guards all wore their matching enchanted Mithril armor, looking at the aide and for any other possible threats. Sneaking an assassin in the midst of a battle was not an unheard of tactic.

"One of the scouts took a look at Verlun. It looks like a massive battle was fought there and a fortress grew out of the ground!" the aide said.

Sigaird tilted his helmeted head to the side, looking at the incoming chat request. He took it.

"King Sigaird, this is Lucy Vernia, lieutenant of the Stone Raiders. I was wondering how your night was going?" The woman sounded completely at ease.

"What do you want and why are you calling? I have better things to do," Sigaird hissed.

"We're going to have to talk about that temper of yours," Lucy tutted.

Sigaird turned beet-red with anger and considered disconnecting. He very nearly did before Lucy spoke up again.

"Tell General Tortessin to prepare his people to assault Emaren. We'll allow your people entry, not because we like you any more than Esamael, but just because he attacked us. See you soon, sweetie." Lucy cut the channel, leaving Sigaird in a state of confusion.

"My king?" the aide asked.

"The Stone Raiders survived and they're making a move." Sigaird turned and continued his march down the corridor. His guards moved around him.

"Find me Lady Merguine," Sigaird said to one of his closest guards. The man nodded and headed off at a speed that belied the heavy armor he wore.

Sigaird opened up a new voice chat with General Tortessin.

"General, something is going to happen to Emaren in the near future. Be ready for whatever happens. Remind your people to not attack any Stone Raiders they see unless they are provoked. Be ready for an opening," Sigaird said before the general could even say hello.

"Yes, my king," Tortessin said.

"Good man." Sigaird closed the channel. Looking up, he saw the guard returning from a side corridor. Merguine and her own guards followed.

"Merguine," Sigaird said.

"Have you seen what happened at Verlun?" Merguine hissed as she fell into step with him. No longer did she wear her dress, but heavily enchanted steel-plated leather armor. Sigaird was more used to this appearance.

"What?" Sigaird asked.

"They were attacked with nearly two hundred and ninety thousand trained troops, the best that Emaren had, buffed, with mobile barriers and no less than four grand workings. Esamael's army used three of the workings, one a Water spirit creator, the other opening doorways to the shade realm, and the last some potent mind magic to get their forces to fight without regret or pause." She shook her head in anger. "Turned them all into berserkers. They were about to use a fourth when they were hit in the rear by the Stone Raiders' minions. They captured the grand working and the survivors surrendered.

"Now, all of the Stone Raiders are gathering at the teleport pad while their allies care for the wounded and get those who surrendered divested of their weapons."

Sigaird's face turned grim. With that many soldiers, the leader must have had the leadership class. It would only make sense, boosting their combat abilities before all the rest of the extras that the force seemed to have at their disposal.

"Seems that they were the sleeping Dragon you were talking about," Sigaird admitted.

"Now, we just have to see what happens with waking a Dragon," Merguine said, not sounding pleased at all with the result.

***

Lord Esamael slammed his hand into the table, breaking it apart as the seer stone he had been watching fell to the floor.

The entire house that Lord Esamael's ally owned and they were using as a command post for the battle in Haugr went silent. Generals, commander's aides, and guards looked away as Esamael beat the table into submission.

"That fucking idiot! I want Loughbreck and all his commanders captured *alive* so that I might show them what happens to those who fail me! How could he lose against such a measly guild!"

No one chose to voice how that measly guild had been supported by more Dwarven Warclans than seen in the last century, as well as the support of three legendary groups that had stepped out of history back onto Emerilia.

"I want an update on our forces!" Esamael barked.

"The forces in Emaren are under heavy siege by General Tortessin's forces. With the barriers, runed walls, and forces there, we can hold the city for another two weeks. Here in Haugr, we have moved through the trading district and are now progressing through the noble housing district. Our mages are now in range of the palace and are using long-range spells to stop any outgoing magic from the palace.

"We have had heavy fighting on the streets with various different groups, from citizens of Haugr, to adventurers and guards. The northern army is on its way, but it will take a number of days.

"Our forces should be ready to assault the palace within four hours. We have secured the southern, western, and northern walls and are pushing to take over the eastern walls," the aide rushed to say, calming Lord Esamael somewhat.

"What of the city rune?" He looked to a different aide.

"Our enchanters believe that they can switch it from the Haugr city guard to our own forces in just a few hours," the aide snapped off.

"Make sure they don't screw it up," Esamael growled.

"Yes, my lord." The aide bowed deeply.

Esamael growled, dismissing the man.

***

"Everyone knows what they're doing?" Josh yelled, looking out over the Stone Raiders gathered below.

A cheer rose from their throats. Their allies had offered to come with them, but Joshua had declined. They had stood together at Verlun, showing that they might be one guild but they had a lot of allies. Now, it was time to show them what they could do when they weren't worrying about defending one location, when they were the hunters.

"Dave, open that teleport pad!" Josh yelled.

The Stone Raiders ran forward in their parties. The teleport pad's runes activated, showing a city being bombarded.

Josh fell in with his Stone Raiders. He dove into the shadows, coming out behind the guards who were around the teleport pad. They were watching the supply wagons that were going through the event horizon instead of being there to fight. Josh cut down three of them before they had time to scream.

Arrows and magic leapt free of the Stone Raiders, killing anything in their path. The guards might be bolstered by the city's runes, but they were goddamn Stone Raiders. What's a bolstered guard compared to a three-hundred-year-old Lich, or a horde of Creatures of Power with a *god* commanding them?

Party Zero stepped through the teleport pad and rushed toward the nearest wall.

"Dave, where are the barrier runes?" Josh moved closer to them.

"I've put them on the map, at least the ones I can sense. Taking them out should drop the barrier," Dave said.

"Good. Now give Tortessin a fighting chance." Josh dove into the shadows again and came out where Dwayne stood with Esa at the teleport pad.

"Esa, secure this city. Dwayne, once our people are all through, I'll head to Haugr with my stealth types. We'll take out the guards at the next teleport pad and you lot come in right behind us. Esa, as soon as that barrier is down and that wall is opened up, we're getting the hell outta Dodge!" Josh grinned. The last Stone Raider made it through the teleport pad.

"Dial up Haugr!" Dwayne barked.

Verlun disappeared as the event horizon collapsed. The circular pad started to move as new runes shifted into position and the circles rotated into place.

***

Malsour ran with the rest of the party. There was no one on the streets except the few defenders running between positions. An alarm started up in the distance before spreading across the city like wildfire.

A group of five guards came out ahead of them, two being caught in a fiery blast, another getting a spear from Steve, and the last two cut apart by Anna.

"I'm surprised you're not Mana exhausted," Malsour yelled to Anna.

"I have a rather high Intelligence, but my strength is my Willpower. I can regenerate Mana like no tomorrow, so I don't get those long headaches like the rest of you schmucks." Anna grinned.

"Hey! As a refined schmuck, I take offense to that," Steve said.

"So, how's Alkao?" Suzy asked.

"Time and place?" Anna complained.

"What? It's not like we've got much chance to talk to you when you're training all of the DCA how to fly and fight!" Induca added. "Sooo, how are things?"

"Guards on the wall!" Dave called out.

Malsour chuckled at Anna's relieved expression. His darklings speared the guards on the wall before they could raise an alarm.

They came to a halt at the base of the wall.

"Dave, you deal with the runes. I can deal with the wall," Malsour said.

"Can do."

Malsour looked for weaknesses in the walls. They had been fused together rather well.

Dave conjured items directly into the walls and then removed them, destroying runes quickly and effectively. Finally, he broke the ones that stopped people tampering with the wall.

Malsour started creating weaknesses in the wall, destabilizing it.

Dave continued destroying the runes that strengthened the wall.

"Incoming!" Suzy called out, her Air creations acting as scouts.

"Steve, stay here with Suzy. The rest of you, move out and intercept the ones charging at us. Malsour, is there anything we can do to speed this all up?"

"A nice explosion would be good in a bit. Just need five minutes to break this thing apart enough so that it leaves a big enough opening," Malsour said.

There was a flash of light to their right a kilometer or two away, followed by a rumbling noise. Malsour looked up to see a section of the wall crumbling where the explosion came from.

"What was that?" Induca moved farther down the street and found a good position to defend from.

"Mana barrier buffer—looks like we got to it and destroyed it. That energy had to go somewhere. Unstable runes make great hand grenades," Dave said.

"Hand grenades? That took out a wall!" Suzy said.

"You got any spare?" Lox asked Dave.

"Oh, I could whip up a batch," Dave said. Small spheres appeared in his hands, energy snaking from one of the floating soul gems into the creations. "Twist the two halves, then throw it. You've got five seconds until they go off."

"Thanks, Dave." Lox walked away.

"Always the coolest gear," Malsour heard Gurren say as Lox handed him a few of the "grenades." Suzy rubbed the bridge of her nose as the rest of the girls were asking Anna again about Alkao.

"Somehow, doesn't feel like we're in the middle of a war zone," Malsour muttered as he shifted a structural support just so, working cracks into the foundations and across to the rest of the wall. Parts started to crumble, falling from the wall and onto the ground outside.

Lox and Gurren tested out their new weapons, throwing them into the middle of the arriving guards. The guards let out their war cries; fire and wind raced to meet them before the grenades went off.

"Well, that was anticlimactic." Anna scratched her head. The grenades had left craters a half foot deep and spread shrapnel out over thirty meters.

The guards might be buffed, but high-velocity shrapnel tore through their barriers and bodies.

"I'm done. Let's get out of here." Malsour stepped away from the wall.

Deia started to cast a spell.

"Let's get a bit farther away before we do that." Malsour started to jog while the others followed.

"Blow it up now," Malsour said when he guessed they were far enough away.

Deia looked back and pointed her hand at the wall.

A ball of burning fury raced at the wall. It hit with what sounded like a thunderclap.

The wall buckled; parts were blown outward as it set off a chain reaction. For a hundred meters in every direction, the wall came apart as if it were made of dominos.

"Hey look, it's the southern army! Hey guys!" Steve said as if greeting a nursery class, waving at the southern army waiting on the other side of the wall.

"Maybe they need an incentive?" Dave asked.

"The damn wall's opened more than a well-used Mithril vein!" Gurren complained.

"I've got it!" Induca cast a spell into the sky.

Malsour looked up as it blossomed into words.

Welcome to Emaren, southern army!

Malsour and Suzy shared a look with Deia. The rest fell into laughter. Malsour couldn't keep up his unimpressed expression anymore and snorted at Induca's antics.

"Next stop—Haugr! Wonder what the capital is like." Steve sounded genuinely interested.

***

Overseer Rendar looked down over Haugr. It was the mage's guild's duty to watch over battles. They made sure that war followed the rules decreed by the goddess Fire and reinforced by the mage's guild.

The guild and college within Haugr had been closed. Those who lived in the town were allowed to leave, or bring their families to the guild for protection. No one dared to attack the mage's guild or college buildings directly. Here and there, they were hit by errant magic or debris moving through the skies.

The Mana barriers took care of the weak secondary effects.

Rendar watched as groups of mages dropped out of illusion spells to deal with those who decided to do as they wanted in times of war. Rendar glanced at their actions, looking away after a few minutes, moving over the city, unseen by those below. There were few who could actually harm him in the city below.

He yawned and looked at the royal palace. Spells were barely making it out of the palace's Mana barriers. Esamael's mages weren't as strong as the palace's, but there were a lot of them, enough to encircle the royal palace and work together to break spells apart before they reached Esamael's people.

The few who did make it through landed on the mobile barriers that covered the ground troops securing all avenues of approach to the palace.

The final attack was about to begin.

"I wonder what will happen to Per'ush if Esamael wins? Probably increase the taxes again. The man loves his taxes." Rendar stretched in mid-air.

He had been alive through Sigaird's brother, father, and great-uncle's rule. He'd watched over Ashal for a time. Now, those people were one hell of a pain to watch. War was nothing new to him; it was just another way to alter the balance of Emerilia.

The teleport pad flickered off for a few minutes. Rendar glanced over to it. "Can't even control a teleport pad correctly. Well, this is probably not going to be better than it was." Rendar sighed.

He turned to look back at the palace. The teleport pad opened and shadowy figures leaped out of it. In minutes, there was not a living guard around the teleport pad.

"This is new," Rendar said with interest, looking at the ragtag-looking group headed through the teleport pad. Their gear seemed almost random but Rendar used Appraisal. His eyebrow rose in interest. He extended out his senses, his bored expression becoming alarmed.

Their gear was strong, much stronger than he'd seen on any other fighting force in Gudalo. It wasn't only that, but their auras. Nearly every single person had an aura comparable to his own.

He opened up a voice chat. It took a few moments before it was accepted.

"Overseer Edwin, this is Overseer Rendar. I have a *situation*."

"Better be important. I don't like being woken up." Edwin yawned.

"I have a group entering the battle between Sigaird and Esamael. Most of them have an aura as powerful as my own," Rendar said.

"One second." Edwin sounded much more serious and less tired from his ordeal. A few minutes later, he was back. The group had now advanced through the city; stealth types moved ahead to take out sentries, the main body not breaking their pace as they charged onward.

"It's the Stone Raiders. Seems that Esamael attacked them earlier today. They won their battle, took out Emaren's walls to let General Tortessin in, and now they're taking out Esamael and his main army. They don't mess around, it looks like." Edwin muttered the last part. "I'm going to wake some people and send support your way if they act up. Though till then, find a Josh Giles. He's their leader. Make sure he knows the rules. It seems like he does, but we haven't had any actual overseers watching them in battle."

Oh joy.

"I'll do my best to find him." Rendar's eyes flicked from one person to the next, or the shadows, trying to find the man.

"Good luck," Edwin said.

"I have a feeling I'll need it."

"Yeah, and I feel like I won't be getting much sleep tonight!" Edwin said, joining him in his thoughts.

The chat closed as Rendar continued to look for Josh.

***

"Look, fireworks!" Steve said as they came out of the teleport pad, leaving Emaren behind and entering Haugr.

"Seriously, what did you upload into him?" Suzy asked Anna.

Anna just shrugged. "Some of the Internet, some random videos and pictures and commonly used sayings. Then I don't know—one-hit wonder songs and memes, whatever they are. A lot of people viewed them so I thought that they might be useful."

Suzy paled as she looked at Anna as if she had just killed her cat. "You uploaded memes into his head! What the hell is wrong with you!" Suzy yelled. She looked at Steve in horror.

Anna was stunned as she thought she saw tears growing in Suzy's eyes. She moved away a bit and looked at Suzy with a worried expression.

They continued on their way, passing dead soldiers as well as guards and civilians.

Dave was using his Touch to look through the city; he updated his map on his interface at the same time, pointing out where sentries were and major groups of soldiers and mages.

He stopped marking his map when he found something odd. "Malsour, I need you to take me to the city rune," Dave said suddenly.

"Sure." Malsour prepared a spell.

"Wait, why?" Deia asked.

"There are some mages messing around with the runes there. They look like they're altering it and there are dead bodies in there, so I don't think that they're Sigaird's people," Dave said.

"They're going to change the rune to buff themselves instead of Sigaird's forces?" Anna asked.

"Yeah," Dave said.

"Okay, then we're coming with you," Deia said firmly.

"Fine with me." Dave looked to Malsour.

"I can do that," he said.

Dave hid his relief. Having Deia out on the battlefield was seriously playing with his nerves. Although he was keeping up appearances of not worrying, he had a couple of invisible spheres rotating around Deia to protect her and their child.

He knew that she wouldn't have stayed behind, but it played on his nerves and diverted his attention. All he wanted to do was take her somewhere far away and safe. Seeing as she wouldn't let that happen, staying right by her side was his next best option.

The ground around them started to descend, slowly at first, picking up speed as dirt was pushed to the side and other materials under Malsour's control pulled and pushed them onward and toward their destination.

Suzy put power into her staff, turning it into a light as they descended.

Dave shared a map with them, adding in where he sensed the mages and their protection detail around the rune.

It was a large circular room with a massive magical circle in the center. Around it were other circular rooms with Magical Circuits embedded into the ground there, turning the whole thing into one massive magical formation.

Earth mages and artificers were altering the different Magical Circuits that came together, changing the formation to their needs.

Soldiers watched one stairwell that ran up into the city guard's barracks. There were more soldiers up above. It had been some time since they saw combat and they were walking around, growing increasingly bored.

Dave conjured some of the grenades; they added to his floating devices.

"Dave, what is with all of the spheres?" Lox asked.

"Different tools. They're rather inexpensive, running off my soul gem, and they'd take a few minutes to make. Keep them just in case as my backup plans," Dave said.

"How are you feeling?" Deia's hand found his in the darkness. Dave sensed the fear in her voice.

"I'm okay, just a whole whack of knowledge running around my cranium, and plenty of ideas to test out." Dave pulled her close to him and squeezed her hand.

"When you collapsed, I didn't know what happened..." Deia trailed off, looking at the base of Malsour's magical lift.

"I'm fine, don't worry," Dave said, side hugging her and kissing her.

She hugged him tightly. Dave could almost sense the sea of emotions under Deia's tough exterior. He squeezed her tighter to reassure her.

"Be there in twenty seconds," Malsour announced.

Deia and Dave untangled themselves, pushing their emotions away for the time being. They had people to fight.

Everyone readied their weapons and their spells. Dave squeezed Deia's hand before she made sure everyone was in position and started to glow brighter. Dave pulled out his conjuring rods, changing into a shield and sword by default.

"Three, two, one!" Malsour said as they came out the opposite side of the stairs, right into the middle of the magical formation.

The artificers, soldiers, and mages looked at them in shock.

Fireballs, blades of cutting air, Mana spearheads, metal spears, and Dave's spheres rushed outward.

Esamael's people snapped out of their shock, but it was too late for many of them, as they died trying to pull up barriers or protect themselves with their arms.

Soldiers rushed to fight them; their supporting mages called on their Mana to form spells. Dave's grenades went off among the soldiers. Steve, Gurren, and Lox had been running as soon as they entered the room. They cut through those who faced them and in minutes the fighting was all over.

Malsour coughed weakly, looking pale as sweat covered his face.

"You okay?" Deia asked.

"Yeah, just getting close to Mana exhaustion," Malsour said.

"All right, everyone move to the stairs. More of Esamael's goons are bound to show up sooner rather than later!" Her words got them moving to the stairs.

"Malsour, if you change forms, will you recover faster?" Dave asked.

"Yes." Malsour nodded.

"Good. I think we have enough room in here for you. I can think of a way to alter these runes, but I can't do all the heavy lifting of moving all the metals and carving out the new runes." Dave moved to the different rooms around the main Magical Circuit, memorizing each of the different interlinking Magical Circuits to understand the magical formation. He stabbed his sword into the floor in places, breaking runes here and there.

Malsour let out a relieved sound as his body grew and elongated; his tail and wings moved outward as his face changed and scales covered his body. He curled up in the middle formation.

"It will take me a few minutes to recover." Malsour lay down his head.

"No worries," Dave said.

"Suzy, get some drones up the stairs. We need to know what's up there," Deia said.

"On it," Suzy said.

"This is a mess," Dave muttered, focused on the magical formation in front of him. The different parts were all in states of change. The mages were having a terrible time dealing with the anti-tampering magic.

Dave conjured and destroyed, used his sword and broke magical spells that had been overlaying the circuits, softening them up for Malsour as a new Magical Circuit and formation filled his mind.

"Oh, hmm, if I did that, then I could counteract their symbol. It only needs a common object with the same or similar Mana signature to connect to. This is pretty simple; reminds me of the amulets that take power from people and put it in the soul gems. Could I?" Dave looked up.

"Looks like they heard us. We've got soldiers coming down!" Suzy said.

"Dave, hurry up with whatever you're doing!" Deia added.

"It'll take some time and I need to talk to Josh."

***

"What is it?" Queen Selhi said as a messenger stepped onto her balcony where she was having lunch overlooking her capital.

"My queen, you said that you wanted to know whenever something happened with the Stone Raiders?" The aide looked nervous.

"Go on." Queen Selhi turned her full attention to the messenger.

"We have had reports of them in Verlun and Emaren. It seems a Lord Esamael of Emaren and his allies are trying to overthrow the king of Gudalo."

"Verlun, the city where they have some traders and they bought their own teleport pad?" The queen sipped fruit juice.

"Yes, my queen. It seems that they arrived as an army was attacking their guild hall," the messenger said.

The queen's eyes thinned as she put her drink down on the table. "What happened?"

"The battle for Gudalo is still ongoing it seems, but the Stone Raiders are sharing the battle with every Player by streaming it. They had a force of just a thousand Players. The army numbers nearly three hundred thousand. A fortress rose from the ground around the guild hall, walls that might be seen around our own palace." The messenger looked to the queen.

"Continue." She waved her hand, a tight feeling in her chest. *Just what did Magistrate Houn piss off?*

"Their allies followed them. Demons, Beast Kin, and Aleph of legend brought their automatons. They came to the call of the Stone Raiders, close allies. Other kingdoms and cities sent forces to show their support. The Dwarves sent several Warclans; Elves sent their rangers. Still, the Stone Raiders rampaged through the ranks of the attacking army," the messenger said.

The queen didn't say anything. Her hand came to rest on the table as she slowly looked over the capital she had grown up in, the kingdom that she had grown like her own child. She had not the time for marriage nor child in her younger years.

We pissed off giants. What will they do once they have defended their home? Will they be sated and let old issues lie, or will they move to make an example of any who might dare to oppose them? I think that the council and treasurer might reconsider their hesitation to stop paying the Stone Raiders.

"What happened at Emaren?" she asked.

"They came through the teleport pad like a group of wraiths, took out the Mana barrier and the walls, and fled again. We don't know where to," the messenger said.

"Find out where they went and see if one of the Players would be willing to share information with us for some gold. I want to know what happens." The queen continued to look out over her capital.

"Yes, my queen." The messenger bowed. The queen waved in their direction. The messenger hurried off to his errands.

Chapter 26: Return of the Stone Raiders

Malsour raised his head to the sounds of battle on the staircase. He shook his neck and stretched out as much as the magical formation would let him. He couldn't even be at his full length within the massive magical formation.

"Good to see you're back to full Mana." Dave continued to go through the various interconnected Magical Circuits.

"So, what am I changing?" Malsour asked, feeling much better.

"Sending it to you now." Dave stuck his head in another room while he accessed his interface and sent the information to Malsour.

"Got it." Malsour read the new formations and circuits. As he read, the components of the circuits started to rise out of the ground; metal and stone floated in the air, forming and changing, being moved around before they came back together and slid back into the ground with ease.

"I missed my Dragon form," Malsour said. It felt as though a weight had been lifted from him as his familiar magic reacted to his very thoughts.

"I can see." Dave looked at several circuits that were changing at the same time as Malsour seemed to read the message Dave had sent.

"I sent you all of the changes." Dave stepped out of the formation.

"Hmm, is this a drain, and then a convert...wait, am I understanding this right?" Malsour lifted his head and looked to Dave, his large split eyes following Dave.

"Yup! Who said to fix the thing when you can make it better!" Dave declared with a grin.

"I don't think that King Sigaird is going to think the same," Malsour said dryly.

"He will if we save his ass," Dave said. "And Josh already gave me the go-ahead."

Malsour shrugged as the last of the interconnecting circuits came together and slotted into their positions. "Well, let's see if this works." Malsour shook himself as he started to become smaller. He walked to the edge of the formation, toward the stairs. Behind him, the main Magical Circuit started to pull itself apart, flying into the air as the different materials moved around and formed into new combinations.

His body finished its transformation as he stepped off the Magical Circuit and the main magical circle settled back into position.

Malsour felt empowered as buffs fell over him. "Not as good as being in my other form, but it will work."

"It'll work, he says," Dave muttered, shaking his head, as he moved to where the rest of the party fought their way up the stairs.

***

"Looks like Esamael's army is making a move," a scout reported.

"Agreed," another said from another direction.

The Stone Raiders had rushed forward. They had been fast and brutal, killing anyone who might raise an alarm before moving into positions around Esamael's army. They'd hidden in various houses, keeping a watch out for any movements by Esamael or Sigaird.

Josh had been about to charge in when Dave contacted him with a plan.

"That man has a damn plan for everything, it seems," Josh muttered.

He let out a breath as newfound strength seemed to flood him. Agility and Strength buffs activated on everyone who wore a guild amulet.

"Once they engage the royal palace's forces, we'll attack. Wait for my signal," Josh said, playing with his daggers.

"You go blind if you play with them that much," Cassie chastised.

"How is that even possible?" Josh grumbled.

Cassie smiled and looked back out of the window they were sharing.

***

There was little that Deia needed to do. Steve, Gurren, and Lox were many levels above the forces they were fighting. In the restricting corridors, they were fighting only four or five enemies at a time. In a nearly one-on-one fight, they were tearing Esamael's soldiers apart.

"That's the last of the soldiers in the stairwell. They've probably sent word to their commanders." Suzy watched through her Air creations she was using as scouts. "I can see more of Esamael's soldiers headed toward us."

Deia rolled her shoulders. Her body felt as if she had just gone through a dozen levels of inputting stat points into Agility and Strength.

"All done down here! Let's go join the fight!" Dave said, Malsour trailing behind him.

"Excuse me, Steve," Anna said.

Steve slammed his shield forward, throwing men back. "After you." Steve waved her forward.

She gripped her sword with one hand, moving into the position Steve had vacated. For one second, it seemed that she was holding her sheathed sword. The next, it was by her opposite hip.

A blade of Air lashed out, cleaving through armor and people alike, leaving just a few soldiers behind.

Before they had a chance to run, Steve sent Mana spearheads into them.

Gurren and Lox finished off their attackers.

"Dude, watch your aim next time," Gurren complained, looking at his gore-covered shield. "Going to take *hours* to clean this off."

"Whoops, sorry. Didn't think it would be such an explosive finish." Steve shrugged.

"Dude, that's gross," Dave said.

"I'm surrounded by pubescent boys in the shape of men." Deia rubbed the bridge of her nose.

"Hey! I meant it as a pun!" Steve said.

"Yeah, the number of puns you made was the problem!" Suzy said.

"How about we leave the puns till later and we get out of here?" Deia suggested.

"Agreed." Lox moved through the soldiers who had been blocking their path moments before. The rest followed.

"I'll take that and that and that," Steve said as he went along, adding loot to his inventory. "All aboard the loot train!" Steve said, rapid-fire accessing the loot tombstones.

"Just another Sunday," Lox said.

"It's Tuesday, isn't it?" Dave asked.

"Doesn't really matter with him." Suzy pointed her thumb over her shoulder.

The ground rumbled as they got to the top of the stairs.

Deia looked back, finding a rune-carved door.

"Don't want people messing up my work," Malsour said.

Deia nodded and checked her map. "Okay, the guild hasn't attacked yet. Let's get over to them and see if we can get in on that action.

"Induca, Anna, Suzy, and I will watch above. Lox, if we're broken up, you're in charge." Deia rose into the air, Induca and Anna with her.

She ran from roof to roof, equipping her bow. She checked it, pulling an arrow from its quiver, ready for anything that might try to stop them.

***

A hungry look passed over Esamael's face as his army let out their war cry. It was louder than the random spells that landed among their formations.

As one, they surged forward, charging up toward the royal palace from every direction. The palace was a series of castles that overlooked the city. On three sides, the hundred-meter tall and smooth castle walls melded into the natural bedrock that they were built on. A slope led up to the entrance of the wall around the castle, crossing a large gorge.

Although it would have been an impressive castle on Earth, this was Emerilia, a land of magic. Scaling ladders could grow to be hundreds of meters tall; mages could call up pillars of earth to push them over the wall.

Esamael's people rushed forward, mages using every way they knew to gain entry into the castle.

The palace fought back: defensive runes, magical traps, and spells being unleashed against the oncoming army. Spells lit up the Mana barrier covering the royal palace.

The battle for Haugr and who would be the king of Gudalo had begun.

"Lord Esamael, there was an issue with the city rune," an aide said, staying out of hitting range.

"WHAT?" Esamael demanded, focusing his ire on the aide who paled, sweating under the pressure of Esamael's aura.

"The city rune—a group of people got into it and then sealed it up. Our forces were killed off," the aide said.

"We're also getting reports that roving patrols have been killed across Haugr," a general said, listening to something as his face paled. "The teleport pad's guards were killed off. None of them were able to raise the alarm."

"Emaren has fallen. The southern army gained access to the city. It looks like someone exited the teleport pad there, broke the walls and Mana barriers," another aide said.

"Why are we only learning this now?" Esamael demanded.

"It seems to have all happened within the last twenty minutes. Our people didn't realize how bad things were in Emaren until the southern army started cutting them down in the streets," a general said.

"Who the hell—" Esamael heard a noise in the background.

Moments later, it was followed by hundreds of other voices. Esamael could barely make out what they were saying.

"Stone Raiders!"

"Sir! We have groups of Players advancing from all directions into the rear of our army's formation," a general yelled.

"Kill them! Kill them all!" Esamael yelled, pointing at the general. Rage contorted his features as spittle flew from his lips.

***

"My king, whatever Esamael's troops did with the city rune, it seems to have been reverted. All of the guards and forces loyal to the crown have regained their lost strength and buffs," an aide said to King Sigaird as he looked down at the forces attacking from every direction.

"Good. It's about time we had something go our way." Sigaird tapped the hilt of his sword.

He wanted to be down with his people, fighting off Esamael's army. Doing so would leave him open to attack. After all, if they killed Sigaird, then there would be no one left to claim the throne.

He heard yells as people ran out of the houses they had been hiding in. They didn't even try to break Esamael's mobile barriers.

"Shit, they're going to get themselves killed," Sigaird muttered, proud that his people would join the fight but knowing it would lead to their deaths.

Their front line met Esamael's and ran through it.

Sigaird's hand stopped tapping his sword as he watched in shock. Over the noises of battle, Sigaird could hear the group's battle cry.

"Stone Raiders!"

Just what kind of Demons are they? They're cutting through Esamael's people as if they're nothing more than level 10 mobs.

***

Dave didn't stop running as he and Party Zero left the cover of the streets around the royal palace, following the rest of their guild that had rushed to meet Esamael's army.

He activated the second part of the city rune. Esamael's people had been working to get the city rune to buff their people, meaning that all of their soldiers were wearing an identifying artifact imbued with a specific Mana signature. They'd already input this Mana signature into the Magical Circuits. Dave copied the signature, but instead of applying a buff, now their artifacts would weaken them, reducing their Intelligence and Strength.

Deia, Induca, Malsour, and Anna worked to cancel any incoming spells and ranged attacks. Suzy threw out pre-made creations; as they fell, they became active. Quickly, there was a small army running with Party Zero or flying around them.

Dave and Steve were firing Mana bolts from their hands. In no time, they were under a mobile Mana barrier.

Lox and Gurren worked in concert with each other, carving a path through the soldiers.

There was no time for the soldiers to recover as the mages unleashed their ranged attacks, killing anyone in the vicinity with their spells.

The barrier fell and the minion army rushed in to kill anyone left. "Move forward!" Deia yelled.

"We got their grand workings! Keep it up!" Josh said over the guild-wide chat.

Dave breathed a sigh of relief; those grand workings could shift a battle quickly. He didn't want to know what Esamael had saved up just in case he needed it.

Grenades appeared around Dave; soul gems fed them power before he threw them through Mana barriers and they detonated.

He turned, using the edge he'd added to his shield, and opened a soldier's neck. He danced under a blade, his own flashing out and cutting the inside of the soldier's legs and then up and across their neck.

Conjured spears took four other soldiers down. The spears disappeared as arrows flew over Dave, taking down several soldiers at the same time. Steve waded into the battle, his axe opening armor and breaking bodies with his massive swings. As he wielded his axe, he fired spearheads from his opposite hand.

Induca turned into a fiery tornado tearing through ranks before cancelling the spell. As she walked into a new barrier group, fiery whips melted through metal as if it wasn't even there.

Anna wasn't hiding her skills anymore. The weakened soldiers were nothing in the face of her sword. She created a wall of Air blades that cut apart anything that made its way into her path.

Malsour cast hexes and curses; people fell down, writhing in pain where his spells landed.

Dave closed his eyes. Soul gems floated around him, gathering the wealth of souls that filled the air. Mana streams exploded from the soul gems around Dave, burning out barrier after barrier and opening Esamael's forces up to magical attacks.

Dave looked around the battlefield. It had devolved into chaos with Esamael's soldiers trying to advance into the royal palace while also trying to fight off the Stone Raiders and getting debuffed at the same time.

The Stone Raiders had turned the formations into a mess, carving their way through. Killing the soldiers was easy. Most of the guild was just using it as an experience farm. They were figuring out the least amount of effort they had to put into getting the most amount of kills. Without the insane buffs and grand workings, Esamael's army weren't even that hard to deal with. There was an issue with them swarming the Stone Raiders, but one powerful spell was good enough to blast open enough room for them to get organized and continue the slaughter.

Lox and Gurren switched to their destruction staffs as the barriers failed. Fuel air bomb explosions detonated against the massive walls of the royal palace, using the walls to direct the blast, killing hundreds with every explosion.

Anna's wind blades cut through tens of people at the same time, no longer blocked by Mana barriers.

It wasn't a battle—it was a slaughter.

Sixty thousand were dead or dying within minutes of the Stone Raiders taking to the field. The royal palace, seeing their enemies fall, were emboldened by their actions, casting spells and using their ranged attacks.

It just added to the body count. Without their mobile barriers, Esamael's soldiers were open to all manner of attacks.

Spells that had been broken on the barriers now washed through the attacker's ranks. Panic quickly started to set in. Here and there, formations were falling apart.

Dave conjured bombs as big as Steve, dropping them from the sky like a bomber might. Soul gems reached out, powering them as they slammed into the ground. The bombs went off, flattening everything in a few hundred meters and tossing many others farther away.

"Get into a circle and use ranged attacks," Deia called.

Party Zero paused their advance, grouping together as they formed a circle, everyone getting a sector as their ranged attacks flared out.

Soldiers were in a panic. Magical destruction was all around and they were now trapped against the royal palace.

At first, a few people started to run out into the city, away from the battle. More and more soldiers tried to flee, many getting cut down in their attempts.

The army had been reduced by half; the shock of it all was getting to the survivors. They stopped trying to gain access to the palace and instead moved to escape.

The Stone Raiders cut down all who tried to escape their wrath.

Dave's bombs broke any large formations that seemed to pull themselves together, wiping out thousands every second.

Some of the soldiers escaped, but most couldn't even get close to the Stone Raiders' parties as they used ranged attacks to kill them.

Chapter 27: Head of the Beast

Esamael looked up as a scream came from near the front of the manor that he and his commanders had taken over.

More yells could be heard through the house. Soldiers and guards pulled their weapons free, ready to deal with whatever came their way.

Undead rushed through the door. Those who had been guarding the manor were now attacking their leaders and friends.

Weapons clashed as the room seemed to darken.

Esamael had his sword out, backing into a corner in case anything made it through his people.

"Hello, Lord Esamael." A man's voice came from behind Esamael.

Startled and scared, Esamael turned around, swinging wildly where he heard the voice coming from. Pain tore through his arm. He heard his sword go flying as his entire being seemed to be trying to tear itself apart.

He looked at a hooded man, holding two wicked curved daggers. Blood dripped from them as Esamael's arm landed on the floor.

He started to scream as he dropped to the floor. Blood flowed from his wound.

"You'll make a nice present," the man said, a cold smile on his face.

"The army has come apart. They're trying to flee in every direction. We've got people out hunting them down," someone else said to the shadowy man.

"Good. Get his arm sealed up and bring him," the obvious leader said.

"Who are you?" Lord Esamael demanded. His blood loss made him feel cold and woozy.

"I'm Josh Giles." The man pushed his hood back and looked down calmly at the recent amputee. His aura flared out.

Cold fear ran through Esamael as a wet spot spread through his pants.

"Whoops." Josh suppressed his aura.

Someone touched Esamael's shoulder, making his body go slack. He was still conscious but he couldn't talk or move as he was picked up and carried out of his command post.

***

Sigaird looked out over his royal palace's walls. The area around the base of the walls and for four hundred meters out was a barren landscape.

Esamael's soldiers lay dead or dying. The few who had surrendered had been quickly secured and stripped of their weapons and armor. The Stone Raiders had them grouped together, already moving them in small groups toward the teleport pad.

Sigaird was in a state of shock. The ground showed signs of the massive magical spells that had been called from the heavens or the depths of Emerilia.

The Stone Raiders were an oddity. They had come in, destroying a force five hundred times their own strength. Their spells and fighting abilities were on another scale.

The army had been broken and fled where they could, lest they be cut down, or surrendered.

What are they going to do with all of those prisoners?

There were nearly a hundred times more soldiers and mages who had surrendered to the Stone Raiders, but none of them thought about trying to attack their new captors.

None of the Player guilds had ever accepted those who surrendered and then taken them from a battlefield. Most had sold them off as indentured servants to other kingdoms.

They had set rates and wages by the mage's college so that they could buy their freedom once again. It was the best way to deal with thousands of battle-trained people.

"My king, a group of Stone Raiders are approaching the royal palace. It seems that they are interested in talking." An aide broke Sigaird out of his thoughts.

"I will greet them. Make sure no one does anything to anger them," Sigaird said.

"Yes, my king." The aide bowed to Sigaird before running off to see his orders were carried out.

Sigaird checked his gear and then started to walk for the main gates. He didn't want to keep the Stone Raiders waiting.

It didn't take long for Sigaird to reach the gate. His mind worked over reasons that they might want to meet with him, his anxiety and fear building in his gut.

These people had defended their home, breached a city and then destroyed another army in the same night. *Thank the gods I listened to Merguine.*

The gates swung open as Sigaird approached. His guards made sure to surround their king, their hands resting on their weapons.

Even though they were hidden in their armor, Sigaird knew that they were similarly nervous.

He made it out of the last gate. The drawbridge lowered to reveal eleven people.

Two Dwarves, a Dwarf Halfling, a High Elf, a Beast Kin, four Humans, a man made of metal, and a Half-Elf looked at him.

Sigaird quickly used his Analyze skill.

Malsour, one of the Humans, had eyes of obsidian black. Josh, another Human, was wreathed in shadows. Deia, the Half-Elf, and Induca, one of the female Humans, floated lightly in the air. Their eyes seemed to glow with inner Fire.

Lox and Gurren, the full Dwarves, had the kind of confidence that only came with battle-hardened veterans, their looks showing that they thought little of Sigaird's protection detail. The other Human woman, Esa, held herself like one of Sigaird's knights, her entire posture showing she was dangerous.

A wolf Beast Kin watched everything with mild interest. Her body language showed that she was unworried by the whole situation.

Anna'kal

Beast Kin

Level 294

Sigaird quickly looked away, scared of offending the high-leveled woman.

The High Elf, Suzy, stood there with a glowing staff. The air distorted around her, the only sign that her creations were around.

Sigaird swallowed hard, wondering how many were floating around, invisible to his eyes. His eyes moved to the last person of the party.

David Grahslagg, the master of magical coding and Dwarven Master Smith.

Spheres with runes on their surfaces and soul gems floated around him lazily. Cold sweat ran down Sigaird's spine. He was looking at the famed Party Zero, and their guild leader Josh Giles and his newest lieutenant, Esa.

"Guildmaster Giles, it is an honor and a privilege to meet you." Sigaird pushed forward despite his anxiety as he bowed slightly to the man who had saved possibly his own life and that of his retainers.

"It's good to finally meet the master of the lands that one of my guild halls rests upon. And please, call me Josh." Josh gave a slight smile, but there was still steel in his eyes.

He's not a man to be crossed.

"Very well, Josh. I do not know how I can possibly repay you. You've done me a great service, not only with the information you have supplied me with, but the defense of my city and preventing further loss of life," Sigaird said gravely.

Josh's face was unreadable for a few seconds. "I have an idea of how to repay not only for our actions in defeating Esamael's forces, but also removing certain elements that were working against the crown," Josh said in a measured tone.

"If it is within my power, I will do it," Sigaird said, his voice confident and reassuring. He had disregarded them earlier, but now, after seeing them, he wanted nothing more than to be on amicable terms. He had watched the recordings from his animal-possessing mages and observed the way that they fought with their allies.

They were a force for change, bringing many groups together in the shape of an alliance never seen before.

Josh nodded. His expression gave nothing away. He opened his interface and sent a message to Sigaird.

He opened the message, taking in a sharp breath. The document provided asked for an incredible amount of gold, or different raw materials.

The sum was so large that it would be felt across Gudalo. To Sigaird, there was no choice.

"I cannot do this immediately. If I can be given some time, I can do this in monthly installments, if that works for you?" Sigaird looked to Josh.

Josh's features broke out into a smile. "Oh, that will work fine. Would you be willing to sign an oath to agree to further discussions?"

Sigaird smiled. The document had been a test.

Smart one, this—see how far he can push and then backing off. He wanted to see if I would keep my word. I didn't think that he would be so reasonable, especially with the treatment he had in Selhi.

"I swear on my life and on my kingdom that we will meet to discuss terms of payment for your aid. Within two weeks?" Sigaird looked to Josh.

"I agree that we will meet in two weeks to discuss the terms of payment for our services," Josh agreed, holding out a hand to Sigaird.

You have made a binding oath

You and Josh Giles have made a binding oath to meet to discuss terms of payment for the Stone Raiders, within two weeks.

"As a gesture of goodwill, I think this will do nicely." Josh glanced to the High Elf. She looked to Josh and then back to Sigaird. Nothing seemed to happen for a few moments until a person came flying through the air landed next to Josh.

Sigaird looked at the man once known as Lord Esamael.

"Thank you." Sigaird waved his guards forward. They grabbed the man, the air-distorting creation disconnecting from his back and flying off.

"He has a paralyzing spell on him. It will wear off in three hours," Josh informed Sigaird.

"I was wondering what you would do with those who surrendered to you?" Sigaird asked.

"There's always a use for mages and laborers. I know that Devil's Crater is about to go into their growing season and Terra is going to need a large workforce to grow," Josh said.

"Terra?" Sigaird asked, confused.

"Ah, our main guild hall. We should meet there for our meeting in two weeks. I will send someone to collect you and guide you to the city. It's linked via the teleport pads." Josh smiled.

Sigaird had even more questions, but he pushed them to the side. "Thank you again for everything. I look forward to our meeting in two weeks."

"See you later!" Josh turned with a wave.

Sigaird watched the legendary figures of the Stone Raiders leaving. He let out a shaky breath, remembering the levels that he had been able to see in their statuses.

Level 294! That Beast Kin was scary powerful. Even though the others didn't have as high of an overall level as her, their presence was almost as suffocating.

He turned and his guards followed him back into the royal palace. His face hardened.

Esamael would be the first to face justice. Then, he would take the Stone Raiders' information, uprooting those who tried to turn traitor. Only once all of those dissident powers were removed could he continue his talks with the southern races.

It was time to unite Gudalo. With the Stone Raiders' support and the Lady of Air's guidance, he felt that it would be but a matter of time.

In one move, he would cut away the negative forces on Gudalo, to bring about an age of peace and unity.

***

"I'm not sure how I feel about this," Josh muttered as the party walked through Haugr, passing groups of soldiers who had surrendered and were being watched by Stone Raiders.

"If we were to leave them here, then they would be executed for treason. Most of them were raised up into this way of living. Lord Esamael gave most of them a home and purpose. Others, he gave gold and made promises. If we kill everyone we fight, then they'll fight to the last man instead of surrendering. People who think that they're going to die anyway are much scarier than people who think they can escape," Anna said.

"I just don't like the idea of having indentured servants all over Terra." Josh sighed.

"It is an acceptable way to try to get them to do something useful with their lives. With Esamael's army destroyed, it's possible that they will find a new path for their lives, leaving behind their hatred and actually working for something they want. They will be fed and clothed as per their contract. If we can't look after them, then the mage's guild and college will make use of them, as specified in the war agreements," Anna said.

"This isn't Earth. Rules are different here," Dave said from where he walked.

"Mage overseers coming in," Deia said.

Lox spat on the ground. "Damn overseers—always watching, never lifting a finger until after the fact."

A group of five mages came to stand in front of the party. The Stone Raiders around them started to look in their direction, ready for another fight if it came to it.

"Hello Party Zero, Guildmaster Giles, and Guild Lieutenant Esa." A man nodded to them all. "I am Overseer Rendar. I was assigned to watch over this battle. As per the war agreements, I saw that you fought along the pre-set guidelines. I ask what you are doing with the wounded you transported through the teleport pad and those who have surrendered to you."

"Don't like to mince words, huh?" Josh said, feeling tired from constantly fighting. Only now was the moon being replaced by the rising sun as he rubbed his face.

"Ugh, I need a shower," he muttered, focusing back on Rendar. "We're healing all those who were wounded in battle, something that we picked up from back on Earth. No matter the person, they're treated the same with medical aid. As for the prisoners, I have been told that we will be making them indentured servants. The mages can take away their binding oath seeing as Esamael is dead. We have quite a number of prisoners, so we might have too many for our upcoming projects."

Dave cleared his throat and looked to Josh.

"If we have any people we don't need and can't support, we will send them your way," Josh said.

"Where are you taking them? If at all possible, we would like to see where they are being held," Rendar asked respectfully.

"We're taking them to Terra. Once we get things figured out, we'll start moving them to different locations. I don't want to have them all in one place. Doing so could give rise to different ideas," Josh said darkly. He did *not* like having all of these people under his command. If he messed up, then they could die. "I would welcome for you to join us. We will probably need some help in seeing if we can improve the facilities that we have."

"Certainly. My other overseers are interested to talk to the king as well as some of the prisoners and look into different issues we've had reported to us. I can accompany you back to this Terra, if that is okay with you?" Rendar asked.

"Certainly. I don't see any reason why we can't leave now." Josh looked to the rest of the party. They agreed with his assessment. They were all looking forward to getting back to their apartments for a shower, food, and sleep.

"One moment while I confer with my fellow overseers," Rendar said.

"We'll be at the teleport pad," Josh said.

Rendar nodded and turned to his people.

The party continued onward as Josh found an invite to Party Zero's party chat. "What, don't trust people to not listen in?" Josh grinned.

"A bit of paranoia is always good." Dave smiled back.

"So is a good jug of ale!" Gurren added.

"As well as some big juicy boar ribs!" Lox said.

"So, what were you hinting at us needing all that labor for?" Josh asked.

"Well, for increasing the size of Terra as well as building other facilities. We've grown a lot in a few months, but there's a limited number of us. Not many of us are going to want to look over the greenhouses, the different facilities we have as well as the expansions for Terra. I think that with magic, those indentured servants won't be hard to keep an eye on." Dave looked to Lox, Gurren, and Anna.

"The binding is very powerful. They are allowed to defend themselves and there are conditions that the mages will be alerted to if they are treated badly. It was made so that people would come to know those who they were fighting. If you know your enemy, you come to understand him—then it's harder to raise your sword against another potential enemy," Lox said.

"Seems the mages are more devious than I thought," Josh said, feeling relieved. He had lost POEs to these soldiers and he, in turn, had killed off their friends, people they had come to see as brothers and sisters.

I wonder who this is going to be harder on, us or them? Josh continued his walk, absently watching as the people of Haugr started to leave their homes, looking at the damage of the battle.

***

Rendar felt apprehensive as he walked to the teleport pad. *These Stone Raiders—they're much stronger than I thought they would be.*

"Everything good?" Josh asked as he arrived. The rest of the party that had been with him had already moved through the teleport pad. There were Stone Raiders and Haugr guards in the area, with a constant stream of prisoners moving through the teleport pad.

"Yes, preparations have been made. I am ready to visit this Terra." Rendar smiled, confused by the odd name for the unknown location.

"Good." Josh smiled and walked through the teleport pad's event horizon. Rendar followed.

They exited the teleport pad and came out inside a large building. A control room looked at the teleport pad; Aleph automatons stood around the room like statues. Rendar would have thought of them as statues if not for the faint Mana signatures.

"Follow me." Josh took them through a doorway opposite to the one that captives were being guided through.

They passed large rooms. In some, there were supplies. In others, wounded were being seen to before being whisked off.

It took a few minutes before they were outside the building. Rendar's eyes went wide as he looked upon Terra. The sprawling city rose around him. Buildings of stone and metal as well as soul gem constructs dotted the skyline. A light source made it seem like day within the cylindrical city.

Dwarves, Humans, Elves, Beast Kin, Demons, and Aleph filled the streets around the building that held the teleport pad.

"These are some of our allies, but most of them were healed after the battle and are staying here to get checked out before going home. Most of the races have gone back to their respective cities. We're currently building embassies for all of our allied people." Josh waved to a group of different large towers. Metal automatons moved over them, changing the crude blocks of stone into actual buildings to house the various allies' embassies.

"This is intriguing; where will your captives be staying?" Rendar asked. He was greatly interested with the city. It was clear that the entire city was what the Stone Raiders were calling their "guild hall."

Just what have they been doing away from prying eyes? A guild with an entire city to themselves!

"Certainly. Come this way." Josh indicated for Rendar to follow him.

It didn't take long for them to leave the people behind. The city was large and there simply wasn't the population there to inhabit all of Terra.

Josh took Rendar to one of the brilliantly glowing buildings.

"Are these one of those soul gem buildings?" Rendar asked.

"Correct. How did you know?" Josh asked, intrigued.

"I heard about it from people who went to Devil's Crater. I didn't think that someone would be able to make a construct this large, though." Rendar looked at the building.

"It takes a hell of a lot of resources, but my resident magic nerd tells me it will work." Josh rolled his eyes, snorting slightly as he led the way inside.

Rendar smiled slightly as they were greeted by the smell of moist earth and plants.

"Josh, I wasn't expecting you to come over here," a Human said, moving through the various crops and different plants in the growing tower.

"Hey, Fornau. Should have guessed you'd be trying to optimize the growing cycle." Josh clapped the man on the shoulder.

"Well, these growing towers are brilliant. Just thinking about their potential is enough to energize me more than a gallon of Xer in the morning!"

"Glad you're enjoying it. Unfortunately, I'm here to show off some of the basic rooms we have here. Also, we might have a whole bunch of people to staff this place so we can get some serious growing started," Josh said.

"I look forward to it. Let me know if you need anything. I'm going to give my report to Dave when I'm done," Fornau said.

"Okay, I'll see you later," Josh said.

Rendar nodded to Fornau out of respect. *I hadn't been able to read his aura and I feel that he's much stronger than his stated level of 54.* Rendar was filled with questions, but now was not the time for them.

They walked through the various levels of the growing tower, reaching rooms that had been set aside for those who would work in the tower.

"Have a look around. These are some of our basic rooms. We're probably going to have different styles, but this one shows all of their major amenities," Josh said.

Rendar walked in and paused, looking around the room. There were four separate bedrooms: two bathrooms, a kitchen, and a living area.

This level of magical coding... Rendar looked through the different appliances, from a heating plate to hot and cold water. There was even a cooling box. The bedrooms were bare, but they had large windows that allowed a person to look out onto the rest of Terra.

Putting them in a place like this? It's comparable to the conveniences that people get on the Per'ush islands. The amount of magical items and artifacts they have here that anyone can use is staggering.

"As long as all facilities are to this quality, then they will be agreeable," Rendar said, not letting any of his inner thoughts show.

He'd been scared that the Stone Raiders wouldn't be able to house and look after all of the prisoners. An influx of nearly two hundred thousand prisoners was no small matter. The mage's college and guild would have had a hard time finding places for them to serve out their indentured service.

"Well, you're welcome to look around and check out the place. Lucy is organizing people, seeing what they're best at, and then moving them around. Going to be a pain to move so many people, but we've got the room for it." Josh laughed and waved at the growing city.

***

Dave and Deia moved to the apartment that they had claimed for their own. All of Party Zero lived on the same floor.

As soon as they were through the door, Dave wrapped his arms around Deia.

"Don't go out there again without me," Dave said over her shoulder.

Deia relaxed; her hands fell on his that covered her belly protectively.

"Don't scare me like that again," Deia said with a shaky breath. Her nerves and fears she had been hiding came to the surface.

"Sorry about that. I didn't think it would happen." Dave gave her a reaffirming squeeze.

For a while, they just stood there, thankful that the other was okay, letting their nerves and fears drain away.

Deia gave Dave a quick kiss. "Okay, I'm going to have a quick shower, and you are too. I need my body pillow!" She pulled him with her as she walked toward the bathroom.

Dave laughed, smiling at her childish antics.

Chapter 28: Roll of the Dice

Dave woke up. As he shifted, Deia's legs and arms tightened around him by reflex as she mumbled in her sleep.

Dave couldn't help but break into a smile at her actions. *Well, looks like I won't be released anytime soon.*

With an excited smile, he opened up his interface, going to the notifications.

Quest Completed: Friend of the Grey God Level 5

Protect your Guild from Lord Esamael's forces

Rewards: Unlock Level 6 Quest

+10 to all stats (stacks with previous class level)

+500,000 EXP

Class: Friend of the Grey God

Status: Level 5

Effects:
+50 to all stats
Access to hidden quests
Access to the Imperial Carrier Datskun
+500,000 EXP

Quest: Friend of the Grey God Level 6

Create transportation network across Emerilia

Rewards: Unlock Level 7 Quest

Increase to stats

Quest Completed: Bleeder Level 4

Protect your Guild from Lord Esamael's forces

Rewards: Unlock Level 5 Quest

+10 to all stats (stacks with previous class level)

+400,000 EXP

Class: Bleeder

Status: Level 4

     +40 to all stats

Effects: Ability to disable Jukal Link

     +400,000 EXP

Quest: Bleeder Level 5

Create transportation network across Emerilia

Rewards: Unlock Level 5 Quest

Increase to stats

Quest: Weapons Master Level 3

One handed and shield 1,000/1,000

Two handed 78/1,000

Dual wielding 9/1,000

Archery 541/1,000

Rewards: Unlock Level 4 Quest

Increase to stats

Passive skills from other weapons increase from 25% to 50% when designated weapon is not equipped. (Example: While using Dual wield blades, one is able to gain 50% of the archery skill's abilities.)

Level 231

You have reached level 231; you have **145** stat points to use.

Character Sheet

Name:	David Grahslagg	Gender:	Male
Level:	202	Class:	Dwarven Master Smith, Friend of the Grey God, Bleeder, Librarian, Aleph Engineer, Weapons Master, Champion Slayer, Skill Creator, Mine Manager, Master of Space and Time, Master of Gravitational Anomalies
Race:	Human/ Dwarf	Alignment:	Neutral Good

Unspent points: 145

Health:	39,300	Regen:	21.76 /s
Mana:	14,280	Regen:	48.80 /s
Stamina:	4,540	Regen:	43.00 /s
Vitality:	393	Endurance:	1,088
Intelligence:	1,428	Willpower:	976
Strength:	454	Agility:	860

He sat there, just getting used to his body. He had been constantly recovering from stat or information overload.

He dismissed his screens and looked at his hands as he moved them. He had been keeping his mind fixed on different things. Having the conjured spheres around him was a good way to divert his attention and strain his Intelligence so he didn't feel out of sync with the world.

His high Intelligence was incredible. It was as if he had been blind before. Now, everything had a richness to it. He didn't just see items; he understood them. Combined with his Touch of the Land spell, he felt almost omniscient.

It was a powerful feeling and one that scared Dave.

What would happen if I was to lose control? The thought surfaced from the back of his mind. A sliver of fear built in him.

It felt as though he had opened Pandora's Box. He had come into the power of a demi-god. When he had seen Deia in the middle of the fight at Verlun, he had needed to assert his control over his emotions. He wanted nothing more than to destroy everything in front of him. He had come up with multiple ways to do it.

It was only Bob's warning and Dave's ability to push away from his emotions that he had controlled himself, using means that were more acceptable for a Human.

He now understood why Malsour, Induca, and Anna contained their power, rarely going full out. If they were to start thinking of themselves as above, or better than their enemies, then they could become terrible existences.

Is this why the Dragons that stay in their Dragon form stay near the Densaou Ring or start to think of themselves as gods?

Deia moved next to Dave, hugging him again and moving her head on his chest.

Dave's thoughts fell away as he smiled. He pushed away her hair covering her face, and tucked it behind her ear. He looked at her calm face. His worries seemed a little bit smaller.

"My firecracker," Dave whispered, kissing her head.

The People of Emerilia and the Players were his people. He might gain great power, but he vowed to protect those he held dear and do his best to act in a way that he could make a future for his family that he could be proud of. He was going to make Emerilia a place where they were free to do as they wished, to live without having to fight and die for the Jukal Empire's entertainment.

Dave sighed. A weight lifted from his shoulders. That promise to himself and to his unborn child comforted him greatly.

Deia yawned and stretched, almost pushing Dave out of the bed.

"Ah!" Dave said, nearly falling off.

"Whoops!" Deia stretched like a cat, a pleased smile on her face.

"First you imprison me in bed, then you kick me out of it!" Dave said, a wicked gleam in his eyes as he smiled.

"What are you doing?" Deia said, wary.

"Payback!" Dave laughed, tickling Deia.

She squealed and laughed, shaking from Dave's tickles and giggling like a little girl.

Dave laughed.

"St—stop! I can't—breathe!" she barely got out. Dave stopped after a few seconds. The two of them fell on the bed, happily tired.

"Rude! Your pretty fiancée wakes up and you tickle her!" Deia pouted.

Dave kissed her pouting lips, a smile on his face as he slipped out of bed.

"Hey! Who said you could leave!" Deia sat up, her eyes thinning as she looked at Dave.

Dave turned, chuckling at her expression. A warm feeling ran through his chest.

"Body pillow, here." Deia pointed at the bed.

Dave wanted to get to work, but he did owe her and with her pout, there was little chance he could deny her.

"Fiiine!" Dave jumped back on the bed.

Deia wrapped herself around him, smacking her lips happily. "Good. Sleep now."

"Aren't you supposed to be the badass leader of Party Zero, not a master manipulator of pouting?" Dave said in her ear, wrapping his arm around her.

"Don't make me take you to the training arena." She looked up from his chest.

"Cuddling!" Dave pulled her from his side onto his chest.

"Ugh! Uncomfortable!" Deia pouted cutely as she half-complained.

Dave laughed at her antics. Her words seemed to push his worries away, making him think about nothing but her. The two of them became lost in their own little world, taking a break from the realities that lay outside of their apartment's door.

*****

Boran-al rubbed sleep from his eyes as he stood from the desk that he had been working at. He looked down on the mass of creatures that covered the ground around the massive crystal tower he stayed in.

The Dark Lord had returned to Emerilia, leaving Boran-al as his commander in his stead.

Boran-al looked at the creatures below with hunger.

He had made a number of creatures in his time. The Alturarans were the embodiment of Dark magic and soul magic. The transplanting of consciousness into an immaterial object.

The Alturarans had sacrificed their biological bodies as the planet had become more hostile. To procreate, they shared consciousness with one another, transplanting it into new crystal cores they found.

Originally, it had been a measure to preserve their race. They found magic, and with it, the strength to change the world.

Though, without their biological bodies, they couldn't understand how to change Alturara back to a place that their old bodies would enjoy. With their twisted consciousnesses, they started to believe Alturara's barren landscape was their paradise.

When they saw a race called the Jukal, they attacked the unnatural biological species, to eradicate their stain from their paradise.

Then, portals connected to Emerilia appeared and they met "Players." Killing them allowed the Alturarans to grow in strength and purpose. They needed to destroy Emerilia, an unnatural world in their twisted consciousness, a world that gave birth to the organic! They led battle after battle with a new purpose.

They had given up their organic bodies to try to survive, to try to escape the death of their world. They survived, but now they were the plague that ravaged organic worlds.

When greeted by the Dark Lord's paladins, creatures of the darkness, they were interested. When offered the ability to grow more powerful, for following the Dark Lord's orders, they were interested. The Dark Lord gave off a similar aura and with his power, he was a person worthy of their devotion! A creature that would lead them to devour worlds with the organic blight!

"Like all good creatures, powerful yet easily bent to the will of their true master," Boran-al said.

He looked to the Alturaran crystals that were arrayed on the tables.

They had been a great and intelligent race, but their weakness came through their procreation. They combined consciousnesses of organic beings inside inorganic materials from two different parents. Many went insane, nothing more than cannon fodder. Some gained the semblance of an identity through the combined consciousnesses.

They lived in madness.

Boran-al shivered with pleasure.

Truly a race of twisted, painful beauty, to be trapped within one's own mind for eternity. To not know the truth of their circumstance. Just troops waiting to be used by the right master. They will serve our purpose well.

He looked to the other end of the valley that the Alturarans rested in. A simple ring mounted in the sand.

The Alturarans called them Gates of Ascendance. Boran-al knew their true name. Portals.

***

Captain Adams watched as the light of the slip stream fell away to reveal a star system.

Her crew went through their procedures. They easily fell into a routine after the first couple of emergences into different systems.

Adams had made sure that they never got used to it, always looking for threats. She didn't need them getting comfortable. They were in enemy territory, after all.

"We're clear for ten light-minutes out," Quinn reported. Everyone relaxed slightly. Many eyes darted to the hologram that was building of the system.

"Fifty percent readiness. I want a comparison of the system. Keep us in the peripheral." Adams changed up her words to keep her people attentive. This long trip had taught her ways to keep her people active and engaged.

"Contact at thirty-two light-minutes out!" Quinn said, her voice a mix of nerves and excitement.

Adams checked her screen and linked it to navigation. With a press of a button, a hologram appeared. She zoomed in on the contact.

An Imperial carrier!

The sensor logs identified the ship. They contained information on every ship that Humanity had run into.

Datskun. A carrier that participated in the war between the Jukal and Humanity.

For all of her life, the Jukal and Humanity's war with them had felt like some kind of fairy tale. She had grown up with the facts and information, but she hadn't been there. She didn't know people who had lived through it. It was history, something that happened to other people. Yet here, now she was looking upon a carrier that had led one of the dozen Jukal fleets into battle against Humanity.

It made everything that much more real.

"We've got a massive orbital satellite system around the planet that the carrier is orbiting. Picking up signals on the north and south poles, as well as on one of the three moons," Quinn continued. No one said anything as she talked.

"Orbital satellites look to be armed. Will need more time to get information from the moons, but looks like there is a large installation within it, facing away from the planet. I am also getting massive power readings coming from the planet's surface," Quinn said.

"Anything else in the system?" Adams asked.

"All other planets look to be uninhabited. I will need more time to go through the information. I am transmitting what we have back to command," Quinn said.

A prompt stopped Adams asking more questions.

Private Message

Sato> Conference.

"I will conference with command. Anders, you're in charge while I'm away."

"Yes, ma'am," Anders said, a steely expression on his face.

Adams touched the relay in her armrest, linking her to one of the two long-range Mirrors of Communication within the ship.

She appeared in what seemed to be Sato's office.

"With all of our information gathered, we have been running simulations and cross-referencing data. We have an eighty-five percent positive result from the simulations," Sato said without preamble.

Adams took in a sharp breath.

Emerilia, the land of magic, exists!

"Observe the planet for two weeks. Release any drones that you have left and then return to base," Sato said.

"Yes, Commander." Adams nodded.

"With this information, things are going to change, and I'll need your strength, Admiral," Sato said.

Adams made to argue Sato's wording, but the look in his eyes stopped her.

"Thank you, sir," Adams said, giving him a terse nod.

"You and your crew have done more than I ever thought possible. Make it home safe." Sato's hardened features turned into a more relaxed smile.

"Yes, sir," Adams said.

It would be a long trip home, but it was clear from Sato's words that she would not be just sitting back anymore.

Epilogue

Dave stood before the grand workings that had been captured from Esamael's armies. From what he could gather, some of them would cause changes to the environment, some would summon beasts or minions, or sometimes they would create massive explosions.

They were rather simple constructs, essentially a spell imprinted onto a grand soul gem. The soul gem gave off much more power than what a person was capable of, so when the grand working was activated, it used the soul gem's power to cast a much more powerful spell than what was imprinted on the soul gem.

The best thing about the grand workings wasn't their destructive abilities. It was their ability to be used anywhere, by anyone. A mage could only cast so many spells; with this, they could be thrown out with ease, doing the work of multiple mages without needing them on the battlefield. This saved the mages who were in the fight from using their Mana reserves and it made the effects immediate.

"What are you thinking?" Malsour looked to Dave. All of Party Zero was sitting around a table, eating, drinking, and winding down from the battle.

"I was thinking that these might be good to use with Dwarven artillery, providing them with a variety of attacks. Imagine if they could fire these into the middle of the enemy, summoning creatures from other realms to fight our enemies and then call down a lightning storm and pure Mana bolts?" Dave said.

For a few moments, Malsour was silent. "I think that whoever we were fighting would have one hell of a shitty day," Malsour said slowly.

Dave nodded.

There was a commotion as Josh and a group of rogues and stealth types moved toward the teleport pads.

"Josh, what are you up to?" Dave asked.

"Cleaning up the trash. We'll be back in a few hours—no need to worry about it," Josh said with a faint smile, only barely slowing down.

Dave's eyes thinned before he nodded. He had a good idea of what they were going to do. He put the grand working down and grabbed his tankard, looking to Deia, who was talking to Induca and Suzy.

He placed his arm around her; her fingers intertwined with his, holding his hand over her stomach as she snuggled into the crook of his arm.

Dave smiled. Emerilia wasn't perfect, but to him it was still a magical and wonderful place.

***

Loughbreck's hand went to the sword next to his chair as there was a knock at the door.

Everyone in the small country home looked at the door, their hands resting on their weapons.

The door opened to reveal an elderly man and his younger assistant standing in the rain.

"Geswald." Loughbreck sighed in relief and stood to greet the man.

"General Loughbreck." Geswald took down his hood. He was drenched from the downpour outside.

Loughbreck snorted and shook his head. "How am I a general? I don't have an army to lead anymore." Loughbreck slumped into his seat, looking at the fireplace with hooded eyes.

The others in the room all silently watched the fire.

"Is there anything left of Esamael's forces?" Loughbreck asked.

"The Stone Raiders tore down Emaren's defenses and then cut down the main army from behind, capturing Esamael and handing him to Haugr." Geswald confirmed the rumors that Loughbreck had heard from his own sources.

"What did the Stone Raiders do afterward?" Loughbreck asked, morbidly interested.

"They captured most of the armies, making them indentured servants under the mage's guild's oversight and then took them to wherever they came from. They were also rewarded with gold and resources from Gudalo. The Selhi nation also paid reparations to the Stone Raiders, an amount that will cut deeply into their treasury," Geswald said. He, too, was cut off from the world, but his information network was much more developed than Loughbreck's.

Loughbreck's hands tightened into fists before relaxing, knowing the futility of his anger.

In the fireplace's flames, he saw the scenes within the Verlun Guild Hall—the Stone Raiders acting like avenging gods as they worked with their POE allies. They really had been a sleeping Dragon; once awakened, the only way to stop them was to kill them all, or be wiped out in turn.

If we'd only left the Stone Raiders alone, we might have won this war.

"We'll rest here for another day and then head for the Elven lands to the south and try to get out of Gudalo," Loughbreck said.

"Well, we can't have that." A cold voice floated through the room.

Loughbreck jumped up, raising his sword in one fluid motion.

"Show yourselves!" Loughbreck yelled. Everyone huddled together as they looked around the small three-room house.

A hooded man stepped out from one of the rooms where people had been sleeping. The shadows seemed to part around him. Behind him, two people in black clothes seemed to materialize out of the shadows.

From the kitchen, four more people stepped out into the main living area.

Geswald made to move for the door outside. The door opened. Geswald didn't have time to look shocked before a crossbow bolt slammed into his chest and came out the other side.

Out of the rain, five more people stepped through the door and into the house. In the corners of the room, metal machines seemed to appear from nowhere.

The hooded man who stood in front of the sleeping quarters pulled back his hood, revealing a face that Loughbreck had studied for weeks.

"Josh Giles, leader of the Stone Raiders Guild, have you come to finish me and my people off?" Loughbreck asked in a cold voice.

"Naturally," Josh said simply. There was no anger, fear, or coldness to his voice. He simply sounded as if he was annoyed, as if killing Loughbreck and the others was just another chore to do.

It made Loughbreck more scared than if Josh had been filled with fiery anger or cold rage.

"Kill them!" Loughbreck yelled, charging forward.

The Stone Raiders loaded crossbows, firing them into the seven or eight people within the house. There was no way they could miss.

Loughbreck was thrown back with the force of the crossbow bolt. He spit out blood as the arrow pierced his breastplate and into his lung.

Josh looked down at the man, pulling out his wickedly curved blades. In a blur of motion, Loughbreck's head was removed from his body.

***

Lady Merguine rested against King Sigaird as they looked out across Haugr.

"So, what will we do now?" Merguine asked.

All around the castle, people were working to fix up the damage that Lord Esamael's army had caused. Even as they removed the broken buildings, there was a sense of excitement within the city.

"First, we get Haugr sorted out, then we can see if we can open our borders to our neighbors to the south and really start to build the republic of Gudalo," Sigaird said.

Lady Merguine nodded, taking a deep breath, comfortable in Sigaird's arms.

"The Lady of Air doesn't like to give her Champions any easy tasks," Merguine complained.

"Hey! It's much more fun for you guys to sort it out!" Air's voice came from above the two, making Sigaird and Merguine jump.

Air floated down next to them. Venfik followed her.

"Air," Sigaird said.

"My lady." Merguine elbowed Sigaird as she half curtsied.

"Now that Esamael and all of his rabble have been cleared out, you'll be free to rule as you see fit and finally advance with the plans that you made with the southern groups to turn all of Gudalo into a republic," Air said.

"You make it sound easy." Sigaird sighed.

"It won't be, but for the coming war, it's a necessity." Air's light and playful tone became somber.

Sigaird's eyebrow rose as he unconsciously straightened.

"All of Emerilia will stand together or they will fall apart. Join with the Stone Raiders and support them. They might be Players for the most part, but they are one of the only groups that the People of Emerilia can rally behind. The other nations, kings, and leaders have too much of a history to do it," Air said.

Sigaird nodded with Merguine. Air might act like a playful child most of the time, not caring about anything, but this was the other side of her.

This was the true Lady of Air, a woman who had never needed to use her divine powers to fight across Emerilia. Instead, her power came from information, the whispers on the wind and correcting the balance of power throughout Emerilia.

If Bob made sure that the Pantheon fought fairly, Air was the one who could create and break empires, alliances and nations.

With Air, her actions were done so that no one, not even the gods, would notice her work.

Emerilia will be continued in Time Of Change.

As a self published author I live for reviews! If you've enjoyed Emerilia, please leave a review!

Hope you have a great Day! ☺

Want a bigger map of Emerilia and the continents? Check out

http://theeternalwriter.deviantart.com/

You can check out my other books, what I'm working on and upcoming releases through the following means:

Website: **http://michaelchatfield.com/**

Twitter: **@chatfieldsbooks**[1]

Facebook: **Michael Chatfield**[2]

Goodreads: **Goodreads.com/michaelchatfield**[3]

Thanks again for reading! ☺

Interested in more LitRPG? Check out **https://www.facebook.com/groups/LitRPGsociety/**

Continue on for Character Sheet!

---

1. https://twitter.com/chatfieldsbooks

2. https://www.facebook.com/michaelchatfieldsbooks/?ref=hl

3. https://www.goodreads.com/author/show/14055550.Michael_Chatfield

In Alphabetical order
Ankol

Dwarf

Dwarven Master Smith. Smithing Art: Metal Spinner. Lives in Grorart Mountain.

Boran-Al

Lich

One of the Dark Lord's Champions. Works directly under the Dark Lord. Creates Creatures of Power and carry's out the Dark Lord's orders. His Citadel was destroyed.

Alastair Montgoa

Arch Lich aka former Lord Vailyn. Gave up his fellow Aleph to have everlasting life; used the centuries to build strength and knowledge

Barry

Dwarf

    Dwarven Master Smith. Smithing Art-Unknown. Wandering smith.

Cassie

Elf/Human Halfling

Holy warrior. Leader of the Golden Sabres. In a relationship with Josh Giles.

Dark Lord

God

Embodiment of the Dark affinity. Created Demons. Normally an ally with the Earth Lord. Always looking a way to tip the power balance of Emerilia in his favor.

Dasano

Dwarf

Dwarven Master Smith. Smithing Art: Metal Press. Lives in Grorart Mountain.

Akatol Dracul

Dragon

Water Mage. Was the second Dragon, Denur's husband. Went mad and started a genocide, disappeared.

Denur Dracul

Dragon

Fire Mage Hailed as 'Mother of Dragons'. First of her race, a creature of power created by the Lady of Fire. Seen as her daughter. Sister to Oson' Deia.

Gelimah Dracul

Dragon
Dark Mage. Brother to Induca, Louna and Malsour

Fornau Dracul

Dragon

Earth Mage. Quindar's mate Malsour and Induca's grand-nephew.

Induca Dracul

Dragon

Fire Mage. One of the youngest from the first generation of Dragons. Sister to Malsour, daughter of Denur, aunt to Quindar, great aunt to Fornau. Member of the Stone Raiders and Party Zero.

Kinal Dracul

Dragon

Louna Dracul

Dragon
  Induca, Gelimah and Malsour's sister.

Malsour Dracul

Dragon

Dark Mage. One of the oldest Dragons in existence, first born of Denur. Deia and Induca's Guardian, Stone Raider and Party Zero member. Brother to Induca. Great Uncle to Fornau Dracul and Uncle to Quindar Dracul.

Quindar Dracul

Dragon
    Wind Mage, wife to Fornau, Niece to Induca and Malsour.

Wokui Dracul

Dragon
    Water Mage

Xednai Dracul

Dragon

One of the first Dragons, had several Dragons. Her son is Fornau.

Gorpal Dunsk

Dwarf

Dwarven Master Smith, lives in Aldamire Mountain, created 3 Weapons of Power - Mace of Fury, Tower Shield, Boots of Smash. Smithing Art: Paint Copy

Earth Lord

God
: Embodiment of the Dark affinity. Created Earth Sprites.

Edmur

Dwarf

Dwarven Master Smith. Had been in the Dwarven War Bands as a Shield Bearer. Former pupil of Quino's Brother to Endur. Smithing Art: Metal's Song

Edwards

Human. Military scientist within the Deq'ual System. Friend of Sato's

Edwin

Beast Kin. Beast Kin representative on ruling council.

Endur

Dwarf

Dwarven Master Smith. Had been in the Dwarven War Bands as a Shield Bearer. Former pupil of Quino's, brother to Edmur, lives in Zolu Mountain. Smithing Art Hammer Blows

Esa

Human

Melee fighter. Member of Mikal and Jule's party. Fought at Boranl-Al's Citadel.

Member of the Stone Raiders. Going out with Jules. Works under Dwayne as a fighter. Being trained for a leadership position under Dwayne.

Lord Esamael

Human.

Lord of Emaren within the Gudalo Kingdom.

Ela-Gal

High Elf.

Warrior living in Aleph, married to Ela'Dorn. Persectued by high elves as heretic.

Ela-Dorn

Orc.

Researcher and professor at Aleph College. Aleph Council Member. Married to Ela-Gal

Fend

Dwarf

Lord Under the Mithsia Mountains.

Geswald

Human.

Trader's Guild Chapter head in Emaren.

David Grahslagg

Dwarf/Human Halfling, in-game character of Austin Zane. Dwarven Master Smith, Resident of Cliff Hill, member of Party Zero and the Stone Raider's Guild. Other names: Austin Zane

Josh Giles

Human

Rogue. Leader of the Stone Raiders. Was a investment broker on Earth, became an E-head. In a relationship with Cassie from the Golden Sabres.

Gimel

Human
  Warrior.
  Fellox Guild Master.

Gorrund

Dwarf

Dwarven Master Smith in Benvari Mountain with Jesal, teaching four apprentices. Smithing Art: Blood Bender.

Goula

Demon
On the Ruling council for Devil's Crater.

Gurren

Dwarf

Shield bearer, member of Dwarven War Band under Lox's command, sent to guide people to Cliff-Hill. Friend of David Grahslagg, Kol's Grandson. Member of the Stone Raiders.

Helick

Dwarf
  Dwarven Master Smith.

Kim Isdola

Human
  Cleric/alchemist. Lieutenant in Stone Raiders.

Ishox

Demon

On the Ruling council for Devil's Crater.

Arch-Mage Jekoni

Human/item

Soul bound to Staff of Growing, over 2,000 years old; missing legs. Held within Dwarven Vaults with other Weapons of power.

Jeeves

AI
Made by Bob to assist the Dwarven Master Smiths.

Jeremy

Human

Fellox Guild member.

Jesal

Dwarf

Dwarven Master Smith, Dave's master smith trainer. Smithing art: Nature's Guide

Jules

Human

Healer. Member of Mikal and Esa's party. Fought at Boranl-Al's Citadel.

Member of the Stone Raiders. Used to be an army medic, E-head without legs IRL. Going out with Esa. Works under Lucy as support, leads the healers of the Stone Raiders.

Joko

Dwarf

Shield bearer, member of Dwarven War Band under Lox's command, sent to guide people to Cliff-Hill. Friend and trainer of David Grahslagg.

Deceased.

Anna'Kal

Wolf Beast Kin/Administrator AI24681

Air mage. Originally a program meant to assist Lo'kal with the running of Emerilia. Anna was uploaded to a Player body and inserted into Emerilia. She became emotionally attached with her charges. When the Beast Kin people were wiped out from Emerilia she went into cold storage, waiting for her father to awake her when a chance came to fight against the prison they had created.

Member of the Stone Raiders and Party Zero. Daughter of Bob.

Lo'kal

Jukal

Scientist, created Emerilia. Awarded the position of the Gray God, maintains Emerilia, its people and Players. Other names: Bob, Bobby McMahnon, The Balancer, Gray God.

Kino

Demon
On the Ruling Council for Devil's Crater.

Kol

Dwarf

Dwarven Master Smith. Gurren's grandfather. Resides in Cliff-Hill. Taught Dave how to Smith. Runs his Smithies. Smithing art: Blind Man's Touch

Lady of Air

Goddess

Embodiment of the affinity Air. Known for causing mischief. Her Champions act as spies and information brokers, tilting the balance of Emerilia.

Lady of Fire

Goddess

Created Dragons, Mages Guild and College. Gave gift of 'knowledge' to the people of Emerilia. Mother to Deia, Lover of Oson'Mal and best friend with Bob.

Other Names: Ignil

Lady of Light

Goddess

Sent Players to kill/capture Dragons to make her own Creatures of Power. Created the race known as Angels. Large rivalry with the Dark Lord.

Lena

Demon
On the Ruling Council of Devil's Crater. Wife to Vrexu.

Lovan

Dwarf
Mithsia Mountain Warclan leader

Lox

Dwarf

Shield bearer. Was the commander of the War Band sent to guide people to Cliff-Hill. Friend of David Grahslagg. Member of the Stone Raiders.

Suzy Markell

Human (IRL)

High Elf (Emerilia)

Austin Zane's secretary and best friend. David Grahslagg's best friend and assistant with running Cliff Hill Smithy and Factory. Summoning Mage. Steven's contractor, member of Party Zero and the Stone Raiders.

Max

Dwarf

Shield bearer, member of Dwarven War Band under Lox's command, sent to guide people to Cliff-Hill. Friend of David Grahslagg. Deceased.

Meda

Dwarf/Elf

Aleph Council member. Deals with the food within Aleph cities and facilities

Melanie

Human
Arch Mage Alamos' Wife.

Melhoun

Water snake made by the Water Lord.
Sealed away.

Mikal

Human

Rogue. Jules and Esa's party member. Member of the Stone Raiders. Friends with Party Zero.

Oson'Deia

Elf/Demi God Halfling

Elven Ranger and Fire Mage. Daughter of Oson'Mal and Lady Fire of the Affinity Pantheon. Resident of Cliff Hill and member of the Stone Raider's Guild, Leader of Party Zero.

Other names: Ouluv'Deia

Penelope

Human
Fellox Guild member.

Pete

Human

Geswald's secretary.

Queen Farun

High Elf
Queen of Raolor.

Queen Mendari Selhi

Human
Queen of Selhi.

Quino

Dwarf

Dwarven Master Smith, lives in Zolu Mountain. Trained the brothers Endur and Edmur. Smithing Art: Internal cutting.

Rola

Dwarf

Dwarven Master Smith. Smithing Art Puppeteer. Lives in Aldamire Mountain.

Sato/Communications officer Sato

Human

Lives in De'qual system.

Communications Officer, becomes Vice commander of Deq'ual military forces. Grandfather original settler.

Emperor Talis

Human.

Ruler of the Xeugrera Empire, located in the Ashal Continent.

Tounk

Dwarf

Shield bearer, member of Dwarven War Band under Lox's command, sent to guide people to Cliff-Hill. Friend of David Grahslagg.

Deceased.

Demon Prince Alkao/Alkao Travezar

Aerial Demon

Melee fighter. Commander of the Third Demon Horde and leader of Xerzit lands. Oldest of the five remaining Demon Prince's of Devil's Crater.

Dwayne Trebault

Human

Melee fighter. Lieutenant in Stone Raiders. Leads and trains the melee fighters in the Stone Raiders.

Venfik

Elf

Lady Air's advisor.

Lucy Vernia

Wood Elf/Human

Lieutenant in Stone Raiders. Spy master, deals with supporting the Stone Raiders and paperwork.

Vrexu

Demon

One of the seven Demon Princes. General in the Devil's Crater Army. Married to Lena, the youngest of the five remaining Demon Princes.

Water Lord

God

Embodiment of the Water Affinity. Created the Mer-People and water creatures. Created the Water Serpent Melhoun. Rival to the Lady of Fire.

Austin Zane

CEO of Rock Breaker's Corporation. Engineer specializing in space vehicles. Background in Astro physics. Other names: David Grahslagg

Wis'Zel

Wood Elf

Bard. Works for David Grahslagg, managing his Ceramics factories in Cliff Hill.